Always
the
Bridesmaid

LINDSEY KELK

HARPER

Harper
An imprint of HarperCollins*Publishers*
1 London Bridge Street,
London SE1 9GF

www.harpercollins.co.uk

A Paperback Original 2015

1

Copyright © Lindsey Kelk 2015

Lindsey Kelk asserts the moral right to
be identified as the author of this work

A catalogue record for this book
is available from the British Library

ISBN: 978-0-00-758233-4

Set in Melior by Palimpsest Book Production Limited,
Falkirk, Stirlingshire

Printed and bound in the United States of America by
RR Donnelley

Find out more about HarperCollins and the environment at
www.harpercollins.co.uk/green

For Janice

My Bridesmaid Journal

Name: Maddie Fraser
Age: Thirty-one but I definitely don't look it, honest
My bride's name is: Lauren Hobbs-Miller
My bride is: My alleged best friend
I have known my bride for: 12 years
How we met: We were flatmates at university
My other bridesmaids' names are: Sarah Hempel, Jessica Hobbs-Miller-Joyce
Three words that describe my bride: ~~Tyrannical control freak~~ Generous, loving, blonde
Three words that describe the groom: Potentially on drugs
The date of the big day is: Too soon for me to lose weight
How I feel about being a bridesmaid: ~~Like I'd rather pull my womb out with a rusty coat hanger and parade up and down Brighton seafront wearing it as a hat~~ Blessed.

Congratulations!

You have been asked to join your bride on this most important journey, one of lasting love and a lifetime of memories. A bridesmaid is not someone who follows her bride down the aisle, but someone who stands beside her in life. Yesterday you may have been a friend, a sister, a cousin, but from today until forever, you are so much more.

This journal allows you to chart every step of your adventure together, from the day your bride bestows this great honour upon you, up until the day you say goodbye to the fiancée she is today and welcome a wife into your life.

Record every moment, write down every feeling and thought and reflection, for this is one of the most special and beautiful privileges in a woman's life.

You are no longer just the person you were when you woke up today.

You are a bridesmaid.

1

Thursday May 14th

Today I feel: Exhausted.
Today I am thankful for: Taxis that can find you with an app.

It is an undisputed truth of the modern age that there are now only two kinds of people in the world: people who call and people who text.

Obviously there are a lot of weirdoes knocking around on social media: that girl from your old job who likes everything you put on Facebook, the boy you hung out with during the first week of university and then ignored for three years but who still added you on LinkedIn, and, most worrying of all, anyone who tries to have extended conversations on Twitter direct messages, *but*, when it comes to genuine, honest to God, help-you-hide-the-body-without-asking-questions best buds in the whole wide world, there are only texters and callers.

My best friend Lauren is a caller. As annoying as I find it, Lauren can't help but pick up the phone, regardless of what it is she has to say. In my humble texter's opinion, we don't need to actually talk about who has been eliminated on *Bake Off*; selected gifs and the odd emoji can express all of our emotions quite adequately. But Lauren loves to call, and that is why I knew something was up when she sent a text message asking me and Sarah to meet her for dinner.

'What do you think she wants?' Sarah asked as we trotted dutifully down the street, right on time. 'Why did we have to come out tonight?'

By the time I got on the Tube I'd run through every possible scenario, and had settled on a kidnapping. Instead of finding her in the restaurant, there would be a sinister man with a random scar, stroking his beard at the bar and demanding a million pounds by midnight, otherwise he would start chopping off her fingers and sending them through the post. Maybe he would FedEx them; the post was a bit unreliable.

'No idea,' I replied. No need to worry Sarah about the kidnapping until it was confirmed. 'It'll be nice to have dinner together, though. I feel like I haven't seen you in weeks.'

Which was a terribly polite way of saying, 'I haven't bloody well seen you in weeks, you massive bastard – aren't you supposed to be one of my best friends?'

'I've been busy,' she said. Not even an attempt to make up a lie. I'd half expected her to show up with a baby bump, but I was relieved to see she was as rail-thin as ever. Well, not relieved, obviously. No one is ever 'relieved' to see their skinny friend is still skinny, are they? And the worst part was, she still had massive boobs. Explain to me how that's fair. 'Work's been shit. I need a new job. Your place is advertising for a PR manager, you know.'

'Are we?' I replied, knowing full well that we were. Sarah unfastened and refastened the top button of her shirt, pulling the collar tight around her throat, muttering to herself.

'I don't know why she couldn't just say let's get dinner?' she said, changing the subject again, still burning up about The Message. 'Why all the drama?'

Because you'd cancel like you have every time for the last month and a half, I replied silently.

'Because she's American?' I suggested out loud.

'She moved here ten years ago,' Sarah argued. 'She does not get to use "because I'm American" as an excuse any more. I'm officially cutting her off.'

'Maybe she's moving back,' I said, hoping it wasn't true. There had been a lot of talk about her poorly mum and pregnant sister lately. And who would want to spend another miserable summer in the UK when you could be drinking cocktails at your beach house in the Hamptons and bothering your sister's new baby? 'She was quite insistent that we had to meet tonight.'

In truth, I was a little bit giddy. I never went out on a week night. Ever. And yes, I know, that sounds sad, but I work a lot and all my best friends are completely coupled up. What's the point of going out when you could be at home with a bottle of wine, making fajitas and laughing uproariously with your boyfriend/girlfriend/blow-up doll? It's fine, I get it, I do the same with my significant other, a great big bottle of gin. And yes, we're very happy together, thank you.

Sarah, on the other hand, did not look giddy. She looked downright miserable.

'She's always so insistent,' she said, tightening her ever-present topknot. Sarah had a look. Sarah always

5

wore her hair up. Sarah always wore perfectly applied black eyeliner and Sarah always wore shirts buttoned up to the throat. And yet, against all odds, Sarah always looks amazing. But regardless, I hated that topknot. I wanted to lop it off with garden shears. But I didn't, because I'm a Good Friend. 'Nothing is ever optional with her. I really didn't want to be out tonight – I just wanted to go home.'

'I'm not sure what you're trying to tell me,' I replied, 'but I've got this weird feeling you're not especially in the mood for dinner.'

She scowled. I smiled.

'Well, your make-up looks nice,' I said, threading my arm through her elbow whether she liked it or not. 'So that's something.'

'Whatever.'

When in doubt, always compliment a woman's eyeliner application.

Sarah let go of my arm to avoid a pack of terrifying pre-teens hurtling down the middle of the street. 'I just don't want to be out all night,' she said, dodging the kids like a pro. 'I'm not in the mood. Who wants to be out in London on a Thursday night? No one. It's full of wankers.'

I caught a glimpse of my overexcited expression in a blacked-out shop window and tried to suppress it before she looked up and slapped it off my face. Wankers and me! If someone wanted to be a full Grumpasaurus Rex, that was up to her. I wasn't going to let it ruin my evening. Probably.

'There you are!'

Lauren was squeezed into a tiny space at the busy bar when we arrived, Tweedleglee and Tweedleglum. Sarah allowed herself to be hugged briefly before ordering a double gin and tonic, while I took on the squeezing of a lifetime. Lauren is deceptively strong. Lauren goes to the gym. I believe these two factors are related but have done no research of my own to back that theory up.

'What's going on?' I asked, dancing around from foot to foot and combing my hands wildly through my hair. It had looked fine when I left the office, well, brown and clean but now, surrounded by so many pretty people, not to mention my two blonde best friends, I was certain it was tangled and greasy and needed to be shaved bald. Or possibly tied back in a ponytail. Definitely, one or the other.

'I'm not telling you until we've sat down,' Lauren said, shaking her very good hair out of her face and into mine. 'I've got a table, and I've ordered champagne – you don't need to get a drink, Sarah.'

Sarah gave her a dark look, slapped a five-pound note on the bar and necked her G&T in two gulps.

'Champagne?' I said. 'What are we celebrating?'

'God, Maddie.' Lauren's eyes sparkled. It actually looked as though someone had already been on the champs. 'Wait, like, ten seconds.'

Despite Sarah's less than chipper attitude, Lauren was still smiling when we got to the table. To her face, we always joked that she was so much better put together than we were because she was American, and behind her back (in a nice way, of course), we reassured ourselves that it was because she'd never had a proper job in her life, but tonight she looked extra shiny.

'So, how are you guys doing?' she asked, allowing the waiter to pull out her seat. 'It's been forever since I saw you.'

'Standard,' I replied. Why hadn't I done something with

my hair? Lauren's blonde mane always curled delicately at the bottom, like a fairy had come along and kissed it. 'Shona got called in for a mammogram, but she'd heard they hurt so she made me go and get one first.'

'Your boss made you go for a mammogram?' Sarah's eyes widened into saucers.

'How does someone make you get a mammogram?' Lauren asked, poking me in the left boob. 'Jesus, Maddie.'

'I don't know,' I said, slapping her hand away. 'It was in my diary – I didn't really think about it until afterwards. I thought everyone was doing it. And don't poke my boobs in public.'

'As if that's even the worst thing she's done,' Sarah said, tapping her fingers on the table and watching like a hawk as the waiter peeled the foil off the champagne cork. 'I think providing hospice care for her incontinent dog was more of an ask.'

I considered this for a moment.

'He was a lovely dog when he wasn't shitting everywhere,' I replied.

'But he was always shitting everywhere,' Sarah countered.

'Did it hurt?' Lauren asked, wrinkling her little nose at the dog-shit banter. 'The mammogram?'

I wrapped my hands around my chest and nodded. 'Even thinking about it hurts. But, you know, they're important.'

'They are,' Sarah agreed. 'When you need them. You're a thirty-one-year-old woman with no family history of breast cancer who spent the afternoon with her tit in a vice to appease her boss. That's different. Is she at least going to get one now?'

'I've scheduled her in for an MRI,' I said in the kind

of quiet voice an embarrassed mouse might use. 'She didn't fancy it after she read my report.'

Sarah gave me the look.

'I don't know why you don't just quit,' Lauren cut in before Sarah could explode. 'You've been her assistant for, like, ten years, Maddie. You could be an assistant anywhere. Wait, don't open that yet,' she ordered the waiter as he gripped the champagne cork. 'I want to make a toast.'

'Jesus, in that case can I have a Hendrick's and tonic, please?' Sarah asked. 'A double.'

'Me too,' I said, raising my hand. 'Thank you.'

'You guys . . .' Lauren's voice had a tendency to get a bit whiny when she wasn't getting her own way. Oddly enough, that didn't happen often. 'I don't want you to get wasted.'

'We won't get wasted,' I promised. 'Just delightfully tipsy. And you know it's not as easy as walking out of the door and into another job. Things are difficult everywhere right now.'

'There are quite a lot of event assistant jobs,' Sarah pointed out. 'Have you even looked?'

'I'm not going to leave one shitty job for another shitty job, am I? And, you know, it's not always awful,' I said, preparing to launch into my well-rehearsed 'Why I Don't Leave My Horrible Job' speech. 'I only tell you the worst parts. It's interesting. I get to do a lot of different stuff, the rest of the company is nice, it's only Shona who can be difficult. And I get to meet a lot of people—'

'Difficult? Can you even hear yourself?' Sarah replied, unconvinced. 'Next you'll be turning up with a black eye and telling us "she only hits me because she loves me". You stay because you're scared to leave. I've known you too long, Mads. You've lived in the same flat for ten years, you've had the same job for ten years—'

'I've had the same best friends for ten years,' I broke in with what I hoped she would take as a threat. 'Maybe I *should* make some changes.'

'I guess you do get to go to a bunch of awesome parties,' Lauren offered. Lovely, peace-making Lauren. 'And you always get a ton of free cake.'

'I do always get free cake,' I said, looking pointedly at Sarah, who had so often been the grateful recipient. 'Thank you, Lauren.'

'But,' she continued with one of her sweet smiles, 'if you left, you might be happier. And we might actually get to see you more often.'

Lauren, the two-faced, backstabbing cow.

'How are you, Sarah?' she asked, ignoring the look on my face. 'What's going on with you?'

'Nothing,' Sarah replied as her G&T was set down in front of her. 'Busy, tired, whatever.'

'Tough day at work?'

'They're all tough,' she said. 'Maddie isn't the only one who needs a new job.'

Lauren cast me a quick glance, which I replied to with wide, nonplussed eyes. When Sarah was in a bad mood, there was very little point trying to force her out of it.

'Let's open the champagne,' Lauren said brightly, beckoning the waiter over with the bottle. 'Before we start talking about mammograms and dog shit again.'

I smiled broadly. 'Just your average Thursday night.'

'This isn't how I had planned this,' she said, reaching under the table into her tote bag and pulling out two elaborately wrapped pink presents. There was a lot of curly ribbon involved. I mean, a lot. 'But I have some news and I wanted to share it with you right away.'

Sarah stared at the presents, stared at Lauren, and took a sharp breath in before downing the rest of her second gin. 'Oh no,' she whispered.

'What?' I flicked my head back and forth between my friends so fast I'm almost certain I could have sued them for whiplash. 'What?'

'Michael asked me to marry him last night,' Lauren announced, fiddling with her hand for a moment, then displaying a diamond ring so big it could only have come from Claire's Accessories. There was no way that shit was real. 'We're engaged.'

I had never seen her look so happy, and Lauren was always happy. Lauren was happy, I was happy, the waiter was happy, and Sarah was . . . oh. Hmm. Sarah did not look happy. In case you were wondering, it takes exactly seven seconds to go from silent awe to awkward silence. Before I knew it, we were right in the middle of one of the most uncomfortable situations I had ever had the privilege to experience. Lauren's smile began to freeze, and her giddy expression turned into tense confusion, while Sarah looked like she was getting a mammogram right there at the table.

'Are you pregnant?' I asked.

Apparently that was not the right thing to ask.

'Jesus, Maddie, no!' Lauren rolled her eyes and pouted. 'I'm hoping he asked because he loves me. It happens. Remember when Sarah did it? Big white dress, church, party, bridesmaids?'

'Oh no,' Sarah said again, this time in a whisper. Her face was ashen and she refused to make eye contact with either of us, even when I gave her a swift kick under the table.

'And that's why I asked you to come meet me tonight,' Lauren went on, in a Keep Calm and Carry On voice. American born maybe, but that girl had the stiff upper lip of a Brit when it was needed. She could pretend something wasn't happening like an absolute pro. 'To ask if you would be my bridesmaids.'

'Of course!' I shouted. Bridesmaids! Lauren's bridesmaids! Lauren was getting married! Argh! I mean, hurrah! 'That's amazing, Lauren – come here.'

Hugging seemed like the socially correct gesture, but in half a heartbeat I went from being ecstatically happy to realizing it would make me the spinster of the group. But still, I gave her a hug instead of stabbing her through the heart with my butter knife. I was raised properly.

'Sarah, isn't this amazing?' I asked, widening my eyes at our other friend across the table while Lauren showed off her ring to the waiter, who politely pretended to care.

But Sarah didn't reply. We should have been screeching and making neighbouring tables offer awkward congratulations, but instead of leaping to her feet and joining the hug, Sarah was staring at her knees with tears streaming down her face.

'Sarah?'

She held up a hand and tried to choke down the tears so that she could speak. Good old emotionally constipated Sarah had finally exploded. She was too overcome with happiness to leave her seat. It was impressive, really – Sarah never cries. When we went to her grandmother's funeral, she was the one who elbowed me in the ribs and told me to keep it together. But our dear friend's unexpected betrothal to a slightly dull man who thought cleaning products were an appropriate expression of love was finally the thing that got to her.

'I think I'm going to be sick,' she croaked.

It wasn't the response either of us had been expecting. 'What's wrong?' I asked. 'Are you OK?'

She looked up, mascara running down her face, lips pursed tightly together, and shook her head, rubbing her hands together like a Topshop-clad Lady Macbeth.

'These are bridesmaid journals,' Lauren said, determinedly upbeat, taking her seat again and tossing the two pink packages across the table, 'so you can write down all the happy memories, like the time I asked you to be my bridesmaids and showed you my engagement ring and Sarah said she wanted to throw up?'

And that was when I noticed Sarah's left hand was entirely without diamond adornment. No engagement ring, no wedding ring.

Fuckityfuckfuckcockbollocks.

'Come on, you two, I'm getting married!' Lauren said before I could react. She waved her newly accessorized hand in the air, too busy looking at her own ring to notice the lack of someone else's. 'What's wrong? Be happy!'

'Sorry, don't meant to be rude,' Sarah said, raising her champagne glass in a solo toast and then draining every last drop. 'Steve asked me for a divorce at the weekend, but, you know, here's to you. Cheers.'

And so, dear diary, on the upside, tonight I was given this lovely journal, but on the downside, I had to endure one of the most uncomfortable evenings of my entire life. On reflection, probably not worth it.

All About You

Being a bridesmaid isn't just a day to wear a pretty dress and have your photo taken!

As well as getting to know your bride even better than you do today, it's a time to learn a lot about yourself. Fill in the answers below and you might be surprised to learn what an accomplished and powerful and wonderful young woman you already are.

Remember, there's a reason your bride chose you!

My hair is: light brown
My eyes are: green
My favourite physical attribute is: boobs
I don't love my: ~~thighs arse bank balance~~ but they're mine!
My three best qualities are: loyalty, sense of humour, perseverance (as evidenced by this journal)
I make a great friend because: I'm a good listener, I remember everything and I always have gin
~~Three~~ things I will practise from this day on for a happier, healthier life:
– Delete all the shopping apps off my phone before I bankrupt myself
~~– Stop looking at my ex-boyfriend's Facebook page~~
– Only look at my ex-boyfriend's Facebook page once a week
– Read all the big literary books Sarah has given me instead of looking at the Wikipedia entries for the ones that win prizes and telling everyone I've read them
– Get fantastic boyfriend and post so many pictures of

the two of us that people I don't know that well unfriend/
unfollow me
– ~~Spend time meditating and getting to know myself so I
can truly be happy~~
– Throw out dry shampoo and bloody well wash hair more
often

2

Friday May 15th

Today I feel: Like eating All Of The Things.
Today I am thankful for: The fact I'm too lazy to go out and buy all of the things.

Knowing I had to work all day Saturday for the McCallan wedding, I had planned to spend the entirety of Friday night on my arse watching some terrible television and working my way through the millions of emails Lauren had already sent about her wedding and hastily arranged engagement party, set for Sunday afternoon. I know, two days' notice. FUN.

So far she'd sent me fifteen different wedding dresses, six venues and enquired whether or not we could get Beyoncé to play the reception – and, officially speaking, we hadn't even started planning properly yet.

Why did I get the feeling this wasn't going to be an easy one?

I was tapping out the politest version of 'No, we cannot get one of the most successful musicians in the world to play the reception, you lovely moron' when the texts from Sarah started. It was her first Friday night as a single woman in ten years, and she wasn't doing well, despite the seventeen 'I'm fine' text messages she'd sent me earlier in the day.

An hour later, she was at my door, Oddbins bag in hand.

'Sorry it's such a shit-hole,' I said, shoving half a pile of magazines off the coffee table onto the floor as she gingerly placed her handbag in their place.

'It's always a shit-hole,' she pointed out, her voice tired and defeated as she handed me a bottle of gin and looked round at the clutter spread all across my flat. Open plan had seemed like such a good idea when I found the place but all I'd really done was double the amount of space I had available to fill with shit. At least she'd had the presence of mind to bring tonic. I never had anything helpful in my cupboards unless you considered an unopened packet of Ryvita and a not quite empty box of Frosties useful. 'I'm used to it – your shit-hole is reassuring. Drinks. Now.'

It's easy to let your flat become a takeaway-box-littered shantytown when no one else is there, but it's hard to defend your appalling housekeeping skills face to face. Ever since Seb had moved out, I'd lacked the motivation to keep the place in order. It was amazing how quickly you could get over dust allergies if you tried.

'I was going to clean this evening,' I lied, 'but I thought essential bonding time with my best friend in the entire world was more important. Do correct me if I'm wrong.'

'You might actually be.' Sarah slapped both of her hands down on the kitchen counter and gave me a grim smile. 'This place is a human rights violation.'

'Shut up and drink your gin,' I said, poking my way to the back of a cupboard to find clean glasses. 'Shona was a real bitch today.'

I'm not proud of myself, but I was putting off talking about the divorce until I had at least one drink in me. I had no idea how to talk about the divorce. If I'd had advance warning, I might have bought in a lot of ice cream and dug up my *Pretty Woman* DVD, because that's what we did when Dave Stevenson stood her up for the lower sixth Halloween disco. I didn't know the protocol for this one.

'I know we give you shit about it, but you need to find a new job,' Sarah said, moving a pile of creased sweatshirts from the settee to the armchair and sitting herself down. 'I can't believe you got a mammogram for her. Your boss shouldn't really get a say in your tits unless you're sleeping with them for a promotion.'

'How do you know I'm not?'

'Because of that time Lauren kissed you at the uni ball to impress Stephan Jones and you threw up immediately afterwards.'

'That was as much to do with Aftershock shots as my aversion to lipstick lesbianism,' I replied. 'I could be a lesbian.'

'You couldn't even get through an entire series of *Orange Is the New Black*.'

'Yes, but that was because I live in mortal fear of going to prison and ending up as someone's bitch,' I pointed out. 'Not because I'm scared of a loving, respectful, consensual partnership with a lady.'

'You're not gay, Maddie,' she said. 'You're just a wimp.'

'Yeah, I know,' I said, chopping up a sad-looking lemon for our gin. 'That's one of the upsides of having a gay sister. You don't run around going "I wish I was a lesbian, it's so much easier", because it isn't.'

Sarah nodded and held her hand out for a red wine glass full to the brim with gin and tonic. 'Remember that girl she was going out with in her first year at Durham? What a cock.'

'It's not just the chaps,' I agreed. 'Women can be just as bad.'

'Yeah, well, I'm pretty anti-man right now,' she said, nursing the glass but not drinking.

Here it was. The Talk. We were going to have the talk and I was going to be supportive and caring and she would leave here knowing that she was an incredible person who, in spite of all the pain she was going through, was utterly and completely loved. I was going to say just the right thing.

'Yuh-huh.'

I suck so hard.

Thankfully, Sarah didn't seem to mind my friend fail and took it upon herself to start talking anyway. I dropped a lemon in her drink, sat myself down and held my glass tightly. All I needed to do was listen.

'Things had been shit for a while,' Sarah said. 'I suppose I got used to it. He was out a lot and I've been working so much . . . you don't realize how quickly things can go wrong. It's got to be three months since we even had sex. I just didn't realize.'

I nodded in silence. Three months. Was that a long time? I'd forgotten.

'Then he comes home one day and out of nowhere he's like, it isn't working, I want a divorce. Just like that, he wants a divorce.'

'So, what actually happened?' I asked, treading as carefully as I knew how. 'What exactly did he say?'

These were the same two questions I'd been asking her about boys since we were eleven. The fact that we were thirty-one and still having the same conversations was impossibly depressing.

Sarah took a deep breath and blew it out in one big huff.

'It's so ridiculous, saying it out loud,' she said, her big blue eyes tearing up already. And as we've established, Sarah is not a crier. 'It was Saturday, he'd been at the football with Michael and some of the others all day. I was a bit pissed off because, like I said, we hardly ever see each other and he was out so late, and he didn't tell me what time he'd be home.'

'So you were perfectly entitled to be annoyed,' I said.

'Exactly,' she nodded, swiping at a stray tear before it messed up her eyeliner. 'So I was making dinner when he got in, and he got a beer out of the fridge and I said dinner was almost ready and could he open the wine, and he said he didn't want wine and I said I wanted wine, and he said he wanted to go out and I said I'd made dinner, and he slammed down his beer on the kitchen top and it spilled everywhere, and then he said "This isn't working". And yeah, it went from there.'

Sarah was still staring at her gin instead of drinking it, but I was halfway down mine.

'It's weird, isn't it?' she said, tapping her bitten-down nail on the rim of her glass. 'You think these things are going to be dead dramatic, and then they're not. You're doing something painfully normal and having a totally average chat, and then, there it is. He just says it, just like that. It's not working. He wants a divorce. Dunzo.'

'Did he actually say he wants to get divorced, though?'

I asked, looking for a silver lining in this epic pile of shit. 'Maybe he means he wants a break. Or he wants to fix things? This might be his way of getting your attention.'

'He's got that,' she replied in a voice so light it felt like her words might float away before I heard them. 'He's already moved out. He slept on the settee on Saturday and went to stay at his mum's on Sunday. He's not coming back, Maddie. He emailed me today to say he's got a lawyer and I should do the same.'

'Oh, bloody hell.' I squeezed her ankle, the most easily accessibly appendage, while she chewed on her bottom lip in an attempt to stop the tears from coming. She'd been gnawing on that thing for so many years I was amazed she hadn't chewed it right off. 'Why didn't you call me before? I could have done—'

'Absolutely nothing?'

I had never felt so useless in my entire life. I wanted to help but didn't know how, and when your entire existence is based around being The One Who Helps, that is majorly distressing.

'I started about a million texts, but I couldn't work out how to say it,' Sarah said. 'Plus I had a yoga workshop.'

I paused, mid-sip. 'You went to a yoga workshop? The day after your husband told you he wanted a divorce?'

'I'd already paid for it,' she said, daring me to argue. 'And what was I supposed to do – sit around and cry all weekend?'

'I don't know whether to be massively impressed or have you sectioned,' I said. 'So that's it? It's happening?'

Sarah tilted back her glass and chugged it down in three big gulps.

'When I try to think about it,' she said, 'it's like my brain shuts down. I can't even process it. Then I'll be sat having a wee and I'll look at my hand and think, do I have to take my wedding ring off? Has he already taken his off? I actually googled how long it would take for the groove to go away.'

She held up her hand and stretched out her bare fingers. I felt my own face crumple a little bit as her tears started to come in earnest.

'Turns out it takes longer than a week,' she gasped, clenching her hand into a tight fist. 'I can't believe that he's doing this and he's happy about it. How can someone who said they loved you every day for a decade suddenly decide they don't any more? I'm sitting at home every night, sleeping in the spare room because I can't stand to be in our bed, and he's *happy*.'

'Do you think he's cheating?' I asked.

She fidgeted with her top button for a moment and then shook her head.

'No,' she said with certainty. 'He said he isn't.'

'Right,' I replied.

'Why?' Suddenly she wasn't looking nearly as certain. 'He wouldn't. Would he? Do you think he is? Have you heard something?'

'Of course not,' I replied instantly, squeezing her foot to calm her down.

Another white lie in the name of friendship.

Of course I thought he was cheating. Why else would he suddenly decide he wanted to abandon his wife and marriage without giving it a second thought? They'd been together since uni, inseparable for a decade, and now he had randomly decided it wasn't working out? I remembered when Seb left me, wonderful Shona reminding me that most men don't leave until they've got the next thing lined up. I scoffed at the time but of course, it turned out she was right in my case. Not an insight I would share with Sarah at this stage, perhaps.

'I don't want to get divorced,' Sarah said, her watery blue eyes meeting my red-rimmed green ones. 'I don't want to have to tell people I'm divorced and sit there while they wonder what's wrong with me or do exactly what you just did and assume he was cheating on me. What's going to happen to me now?'

I stared blankly at the TV that I'd muted when I heard the doorbell but not turned off. A cartoon played silently in the background, a happy dysfunctional family, husband, wife, three kids.

'I don't know,' I said, not wanting to lie any more than I had to. 'But I do know we'll get through it. I don't know what else to say that won't sound like a load of annoying clichés.'

'I'm only thirty-one,' Sarah said, gripping the stem of her glass until her knuckles turned white. 'I'm not the first person in the world to get divorced, am I? Better now than ten years down the line when we'd have two kids in the mix, isn't it?'

'Course.' I wondered how many times she'd told herself that already this week. 'You're totally right.'

'All I want is to not feel like this any more,' she said wearily, putting down her glass and pressing the heels of her hands against her eyes. 'It's like the worst hangover ever. I feel sick and empty, and every time I forget about it for a moment, it comes back and punches me in the face. And the only person who could make me feel better about it is the person who's causing it. I hate him so much I can see it, but all I want is for him to come home and tell me he's changed his mind.'

That part I recognized. 'Really? You'd take him back?'

'I don't even know,' she laughed, sounding sour. 'I don't know what I'd do. How would I ever trust him? I'd always be waiting for him to do it again, wouldn't I?'

For want of a better response, I shrugged.

'So what the fuck do I do now?' Sarah asked, dropping her head against the back of my saggy settee. 'Am I just supposed to sit here until it stops feeling like someone ripped my insides out with a fish hook?'

'Would it help if I made you a kale smoothie?' I offered.

'It might,' she said, pulling my hair. 'But I think I'd rather have another gin.'

'Good because I don't have any kale.' I grabbed the bottle off the coffee table and topped her up. 'Let me get the tonic out of the fridge.'

'Don't bother,' she said, taking a glug then holding up her glass. 'To fresh starts, Maddie. Cheers.'

'Cheers,' I echoed, wondering whether or not there ever was such a thing as a fresh start, or whether you just picked up a new set of problems.

I can't believe Sarah is getting divorced. It's bizarre: I've known her for two-thirds of my life, and for the first time ever, I have no idea what to say to her.

Divorce. She's getting a divorce. I don't know anyone who got married and isn't married any more other than Lauren's parents, and I don't really *know* them. It's so weird. When you're single you don't think about that bit, even though in this day and age you're fully aware of that bit. Getting the ring on your finger is the goal: the white dress, the John Lewis wedding-present list, worry about the rest of it afterwards. Getting married means you've won, and I hate thinking like that, I do, but let's be honest, that's just how it is. In our super progressive, equal rights, modern society, it's the one thing no one wants to say but everyone is thinking, however messed-up it is.

Until you're married, you're a loser, no matter how great you are at everything else. But what does that make someone who gets divorced?

Divorce is something that happens to my parents' generation, not my friends. Like in year nine, when everyone's mum and dad suddenly split up and no one talked about it until Jane couldn't come to your ice-skating birthday party because she 'had to see her dad on Saturdays'.

Shit, who will get their cat? They both love that cat. Won't somebody think of the children?

3

Saturday May 16th
Today I feel: Sore.
Today I am thankful for: Shaving my legs this morning when I couldn't really be bothered.

I am so confused as to what happened today. All I do know is that it has ended with a strange man in my bed who I cannot ask to leave because it's impolite, but who I really wish would leave because I'm starving and want to eat some biscuits, and if I don't, I'm worried I might very well eat his arm in the night.

It started out as a normal day. Well, normal apart from the wedding/divorce debacle of Thursday night and then the depressing divorce-and-gin fest of Friday night, obviously. I got up, I texted my friends, they didn't reply, and I went to work. The only difference was that my text to Lauren was all about her wedding, rather than last night's telly, and my text to Sarah just said 'Are you OK?' She'd left at ten o'clock last night, teary with mother's ruin but refusing the offer to stay over with a curled lip at my shabby sofa and the mountains of washing covering the spare bed. Fair play, really.

Ahhh, work. The McCallan wedding.

One of the fun things about working for an events planner is you never know exactly what you're going to be doing from one day to the next, other than working yourself into a blind, desperate pit of no return seven days a week, obviously. Thanks to ten years in the trade, I am now a passable florist, competent seamstress and an excellent mixologist. Nevertheless, I wasn't too happy when I got to the reception venue to find out two of the waitresses couldn't be arsed to get out of bed and come to work, meaning I had to save the day by putting on a pinny and serving a room full of drunk people an absurdly expensive chicken dinner.

It's amazing how terribly people treat wait staff sometimes. I ask you, how hard is it to say please and thank you? I'd say their mothers would be appalled but most of their mothers were there and quite frankly, in a lot of instances, the mothers were the worst. After spending a year planning every last moment of the McCallan's big day, running around on the actual day of the wedding, fetching and carrying dirty dishes, while every single assembled guest refused to look me in the eye didn't half test my moral fibre.

And then I saw him.

He was easy on the eyes, there was no getting around it. His eyes were brown, but a light brown – sort of gold, when you looked at them – and his black hair was shaved close to his head, giving him an air of an Action Man; but somehow, it worked. He had gorgeous full lips, and when he smiled at me I wanted to burn every pair of knickers I owned because I would never, ever be needing them again. He looked solid but smiley, like he'd always have a joke to tell you, and even while he was charming the pants off your parents he'd have his hand on your arse, and at the end of the night, when you'd had one too many, he'd feel you up a bit in the taxi.

'Hello, everyone.'

Action Man was actually the best man. When it was his turn to give a toast, he didn't even need to clink his glass. As soon as he stood up, everyone turned around and sat up straight. Without even asking myself why, I tightened my ponytail and bit some colour into my lips. Be still my beating heart.

'As most of you already know, I'm Will, the best man,' he said. 'Or at least I'm the best one that was free today and had his own suit.'

I leaned against the wall, cupping my elbow in one hand, and pressed a fist against my mouth. He wasn't so tall but he was tall enough, and his jacket hung perfectly from his shoulders, the result either of excellent tailoring or of excellent shoulders, it was hard to tell, but his easy stance and the way he looked around the room, totally comfortable in a situation that others found unbearable, gave me the biggest ladyboner.

Here's the thing. I've always loved weddings. When I was little, I would run around the house wrapped up in a bed sheet screaming 'I do!' at the next-door neighbour, and when I was seven and my aunt got married, I didn't take my bridesmaid's dress off for two weeks. And that was only because I had the measles and threw up on it. Since then, I've been a bridesmaid five times and I would do it five more times if someone asked. How is it not fun? The dress shopping, the hen night, the penis head-bands, I love all of it. And then there's the actual wedding:

you get a new frock, you get a free feed, you get to drink from the crack of dawn right through to the next day and not even your parents can complain about it. Weddings are the best.

But after hearing Sarah and Lauren's news on Thursday, for the first time ever I was beginning to feel the onset of matrimonial fatigue. All of a sudden, everything that had once made me clap with delight had me rolling my eyes instead. Oh, you're pretending to run away from a dinosaur in your pictures? How original. Choreographed first dance to the song from *Dirty Dancing*? *You guys!* It was horrible. Even the thought of stealing macarons from the dessert table didn't help. I was over macarons. And when a woman declares herself over macarons, you know something is wrong. By the time the speeches had begun, it would be all I could do not to launch myself at the bride and groom and start screaming, 'This is a sham! True love is an illusion! We're all going to die alone!'

And for an assistant wedding planner, that was less than ideal.

And so the undeniable hotness of the best man made for a very welcome distraction on an incredibly shitty day.

'I've known Em and Ian for donkeys,' Will went on. Addressing the room, making eye contact, not using notes. All very impressive. 'And between you and me, I couldn't have been happier when he told me they were getting married. In fact, when he told me he was going to ask her, I cried. And then, when he sent me a text to say she said yes, I cried again.'

All the mums began to sniff and coo in unison, while all the single women pulled out lipsticks and powder compacts as they readied themselves to go to war.

Will was doing a good job.

'You see, it's hard to meet someone these days.' He gave a little shrug and looked over at the happy couple. 'These two met at a wedding, if you can believe it – my little sister's wedding, actually – and I know it's a cliché, but I knew they were going the distance as soon as they started going out. Actually, let me clarify that first bit again. It's not hard to meet someone. It's hard to meet someone special.' He cleared his throat and let his voice crack a little, and I may or may not have let out a little squeak.

'When Ian started seeing Emma, he changed, and I don't mean that in a bad way. Whenever we saw each other, he couldn't stop saying her name. He brought her to the football and let her wear the scarf that his dad bought him when he was six, and then, when he changed his Facebook status *and* his profile photo, I knew it was only a matter of time.

'I think, when you meet someone who you love so much that you're happy to tell Mark Zuckerberg and the world that they're yours, you ought to lock it down. There was never any doubt for him. As soon as they met, no one else even existed to Ian. That's why I'm not going to stand here and make jokes about his suit and his haircut. Although I clearly could.'

Cue genuine laughter. Cue me flushing from head to toe as Best Man Will picked up the Libbey Embassy champagne coupe that I'd had to order in especially because the bride wanted coupes and not flutes and raised it high in the air.

He was staring right at me.

Not at the little redheaded bridesmaid who was trying to squeeze her arms together to make her demure lilac gown show a bit more cleavage, or at the hot blonde guest who had been crossing and uncrossing her legs throughout the entire speech.

He kept looking at me.

Flushed in the face from running in and out of the kitchen, hair yanked back in a utilitarian ponytail, mascara all over my face after a champagne-opening incident that left me and three other people smelling like a piss-up in a very fancy brewery.

And I had checked – my shirt wasn't unbuttoned or anything.

'So if you would all join me and raise your glasses. To the bride and groom.'

As everyone shuffled out of their seats, the women struggling to stand in their too-high heels that would soon be kicked off and replaced with flip-flops, I blinked, breaking the connection. When I looked back, he was smiling at the bride and groom, the moment gone.

Breathing more heavily than is healthy, I slipped back into the kitchen looking for a drink of my own.

'Sorry to bother you, but have you got a light?'

Hours later, when the buffet had been reduced to nothing more than a few stray cherry tomatoes and the odd splodge of tartar sauce, I was hiding at the back of the venue, holding a Marlboro Light, tearing up at the picture of Lauren's engagement ring on Facebook and trying to work out how to ask Sarah if she was OK again without saying 'Are you OK?', because clearly she wasn't. When I looked up, a man in a suit (strangely enough) was holding out a cigarette of his own. I blinked a couple of times, my eyes adjusting from the bright white light of the iPhone screen to the semi-darkness of my hidey-hole.

'Oh, um, I haven't actually got one,' I said, squinting. It was one of the ushers. The one whose trousers were an inch too short. You tend to notice strange things when you work two weddings a week for three-quarters of the year. 'Sorry.'

'No worries,' he said, putting the cigarette back in the pack of ten in his inside pocket. He was awfully tall; I supposed that explained the trousers. 'I'm supposed to have quit anyway.'

'Probably best then.' I shuffled from foot to sensibly shod foot, flicking my unlit cigarette between my fingers and tucking my phone back into the waistband of my skirt.

He nodded, pressed his lips together and stuck his hands in his pockets.

'Did you lose your lighter?' he asked.

Oh good, awkward conversation. I loved those. Why couldn't he leave me alone so I could bunk off and text my friend in peace?

'Oh no,' I replied, preparing myself. 'I don't smoke.'

The very tall usher looked at me strangely.

'You don't smoke?' he asked.

'No.'

'But you're standing outside holding a cigarette?'

'Yes.'

He took in a short breath that sounded like he was going to say something, then shook his head and stopped himself. Then did it again and didn't stop himself. More's the pity.

'I'm sure I'm going to regret it, but can I ask why you're standing outside holding a cigarette without a lighter if you don't smoke?'

It was a fair question; I just didn't want to answer it.

I wanted to read some showbiz gossip on my phone, text Sarah, call Lauren and pretend I hadn't just pissed away an entire Saturday at someone else's special day. It didn't matter if you were wearing Jimmy Choos or a pair of Clarks – if you were on your feet for nigh on twelve hours, you were in pain.

'My boss smokes,' I said, shaking a full box of Marlboros at him. 'And she takes cigarette breaks all the time, so she can't stop me from taking them. So, you know, as far as she's concerned, I've got a very healthy two packs a day habit. Or unhealthy, as the case may be.'

He looked at me. 'You're not serious?'

I looked back at him.

'Oh my God, you are.'

'She thinks smoking is better than eating,' I replied. 'Fewer carbs.'

'But smoking will kill you,' he said, looking at his own pack with a regularly repeated lecture playing over in his head. 'She does know that, doesn't she?'

'We get private health insurance,' I said. 'So it all works out.'

'Fair enough.' The usher put his cigarettes away and scrunched up his face for a moment, staring at me. 'I hate weddings,' he said.

'Really?' Who went around saying they hated weddings while they were at a wedding. 'Why?'

'There's so much standing around,' he said wearily, pushing wavy brown hair off his forehead. Earlier it had been all slicked back and crunchy-looking, but by this point in the proceedings his locks had let loose. He needed a good shot of Elnett; he had to be single. 'And there's never anywhere to go. I just want to sod off somewhere and have a sit-down.'

'Once I did a wedding that had a mini cinema,' I said, nodding in agreement, 'but the bride got angry because everyone sat in there all night instead of dancing to the band she'd paid a bloody fortune for. In the end she made us turn the film off and shouted at everybody.'

'What film was it?' he asked.

'*Ghostbusters*. The groom picked all the films from when they'd been dating but he did too good a job.'

'I'd give my right arm to sit in the dark and watch *Ghostbusters* right now,' he said, sighing. His skin was quite pale and his eyes were quite dark and he really was awfully tall. At least a foot and a half taller than me. Teetering around too tall territory. Just the right height if you wanted something down from the loft, but a nightmare to sit next to if you were flying economy.

'They had ice cream and beer as well,' I added, trying not to look at his visible ankles.

'I might never have left.' He paused for a moment and then smiled.

He was nice looking when he smiled, a bit less gawky and angular, a realization that only made me feel all the more uncomfortable. I felt myself breathe in slightly and brushed a few stray strands of hair behind my ear.

'Maybe my fiancée will let me have one at my wedding.'

Stray strands of hair be damned and belly be bloated.

'And these bloody penguin suits,' he said, ignoring me and pulling at his stiff collar. 'If I took my tie off, I'd look like one of you.'

'One of you?' I asked. What the cocking cock was that supposed to mean?

'Oh. Oh!' he said, hands stuck midair as though he

were showing me he had caught a fish thiiiiis big. 'I didn't mean anything by it. Just that, you know, I'm dressed like a waiter.'

As soon as he'd said it, I could tell he wanted to take it back. Unfortunately for him, I was not in the mood to let anyone off with anything.

'And what's wrong with being a waiter?' I asked.

He looked even paler than he had two minutes before. 'Nothing. But I'm a lawyer.'

He couldn't have been anything else in the world, could he? He *had* to be a lawyer.

'And you think being a lawyer is better than being a waiter?'

'I was just trying to say how funny it is that we're both wearing black and white, when I'm at the wedding and you're just a waitress,' he said.

And there it was. The shovel hit the soil and suddenly he was tit-deep in a hole he couldn't possibly dig himself out of. Just a waitress? *Just* a waitress?

'Not that I think being a lawyer is better than being a waitress,' he said, the panic setting in. 'I think it's brilliant that you're a waitress.'

I was so angry, I was very nearly ready to be slightly rude.

'Is it?'

No one had ever made those two syllables sound like such a threat.

He was flustered. I was angry. It was a perfect British combination. I think we both knew it was time for him to give up and walk away, but I knew he wasn't going to: lawyers never could.

'Absolutely. I look like a penguin.' The usher pressed his arms against his side and kicked his legs out. He looked so ridiculous that I almost softened. 'I think you're more of a panda.'

And then I stopped almost smiling.

'How come you're a penguin and I'm a panda?' I asked, breathing in again. Had he just called me fat? 'Because I'm a woman?'

'Pandas are good!' he replied, exasperated. 'Pandas are better than penguins!'

'Maddie?' Shona's voice cut through the darkness.

'Christ.' I pulled my cigarette back out, broke off the filter and ground it against the wall before Shona could bust me. 'Whatever.'

'Pandas *are* better than penguins,' he said in a sulky voice. 'So much better. Everyone knows that.'

I shook my head and turned on my heel, striding back towards the kitchen as quickly as my ugly practical shoes would carry me.

Wanker.

4

'*MADDIE!*'

'I'm here!' I picked up pace and ran into the kitchen, to find my boss waiting for me. 'What's wrong?'

'Nothing,' she said. She was sitting on a stool, leaning her elbows on the big stainless-steel island in the middle of the kitchen. 'Everything's fine. Do you want a drink?'

Sometimes this happens. Sometimes my boss Shona forgets she's a she-beast who would be better occupied guarding the gates of hell and likes to pretend we're friends. This is how you know she's a properly evil mental case. The truly psychotic are not consistent.

'Go on, then,' I said. I didn't know if it was a trap or not, but I am not above taking a free drink when it's offered.

She poured two glasses of champagne into water glasses and pushed one towards with me something resembling a smile. I took it, peeking at the phone in my pocket while she chugged. Shona might tolerate drinking and smoking on the job, but carrying your phone while you were waitressing? She'd replace my champagne with lighter fluid, spark it up and still make me drink it. There was a message from Sarah but it was going to have to wait two minutes until I could escape.

Looking up at my boss, I saw that she was already three-quarters of the way through her Veuve Clicquot. Shona was tall and thin with white-blonde hair that sometimes looked fantastic and sometimes looked as though she needed to shave it off and start again. Today fell somewhere between the two.

'I don't think we're going to need you to serve for the late shift,' she said, refilling her glass and not refilling mine. 'I was going to send a couple of the girls home, but why don't you just knock off early instead.'

'Thanks,' I said, utterly relieved.

'I don't mean leave,' she expanded. 'I just mean you don't have to waitress. I still need you here to make sure everything runs OK. I'm probably going to go home after this.'

Oh, Shona, you card. It was only ten and I knew full well that we had the venue booked until two a.m.

'Going somewhere nice?' I asked through gritted teeth.

'Maddie, I'm exhausted,' she announced, rubbing both of her hands over her face. 'Ever since that slacker Victoria quit, I've been doing two people's jobs. I need a bath, another seven drinks and an early night. You can handle this – I trust you.'

Fighting the urge to charge her with the carving knife resting on the butcher's block to my left, I pasted on a smile. She was my boss, she was allowed to leave early. Even if I had arrived two hours before her, done all the prep and spent three hours serving at the reception while she sat on her arse in the kitchen drinking herself stupid.

'Speaking of Victoria—'

'The slacker.' Shona nodded.

'Such a slacker,' I replied with far too much enthusiasm. 'Can't believe she just left like that.'

'Standard,' she replied. 'She was crap anyway.'

For the record, Victoria is neither crap nor a slacker, she's a very nice lady who happened to marry a man who used to work with us who Shona fancied. Probably best that they've both left now, for their own safety.

'Actually, I meant to ask, is her job still going? Have we hired anyone yet?'

Across the island, Shona lowered her glass from her lips and nursed it in both hands. Very, very slowly, I reached out for the carving knife and placed it in the sink behind me.

'Victoria was crap,' she said in a crisp voice, never taking her eyes off me. 'Compared to me. Compared to most other people in the industry, she was brilliant.'

'OK.'

I wished I could have recorded that and sent it to Vic. It might have made up for the time Shona emailed the entire office asking them not to eat snacks in front of her because she'd just joined Weight Watchers and we should all support her in her weight-loss journey. It was just about the nicest thing she'd ever said about anyone.

'But you won't get that job, Maddie. So don't embarrass yourself by applying for it.'

For some reason, it seemed as though I had suddenly decided to stop breathing. What?

'You're a decent assistant, Maddie, but there's a lot to learn and a long way to go. You know I'm not an event planner, I'm—'

She cued me to complete the line.

'An experiential architect,' I said, trying not to be sick in my mouth.

'An experiential architect,' she confirmed. 'And let's be honest, you're not cut out for management, are you? I know I can say that to you without hurting your feelings because we've known each other for such a long time.'

Too long, some might say.

'If you were working for anyone else, I'm not sure they would have been as patient as me,' she said, raising her glass and sipping. 'I'm so used to you, it's like I hardly notice how you let me down me sometimes.'

I didn't say anything, I just nodded.

'I mean, you'd have to apply like everyone else, submit your CV, interview with Mr Colton,' Shona's eyes sparkled at the very thought. 'And to be honest, he's so totally threatened by me, your being my assistant for so long would probably go against you.'

'It would?'

'That's if they even gave you an interview,' she said, wincing at the very thought. 'I know everyone likes you, and your job must seem like a lot of fun, but moving up would mean a lot of responsibility. You would literally have to be me.'

I'd have to lose three stone, fuck up my hair and start taking motivational tips from Darth Vader first.

'Don't overreach, Maddie. When you shoot for the moon, you end up with your face in the mud.'

I blinked several times and gently reminded my lungs that I needed them to work for me to go on living. They weren't convinced. It had been a bloody long day.

'I thought it was reach for the moon and you might land amongst the stars?' I said. 'Isn't that the saying?'

'To be in the stars, you've got to be a star.' Shona gave me a sharp, kindly look. 'Do you feel like a star, Maddie?'

I looked down at my slightly too-small-across-the-bust shirt, knee-length black skirt and nana-approved shoes. I did not feel like a star. I felt like a girl at the end of year nine who has grown out of her school uniform but her mum doesn't want to buy her a new one until September.

'Do you know what –' she slipped off her stool in her three-inch black patent heels and sleek grey dress and knocked back the dregs of her drink without so much as a champs shiver – 'why don't *you* take the rest of the night off? No point in having an assistant around if her head's not in the game anyway, is there? I'd only spend all night worrying and double-checking.'

I wasn't sure how I'd managed to be so thoroughly insulted and abused but still get away with an early finish, so I kept my mouth shut and my eyes down. Shona rounded the kitchen island and patted me on the shoulder.

'Go home and think about what you're suggesting,' she said as I flinched. 'Ask yourself if you really want to put yourself through it. I can't guarantee that your job will still be waiting for you if you decide you want to play at being me and it all goes wrong.'

'That's not—' I started to explain but she cut me off with a sad shrug.

'It's just not who you are, Maddie,' she said with a sympathetic smile. 'You're an assistant. You're good at that. Mostly. Don't rock the boat.'

Left alone in the kitchen clutching the bottle of champagne, there was nothing for me to do except storm back outside into the gardens. The party was in full flow inside, big picture windows lit up with flashing lights and silhouettes of people much happier than I was. Or at least more drunk than me. Pouting, I considered the champagne and decided it was churlish to waste it just because I didn't want it. Besides, nothing said thirty-one and going nowhere better than binge-drinking alone.

Staring blindly into the party, I was vaguely aware of a vibration against my right thigh. Phone. It was my phone.

'Oh no, Sarah,' I remembered, throwing myself down underneath a tree like a fifteen-year-old with a bottle of White Lightning. *'You home?'*

This was followed by a sad-face emoji and a gun. And that was followed by two Martini glasses and a dancing girl. The phone rattled in my hand as I tried to decipher the pictograms while swigging champagne out of the bottle. Class act all the way.

'Tell me you haven't killed yourself.'

'If I'd killed myself, I couldn't tell you, could I?' I typed. *'I'm still at work, you ok?'*

Turns out there wasn't a better way to ask that question.

'No.'

And no better way to answer it.

'Have you seen FB?'

'No.' I typed, wondering what fantastic news awaited me on the wonderful world of the Internet. *'What?'*

There was a pause, followed by three little grey dots on the screen.

'Seb's missus had the baby.'

If only they had stayed dots.

Seb had a baby. There was a baby Seb. A tiny, red-faced, screaming mini Seb.

And it wasn't mine.

Seb. Formerly Bash or Sebby, latterly Knobjockey, Cockchops and, most recently and accurately, that absolute bastard who systematically pulled apart every single one of my organs like Cheestrings before getting to my heart, taking it out, freezing it, defrosting it in the microwave, freezing it again, defrosting it and freezing it one last time until all that was left was a leathery bit of offal that would nourish neither man nor beast. I was still getting letters from Direct Line about his car insurance renewal and he was married with a baby.

'*So?*'

I tapped out the letters, totally not imagining the former love of my life sitting in a fancy private hospital room holding his new baby while his sweaty but beautiful wife smiled at him knowingly. I had some dregs of champagne and a shirt that was a size too small. The only thing that could even this out was a kebab on the way home.

'*I've got to get back to work.*' Lying was so much easier through the medium of text. '*See you tomorrow?*'

'There you are. I've been looking for you.'

A very tall man appeared from nowhere in the semi-darkness before she could reply, and for a split second I was very worried that I might not live to see that kebab.

'That's not an incredibly creepy way to address someone you don't know,' I replied. It was the insulting usher. 'I definitely didn't think you were going to kill me.'

'Sorry,' he said, clearly not meaning it. 'Not smoking again?'

'No, this time I'm not not drinking.' I held up the champagne bottle and didn't smile. 'Cheers.'

He crouched down beside me and took the bottle, helping himself to a swig.

'You might be the most interesting waitress I've ever met,' he said, handing the bottle back. Even in a squat he was massive. I'm pretty standard height at five four-ish, but he had to be pushing six five. He would be a very helpful man to know if I needed any light bulbs changing.

'Thanks,' I replied, sipping my booze straight out of the bottle in as ladylike a fashion as possible. 'I try.'

No point explaining I wasn't a waitress. Might as well be a waitress anyway: most of the waitresses I met did something else. They were actresses or models or musicians or they were at uni studying something fantastic. That or they had lovely families at home and they waitressed as a part-time thing. All I had at home were fourteen back issues of *Marie Claire*, three still in their mailing bags, and a stale chocolate croissant that I would probably eat when I got home, regardless.

'I wanted to apologize,' he said. 'I think I was rude earlier.'

Seb had a baby.

'What?' I looked at him, confused.

'Earlier, I was a bit out of it.' He folded himself up into an oversized-schoolboy sitting position. 'It feels as though I ought to say sorry.'

'You *think* you were rude?' I said. 'And it *feels as though* you ought to say sorry? Don't knock yourself out, whatever you do.'

'All right, I *was* rude and I *am* sorry,' he replied, overenunciating but still not leaving, which was all I wanted him to do. 'I'm having a very bloody bad day.'

I took another sip and then laughed.

'My boss just told me I'm shit and I'll never get promoted, one of my best friends is getting divorced, the other is getting married, and my ex-boyfriend literally just had a baby with his new wife. As in, an hour ago.'

'Not ideal,' he said, combing his hair back off his face. It had completely given up any semblance of style and was starting to curl up over his collar. I thought he looked much better now, less like a young Tory backbencher and more like he'd just come in from taking the dog for a walk before bed. 'Did you not know he was having a baby?'

Trust a man to completely miss the point.

'I did,' I said, 'but it's still weird to think that there's, like, a new human out there that's half of him.'

The usher thought on it for a moment, his eyebrows coming together slightly, and then he nodded.

'Why does your boss think you're shit?' he asked, taking the champagne again. Without asking, again. 'Are you?'

'I don't think so.' Blunt but fair. 'She's not the nicest person in the world. Or the most reasonable. Or the most sane.'

'Then why do you work for her?' He stuck out his tongue as he tried to balance the empty champagne bottle on the uneven grass. Someone was a bit drunk and, unfortunately, it wasn't me. 'Can't you be a waitress anywhere?'

'I suppose I just can't imagine it,' I said. 'I've been doing this for so long, I'm probably a bit frightened of being the new girl. And what if she's right? What if I am shit?'

It's strange how some things are easier to say to strangers than your best friends. I knew I wasn't bad at my job, but there was every chance I wasn't brilliant at it. It wasn't like I'd won any awards or been headhunted or anything. The idea of applying for a new job and not getting it, or worse, getting it and then fucking it up, scared me senseless.

'I don't believe it for a second,' he said, reaching out to robotically pat my shoulder with a stick-straight arm. 'Apart from the fake smoke breaks and getting drunk under a tree during the reception, I bet you're a brilliant waitress.'

'The best,' I confirmed, pushing the carefully balanced bottle over with my foot, much to his dismay. 'What's been so bad about your day, anyway? You're at a wedding. You're *in* a wedding. What can possibly have been so bad?'

He closed his eyes and shook his messy head. 'You don't want to know.'

'Well, no, I don't,' I agreed. 'But you brought it up and I've asked now, so it would only be polite to tell me.'

'What on earth is going on out here?' A voice chimed in the darkness, and the silhouette of another man approached. 'Am I interrupting something?'

'When has that ever stopped you?' The usher unrolled himself and climbed unsteadily to his feet. 'We're having a chat.'

Be still my beating heart, it was the best man.

'Looks like it,' he said, nudging the empty bottle with his toe. 'Has he been a naughty boy?'

'Please shut up, Will,' the usher said, digging his hands deep into his pockets. 'We were just talking.'

'About me?' He grabbed the knot of his dark blue tie

and pulled it away from his neck before unbuttoning the top two buttons of his shirt. He was a very attractive man. Just looking at him made me feel all flighty and unnecessary. 'Whatever he told you, it's not true.'

'Strangely enough, you're not my only topic of conversation.' My champagne-swilling buddy was not nearly as impressed with Best Man Will as I was. 'What do you want?'

'I came out for some fresh air – things are getting a bit much in there,' he said, cocking his head back towards the reception. 'Shouldn't you be inside with your fiancée?'

The usher stepped back. 'Shouldn't you—'

'I should be a lot of things, but I wouldn't worry about them if I were you,' Will cut in before he could finish. 'Let me guess, he's making an arse of himself, being horribly offensive and sulking like a little girl?'

'Sort of,' I said. 'Although I'm not sure it was all on purpose.'

For a moment they stood staring at each other, Will with his collar and tie undone and a big grin on his face, and the usher all buttoned up and vibrating with a very British rage. It was like *EastEnders* versus *Downton Abbey*. Sitting under a tree where I'd been directing the bride and groom portraits a few hours earlier, watching these two random blokes square off to the sounds of the Village People, it felt as though my very odd day was complete. They were either going to knock seven shades of shit out of each other or kiss.

'Kiss!' I shouted.

They both turned round and stared. I shrugged and reached for the disappointingly empty bottle.

'Right, well . . .' The usher adjusted his cuffs, tugging

the white fabric down below his jacket sleeves and breaking the testosterone-fuelled spell. 'I came to apologize and I've done it. I hope your day improves, but I should warn you, talking to this arsehole isn't going to help.'

'Ouch,' Will replied, immediately dropping down onto the ground beside me. 'Ouch, Thomas.'

'Your name is Thomas!' I clapped, realizing he hadn't introduced himself, but then Will casually draped his arm round my shoulders and I lost the ability to speak.

'Tom,' Thomas said, rubbing his hand against the back of his neck. 'It's Tom.'

'It's Thomas,' Will whispered in my ear. 'Everyone calls him Thomas.'

Why was he touching me? How could I make him keep touching me? And then how could I turn that into him marrying me and making a baby so I could put it on Facebook for Seb to see?

Thomas the usher didn't look nearly as happy about my current situation as I was. He gave me one last warning look before turning back towards the party.

'Bye, Thomas,' I called.

'Yeah, bye, Thomas,' Will echoed, laughing as he turned towards me. 'You're funny.'

'Am I?'

I certainly didn't feel funny. At least not funny ha-ha.

'Yeah.' He peeled his arm away and leaned back on his elbows to take a better look at me. I knew that after a long day at work and several hours in a steamy kitchen I didn't look my best, but there was nothing I could do now, so I kept my eyes trained on his right ear and hoped for the best. 'What's your name?'

'Maddie,' I said, a horrible squawk of a laugh bubbling

from my lips, as though my name was the funniest thing I'd ever heard. 'Are you having a good time?'

'Maddie,' he repeated, ignoring my question. 'What did Thomas want?'

'We were just talking.' I waved my hands around aimlessly. 'About nothing. He wasn't being a knobhead.'

'Makes a change,' he drawled. 'Doesn't matter though, does it? At least he's gone. You're safe now.'

'Am I?' I asked. Isn't that what murderers say right before they kill you?

We were completely alone, no one around but random shadows thrown across the lawn by the party going on inside and a Kanye West soundtrack that I would not have chosen for this moment.

Will was still staring at me, a big smile on his face. It was most disconcerting.

'I liked your toast,' I said, smiling back, possibly looking a bit like a loon. 'Very important job, best man. You were great.'

He ran his hand across his five o'clock shadow, still considering me. I surreptitiously licked my lips and combed a few loose strands of hair behind my ears.

'Very important job,' he agreed finally. 'But it's been a long day. Too much standing around for my liking. I'm knackered.'

'It has been a long day,' I agreed, smoothing the back of my hands across my shiny nose. 'At least it's almost over.'

'You're done for the night?' he asked.

I nodded. He nodded back, and then, without warning, slapped my bare thigh so hard I let out a yelp and bit my lip.

'Listen, Maddie, I was actually planning on sneaking

out when I saw you out here,' he said, jumping to his feet and holding out his hand. 'Don't suppose I can give you a lift anywhere?'

This was it. This was the moment. Or at least, it felt a lot like a moment. The kind of situation that a girl who blow-dried her hair properly and got professional manicures would know how to deal with. I glanced down at my bare, bitten-down nails and breathed in. Think of the money you'll save on a taxi, I told myself. It's just a lift, I told myself.

'That would be very nice of you,' I said, pushing my shoulders back and trying to look more confident than I felt. 'But I don't want to put you out. Which way are you going?'

He smiled again, and this time there was no mistaking what he meant.

'I'll drop you off,' he said, helping me to my feet without asking where I lived. 'Come on.'

'Only if it's on your way,' I said, holding back a Tigger-like bounce in my walk when he did not let go of my hand. 'Really.'

'Maddie, I will drop you off,' he said again, squeezing my fingers as we walked towards the car park. 'It's not a problem.'

And that was how, for the first time in thirty-one years, I woke up with a strange man in my bed.

5

Sunday May 17th

Today I feel: Slutty in a good way.
Today I am thankful for: Netflix, Lauren and Mini Cheddars.

I woke up first the next morning, Will still face down in his pillow, snoring and enjoying the deep, restful sleep of a man who had performed. I hadn't slept quite so well. I don't know how anyone can relax in bed with a complete stranger, even if they've just seen every last little bit of you, up close and personal. Actually sleeping with someone is a lot more intimate than sleeping with someone, as far as I'm concerned.

Rather than wake him up and have to actually converse with the man, I did the only sensible thing I could do. I snuck out of bed, locked myself in the bathroom and panicked. I'd had a one-night stand. I was fairly certain it had been a good one, but it had been a while, and despite what people might say, it was nothing like riding a bike. Or if it was, I was doing it wrong.

'Hello, what's wrong, are you OK? You're still coming to the party, right?'

Lauren would know what to do. Sensible, sweet Lauren.

'I brought a man home,' I hissed into my phone, shoving a towel under the bathroom door to muffle the sound of my voice. 'Last night. I did it with a man. He's still here. What do I do?'

'Go you!' she replied, only sounding slightly surprised. 'Is he hot? Do you like him? Is he coming to the party?'

'He is hot,' I said, examining myself for love bites and thankfully coming up clean. 'I think I like him, and no, he isn't coming to the party.'

'Oh.' She only sounded slightly disappointed. 'I think I've overcatered. How did you meet him? Tinder?'

'I deleted Tinder off my phone to make room for the Taylor Swift album.'

'The last one?'

'Yep.'

'Totally worth it.'

'Totally worth it,' I agreed, randomly taking the lids off my various lotions and potions and wondering which one would make me look less grey. 'He was at the wedding I worked yesterday.'

'Nice.' Lauren sounded genuinely impressed. 'Good work.'

I patted a thick white moisturizer onto one cheek. 'Thank you?'

'Maddie, it's not even nine a.m. on a Sunday,' she yawned. 'Did you want something, or did you just call to brag now I'm practically an old married woman?'

'I don't know what to do,' I whispered, closing the toilet lid and sitting down carefully, wiping off the cream with a tissue. 'I've never done this before.'

'You've never brought a guy home before?' I could hear her racking her mental archives even as she spoke. 'Jesus, woman. You're two years late on your rebound.'

'Just tell me what to do,' I said, wondering whether or not he would stay asleep long enough for me to paint my toenails. Of course they didn't matter last night, but they mattered this morning. If only to me.

'Baby's first one-night stand,' Lauren cooed. 'This is so awesome. I am so touched that you called me. Not that you could call Sarah right now, I guess.'

'Yeah, I can't imagine that call going well,' I replied, wincing. 'Now back to me. Please.'

'Go easy – you want to look totally natural. Clean your teeth, wash your face, put on mascara and lip balm, maybe a little powder if you're shiny, but that's all,' she instructed. 'What are you wearing?'

'Last night's shirt and my not terribly attractive knickers,' I said, sniffing myself. 'Are you turned on?'

'You want to look cute and comfortable,' Lauren said. 'Like, a loose sweater, something lived-in, like you wear it all the time. But a nice one. Do you have any cashmere?'

'No, I don't have a nice, baggy, post-coital cashmere jumper in my bathroom,' I replied. As if I wasn't stressed enough about my chipped toenails, now I had to worry about not having enough premium knitwear to flounce around the house in as well? 'Forget what I'm wearing, what do I actually do?'

'Honey, if I've got to tell you that, I'm not sure how you got him home with you in the first place.'

'I don't mean sexing,' I whispered. Maybe I should have called Sarah. Or my mum. Or anyone else alive. 'I mean, what do I do? What do I say?'

'I don't know,' Lauren replied. 'Just be cool.'

Oh. Be cool. Of course.

'Act like it's no big deal,' she carried on before I could kick her arse. 'Or just tell him you have plans and he has to leave.'

'OK.'

'You do want him to leave, right?'

I stared at the patchwork paint job on my toes and considered this.

On one hand, he was a handsome man who wanted to put his penis in me and owned his own car. On the other hand, he was, to all intents and purposes, a stranger who had willingly put his penis in me without so much as asking my last name. I probably did want him to leave. He probably wanted to leave.

'It's just a one-night thing,' I said, convincing myself. 'He was the best man at the wedding. Everyone wants a shag at a wedding, don't they?'

'He was best man?' Lauren asked. 'And he went home with you?'

'What's that supposed to mean?'

She guffawed down the line with her throaty American laugh. Lauren has an excellent laugh. It's big and deep and makes women clap and men's underwear fall off. 'I'm just saying the best man usually has the pick of the crowd. Good going, girl. You needed to get back on the horse.'

'It's nothing like riding a bike and it's nothing like riding a horse,' I grumbled. 'Why do people say that?'

'Maybe you're doing it wrong?' she suggested.

Dear God, my greatest fear come true.

'Maddie?'

'Lauren?'

'Where are you?'

'Bathroom.'

We've been on the phone for kind of a while – you should probably go.'

'Yeah,' I said, fluffing my hair and then immediately smoothing it down. 'It's fine, isn't it? Totally fine.'

'See you later,' she said. 'I want to hear all the gory details.'

'A lady never tells,' I replied. 'And you're disgusting. Love you.'

I hung up, stashed my phone in with the spare loo rolls and stared into the mirror. My green eyes were a bit red, but I had eye drops that could fix that. My hair was my hair and didn't look any better up or down, so I decided to leave it down for sexy flicking-around purposes, and as for the rest of it, he'd already seen me completely naked from every angle so there wasn't a lot I could do about any of that.

At least it was one less thing to worry about.

'Now all I need is a baggy, lived-in, sexy jumper that's nice,' I told myself. 'And the job's done.'

'Morning.'

When Will emerged from the bedroom, I was carefully padding around my kitchen in slouchy sports socks, a sort-of clean T-shirt and the Marks & Sparks cardigan my mum had left last time she came to visit. It was a carefully put-together outfit based on something I'd seen in a Nivea commercial slash the clothes that were in my bathroom and seemed all right for the 'Oh hi, random man I brought home with me last night, hair toss, hair toss' attitude I was attempting to give off.

'Morning,' I squeaked.

Will was standing in the middle of my flat completely stark bollock naked. Bollock being the operative word. This never happened on Nivea commercials. My mother's cardigan was aghast.

'I was starting to wonder where you were.' He stretched, man parts flopping as he went, and wandered across the room to park himself on a bar stool in front of the breakfast bar. Naked. 'I thought you'd done a runner from your own house for a minute.'

'I was going to make coffee,' I said, trying very hard not to look at his penis. But it was like staring into an eclipse: you knew it was bad for you and you still couldn't help it. 'Would you like some coffee?'

'Love some,' he replied, staring out of my window. Oh dear God, the neighbours. Mrs Meakin's heart wouldn't be able to take something like this.

'So, big plans today?' I asked, shaking as I pulled out the cutlery drawer. Femme fatale I was not.

'No,' Will replied, still naked. 'I'd more or less written the day off for a hangover. You know how weddings can be. Happily, not the case.'

'Yeah,' I nodded, trying not to spill the milk. 'Weddings, eh?'

'I've got some work to do.' He tapped his fingers on the kitchen counter and gave my flat the once-over. Happily it was a bit cloudy out so you couldn't quite see how incredibly filthy it was. Job number one after he left, dusting. Actually, that would be job number three after I'd Dettoxed the stool he was sitting on and had a brief lie down. 'But, you know, nothing major.'

'You've got to work?' I asked, but in a totally cool way. 'I don't actually know what you do.'

'I'm an associate at a law firm in town,' he said, resting

his elbows on the counter while I expertly boiled the kettle. 'I went to law school with Ian.'

I was cursed only ever to be penetrated by men in the legal profession. I suppose it could be worse, but really, was a doctor or an architect too much to ask for?

'That other man was a lawyer,' I said, memories coming back to me. 'From last night. The usher.'

'Thomas?' Will pulled a sour-milk face. 'Yeah, he was in law school with us but he dropped out, so he didn't qualify when we did.'

'Why did he drop out?' I sniffed my own pint of semi-skimmed and thanked the gods of Cravendale for lasting one day past their best-before date.

'I don't remember,' he shrugged, accepting his mug of instant coffee as though it was a golden chalice full of unicorn tears. 'Because he was shit, most likely.'

It seemed as though I shouldn't take Thomas's pep talk from the night before too seriously after all.

'Do you like it?' I asked, sipping my coffee and considering him a little more closely. He didn't seem to be in any rush to leave. Maybe I could afford to be very slightly optimistic. 'Being a lawyer?'

'I don't like the hours,' he replied, scratching his stubble. On his face, not his neatly topiaried man parts. 'But the money's good. And it's interesting. Do you like your job?'

'Most of the time,' I said, not wanting to go into the details. That seemed like a drunk-under-a-tree–with-a-complete-stranger conversation, not a bright Sunday morning didn't-you-have-your-penis-in-me-a-few-hours-ago-stranger conversation. 'Unless I have to play waitress for a lot of drunk people. I work for the company that planned the wedding, I was only waitressing yesterday to help out.'

'Sounds fun.' He glugged his coffee and smiled. 'I can't imagine spending every weekend at a wedding. It must be knackering.'

'Well, we do all kinds of things,' I replied, almost for one second forgetting he was naked. And then remembering again. 'Weddings, birthdays, anniversaries. Sometimes corporate stuff. I'm working on a birthday thing and an engagement party at the moment. Keeps me on my toes.'

'The last party I had was for my eighteenth,' Will said. 'My best friends got me a dodgy stripper and my mum cried. We had it in the village hall. Good times.'

'Our events tend to be a bit more involved than that,' I said. I wanted to be diplomatic, but I also wanted the image of a ropey middle-aged village stripper with a fag hanging out of her mouth while she rubbed her boobs on eighteen-year-old Will's face out of my head ASAP. 'But I've organized burlesque performances before.'

'Do you fill in for the dancers if they call in sick as well?' he asked with a shimmy that should never be performed by a naked man, no matter how handsome. 'Is there something you want to tell me?'

I stood in the middle of my messy kitchen, in my carefully careless outfit, holding my ancient Garfield mug and staring at the nude stranger on the bar stool.

'God, I was only joking,' Will said, abandoning his stool and coming over to me. I swallowed hard and looked up at him for as long as I could stand to make eye contact. Which was about four seconds. 'I'm not asking you to strip for me or anything. Not right now, anyway.'

'I don't do this,' I said, holding my mug of hot coffee away from his body and ignoring the semi that was starting to bother my thigh. 'I don't usually go home with people.'

'You don't have to explain yourself,' Will said, still standing in front of me, his peen properly waking up and poking me in the leg. 'I'm not judging you.'

'I bet everyone says that, though, don't they?' I tried to reach the kitchen top to put my mug down but it was too far away. 'I bet everyone says "Ooh, I don't usually do this".'

'I don't know,' he muttered into my ear, his hands circling my waist and resting on my bum. 'I don't usually do this either.'

There wasn't enough time for me to work out whether he was making a joke, telling the truth or taking the piss, because the next thing I knew, we were awkwardly clambering down onto the floor, my mum's cardigan was off and we were doing it on the kitchen floor.

Which is a part I will leave out when I tell the grandkids about how we met but have already texted to all my friends. Obviously.

Being a bridesmaid is a huge honour but it's also a celebration! Tell us all about your bride and your special friendship in the spaces below:

Tell us about the day you met your bride:
We were flatmates at uni and I was very excited to meet a proper American. She bought our love with Peppermint Patties and Reese's Pieces and Maybelline Great Lash mascara. It was a simpler time.

What were your first impressions of her?
I thought she was incredibly glamorous because she was from New York and she had really cool clothes, like proper Levis and Abercrombie & Fitch jumpers, and she said 'sneakers' instead of 'trainers'. She was sweet and funny and thoughtful, and even though she was nice, she was never a drip. She just seemed so much more grown-up than us.

What were your first impressions of her husband-to-be?
Before I met him, all I knew was that Michael had bought Lauren a Swiffer sweeper for her birthday. Entirely without irony. When I met him at Lauren's party, we had a perfectly nice conversation about dinosaur erotica and the price of Kentucky Fried Chicken. I still haven't got over that Swiffer though.

Share a happy memory from when you met your bride-to-be:
Lauren had never had a drink until she moved to England. We changed that pretty quickly and introduced her to snakebite and black. Unfortunately she drank one too many

and threw up all over the Student Union toilets and was barred for the rest of the semester. Maybe you had to be there.

What life lesson have you learned from your friendship?
She was the first person who made me look at the wider world and realize there was more out there. She also taught me how to make fajitas, and you can't put a price on something like that.

6

Sunday May 17th, evening
Today I feel: Full.
Today I am thankful for: Food.

'Bloody hell.'

When Lauren had sent out the e-vites for her engage-ment party at her dad's house, we figured we were looking at a lovely Sunday afternoon of handmade sandwiches in the living room with a glass of Pimm's in the garden if we were lucky.

It was ten years since we'd been to Lauren's dad's house. Lauren's dad had moved.

'How is this somewhere people actually live?' Sarah asked, handing her coat to one of the two people clam-ouring over it at the front door. 'Are they his servants? Does he have servants?'

'I don't know,' I whispered, taking a glass of champagne from another bow-tied helper. 'When did he get this rich?'

We knew Lauren was From Money, but the last time

I checked it wasn't Scrooge McDuck money. I half expected to open a cupboard and have bags of gold coins fall out and smother me.

'Maybe he won the lottery and she didn't tell us,' Sarah suggested as we were shown through the house and out into a marquee in the back garden. 'Maybe she thought we'd feel weird about it.'

'She would be right,' I replied. 'This is insane.'

A string quartet played in the corner of the marquee and fairy lights were strung all across the ceiling, fighting the dismal British weather to create a happy atmosphere. In the middle of it all stood Lauren, happily clutching Michael her Swiffer-loving fiancé's arm.

'Hey!' She broke away the moment she saw us and rushed over as fast as her four-inch heels would carry her. 'You're here!'

'Nice shoes,' I said, accepting a hug and a kiss on the cheek.

'Thanks,' she said, kicking up a heel as she hugged Sarah. 'I was thinking about these for your bridesmaid shoes, actually.'

'All the better to break an ankle in,' I replied. 'So, um, when did your dad become the head of an international drug cartel? Because that's the only person I can imagine would live in this house.'

'Oh, haha,' she replied, taking a glass of champagne from another waiter.

Sarah grabbed a second, her first almost finished. 'What?' She shrugged.

'He's an estate agent,' Lauren said, waving at more people as they arrived. 'He gets good deals on houses.'

'Especially when he has the previous owners killed,'

Sarah added. 'I've always got a Mafia vibe off your dad. Is that how he ended up in America? Is that how he met your mum?'

'He's not in the Mafia and he doesn't run a drug cartel,' she replied. 'He's just having a good year. And since my mom got remarried, he doesn't have to pay her alimony any more. That probably helps.'

'Is your mum here?' Sarah asked, checking the marquee with fear in her eyes. 'Please tell me she couldn't make it.'

'She couldn't make it,' Lauren said, entirely unimpressed. 'It's a long way for her. She sent flowers. She'll come for the wedding, obviously. I don't know why you're so afraid of her.'

'Lauren, your mother is the only woman on earth who has ever knocked me out,' Sarah replied, rubbing her jaw to nurse a ten-year-old injury. 'And she's thirty years older than me.'

'You did hit on my dad,' she pointed out. 'It wasn't totally undeserved.'

'I didn't know he was your dad,' Sarah sulked, rubbing her jaw as though the punch had happened yesterday. 'And looking at this place, I wish I'd tried harder.'

'You could have been mother of the bride,' I said, patting her on the back. 'It would have been beautiful.'

'If you're going to invite drunk nineteen-year-olds to you dad's company Christmas party, you should provide some sort of handout to tell them who they may and may not kiss under the mistletoe,' she said. 'Totally innocent mistake.'

'You had your tongue so far down his throat, I nearly threw up,' Lauren replied. 'You're lucky I ever spoke to you again.'

'This is a beautiful party,' I said loudly, watching as tray after tray after tray of food was brought out and passed around. 'That is my official and professional opinion. Who did you use?'

'For the party?' Lauren asked. 'No one. My step-mom put it together.'

I stared blankly. 'In two days? She did all this in two days?'

She nodded.

'God, maybe Colton-Bryers should hire her,' I muttered. 'At least you've got good help for the wedding then.'

'But you're going to help me with the wedding too, right?' she said, sipping her champagne. 'I don't want to be an asshole since they're throwing me this party and everything, but I don't want my stepmother planning my wedding. Besides, you're an actual wedding planner. And it would be way more fun if the three of us planned it together.'

Yes, I thought, saying nothing. It would be way more fun. Planning a wedding with bridezilla, a divorcée and a spinster. Sob. It seemed pointless trying to remind her I was an events organizer and not just a wedding planner so I didn't. I just sulked about it silently, alone.

'So where are you at?' Sarah followed Lauren over to a plush white sofa set up in one corner of the marquee and sat down. 'Is the whole thing planned and booked and paid for already?'

'Oh I wish,' she said, giving another new arrival a wave. 'I don't know how you do this every day, Maddie. Every time I think I've decided on something, there are another ten things to work out.'

'That's why it's a job,' I said. 'It's more work than you realize.'

'Thank God I have you to help me,' she beamed across the table. 'My own personal wedding planner.'

'Yeah, of course.' I returned her smile, barely. One more time, not a wedding planner. 'Have you decided on a date yet?'

'I wanted to talk to you guys about that,' Lauren said, looking slightly shifty and curling the ends of her blonde ponytail around her index finger. 'So, it's like this. Michael's grandma is over there.'

She pointed at an elderly lady in a wheelchair who was wearing the most spectacular hat I had ever seen.

'She's really sick,' Lauren whispered.

'She looks all right to me,' Sarah replied. 'What's that she's drinking?'

'Whisky,' Lauren said. 'I kept having to top her up so I just gave her the bottle.'

'And now she's drinking out of it with a straw?' I asked.

'Whatever, she's sick,' Lauren said. 'So we're definitely going to have to get something figured out sooner rather than later if we want her there.'

'I think you're going to have to do it this afternoon if you want her there,' Sarah said with a frown, unable to take her eyes off the woman. Really, it was the most amazing hat.

'How soon is soon?' I asked. 'New Year's maybe? Next spring?'

'Like, August?' Lauren pulled up her shoulders in a faux wince.

'That's not that soon,' I said, calculating on my fingers. 'That's fifteen months, totally standard.'

Lauren smiled with all of her teeth and an apology in her eyes. 'Like, this August?'

'This August?' I asked. 'As in three months from now?'

'The first, actually,' she confirmed, looking to me for support, but I had nothing. 'It'll be OK, right? Maddie?' I stared blankly across the table. Two and a half months.

'My dad said he'd pay for the actual wedding, and my mom is going it pay for my dress,' she said, flipping her eyes between the two of us. 'And I'm not doing some crazed pre-wedding diet that's going to take six months, so that's not a thing.'

'People don't plan their weddings so far in advance just so they can lose a few pounds,' I said, deliberately not catching Sarah's eye. We all remembered her pre-wedding diet. They were dark days. Dark, Slim-Fast-filled days. 'It takes time to make the dress. The ones you try on are samples. Most designers make every dress from scratch when you order it.'

'But you'll be able to help me, right?' she said with pleading eyes. 'I just want it to be perfect.'

'Of course I will,' I replied automatically. 'But if you want to organize a wedding in three months, you're going to have to make compromises.'

Why did I suddenly feel like I was at work? Oh, that's right, because my best friend had just hired me to pull together her wedding in three months and she was planning on paying mates' rates, i.e. nothing.

'It's going to be fine. It'll be awesome,' she said. And she was smiling again, clearly having stopped listening to me halfway through. 'I just know you're going to help me have the perfect wedding. I've done some research to help you. Do you think we could get the carriage they used at the royal wedding? They can't be using it now, right?'

Before I could say anything, she reached underneath the sofa, pulled a giant powder-blue ring binder out of her tote bag and dropped it onto the table in front of me with a thud.

'This is where I'm at so far,' she said, brushing her hair over her shoulder, all business. 'Do you want to go through it now or do you want to take it with you and get back to me later?'

'I think I might take it with me,' I said slowly, leafing through the pages. Vintage Rolls-Royces for the bridal party, Routemaster bus to take the guests to the reception, Monique Lhuillier, Vera Wang, Jenny Packham, fireworks displays, swans, doves, swing bands, pick-and-mix counter for the reception, chocolate fountain, champagne fountain, sherbet fountains . . . it was my all worst nightmares wrapped up in a best-friend bow. I wanted to help Lauren, but I couldn't help feeling a bit sick. 'You know, I might not be able to get all this for August.'

'Of course you will,' she said confidently. 'You're amazing.'

'I mean, yes, I am,' I agreed. 'But putting this together this quickly is going to be a full-time job, and at last count I already have one of those.'

'Can I get you anything at all?' A waitress appeared at my elbow, pad at the ready.

'Three champagnes please,' Sarah said quickly. 'Do you two need anything?'

Against all the odds, the party was fun. I made a deal with Lauren to keep Sarah away from her dad, and Sarah made a deal with me to keep a glass of champagne in her hand at all times. Thank goodness I'm used to managing conflict on a daily basis.

'He is fit, though,' Sarah said, leering at the aforementioned father from our new perch outside the marquee. 'For an older man, I mean.'

'He's Lauren's dad,' I said as I looked over at the sixty-something-year-old man clutching the arse of his thirty-something-year-old second wife and gipped. 'I just don't get it.'

'He's a silver fox,' she said, actually swooning as he flicked a hand over his far-too-luxuriant-for-my-liking grey locks. 'Imagine all the things he could teach you.'

'Like the current value of a shilling and what things were like "when he was a lad"?'

'Piss off.' Sarah slid her finger inside the top button of her silk blouse and pulled it away from her neck. 'I bet he knows his way around a bed.'

I stuffed a piece of puff pastry into my mouth. 'I think I'm going to be sick.'

'Ladies, I've been thinking.' Before Sarah made me actually vomit, Lauren dropped into the third chair around our little iron table and all sexual theorizing about our best friend's father ended abruptly. 'I'm so sorry about you and Steve. I feel as though messing around with all my wedding stuff is going to be difficult, given everything that's going on, so if you don't want to be "involved", I completely understand.'

Sarah, half-cut and half awake, gave a loud sniff.

'If I'd known, I never would have done that dumb dinner announcement thing.' Lauren continued, crumpling her pretty face in a frown, and I knew she meant it – she was the most considerate person I knew. 'I got carried away.'

Sarah smiled awkwardly and shook her head. 'And you should be getting carried away – you're getting married,' she said, reaching out for Lauren's hand. 'Things are weird, yeah, but I want to be a help. I'm sorry if I've been weird.'

'You haven't been weird at all!' Lauren said, dashing round the table to give Sarah a hug. 'You're going through something so awful, and this is shitty timing. If I could change it, I would, but with Michael's grandma and all . . .'

I glanced over at the little old lady in the spectacular hat. The bottle of whisky in her lap was empty now, but the bottle of gin she'd moved on to looked fairly full so I assumed she was all right. And my own personal hero.

'It'll be fine,' Sarah promised. 'It'll be better than fine. I'll be fine and the wedding will be fantastic. Give me something to do – I'm always happiest when I'm busy.'

'I hate to interrupt . . .' Michael, never Mike, leaned over his new fiancée's shoulder and squeezed her shoulder. 'But my mum and dad are leaving.'

'Congratulations, Michael,' I said, beaming at the groom. 'Now remember, if you break her heart, I'll have to kill you.'

He stepped back and stared at me.

'Why would you say that?' he asked with big brown Bambi eyes. 'And at our engagement party?'

No one could accuse Michael of being sharp enough to cut anything. He was very nice and clearly loved the shit out of my friend but I would never forget the time he was discussing films with Sarah and told us all he thought the sequel to *Dumb and Dumber* was the most underrated film of all time.

'It was a joke,' I said, looking to Sarah and Lauren for support and finding none. 'I was just kidding.'

'That's a terrible thing to say,' he said, gripping Lauren's hand tightly in his and pulling her away from the table to stand by his side. 'And you're supposed to be planning our wedding?'

'Technically, I'm a bridesmaid,' I replied. 'I'm *helping* to plan the wedding. But I didn't mean to offend you.'

'Such an awful thing to say,' he said to Lauren. 'You know I would never hurt you. Why would she say that?'

'I know.' Lauren narrowed her eyes at me and shook her head. 'Don't worry about Maddie, she thinks she's funny.'

'I *am* funny, aren't I?' I hissed at Sarah, who shrugged in response.

'Not as funny as he is,' she replied. 'But I don't think he's making me laugh on purpose.'

'I'll be over in a moment, honey,' Lauren told her still horrified fiancé. 'Don't let them leave until I've said goodbye.'

He nodded dutifully and trotted back across the room long legs lolloping, with the look of someone who had just been told his puppy was terminal.

'Sorry,' I said, hanging my head in uncertain shame. 'Sensitive, isn't he?'

'What about the bachelorette?' Lauren suggested, ignoring me completely. 'We haven't been anywhere together in forever. We should do something just us girls.'

'That could be fun,' Sarah said, looking to me for confirmation. I nodded blankly, slyly checking my phone for a message from Will. Perhaps something along the lines of 'top shag, will you marry me?' but alas, nothing. 'When do you want to go?'

'Next month?'

'Perfect. Maddie, what weekends are you working next month?'

'Huh?' I said, putting my phone away. 'What weekends what?'

'It's not her fault she's being stupid,' Sarah said, batting me in the head with her clutch bag. 'She's all shagged out.'

'Oh!' Lauren blinked and clapped loudly. 'Oh my God I forgot to ask you!'

'Yes,' I said, not wanting to make too big a deal out of my shagtacular night in front of Sarah. I had given her the briefest of details in an attempt to distract her from goosing Lauren's dad at the buffet table earlier, but I had a feeling the soon-to-be divorced didn't want to hear too much about their friend's amazing one-night-stand at their other friend's engagement party.

'And?'

They both stared at me with expectation and it felt weird.

All I'd brought to the table for the last two years, relationship-wise, was how much I missed Seb, and now, out of nowhere, I was the centre of attention. Sarah was getting divorced, Lauren was getting married, I was the only one with shagging stories. Even though they were my best friends, I got the impression that they felt sorry for me sometimes. Having someone new, something promising to talk about, felt like a relief.

'He's . . . I don't know,' I said, confused and oddly shy. 'I like him.'

'Ooooh, you like him!' Lauren did a little dance in her seat. 'Are you bringing him to the wedding?'

'I think it's a bit early to be thinking about that,' I scoffed.

It wasn't too early. I had thought about it endlessly, ever since he'd left that morning.

Sarah stuffed a whole tomato and goat's cheese bruschetta into her mouth as a waiter with a shocked face reeled from the drive-by food-snatching. 'Tell us everything.'

'His name is Will,' I started.

'Will what?' Lauren asked.

'Oh,' I replied, cringing. 'I don't actually know.'

'How old is he?'

'Don't know.'

'What does he do?'

'He's a lawyer!'

'Oh.' Lauren frowned. 'Not another one.'

'How do you know Will isn't some amazing lawyer who works for a charity or saves children from sweatshops or stops make-up companies from testing lipsticks on rabbits?' I asked.

'Is he?'

'I don't know,' I admitted. 'I know he's a lawyer, I know he was Ian McCallan's best man at the wedding yesterday, I know he likes to sleep on his left side and I know he likes to walk around my flat starkers in the morning.'

'What does he look like?' Lauren asked, tapping away at her phone while Sarah rolled her eyes.

Rude.

'Dark hair but really, really short,' I said. It felt strange talking about him like this as though he was someone I'd seen on TV, not someone real. 'Nice smile, like, you just want to laugh every time you see it. Golden-brown eyes, great bod.'

'Give me a comparison.'

'Um, George Clooney before he went grey?' I said. 'Only English and without the gay rumours.'

Lauren squinted at me angrily. 'George is married now! You've got to quit saying that shit.'

'Elton John was married,' I replied. 'And he works in Holborn. And one of the ushers from the wedding really doesn't like him.'

'Yeah, well, he probably fancies you as well,' Sarah said. 'Men only ever fall out over women and football.'

'Oh, he plays rugby! I know he plays rugby,' I replied. 'And the usher didn't fancy me – he thought I looked like a fat panda, plus he's engaged. Will says he's a knobhead and I'm inclined to agree.'

'Is this him?' Lauren held up her phone to reveal an iPhone plus-sized photo of the man I'd been having sex with not three hours earlier.

'Bloody hell, how did you do that?' I asked, grabbing the phone out of her hand. I fancied him so much I could hardly stand to look at him.

'Facebook? I put in Ian McCallan and the wedding photos came up. Ladies, meet Will Jennings. His profile is private but the dumbass who just got married still has his set to public.'

'Maddie Jennings,' I said. Online stalking was the best. 'I like it.'

'Have a minute,' Sarah warned, balling up her napkin as she finished her food. 'What happened last night?'

I didn't know what to share. We'd snogged like teenagers, and as soon as we were through the door my knickers were round my ankles. It was such a long time since I'd felt anything for anyone, to feel so wanted and to want someone else so much was totally overwhelming.

'Honestly?' I asked. 'You want the details?'

'I do!' Lauren squealed.

'I mean, did you talk about seeing each other again?' Sarah overruled. 'Are you properly going out?'

'Well it's only been one night so far. Also, I don't think people actually have the "are we going out together?" conversation in their thirties, Sarah,' I said. As if I've got any idea what I'm talking about. 'But yes, we did make plans. He said maybe Wednesday.'

'Which one of these is the usher that fancies you?' Lauren interrupted, waving a group shot from the wedding in my face.

'This one.' I took the phone and enlarged it to show Tom the Usher. 'But he doesn't fancy me, honestly – he was just awkward. It was a painful exchange.'

'He totally fancies her,' Sarah whispered to Lauren. 'Let me see him.'

'He's kind of nice too,' Lauren said, passing the phone around the table. 'Is he a giant or something?'

'He is ridiculously tall,' I confirmed. 'I think this one is his fiancée.'

I swiped through to the next page to show the brides-maids, zooming in on the obscenely attractive blonde girl who I was fairly certain was called Vanessa.

'Shit.' Sarah leaned across the table along with Lauren to get a better look. 'I thought you weren't supposed to look better than the bride on her wedding day.'

'I'm putting the two of you in trash bags,' Lauren muttered, tapping on the screen. 'Tom Wheeler. Maddie Wheeler. I kind of like it.'

'I wouldn't change my name anyway,' I said, going back to the picture of the groomsmen and staring at the screen. Gawky Tom on one end of the photo, laughing Will at the other.

'What happened to Maddie Jennings?' Sarah asked.

'She went to prison for killing her best friend,' I said, looking up for signs of more canapés and handing the phone back to Lauren. 'Now, tell me more about these trash bags. I need to get them ordered.'

Being a bridesmaid can be hard work! But your bride chose you because she knows you're the woman for the job. Use this space to remind yourself of your own unique qualities and why your bride can rely on you during this special time.

If you could be anyone, who would you be?
It's taken me 31 years to find a pair of jeans that fit properly – I'm not starting that all over again. I'll stick with myself.

If you had to choose between world domination or world peace, which one would you pick?
Would I still be in charge if I chose world peace?

Who or what inspires you?
Lorraine Kelly. Imagine getting up that early for that many years and still having a smile on your face.

What is the one thing you wish you could do if given the chance?
Not end up alone.

Where do you see yourself five years from now?
Still trying to answer this question.

7

Monday May 18th
Today I feel: Conflicted.
Today I am thankful for: Nurofen and Dolly Parton.

'Maddie, can I talk to you for a minute?'

It's not every Monday morning I'm yanked into the gents' toilets by the head of HR, but I'm a curious soul so I went along with it.

'Is something wrong?' I asked while Matilda Jacobs checked to make sure all the stalls were empty. I wasn't sure what would happen if they weren't; what was the poor sod supposed to do, go to HR?

'No,' she replied, washing her hands. 'It's just that this is the only place we can talk without Shona listening.'

'How have I never thought of this before?' I wondered out loud. That was why they paid her the big bucks. 'She's not in today, though, it's fine. What's wrong? Why do we need to be Shona-proofed?'

Matilda was a decent woman. She'd been at the company

almost as long as I had, only she'd started as the HR
assistant and now she was head of the department. I'd
started as Shona's events assistant and I was now Shona's
events assistant. You can see how our career paths have
not enjoyed the same trajectory.

'You know we're advertising Victoria's job?' she asked,
folding her arms over her enormous bosoms. It was the
only word for them. They were bosoms.

'I do,' I replied. 'Actually, I've got a CV for you.'

'So you are going to apply for it?' Matilda's eyes were
as big as saucers. 'That's fantastic.'

'Oh, no,' I said, cutting off her enthusiasm. I had Sarah's
CV. As much as the idea of working with my best friend
made me want to do a little sick, I could hardly refuse
to help her out right now. 'Wait, what? Why?'

'Because Shona emailed me this morning and told me
in no uncertain terms that I was not to accept an application from you for the position,' she said.

Shona. What a massive bastard.

'Of course, I told her if you wanted to apply, we were
legally obliged to put you through the process, the same
as any other applicant.'

'But I haven't applied,' I said, panic starting to rise. 'I
have a friend who wants to apply for the job. I'm not
going to apply for it.'

'Yes you are,' Matilda replied. 'I want a CV on my
desk by the end of the day.'

'No, really, it's fine,' I insisted. 'I'm very happy doing
what I'm doing now. The management side of things
doesn't interest me that much.'

Matilda stood very still, looked me square in the eye,
and smiled.

'Maddie,' she said. 'You're being an idiot.'

I wasn't sure that line came out of the HR best practice handbook. 'I am?'

'You are,' she confirmed. 'I'm not asking you to apply to be CEO. I'm asking you to apply for a job you have, to all intents and purposes, been doing for the last nine years. Only I'm asking you to do it for more money, better benefits and without reporting in to a woman who told the MD he couldn't promote you because she was worried you were taking crystal meth. You didn't hear that from me.'

'I wondered who was leaving those rehab brochures in my pigeon hole,' I breathed. 'Why are you telling me this now?'

Matilda looked up at the polystyrene panels in the ceiling. 'Victoria was a very good friend of mine and Shona is not my favourite person in the world.'

'So it's not because I'm really, really good at my job then?' I asked, slightly deflated. Matilda replied with an expression I hadn't seen since year ten maths class.

'I'm not here to blow smoke up your arse, Maddie,' she replied. 'I'm here to do the best for the company. You should be applying for this job, bottom line. The fact that it will piss off a woman who gave me a six-month subscription to gay.com for my secret Santa last year is a happy coincidence.'

'I didn't know you were gay,' I said.

'Because I'm not,' she replied. 'She told me at the Christmas party that I give off a vibe and should probably get nice shoes if I didn't want everyone to think I was a dyke.'

'Classy.' I'd missed that party because I was in the office sticking Swarovski crystals onto one hundred tealight holders for a winter wedding the following day. Good times.

'You can email the CV or bring it over, whichever is less likely to cause a fuss. I know she monitors your emails.'

I did a double-take. 'She does what?'

'She reads your emails.' Matilda nodded. 'Technically all managers can read their employees' emails, but Shona is the only one who takes advantage of the privilege. I think she's also your next of kin according to your company pension, so let's hope nothing happens to you before you get on the phone to Legal & General.'

'Is that a joke?' I asked as she pushed past me, folding her sleeve around her fingers to open the door.

'The fact that you've got to ask is why you should apply for this job,' she called back. 'Do it now, Maddie.'

'Morning, Maddie.' Paul the Perv, deputy sales director, walked in as she walked out and gave me a wink. 'Any particular reason you're in the gents?'

'I'm not sure,' I said.

'Let me be the first to welcome you,' he said, unzipping and beginning to pee right next to me. 'You're welcome in here any time.'

'Thanks, Paul,' I said, heading straight for the door.

It's just like they always say. You go nineteen months without seeing a single penis, and then two come along at once.

It should have been a relaxing couple of days. Shona was on an overnight with a PR, checking out some new hotels they were looking after so we could use them for future events, and I didn't have anything especially pressing on my agenda. I was looking forward to getting some paperwork out of the way, finding a caterer for Lauren, maybe doing a little light online shopping and leaving dead on the dot of five-thirty.

I settled in to my ergonomically sound and bloody uncomfortable chair, cupped my mug of tea in one hand and opened my email to IM Sarah for advice on the job front. Only I couldn't. HR wanted me to apply for a job that she wanted. She'd asked me if I thought she was in with a chance at Lauren's engagement party and of course, I'd said yes. Because, according to the CV she had sent me that evening, she was definitely qualified for it. Plus she had more than enough on her plate with the Stephen situation. I'd never seen her so messed-up about anything; I didn't want to make things more difficult for her. This definitely had to be an in-person conversation. I couldn't talk to her about this on email.

Instead I clicked on Lauren's name in the instant messaging bar, sent a dancing lobster and waited for her to respond.

'*You've got crabs????*' she typed immediately.

'*No, I haven't got crabs,*' I replied. I'd know if I had crabs. Wouldn't I? '*I've got a work problem, I need some advice.*'

'*Sounds like a Sarah problem TBH.*'

Like I didn't know that already.

'*I can't ask Sarah, that's why I'm asking you.*'

'*Thanks.*'

'*Don't get offended,*' I typed as quickly as I could, one eye on Shona's glass-walled office beside me. In some ways I preferred it when she was in there: at least then I knew where she was. Having her out and about was like knowing there was a spider somewhere in the flat but not knowing when it was going to jump out at you. '*They've asked me to apply for a promotion at work but it's the same job Sarah wants to apply for.*'

'*Sarah is applying for a job at your place????*'

Lauren loved to overpunctuate. As the child of two English teachers, it genuinely caused me physical pain.

'*Yes,*' I replied. '*But I think it would be weird if she worked here.*'

'*She didn't tell me she was looking for a new job. She's gone radio silence on me. Do you think she's mad at me because of the wedding?*'

'*I think she's upset about Steve.*'

'*It's so crazy. They're really really getting divorced?*'

'*They're really, really getting divorced. It's bad.*'

For a moment she didn't say anything.

'*So she won't need a plus-one for the wedding?*'

I sat staring at my screen for a full minute.

'*Sorry,*' Lauren typed, adding a crying puppy for good measure. '*Joking. Job. You want it?*'

'*Think so,*' I replied. '*It would be more money. Wouldn't have to work for Shona.*'

'*Is she going to be mad?*'

'*Yes,*' I confirmed, running through the revenge scenarios that could await. '*She told me not to apply and asked HR not to give it to me.*'

Lauren replied with a winky face.

'*Wait, wrong one,*' she tapped, following up with a shocked emoji. '*And you're not going to tell?*'

'*No.*' Wasn't that the whole point of this conversation? '*She's so upset about the divorce, I don't want to upset her more.*'

'*I can't believe they're getting divorced,*' Lauren replied before a little blue link appeared in the conversation. '*What do you think of this dress?*'

'*Nice,*' I said, without clicking on it. '*It's so weird. I know it's happening but it doesn't feel real.*'

'*I guess we hardly ever see him,*' she said. '*How long is it since he came out with us?*'

'*I know, I think things were worse than she wants to say.*'

I could understand why Lauren was struggling with the concept. When I woke up on Monday morning I only remembered Sarah was getting divorced when I found our wine glasses from Friday night under the sofa. Sarah probably hadn't even slept. It was this big, huge, giant thing, and nothing had prepared any of us for what it actually meant. It's so strange how something can affect one person in such a huge way and only have a ripple effect on others. My heart hurt to think of how hard it had to be for her.

'*I think you should apply for the job,*' Lauren typed.

'*You do?*'

'*If the company have asked you to, it'll look bad if you don't. They must think you can do it. Sarah will understand. Just tell her they offered it to you.*'

'*I've got to interview, they're not just giving me it,*' I explained. Underneath the stress of Shona finding out, of upsetting Sarah, and the general terror that I would somehow fuck it up, there was a part of me that was so excited. '*But could be fun?*'

'*Deffo,*' she agreed. '*And my wedding will be great practice!!!!!*'

I'm so lucky to have such good friends.

Lauren always says the best way to get over a man is to get under another one. Maybe she's right. When I got home, there was a letter addressed to Seb on the doormat, and for the first time I picked it up and stuck it in the box on the telephone table (that had never had a telephone on it) without even considering bursting into tears. Definitely growing as a person.

Plugging in my phone, I dumped myself on the settee and turned on the telly, my mind overrun. Lots to think about, lots to think about. I had to tell Sarah I was applying for the events position, I had to figure out how to work Kevlar into a passable outfit for the office once Shona found out I was applying for the job, and I had to plan my best friend's wedding. So of course the only thing I could think about was why I hadn't heard from Will. My own brain was failing the Bechdel test. I was the worst fourth-wave feminist ever. He would be in touch; he was probably still at work. Lawyers didn't work normal people shifts. Seb used to be in the office until all hours. But then Seb was having an affair . . .

No.

We're both playing it cool, that's all, I told myself, forcing myself up to flick on the kettle before hitting the biscuit tin. He's got my number, he knows where I live. If he wants to call, he'll call. After all, the sex was brilliant, if I did say so myself. Why wouldn't he call? That was not the last I'd seen of Mr Will.

8.02 p.m.

It was *absolutely* the last I'd seen of Mr Will. Oh God, oh God, oh God. It's been twenty-nine hours and I haven't heard from him. He hasn't texted or called or added me on Facebook or looked at my LinkedIn profile. I think I just had my first ever one-night stand and it feels horrible. Why hasn't he texted me? I know the rules say wait three days, but no one really waits three days, do they? This is horrible. I feel like such a slag. What did I do wrong? My poor vagina. She does not deserve this!

8.34 p.m.

I'm going to text him. I mean, he gave me his number
– he wants me to use it, surely? And it doesn't matter
who texts first, we've already slept together. I can send
a little message that's just a 'hi!' and it's fine. This is
ridiculous. If I hadn't had sex with him, I'd send him
a text message. If he was just a man or a woman I had
met and liked and had stuff in common with and
wanted to see again, I would text him. I'm going to
text him.

8.56 p.m.

I sent the text. I just said 'Hi! So happy Monday is over!'
That's OK, isn't it? That's totally normal. That's like, hey!
What's up! I'm not crazy! He'll reply to that. And you
know, if he likes me, it won't matter who texted first or
what I said, he'll just be happy to have heard from me.
It'll probably be a funny anecdote in the wedding
speeches. 'She couldn't wait to hear from me so she
texted me first and I was so happy!' Actually, I think I
texted Seb first. So it's fine.

9.13 p.m.

Hmm.

9.33 p.m.

There are more than a million good reasons for him not
to have replied to that message yet. Men don't check
their phones all the time, do they? They can't put them

in their pockets in case it gives them cancer of the nads. He probably hasn't got his phone.

9.45 p.m.

He's definitely seen it. There's no way he hasn't seen it. Maybe he's just playing it cool.

10.07 p.m.

What the fuck was I thinking? I should NEVER have texted first. That's probably the reason it didn't work out with Seb. Our entire relationship was founded on him having all that power over me, knowing that I caved and texted him because I was so desperate to have him in my life. And it was such a stupid message – I didn't even ask him a question! How is he supposed to reply if I don't ask him a question? That's messaging 101. I am so bad at this. And now I've ruined it forever. I'm going to run a bath and leave my phone in the other room and think very carefully about THAT TIME I TEXTED A MAN FIRST AND RUINED MY LIFE.

10.42 p.m.

A text! But it's from Lauren. Wanting to know if I have an 'in' at Vera Wang.
  So it begins.
  I'm going to bed. I'm being ridiculous.

11.17 p.m.

Just checked. Nothing.

11.33 p.m.

Still nothing.

11.45 p.m.

He replied! HE REPLIED.
   He sent me a smiley face! What does *that* mean?

12.04 a.m.

God, I almost wish he hadn't sent anything at all . . .
How do I reply to a smiley face? This is insane.

12.32 a.m.

A bloody *smiley face*? REALLY?

Weddings are all about love and commitment, not just the love between the bride and the groom but the love shared between everyone in attendance. Love can come in a thousand different shapes and sizes. Take a moment to think about this: what does love mean to you?

There's no love like puppy love! What was the name of your first boyfriend?
Gowri Gopalan. We were both seven. It lasted from morning playtime until afternoon break.

When was the first time you ever said I love you and meant it?
To Seb, two months after we started going out. He said it first when we were on a night out, but I thought he was drunk and being stupid and I couldn't say it back. I had to wait until we got home and I thought he was asleep, and then I said it and he smiled and kissed me on the top of my head and said, 'Shut up, Maddie.'

If you could tell the bride and groom something you've learned about love, what would it be?
My mum and dad always say they don't go to bed on an argument. I would say, if he's got nothing to hide, why won't he let you use his phone to order a pizza?

8

Half asleep and barely caffeinated is never my ideal state, but Tuesday morning had decided it wanted to be especially shitty. Sarah wasn't responding to my cheery texts suggesting we meet so I could break the news about the job, Lauren had sent me fifteen summer wedding Pinterest links by 8 a.m. and I was already on the bus when I saw the deodorant marks on my jumper. Then I burnt the top three layers of skin off my tongue with a cup of molten lava trying to pass itself off as a flat white. And as if I wasn't already feeling enough like a shit grown-up, no matter how many times I slung my handbag at the key card sensor, the gate to the building would not open.

'Oh, bloody hell,' I lisped painfully, pressing my hand to my heart as Matilda pressed her security pass against the wall and it flung open immediately. 'Sorry, you made me jump.'

'Good,' she said, giving me a tight-lipped smile. 'You won't be nervous, then. Come with me – you've got a meeting with Mr Colton.'

'When?' I said, nervous.

'Now,' she replied. 'Let's take the stairs.'

I feel as though it's worth pointing out that we work on the fifth floor of our building, and expecting someone to walk up five flights of stairs in high heels when they've barely slept because they were obsessing over the meaning of some ill-thought-out emoji communication and then putting them in a meeting with the MD of their company is incredibly cruel. And on top of that, she expected me to make polite conversation as we went. The woman is a monster.

'Do I look OK?' I asked, pulling at my jumper.

'Maddie –' she held open the door to our floor, looking cool and composed while I offered her a sweaty thank you – 'I think we both know that if you have to ask, you already know the answer to your question.'

It was fair. Short skirts and ankle boots looked cool in theory, but when you were unexpectedly called in to see the boss, it looked like you'd put on the bottom half of a cowgirl costume. Sarah would look amazing in this outfit. Lauren wouldn't be caught dead in this outfit. I was probably about to die in this outfit, so that left me somewhere between the two.

'Madeline.'

Mr Colton was already in the HR meeting room. Mr Colton was wearing a suit and a tie. Why had I chosen today to mix it up a bit? This is what happens when you decide you're cool enough to have a one-night stand. First it's going home with strange boys, then it's the misguided belief that you have the ability to put together an 'interesting' outfit.

'Mr Colton,' I replied, taking the seat opposite. Matilda followed me in and popped herself down in the chair next to the boss. 'You look nice.'

He looked at me over the frame of his fancy glasses.

'Great thooz,' I said, smiling broadly. I tried a bit harder with my burnt tongue. 'Really nice shoes. Classy.'

'Thank you, Madeline.' He took a piece of paper from Matilda, exchanging it for an 'Are you sure?' expression.

The only people who had ever called me Madeline were my father and my sixth-form tutor, which gave this whole interview a feeling of being called into the headmaster's office. I was thirty-bloody-one – why did I still feel like a naughty little girl?

'Thorry if I thound funny, I burnt my thung.'

'You've been with us for quite some time now, haven't you?' he said, scribbling some notes on what I assumed had to be the CV I had hastily pulled together for Matilda. 'Nearly ten years as Shona's assistant?'

'Thee's very good at what thee does,' I replied. It wasn't a lie. She might be an unpredictable twatbag of a boss, but she was bloody brilliant at throwing a party. I rubbed my tongue on the top of my mouth until I got the feeling back. 'I've learned tho much.' Try again. 'So much. So.'

Thank God.

'She is very talented,' he agreed, and handed the CV back to Matilda, steepling his fingers. 'You've never talked to us about a promotion before, Madeline, is that correct?'

'It is,' I said, shifting in my seat. My bare thighs were stuck to the leatherette and it was Not Comfortable.

'Then why do you think you should get one now?' Colton asked. 'What makes you think you'd be a great events manager?'

I looked over at Matilda and fought the urge to say 'because she told me so.'

'Because I am excited about the opportunity,' I said

slowly, encouraged by the head of HR's encouraging nods. 'I have the experience and I think I'm ready for more responsibility?'

I didn't mean to make it sound like a question, but it didn't sound like something I would say. Two weeks ago, I'd spent three days trying to find three trained seals to perform at a one-year-old's circus-themed birthday party. Surely that was enough excitement for anyone?

'Obviously, where possible I do like to promote from within the company,' Colton said. 'And you have definitely put in the hours. But without wanting to discourage you, this would be a big step up the ladder. As part of the selection process, we're asking you to do a piece of work. A test of sorts.'

'A test?' I asked, visions of a Hunger Games-style arena running through my mind. I could never pull off that kind of leotard and I'd be dead inside ten minutes.

'We'd like you to take on a special project,' Matilda elaborated. 'Victoria left behind a number of events. Shona has taken on the majority of them, as I'm sure you know, but this one only confirmed yesterday. We would like you to manage it.'

I opened the folder she handed me and leafed through the pages inside. Gay couple, adopted baby, big celebration. No request for zoo animals. Yet.

'We'll still be advertising for the position,' Mr Colton replied while I flipped through the event request form, 'and interviewing accordingly, but as I said, I would very much like to promote from within. Someone we already know is a team player. Someone we trust.'

I looked up abruptly.

'Does Shona know?' I asked. It suddenly occurred to

me that this could be a test. Matilda was going to pull her face off and it would be Shona underneath and she would punch me in the stomach until I wet myself while Mr Colton stood on the table and did a tap dance.

'I'll tell your manager,' Matilda said. 'We've got a new person starting on Friday who I'll be placing in your team. She'll be able to take on some of your responsibilities while you're on the project, but you will still be Shona's events assistant – I can't take you out of the job entirely.'

'No, I totally understand,' I replied, my pulse thumping in my ears. 'That's fine.'

A half-decent shag and a sort of promotion all inside a week. These were the things dreams were made of. I should buy a scratch card on the way home.

'Well then.' Mr Colton slapped both of his palms on the table, making me jump out of my seat, leaving half an inch of each thigh behind me. I shook his proffered hand with a grimace, my eyes watering. 'I'll leave you with Matilda to sort out the details. This is a wonderful opportunity, Madeline. I'm excited for you.'

'Thank you very much, Mr Colton,' I said, giving him a little bow. 'I'm super-duper excited.'

He threw one more uncertain glance at Matilda and left the office, shaking his head to himself.

'I've already buggered this up, haven't I?' I asked, my stomach falling through the floor at the thought of losing a job I didn't even know I wanted.

'You're going to be fine,' Matilda said. 'Now sit down and pull your skirt down. It's tucked in your knickers at the back.'

I reached around my bum, trying to pull my mini out of my pants.

'No,' I said, sitting down and dropping my head on the table. 'No, it's not.'

'Oh,' Matilda frowned. 'Then, as your HR manager, I'm going to have to recommend you get a new skirt.'

'Fair,' I replied.

'And as your friend as well,' she added. 'It's doing you no favours, Mads. You haven't got the arse for it.'

My dating experiences have been few and far between since Seb, but I do know that you should never agree to go out with a man on the same day that he requests the pleasure of your company. Which is why, when Lauren and Sarah asked, I told them Will asked me out Tuesday afternoon, not Wednesday lunchtime, for our Wednesday evening date.

So what if I was breaking rules, I thought, tossing my hair like a middle-England Beyoncé – they'd already been broken. One-night stands weren't supposed to develop into real relationships, but here we were, sitting in a pub on a Wednesday night, and maybe it was the gin and tonic I'd shotgunned but I felt great about my life choices.

Even if he was fifteen minutes late.

I felt less great about the voicemail from Lauren asking if we could get breakfast before work on Thursday to go over 'a few more ideas' that she'd had.

That woman had already treated me to more ideas than every single bride I'd ever worked with, but at least every third suggestion was ridiculous. Yes, Lauren, you can have a candyfloss machine at your reception. No, Lauren, you can't have Katy Perry serving that candyfloss just for Michael. Yes, Lauren, you can have butterflies released as you say your vows. No, Lauren, we can't breed your own special hybrid butterfly in time.

Reluctantly checking my phone and ignoring the three new emails from my beloved bestie, there was nothing from Will. As an On Time Person, lateness was not on my list of must-haves in a boyfriend, but these things happened. It could have been traffic, he could have got stuck on a phone call at work, who knew? He was the one who had asked me to meet him, after all. Why would he cancel?

'Another drink?' the wizened old landlord shouted across the room.

Will had suggested the Butcher's Arms, a proper old pub, for our liaison. Perhaps not the venue I'd have selected, but it did have a certain charm. Unfortunately, it also had this nosy old bugger who hadn't left me alone from the moment I'd walked in.

'I'm all right, thank you,' I called back with half a smile. All the little wooden tables around me were populated by what were clearly regulars. A couple of other old men sharing a pint, one sad-looking couple with half a shandy and a large white wine in front of them, and, in the corner, a French bulldog who had been nursing a port and lemon since I'd walked in. God knows where his owner was.

'Go on, have another,' the landlord said, picking up a glass before I could decline again. 'He's running late, is he?'

'Uh, yes?' I replied, taking another quick look at my phone. Almost twenty minutes.

'Stuck at the office?' In went a very generous measure of gin.

'I suppose?'

And then the glass got a glance at a bottle of tonic. 'Ooh, has he not told you where he is? What a tinker. Ice and a slice?'

'Yes please.'

'I shouldn't worry about it, darling,' he said, bringing the drink to my table so I could fully enjoy his decision to shun traditional dentistry up close. 'You two married?'

'No,' I said, accepting the drink with as much grace as I could muster. Oh good, he decided to sit down.

'Engaged?'

'No.'

'Living together?' he pressed.

'We've only just met,' I said, taking a tiny sip of the drink. Dear God, that was strong. I wasn't even certain it was gin – there was a definite hint of turps about it. 'It's fine, he's a lawyer, he works late.'

'Oh no, love,' The landlord pulled a filthy bar towel out of the back of his trousers and wiped down my table before blowing his nose into it and shoving it back into his belt. I pulled my elbows away and put my hands in my lap, turning green. 'Knock it on the head now. How late is he?'

'Twen— ten minutes,' I lied.

'If he can't be on time for a pretty thing like you at the beginning, he never will be. You don't want the unreliable ones, trust me,' he said with a wink. 'I've seen it all in here. Whenever she gets in before he does, someone leaves in tears.'

'I'm sure it's nothing,' I said through gritted teeth, desperate to spill my drink across the table and actually clean it. Whatever he'd given me had enough alcohol content to kill the germs he'd just wiped all over the surface. Maybe. 'He'll be here in a minute.'

'It isn't a good sign, though, is it dear?' The woman sitting at the next table with her miserable husband gave me a sympathetic frown. 'He's right, it's all about how he treats you in the beginning. Have you read *The Rules*?'

'Have you?' I asked, somewhat shocked.

'That's how I got my Bobby here,' she said with great pride. 'Always end the phone call first, keep them on their toes.'

Another check of the phone. Nothing. Twenty-five minutes.

'Get yourself online.' The landlord took over again, with the nodding dog support of Bobby and his good lady wife. 'I like that Tinder myself, but I've heard good things about Match.com as well. What's the one they do at the *Guardian*?

He stooped back underneath the bar and clucked his tongue at me.

'You're still a youngster,' he went on. 'No point in hanging around pubs waiting for lawyers who are half an hour late to show their face.'

'Ten minutes,' I corrected. 'And I'm actually thirty-one.'

Bobby and the landlord sucked their breath in through their teeth. Their discoloured, crooked and occasionally missing teeth.

'She looks good on it,' Bobby's missus admonished. 'You two leave her alone.'

'Thank you,' I said, braving a bigger sip of the gin, wondering if it had been made in the bath upstairs. Hendrick's it was not.

'Doesn't change the facts, though, does it, girl?' she said. 'Whether you look it or not, you're not getting any younger. I should lock this one down while everything's still where it started. You need to get yourself wed.'

'I thought I should be breaking up with him because he's not here yet?' I replied, defensively crossing my arms across my perfectly-pert-thank-you-very-much boobs. 'What happened to *The Rules*?'

'Out the door,' she replied. 'I know it's controversial with some women, but tell me, have you thought about faking a pregnancy?'

Fifteen minutes more advice on my love life was all I could take. It was seven thirty-five, I was hungry, I was tired, and thanks to the most disgusting gin I'd ever had the privilege of tasting, I was already half-cut. It was just as well. Buzzed Maddie wasn't nearly as distressed over Will standing her up and turning off his phone as Sober Maddie would have been. Buzzed Maddie just wanted to get inside before it started raining on her expensive blow-out and then show it off to the Domino's delivery man. It was only right that someone should see it, after all.

The weirdoes in the pub were wrong, I told myself, jumping off the bus and beginning the ten-minute walk home. Thirty-one wasn't old these days – I didn't need to rush into anything. Lauren was the same age as me and she was getting married. Although Sarah was the same age as me and she was getting divorced. Seb was the same age as me but his wife was three years younger, only twenty-eight. I wondered who would get remarried first, Sarah or Steve. And would she marry an older man? Would he marry a younger woman? When we were younger, in school and in uni, we all dated people our age, but now the age gaps were starting to become more apparent. I wondered why. Were women looking for older, more mature men or were men looking for younger women with less baggage than their contemporaries? God help any woman over the age of twenty-nine if it was the former.

I was literally two minutes from home when the heavens opened and of course I didn't have an umbrella.

'Shit,' I muttered, holding my handbag over my head as my bouncy curls started to flop and running through the puddles as fast as my gin-soaked legs could carry me.

And right there, huddled up next to my front door, was Will.

'What the fuck are you doing here?' I asked, handbag falling to my side, all thoughts of protecting my hair forgotten.

'What do you mean, what the fuck are you doing here?' He looked gone out. 'I've been waiting twenty minutes and now I'm piss-wet through.'

'*I was at the pub,*' I shouted. Was shouting at a man on your first date proper in *The Rules*? Probably not. 'Waiting for you.'

'But I was at the pub,' he said, pulling his suit jacket around himself as an especially big raindrop ran off the end of his nose. 'I was waiting for you.'

Clearly he was not at the pub I was at, otherwise he would also be quite drunk and reconsidering all his life choices.

'At the Butcher's?' I asked.

'Yeah,' he replied. 'Round the corner.'

Oh fuckknuckles.

'You were at the Jolly Butcher,' I said. 'On Cambridge Street.'

'Yeah, the Butcher's round the corner,' he said, annoyed. 'Where were you?'

'The Butcher's Arms,' I said, equally annoyed and wiping mascara out of my eyes. 'In Holborn.'

Will looked incredulous. 'Why were you there?'

'Because that's the Butcher's, not the Jolly Butcher,' I replied, sanity snapping. 'Why didn't you call me?'

'My phone's dead,' he said, wiping the rain off his face. 'I was ten minutes late, I thought you might have left already, so I came round and stood on your doorstep in the pissing-down rain.'

When you thought about it, pub fuck-up aside, it was actually quite romantic.

'How long would you have waited?' I asked, fighting a smile. 'Just out of interest.'

'All night,' he replied. 'Obviously.'

'Maybe I'll pop back out and see if you're still here when I get back,' I said. He grabbed hold of my hand and pulled me in for a long kiss, his mouth warm against the cold rain.

'Maybe you'll open the door and we'll get out of these wet clothes,' he said, kissing me again. 'Christ almighty, woman, what have you been drinking?'

'It was supposed to be gin,' I said, rummaging about in my bag for my keys while Will kissed the back of my neck. 'But you might need to check I haven't gone blind in the morning.'

'Is that an invitation to sleep over?' he asked, grinning.

'Well, I did leave you standing on my doorstep in the pouring rain, didn't I?' I said, holding up the keys with a triumphant flourish. 'I suppose I could see my way to putting you up for the night.'

As the rain started to slow, he cupped my face in his hands and wiped away the smudged make-up under my eyes, pressing his lips to mine once more.

'That's very decent of you,' he said. 'Now unlock the door before I get carried away and have to give you one on the doorstep.'

'Such a romantic,' I whispered. 'Get your arse inside, I'm freezing.'

Rules, after all, were made to be broken.

9

Friday May 22nd
Today I feel: Like a bit of a knob.
Today I am thankful for: Sarah Bloody Hempel.

When Shona stopped by my desk on Friday morning, I couldn't help but feel slightly faint. The look on her face suggested she had been informed of my special project. That or she'd finally found out about the Shona Matthews versus Joffrey Baratheon meme that had been flying around Facebook for the last month; it was tough to say.

'Matilda sent me an email about you applying for Victoria's job,' she said. 'How exciting.'

'Exciting?' I asked, my fist closing around my biro. I know they say the pen is mightier than the sword, but what I wouldn't have given for a machete at that exact moment.

'Yes,' she nodded. 'I'm sure you think I overreacted when you brought it up at the McCallan wedding, but I was just testing you.'

'You were?' She was?

'Honestly, Maddie, I think it's a fantastic opportunity.' Shona looked intently at me with her best sincere smile. 'I hope you don't mess it up. Now, do you think you could find your way into my office? I want you to meet my new assistant.'

I nodded.

So nice of her to make it sound as though I'd already been replaced.

'Now, maybe?' she said. 'If it's not too much trouble?'

Oh dear God, what had I done?

'Maddie, I want you to meet Sharaline,' Shona said, pointing at a very young, very eager-looking girl sitting in my chair in her office. 'Sharaline is going to be helping us while you deal with your situation.'

My situation? Was I suddenly an unwed teenage mother from the fifties?

And more importantly, *Sharaline*?

The girl in my chair jumped up and stuck out her hand with an exuberance that made me tired just looking at her. Obviously I noticed all the important things first. Great hair, sort of a very clean white blonde but with bluish tips. The kind of thing that would look like a fright wig on normal people but worked on her. Not upsettingly skinny, but great legs and brilliant boobs and, most distressing of all, it didn't look like she was wearing any make-up. None. Not even mascara. And she did not look like shit.

How very dare she?

'You must be Madeline,' she said, gripping my hand with both of hers and pumping my arm enthusiastically. 'I'm Sharaline.'

'It's Maddie – hi,' I said. After my disappearing-mini

debacle on Monday I'd gone for a more becoming floral midi skirt and little leather lace-up flats, but instead of looking chic and on trend, I looked like Sharaline's maiden aunt.

SHARALINE.

'Nice to meet you,' I said. 'How old are you?'

'Twenty-two,' she said, sitting back down in my chair and leaving me to perch on a high plastic stool. 'I graduated last year but I spent some time travelling.'

'Fantastic,' I replied. 'Whereabouts?'

'Oh, you know –' She waved a hand in a carefree gesture that would soon be beaten out of her. 'South East Asia, India, Central America, South America. Everywhere everyone else has already been.'

'Maddie went to Butlin's with her parents last year, didn't you, Maddie?' Shona asked.

'It was a Pontins,' I muttered. 'A family reunion thing, you know?"

'Where's Apontins?' Sharaline asked. 'Is it in Australia?'

'Isn't she fantastic?' Shona said. 'I like her already. Our first ever graduate trainee.'

'I started right after graduation,' I pointed out. 'Wasn't I a graduate trainee?'

'Let's hope not,' she replied with an eyebrow raised, flicking through some papers on her desk. 'Wouldn't say much for the programme. Anyway, since we're already halfway through the morning, shall we get down to it?'

Yes, this was going to go fabulously well, wasn't it?

'What I thought would be best,' Shona went on, 'would be for you to carry on dealing with the day-to-day tasks and for Sharaline to take on new business as it comes in. That should make things cleaner, don't you think?'

I nodded. 'When you say day-to-day tasks . . . ?'

'I'm going to give Sharaline things that she'll be able

to pick up easily, the business stuff,' she clarified. 'But you know how I like things, Maddie. There doesn't seem a lot of point in wasting Sharaline's time trying to teach her how I like my coffee when she's here to learn the business.'

'Well, what if I get Victoria's job?' I asked. 'Then who will know how to make your coffee?'

Shona's head popped up and she let out a tiny, stifled laugh.

'Sorry,' she said, pressing her hand against her chest to calm herself. 'Absolutely. Actually, I'd like to go over some of the new projects with her now, so why don't you go round to Starbucks and get us both something to drink.'

Sharaline, who had been blessedly quiet through this exchange, suddenly found her words. 'I'd love a flat white,' she piped up. 'Non-fat, obvs.'

'Obvs,' I replied. 'Non-fat for Sharaline.'

Sharaline. It's really not a name. Her awful parents.

'Fantastic.' Shona was still smiling when I stood up to leave. 'I think we're going to be a very happy little family.'

To be fair, sitting in that office with the two of them was starting to feel a lot like spending time with my family.

By the time the end of the day rolled around, I couldn't wait to get out of the office. Between doing my regular job, showing Sharaline how to do everything, twice, counselling Sarah and wedding planning with Lauren, I needed a drink. Will had been sending adorable texts all day, but he hadn't suggested we make plans and so I made some of my own, determined not to spend my evening Facebook-stalking him and drunk-dialling him at three a.m. to scream *'Why don't you call me?'* at him while listening to 'All By Myself' on a loop. I was switching my sensible work flats for my break-an-ankle Friday-night heels when the lift doors opened and a surprising figure walked in.

'Oh!' I said, one shoe on and one shoe off. 'It's you.'

It was the very tall usher from the wedding.

'Tom,' he replied, looking at me and then looking around the office. 'Am I in the wrong place?'

'Depends what you're after.' I hobbled out from behind my desk. 'How can I help you?'

He ruffled his hair, entirely product-free today and all the better for it. 'Aren't you a waitress?'

'I was filling in for one of the waitresses,' I said, wondering what he was doing in my office. 'I'm part of the events team here. But I am super pro waitresses.'

'Who isn't?' Tom asked, pushing back his hair again. 'Anyone who facilitates eating and drinking is all right with me.'

'Glad we've got that sorted,' I said. 'I'm assuming that isn't what you came to tell me, though?'

'Oh. No.' I felt like he was staring at me, but it was possible he was just so tall it was hard to see me down here at normal person height. 'Are you only wearing one shoe?'

Ah. He *was* staring.

'Yes,' I replied. 'Is *that* what you came to ask?'

'I'm supposed to pick up some stuff that was left behind at the reception,' he said, eyes still trained on my feet. Probably got a weird foot fetish or something.

'Ah, yes,' I said. 'I'll get the box.'

Well, this was interesting. I had left a message for

Vanessa, one of the bridesmaids, to let her know we had a box of lost and found, and he definitely wasn't a girl called Vanessa. She had to be his fiancée. Not only was he a tall lawyer, he also did fetching and carrying on her behalf. Lucky cow. I tried to remember which bridesmaid was which, but the McCallans had about twenty-five of them (OK, six) and I just couldn't be sure. I was fairly certain that it was the stunning blonde. There was a definite correlation between hot girls and tall men. I blamed online dating – they could round them up by size much more easily these days. It meant the rest of us had to try twice as hard if we wanted to snag a decent one out in the wild.

'There's some nice stuff in there,' I said, handing him the heavy box that had been doubling as my footrest all week. Tom took it as though it weighed nothing, picking out what looked to be a real fox fur stole complete with head and feet and pulling a face. 'Apart from that, obviously. Who wears a dead fox to a summer wedding?'

'You'd think I'd remember Ivana Trump being there, but I'm drawing a blank,' he said, dropping it back into the box and wiping his hand on his trousers. He shifted the box around in his arms and nodded at the bustling office behind me. 'So you're actually an events organizer?'

'It's not exactly MI5,' I replied. 'But I don't like to brag. How's, you know, lawyering?'

My eloquent and witty banter is one of the main reasons I'm constantly fighting men off in the streets.

'Technically, I'm a barrister,' he said with a smile. 'I just qualified.'

'Congrats. And that's different to a lawyer?'

'It's still practising law, but—' Tom looked at me, paused and then nodded. 'Yes. It's different.'

He was right to think it wasn't worth explaining further.

'So you don't work with Will, then?' I asked, mention-itis spilling out of my mouth so super casually even I wasn't sure whether or not I genuinely cared. 'And, you know, the groom? Ian?'

'I did undergrad law with them,' he said, a somewhat suspicious look coming over his face. 'But I didn't qualify at the same time.'

'Yeah, Will said that,' I nodded sagely, as though it were perfectly natural for Will to be telling me such things. In reality, our post-date conversations hadn't gone much further than gifs, three-words sentences and a picture of his penis, but whatever – he didn't need to know that. 'About you, er, not finishing.'

'Is that right?' Tom had gone from genial strapping young man to towering furnace of brooding rage faster than you could blink. It was quite sexy, if you're into that kind of thing. 'And what else has Will said?'

'Oh, you know.' I flapped my hands around and tried a coquettish laugh. He was unmoved. 'It's Will.'

'I do know,' he said, shrugging off his rage and taking a step sideways. 'So you've been speaking to him, have you?'

'Yeahnnabitwhatever,' I burbled, not quite settling on any real words. 'We're going to get a drink after work.'

'You're meeting him tonight?' he asked. 'Really?'

I couldn't quite put my finger on what was getting my back up most: the tone of his voice or his look of utter disbelief.

'Why?' I asked. It's hard to look confrontational in one shoe, but I did my best.

'It doesn't matter,' Tom said, as much to himself as to me. 'Nothing to do with me.'

'Your words not mine,' I replied.

He took a deep breath and shook out his shoulders. 'I'm sure you'll have a delightful time. Going anywhere nice?'

'I can't remember the name of the place.' I tapped my finger against my lips with Inspector Clouseau-like forgetfulness. I wasn't telling any outright lies – he had said we should get a drink after work one night. He just hadn't said which night. 'Somewhere near his office.'

'The Plumtree? He's meeting you at The Plumtree?' He sounded incredulous. Why wouldn't Will want to meet me for a drink at The Plumtree? What a wanker.

'I can't remember,' I said with a shrug, ready for him to leave. 'Something like that.'

'Well, have a lovely time,' he said stiffly.

'I will, thank you,' I said, repeating the name of the pub over and over and over in my head. 'I will have a lovely time.'

Tom jogged the box up and down in his arms. 'I'd better get off,' he said, breaking our stand-off. 'Who knows how long this woman can cope without her dead fox?'

'I know, it would be on my mind,' I said, dashing round him to press the lift button. 'Thanks for picking it up.'

And thanks for sodding off, I added silently as the lift doors closed on his curious expression. As soon as he was gone, I grabbed my phone and texted Sarah.

'*Change of plan*,' I typed, '*meet me at The Plumtree in Holborn.*'

'Why do you always attract lawyers?' Sarah asked over her second gin and tonic. 'Are you secretly a criminal mastermind?'

'I'm not attracting this one,' I reminded her over my

first. She'd necked an entire drink while I relayed the Tom–Will story and, let's be honest, it wasn't a long one. 'He was just picking that box up from the office. The point is, he's clearly got something against Will but he wouldn't say what.'

'Tall, handsome and well trained,' she sighed, poking at the lime floating in her drink with the tiny straw. 'You do need to get over this legal eagle thing, though. It's not good for you.'

I stared wistfully out of the bar window. 'But I do like the idea of telling the teachers at parents' evening that my husband is late because he's been in court all day.'

'You're sick,' Sarah said. 'Don't you think it's a bit weird that you've been the full nun ever since you broke up with Seb and the first person you shag is basically his clone?'

'I can't believe he's had a baby,' I said, curling a strand of hair around my finger. 'Seb had a baby.'

'Do you want to look at pictures of it and say mean things?' she asked. 'Because I've been keeping an eye on it and they'd better hope he grows into himself.'

'You can't say mean things about a baby,' I admonished my best friend, as though I hadn't been staring at it on Facebook all week and thinking exactly the same things. 'Anyway, it doesn't matter. Me and Will are going to have gorgeous babies. Two. Both boys. It's going to be fine.'

'I worry about you,' Sarah said in a low voice, sipping her gin. 'I really do.'

'Never mind me.' I craned my neck to check out the men at the bar and looked at my watch. It was only 6.30. Still very early. 'What about you. What's going on?'

Sarah's shoulders curled up for a moment before she forced them back down. 'Back to lawyer talk – I went to talk to one. This woman at my office got divorced last year and she recommended her. It sounds stupid, but the divorce is going to be harder because no one fucked up. The only way we can get it done now is if one of us sues for adultery or unreasonable behaviour. I don't want to wait two years to prove separation.'

'There was that time he came in shit-faced and ate all the chocolate out of your advent calendars and knocked over the tree,' I said. 'That was pretty unreasonable.'

'I think it's going to take more than that to convince a judge,' she said. 'I did think about going round to his mother's house and kicking a few windows in to speed up the process, but I'll be damned if I'm paying for that witch's double-glazing.'

'Fair.'

'The best bet is for me to meet an incredibly attractive and successful man who wants to sweep me off my feet,' she said, pausing to tighten her topknot. 'And then he can sue me for adultery. My lawyer is actually telling me to go out and get laid. She actually said I need to get back on the horse.'

'Why do people keep saying that?' I asked. 'If I had a horse and I fell off it, I would never get back on. I would sell it for glue and have a happy life full of no horses and free Pritt Sticks.'

'Don't worry,' Sarah said, gulping down the rest of her drink. 'I can barely stand to look at the horses. If a horse came near me, I'd probably punch it in the face.'

'On the plus side, you've still got more experience than anyone I've ever met,' I reminded her. Sarah had been very social while we were at university. It was a pretty big surprise to everyone when she got married so young, but as she explained at the time, she'd sown more oats than Quaker and she was ready to settle down. 'So that's something.'

'Surely Lauren has outdone me by now?' she said, scratching her nose. If I didn't know her, I'd want to slap her. She was far too pretty for someone wearing NHS specs. 'And you're on the market now.'

'I feel like I've been on the market for ages.' I pushed my toes in and out of my shoes. They were higher than I remembered and the balls of my feet were burning. 'Like, a rubbish market where you get secondhand DVDs and fake Man United shirts.'

'You're on the New York stock exchange,' Sarah said, smiling. 'You're Harrods. Maybe not Harrods – it's a bit tacky. How about Harvey Nicks?'

'Thanks.' I gave a smile back, eyes darting over to the door when three men walked in. Nope. 'I really hope you find the courage to let a stupid hot man shag you rotten and allow your husband to sue you for adultery.'

'You're so sweet,' she replied. 'Have you heard from Lauren this week? She's been so quiet.'

'It's all going to be fine,' I lied. 'I've had a few emails.'

I'd had seventeen emails, one hundred and thirteen text messages and one hour-long phone call. In the past forty-eight hours.

'I'm trying not to freak out,' Sarah said, beaming at the waitress when she offered to bring us another round. 'And I want to be there for her, but it's going to be diffi-cult at best.'

'I know,' I said, necking my G&T to make room for the next. If I was going to continue to lie so impressively, I would need more alcohol in me. 'But I'm going to be there to buffer her. If you start feeling overwhelmed, we can choose a safe word and I'll get you out of there. Something like "banana".'

Sarah's face immediately did that strange tightening thing that people do when they're about to start crying.

'Oh God, that wasn't your actual safe word, was it?' I asked, mortified and horrified in equal measure.

She shook her head. 'How am I going to help my friend plan a wedding when I'm going through a divorce?' she muttered, running her finger over the spot where her wedding ring had been. There was still an indentation, but only just. Ten years erased in a little over a week.

'You're going to be fine,' I promised. 'And if need be, very heavily drugged. Lauren's mum has always got all kinds of exciting American pills. We'll sort you out.'

She nodded, trying to convince herself that she agreed with me.

'Have you seen him yet?' I asked. 'Stephen?'

'No,' she said. 'I haven't seen my husband in almost two weeks. How mental is that? It's the longest we've ever been apart. I just keep thinking, what if we hadn't had that stupid row about wine . . .'

She drifted off for a moment, staring out of the window. 'Fuck it – sorry, Mads. I don't want to ruin your evening,' she said.

'Not even,' I said, kicking her gently under the table. 'Do you want to leave?'

'No,' she said, giving herself a shake and settling back in her seat. She turned her attention away from the window and towards the dark, wood-panelled bar. It really was wall-to-wall suits. If I didn't already have an agenda, I'd be giddy as a kipper, there was so much three-piece porn. 'What made you choose this place? It's so not you.'

'So, you'll laugh –' I started, knowing she in fact would not – 'but I thought Will might be here.'

Sarah looked me dead in the eye.

'You dragged me halfway across London to drink over-priced gin in a sausagefest pub because you thought the bloke you shagged on the weekend might be here?' she asked as the waitress put fresh drinks in front of us with a smile neither of us returned. 'Are you serious?'

'Yes?'

'And you didn't tell me?'

'No?'

Sarah took a long sip of her G&T and studied me through her non-prescription lenses.

'Does he know you're coming?'

'No,' I said, tapping my fingertips against my glass.

She took another sip and considered the information.

'You should have told me,' she replied eventually. 'And you should have got changed. What the fuck are you wearing?'

'It's nice!' I squealed, looking down at my navy blue dress with its little white collar. 'Isn't it nice?'

'It is nice, yeah,' Sarah replied. 'That's the problem. Aren't you trying to get this bloke to sleep with you? That dress makes you look like you want to buy a carton of Ribena and then skip down the beach holding hands.'

Didn't sound like a bad afternoon out to me.

'It's not like you've got them out, is it?' I said, pointing to her buttoned-up shirt and high-waisted shorts combo. 'Everyone knows men hate shorts over tights.'

Sarah regularly told me she wore them as a rape deter-rent when walking through East London on her own,

115

and Lauren regularly waited for her to go to the toilet to tell me they were an all-out penis repellent, be it consensual or otherwise.

'Good, I hate men,' she said, smoothing down her shirt front. 'Anyway, I don't dress to pick up lawyers. I dress to pick up tech entrepreneurs and men who are too old to be in bands but haven't given up the dream.'

'I'm dressed like a four-year-old,' I realized. 'This is why I never pull, isn't it?'

'There are so many reasons why you never pull,' she said, nodding. 'Now, in a vain attempt to take your mind off your ridiculous dress, what's happening with that job? Did you give HR my CV?'

'Too late,' I said, staring at the doorway and not really hearing her. 'That's Will. He just walked in.'

As the double doors flew open, a power ballad started playing in my head and Will strode towards the bar in slow motion while tossing his head back in uproarious laughter at something one of his dodgy-looking friends had said. Honestly, he had to be the most attractive man I had ever seen. It was beyond me why everyone woman in the bar wasn't trying to hump his leg as he walked.

'Which one?' Sarah asked, destroying my soft-rock fantasy and craning her neck as Will and his three friends sauntered over to the bar. 'Which one is he?'

I tried to nod towards him without drawing attention to myself. It was very strange, desperately wanting him to notice me and at the same time wanting to disappear into a hole underneath the table and find myself mysteriously transported to my settee, under a blanket, watching reruns of *Friends* and eating a very big pizza.

'Blue striped tie,' I whispered. 'Brown man-bag. Close-shaved head.'

'Oh, I recognize him from the photos. He's fit,' Sarah said, absently rubbing the leg of her corduroy shorts as she stared. 'Good work. Are you going to go and say hello?'

'No.' I looked at her as though she was quite mad. 'Why would I do that?'

'Because you dragged me out to Holborn to sit in a pub just in case a man you shagged might show up? And he has?'

'So?' Sometimes she was very stupid.

'You've lost me,' she said. 'You came here to talk to him and now you don't want to talk to him?'

'I want him to come and talk to me,' I said, my entire body still burning. 'I'm not going over there. He'll think I came here on purpose.'

'Mads, you did come here on purpose.'

'But I don't want him to know that, do I?'

I wanted to give her the benefit of the doubt – she was newly separated, after all – but fucking hell, how dense can you be?

'So we sit here, drinking our drinks, chat shit and wait for him to notice you?' Sarah asked.

I pulled out my lipstick and coyly reapplied. 'Yes.'

Sarah rolled her eyes and sat back in her chair, chucking her G&T down her throat. 'Fine. So how many emails has Lauren really sent you about the wedding?'

Thirty-seven minutes and another drink later, Sarah was starting to get annoyed. We'd discussed Blake Lively's baby, the appropriateness of thigh-high socks and exactly what Diet Coke was made of, and I was definitely getting a bit too tipsy for my own good.

'You don't think it's a bit silly sitting across the bar

from a man you've had sex with twice and pretending you haven't seen him?' Sarah asked, hoisting up her tights. 'You're thirty-bloody-one, Maddie. Go over and say hello.'

'But what if he's seen me and he's ignoring me?' There were no two ways about it, I was starting to panic. Ever since he'd walked into the bar, I'd been anxious. My brain was full of gin and adrenaline, and it was all getting to be a bit too much.

'Then he ought to have his balls chopped off and posted home to his mum,' she said, slamming her glass down on the table. 'You've got five minutes to go and talk to him or I'll go and talk to him for you, and then it really will feel like we're sixteen again.'

'What do I say?' I said, turning to look at my quarry. 'What do I do?'

'Maddie, two days ago, you saw fit to get naked with this man and let him put assorted parts of his body inside assorted parts of your body—'

'Not that assorted,' I interrupted. 'It was pretty straight-forward stuff.'

'Shut up,' Sarah instructed. 'What I'm saying is, if you can have sex with a complete stranger but you can't have a conversation with him, something's wrong. And not with him.'

I knew she was right, but this was definitely one of those 'easier said than done' scenarios. Dropping your knickers is considerably less emotionally dangerous than saying 'I like you'. Everyone knows that. Only someone who has recently gone through the trauma of hearing someone say 'I don't like you at all and would like a divorce, please' would think otherwise.

'Has he given you any reason at all to think he might

be a wanker?' she asked. 'Other than by being a man.
Which isn't his fault.'

'No,' I said, spinning the cardboard coaster on the table-
top. 'He's been nice. Very texty.'

'Then go and say hello,' she said, pointing across
the busy bar to where Will stood with his back to me.
'You're on your way to the bar, you're dead casual, you're
here meeting me, you're not a mental who tracked him
down because you were too impatient to wait for him to
ask you out again, and then we're going to get some
dinner because I'm fucking starving and all they've got
here are Kettle Chips. Isn't there a Nando's around here?
Do you fancy Nando's?'

I did fancy Nando's. I fancied it a lot more than trot-
ting across the now very crowded bar and interrupting
Will when he was with all his friends on a Friday night.
What was I thinking? This was the worst idea ever. I'm
destroying this before it has even started, I told myself.
I'm standing right in front of him. I'm—

'Maddie?'

'Will?'

I'm an idiot.

'Hello!'

He pulled me into a big, filthy, squishy hug, right
there, in front of everyone, and kissed me on the cheek.

I'm a genius.

'Hello,' I said, determined not to stutter or blush or
fall over or do any other terrible things that would make
for a fantastic story at brunch tomorrow but basically
ruin my life. Not to make too big a deal out of this.
'What's up?'

'Just getting a drink with the boys,' he said, waving
his pint at three other men in shirts and ties of assorted

muted colours. 'Boys, this is Maddie. She was at Ian's wedding at the weekend.'

The boys waved and smirked and let their eyes dart over my covered-up breasts. Sarah had been right about the dress. Between the beers they'd been putting away and the warmth of the bar, they all had bright pink cheeks and sheepish grins, giving them a definite air of overgrown schoolboys. Every man looked sexy in a suit and every man looked ridiculous when he rolled up his sleeves and undid his tie. Top button undone and tie loosened, hot. Top three buttons undone and tie completely unfastened and you're Paul the Perv at the office Christmas party. It was one small step away from tying it round your forehead and doing the dance to 'Wig-Wam Bam'.

'Twice in one week,' he said, smiling. 'How lucky am I? What brings you to this neck of the woods?'

'Stalking you,' I replied, gurgling with manic laughter.

Will stared at me for a moment.

Oh, Maddie, shut up . . .

And then he laughed.

'I was meeting my friend Sarah,' I said quickly before he had a chance to realize I wasn't actually joking. I pointed back at our table where Sarah was staring intently at the screen of her phone. 'She works round the corner.'

She didn't work round the corner, but he could work that out in his own time.

'Love it when you bump into people,' Will said, still smiling. His friends closed ranks and moved ever so slightly away from us, leaving us to our actual official conversation. 'How's the rest of your week been?'

'Shit,' I replied automatically. 'We've got a new assistant and she's ridiculous.' SHARALINE. 'How about yours?'

'Manic,' he said, nodding. 'Took on a huge new case. Been in the office till midnight more or less every night other than Wednesday.'

'Wow,' I said, copying his head-bobbing. My lipstick felt too thick and my mouth felt too dry – it was horrible. 'That sounds tough.'

'I leave the work at work – it's the only way to cope,' he said, smiling again, and I stopped worrying about my lipstick. Mostly. 'What's on the agenda for tonight then?'

I wondered if he'd fancy getting a Nando's with me and Sarah.

We're probably leaving soon,' I said, leaving the offer of Portuguese chicken off the table for the time being.

'Yeah, these lightweights were talking about going home as well,' he said, rubbing his stubbly head. 'Friday gets harder when you get older, doesn't it?'

I wanted to rub his stubbly head. And then I remembered how his stubbly head felt on my thighs and suddenly I came over all unnecessary. Who knew Action-Man hair could be so bloody sexy?

'Yes,' I said robotically. 'Friday is hard.'

'Well, if you're leaving and I'm leaving . . .' Will leaned forward until I could feel his breath in my hair, on my neck. 'Why don't we leave together?'

'I thought you were tired?' I said, blushing, stumbling and stuttering all at once.

'Not that tired.' His hand moved down my waist to rest right on a place that could still be considered socially acceptable. 'I'll get my card from behind the bar and I'll meet you outside in five. You flag down a cab.'

'OK,' I mumbled, wondering how to break my abandonment to Sarah. 'I'll be outside.'

With one last slutty look he smiled, squeezed my hip

and turned back to the bar. With one last trip over my own feet, I ran across the room.

'Well?'

'He wants to go home,' I said very quickly. 'He wants to go home right now.'

'Loser,' she said, slipping her phone in her bag. 'Nando's for two then.'

'Oh . . . no.' I pulled my best 'please don't hate me' face, knowing that she was well within her rights to hate me. 'He wants to come home with me.'

'But you're not going home,' Sarah said. 'We're going to Nando's.'

I pursed my lips and tried to think of the best way to put it. 'Yes, we were going to do that,' I agreed. 'But if I went home with him instead, would that be a terrible, terrible thing?'

'You're asking if it would be bad to ditch your lifelong best friend, who is going through a horrible separation and has always been there for you, just so you can go and shag some bloke you met at a wedding last weekend?'

'That more or less covers it, yes.'

'You're the worst friend ever,' she declared.

'I am.'

'And you owe me a massive one.'

'The biggest one ever.'

Sarah looked across the room at Will and then back at me.

'You like him, don't you?' she said, pulling the strap of her leather messenger bag over her head.

'I do,' I said, colouring up from gin and vulnerability. 'I like him.'

'Then go on,' she said, waving me away. 'Consider me your fairy wingman. Have fun and I'll see you tomorrow.'

'Thank you,' I said, wrapping her up in a huge hug. 'I'll make it up to you. Whenever you're ready, I'll be the best wingman ever. I'll be Goose.'

'Goose died,' she said, standing up and readjusting her tights.

'Iceman?'

'Iceman was a wanker. You're already Iceman.'

'And don't forget I owe you a Nando's as well,' I said, hoping she'd hold me to it. 'See you in the morning.'

Twenty minutes later, when I was still standing outside on my own watching cab after cab after cab pass me by, I started to wonder if I'd made a mistake. Sarah was long gone and gangs of girls rolled by me, holding on to each other and laughing at a joke I would never be invited to understand, while I hung around in the street, handbag over my shoulder, legs crossed at the ankle as though no one was keeping me waiting.

The bar was so busy now I couldn't see what was happening in there, and as much as I wanted to go back in and get Will, I didn't want to be that girl. I didn't want to be demanding. I wanted to be cool and not bothered and whatever. Not that I had ever been either of those things in the history of ever.

A bright orange light came tearing down the road and I stuck out my arm. I just wanted to go home.

'Perfect timing.'

Just as the taxi pulled up to a halt, Will appeared out of nowhere and slung his arm round my shoulders.

'Yeah,' I replied, clambering inside as he held the door open for me. 'I thought you weren't coming.'

There was a forced lightness in my voice that made me feel a bit sick at myself.

'Sorry, took ages to get my card back,' he said, settling in beside me, warm hand on my cold thigh. 'I wasn't that long, was I?'

'Long enough,' I said, arching my eyebrow and losing the fight before it had begun. 'It's fine.'

'When women say it's fine, it never really is,' he said, pressing his face into my neck as I gave the driver my address. 'How am I going to get back on your good side?'

'I don't know,' I said. I would remain a cool, calm, detached ice queen. Even when his hand was already up my skirt. 'I've got some jobs that need doing in the flat?'

'I can think of a job that needs doing,' he whispered, his fingertips finding the edge of my knickers. Thank the Lord I'd worn nice ones.

I wonder how many times a day, on average, people thank the Lord for things he really doesn't want to be thanked for?

Being part of a bridal party is a lot like being part of a family. You don't get to pick your brothers and sisters and everyone must take care of their chores to keep the household running! But more importantly, just like a family, you and your fellow bridesmaids and ushers will become a family in the time leading up to the wedding, making sure things run smoothly for your bride and groom on the day.

Use this space to remember how important your own family is to you and take a moment to be thankful for all the love that brought you to this day in your life.

Your mom's name: Tracy
Your dad's name: Peter
Brother(s)'s name(s): Daniel Michael
Sister(s)'s name(s): Eleanor Jane
Do you have any cousins? Yes, but only one and we don't talk to him because he went on *Big Brother* after it went to Channel 5 and is officially a 'disgrace'.
Tell us about any nieces or nephews you might have: I only have one and she is reasonably new so there isn't much to say. She's quite pink and doesn't cry too much. I suppose that's a bonus.
What qualities do you share with your mom? Big boobs, irrational love for tomato sauce, allergic to cats.
And what qualities do you share with your dad? Brown hair, green eyes, sense of humour, inexplicable need to eat an entire box of Quality Street every Christmas Eve even though it makes us throw up, undying love of *Game of Thrones*.

10

Sunday May 24th

Today I feel: As though I might be adopted.
Today I am thankful for: Give me a minute . . . I'll think of something.

Given that I get very few weekends off in the summer and I had already spent last weekend at a wedding and then planning my own friend's wedding for free, I thought it was very good of me to agree to spend Sunday with my family when I could have been sitting on my arse watching whatever bad films were on ITV2. I was such a good daughter.

'It's looking at me funny. Why is it looking at me funny?'

'Maybe because you're looking at her funny,' my sister replied, taking my new niece out of my arms and placing her back in the travel cot. 'What's all that crap over the back of your cardi?'

'Must be from the train.' I pulled my cardigan off and shoved it into my handbag. Train, kitchen floor, whatever.

Will had popped back round this morning on his way to rugby; these things happened. 'You look well.'

'Do you mean I actually look well or do you mean I look fat?'

'I was actually thinking you've lost the baby weight quickly,' I said, staring into the baby's green eyes. It stared back but said nothing. So confusing. 'So, yeah, I meant what I said.'

'I haven't been trying to lose it,' Eleanor said, yawning. 'But I'm exhausted all the time and I haven't slept for months, so that's got to be good for burning calories, hasn't it?'

'Are you breastfeeding?' I asked.

'Yes,' she replied. 'Don't pull that face. You'll have to do it one day.'

I wished I were as certain as she was.

'Look at my girls!' My dad came booming into the room as my dad is wont to do and launched himself on me. My dad is not a slender man. It was not comfortable. 'Your mother says dinner is ready and you're to get yourself to the table before Daniel eats it all. Shall I stay in here with madam?'

'No, she's fine,' Eleanor said, pulling on a jumper and peering from underneath it at baby Emily. 'She'll let us know if she wants anything.'

My little sister has been a parent for exactly five weeks and she's already better at it than either of ours.

'You just leave her?' I asked, staring at the baby.

Eleanor shrugged. 'Where's she going to go?'

My parents don't live in the same house I grew up in, but for some bizarre reason best known to them, when they moved they decorated the new house to look exactly like the old house. It's very disconcerting.

Lindsey Kelk

'Now, who wants how many Yorkshire puddings?'

In the new old dining room, Mum was looming over the table holding a giant bowl full of Aunt Bessie's finest.

'Mum says Sarah's getting divorced,' Dan said, grabbing the gravy boat and pouring half the contents all over his plate before anyone else had a chance. Dan, love him though I do, is a complete wanker. How his girlfriend has managed to put up with him for so long is beyond me. 'What's going on?'

'Who told you?' I asked Mum as she untied her apron and beamed vacantly.

'Who told me what?'

'Who told you Sarah is getting divorced?'

Mum pressed her hands to her heart and pulled a face she usually reserved for Children in Need or whenever she found out another BBC TV presenter was a paedo. 'Her mum told me,' she said, ladling mint sauce all over her lamb. 'She's very upset.'

'I find that hard to believe,' I replied. 'She never liked him.'

'Well, it's distressing, isn't it?' Mum said, clearly not wanting to relay the exact conversation. 'Anyone would be upset.'

'What happened?' Eleanor asked. 'Did he cheat on her?'

I shook my head. 'She says he didn't.'

'Hmm,' Mum sniffed. 'He says he didn't.'

'And I see Seb had his baby,' Dad said, lifting his wine glass. 'Have you spoken to him?'

'Should we send him a card?' Mum asked. 'I'll send a card.'

I put down my fork and stared at my parents. 'Are you still Facebook friends with Seb?'

'Of course we are,' Mum replied. 'Why wouldn't we be?'

'Because we broke up and he's married to someone else?'

'He was part of the family for a long time,' Dad said, waving a lamby fork around to diffuse the tension but only succeeding in sending a lump of meat into Eleanor's lap. 'That's what FB is for, isn't it? Keeping in touch with people?'

'No, it's for stalking people and passing judgement on the lives of others,' I said. 'You're Facebook friends with my ex-boyfriend but you're not Facebook friends with me? And don't call it FB, it's weird.'

'We thought it would be awkward,' Mum explained. 'We didn't think you'd accept.'

'They're Facebook friends with me,' Eleanor chimed in.

'And me,' Dan said. 'And Rachel.'

Now I was annoyed. 'You're Facebook friends with Dan's girlfriend?'

'They're friends with Jessica, as well,' Eleanor added. 'And Emily.'

'Oh, OK then,' I said. 'It's just Dan, Dan's girlfriend, Eleanor, her wife and their baby?'

'You're making a drama out of nothing as usual,' Mum tutted. 'I'll send you a friend request.'

'Don't bother,' I said, digging into my mashed potato. 'I'd only put you on restricted view anyway.'

'She didn't want to interfere with your adventures,' Dad said, giving me a nudge. 'All those boys poking you.'

'Please, I'm trying to eat,' Dan groaned. 'And no one's poking her. She's unpokable.'

I was dying to tell them all about Will, but it was too soon. The second I mentioned his name, it would be the only thing I heard until our tenth wedding anniversary. I'm not sure when it happens – maybe it's something to do with puberty – but as soon as you start showing an interest in the opposite sex, your love life becomes open season for every dinner-table conversation until you settle down and start boring everyone.

Seb and I broke up ages ago, and yet he still came up in conversation every time I came home because they couldn't not mention him; they couldn't not ask me the relationship question. Nature abhors a vacuum, and the vacuum nature abhorred the most was the one in my vagina.

'No new young man on the scene, then?' Dad asked. 'No dashing suitors we should know about?'

'None you should know about,' I confirmed.

'And now Sarah's back on the market, you've got even more competition,' Dan added.

'Thanks, Dan.'

'Sarah's fit, though.'

'Thanks, Dan.'

'If I was single, I would.'

'All right, Dan.'

'How's Lauren?'

'Getting married.'

'Lauren's fit as well.'

'Oh, that's exciting.' Mum swapped her 'not Rolf Harris as well?' face for her 'Oh, Des Lynam's on the TV!' expression. 'Has she asked you to be a bridesmaid?'

I nodded, chewing thoughtfully. 'Yep. It's just a bit weird, because Sarah is getting divorced, and Lauren is getting married, and it's all happening at the same time and—'

'Guess what – I'm going to Japan for a shoot next

week,' Dan said. Dad reached over and ruffled his curly brown hair. 'Should be interesting.'

And so the sibling one-upmanship begins.

'That's exciting,' Dad continued. 'You haven't been there for a while, have you?'

'Been a few years.' Dan shrugged. 'It's just Tokyo, just for a couple of days.'

Just Tokyo. Like I said, Dan is a bit of a wanker.

'What about you, Ellie?' Mum asked. 'Anything exciting happening?'

'I had a baby,' she replied. 'I'm knackered all the time. This here is the most exciting thing I've done all week, which should tell you all you need to know.'

'It's so nice to have you all together,' Mum said, ignoring her youngest daughter's response. 'So lovely.'

'How about you, Maddie?' Dad asked. 'Put on any good parties lately?'

'I booked the Chuckle Brothers to turn up at some-one's fortieth last week,' I said, pulling my hair back into a ponytail. 'And I'm sort of up for a promotion at work.'

Mum slapped my hands away from my head. 'Don't play with your hair at the table. A promotion? What sort of a promotion? You won't be doing parties any more?'

The excitement in her voice was heartbreaking. Neither of my parents really understood my job. They were both English teachers and their experience of 'a fancy do' stretched as far as renting the nice room above the pub and ordering in some M&S party platters.

'It's still events,' I said. 'But I'd be a manager instead of an assistant.'

'Have you thought any more about teaching?' Dad asked, clasping his fork so tightly I could see his knuckles turning white. 'Because you know we always said we'd pay for you to go back to university.'

'I'd be a rubbish teacher,' I said. Dan and Eleanor nodded. 'And I don't need you to pay for me to go back to university.'

'You needed them to buy you a flat,' Dan pointed out. 'Which you still live in.'

'That's our retirement fund,' Mum said, answering for me. 'Maddie is looking after it for us.'

'You haven't been round there lately, have you?' Dan muttered through a forkful of peas.

'You'd be such a good teacher,' she went on, wrestling with an undercooked Brussel sprout as she spoke. 'Surely you don't want to play at parties forever.'

'I'm not playing at parties,' I said, tired of having the same conversation a thousand times over. 'And I don't want to be a teacher.'

'You don't want to be anything,' Dad announced, placing his fork down with some force. 'Life isn't all fun and games, Madeline. You can't expect to just muddle through.'

I don't know exactly what I did to deserve a 'Madeline', but my dad looked like he was properly pissed off.

'OK,' I said slowly, looking around the table for help and finding none. 'That's not true. Just because I don't want to be a teacher doesn't mean I don't want to do anything. This promotion would be a lot of responsibility. It's a big job.'

'Hiring the Chuckle Brothers to show up at someone's fortieth birthday party,' Dan added. 'Sounds massive.'

'Just because you don't understand what I do, doesn't mean it isn't difficult,' I replied calmly. 'You couldn't organize your arse from your elbow if Rachel didn't tell you which was which.'

'God help you when you have a baby,' Eleanor said as Emily started crying in the other room. 'I don't know how you'll manage when you've got actual important things to worry about.'

I turned in my seat to give my baby sister the full weight of my 'Excuse me?' face.

'Ooh, Sarah's mad at Lauren and Lauren's upset with Sarah and I can't decide what I want to do with my life even though I'm thirty, why don't I go and plan a party for some rich git who's got more money than sense,' she said in a sing-song voice that she pretended was jokey. 'Poor me, poor me, poor me.'

Dan coughed to clear his throat. 'She's thirty-one.'

'Isn't it all a bit, I don't know, pointless?' Eleanor said, looking me directly in the eye. 'Don't you get bored of planning parties for other people? I don't know how you can be bothered to get up in the morning – it just seems so empty.'

Oh. Oh no. Now I was mad.

'Are you fucking kidding me?' I asked calmly.

'Madeline! Language!'

That Madeline I probably deserved.

'What?' Eleanor hadn't even stopped eating to insult me and her baby carried on wailing in the background. 'Everything is so superficial, Maddie. I don't want to be rude, but the more you talk about things, the more it sounds a bit pointless.'

I looked at my little baby sister, stunned. 'You're saying my life is pointless?'

'I said your job, not your life, but it's not as though you're curing cancer, is it? Maybe pointless isn't the right word,' she mused, trying to find the exact phrasing with which to trash all my life choices. 'Empty. It's empty.'

I take back everything I said about her being a good parent. You can't be a good parent when you're a shitty human being.

'*What are you talking about?*' Shouting was not allowed at the Fraser dinner table, but it was either control my voice or control my fists, and punching was definitely more frowned upon. '*How is my life empty?*'

'None of it *means* anything,' replied the twenty-five-year-old married mother of one. 'All this stressing out over nothing. I'm not having a go at you – I'm trying to put it in perspective. You've got too much time to worry about things that don't matter. When you have a baby, you'll get it.'

'Oh, Els, she's going to kick your arse,' Dan said, shaking his head into his dinner and grinning.

'Daniel . . .' Mum gave him a light warning for the use of the word arse before turning her attention to her daughters. 'Now you two stop it. Eleanor, your sister's life isn't pointless. And Maddie, Eleanor's right.'

'What?'

'Sorry, not what.'

'What?'

'Your life is not pointless – Eleanor didn't mean that. But everything does change when you have a baby,' she said, flapping her hands around in the air. 'You'll see. You won't have time for your nonsense.'

Is justifiable homicide a thing in England? Or is that only on American police shows?

'What if I don't have a baby? What if I don't want a baby?' I asked. 'What if I can't have a baby?'

'Oh, Maddie!' Mum's hands flew back to her chest. 'What's happened? Is it your Fallopian tubes? Because your aunt Ivy had a terrible time with her tubes—'

'Classic,' Eleanor interrupted. 'Let's make it all about you.'

'Oh my God.' I leaned my head as far back as it would go and took a very deep breath before responding. 'You're the one that made it about me. You're the one who just said my life doesn't mean anything.'

'That's not what she said,' Mum said.

'It sort of is,' Dan said.

'*I don't have an empty life,*' I shouted. 'I have a *brilliant* life. I have friends and a job and I'm seeing a very handsome man who is a lawyer.' I stood up and slammed my hand on the table for good measure. 'Yes, a lawyer.'

'A blind lawyer?'

'Shut up, Dan!' my mother and I shouted at the same time.

'I happen to love my life, thank you very much. Yes, I plan parties for a living, and yes, I spend a lot of time talking about my friends, but there's nothing wrong with that. I care about my friends. I don't have too much time on my hands, so don't worry about that. I work eighty hours a week, I go to *yoga* and *spinning* and *book club*, and, yes, I see my *friends*. Friends who are having dinner at Ceviche right now while I'm sitting here trying to have a nice family dinner with *you*.'

'*When do you go to yoga?*' Eleanor yelled.

'*I go sometimes,*' I yelled back.

'What's a *ceviche*?' Dad asked.

'It's raw fish,' I said, slightly calmer. 'It doesn't matter, Dad.'

'I thought raw fish was sushi?' he whispered to Mum. 'Have they changed it?'

'It's different to sushi,' Dan replied. 'More Spanish and pretentious.'

'It's not pretentious, it's delicious.' I breathed out hard. 'And for the love of God, Eleanor, can you not stop that baby crying?'

'We're letting her cry,' she replied calmly. 'She's a baby, she's supposed to be making that noise. I'm not sure what your excuse is.'

'Can we all calm down and finish our dinners please?' Mum said in a voice so high-pitched I thought the windows would shatter. 'I've got an apple crumble in the oven for pudding.'

'Ooh, crumble,' Dad said.

'Now, Maddie.' Mum took a deep breath and cut up a tiny piece of lamb while the rest of the table stared at their plates. 'Tell us all about this lawyer.'

11

Wednesday May 27th
Today I feel: AMAZING.
Today I am thankful for: BEING AMAZING.

I don't know what I've been worrying about.

It turns out I am, as I secretly expected, amazing at everything, not just sitting on the settee eating Quavers as my sister seems to believe. Although I'm also good at that because I'm GENERALLY AMAZING.

Admittedly my meeting with the couple who wanted us to plan their baby-naming didn't get off to the best of starts, but I think I got there in the end.

'Hi, I'm Maddie,' I said as I entered the meeting room armed with high heels, several notebooks and Sharaline (sigh) by my side. 'It's so great to meet you, Mr and, uh, Mr Dickenson.'

'Andrew and Christopher, please,' Andrew said, pointing at himself and his husband. 'I took his name. Who'd want to be Andrew Higglebottom all their life? Silly name.'

'And this is Sharaline.' I gestured towards my intern. Speaking of silly names. 'Can we get you anything to drink? Coffee, tea, a glass of champagne maybe?'

'I wouldn't turn down a glass of fizz,' Christopher said, flashing a very elaborate diamond wedding band as he did so. Fantastic, I thought – big budgets ahoy. If I got the job full time, I'd be on commission. The bigger the diamond, the bigger the party and the bigger the pay cheque for Maddie.

'Sorry we kept cancelling last week – things have been rather hectic.'

'I can only imagine,' I replied, waving away the apology but secretly catching it and putting it in my back pocket. I had been so convinced they were going to cancel the party, I hadn't slept properly in a week. 'You have a baby on the way – you must be insanely busy.'

'You can't even imagine,' Andrew said. 'Do you have children?'

'Oh God no!' I laughed madly, reaching for the remote to turn on the projector screen across the room. 'Ew.'

Andrew and Christopher did not join me for a chuckle.

'My sister just had a baby, though,' I said, scraping my fringe out of my face.

Still nothing.

'And she's gay.'

'Did you organize her baby-naming party?' Christopher asked hopefully.

'No, she had a very traditional christening,' I said, sorting through my folders. 'It was lovely, actually.'

They glanced at each other, sharing a look last seen on my parents' faces.

'Have you planned many of these kinds of events?' Andrew asked.

'So many. You're in such safe hands,' I said, swiping too roughly at my iPad screen and promptly throwing it across the room. Climbing out of my chair, I slunk across the room to pick it up.

'When we called, we originally spoke to someone called Victoria?' Andrew said. 'Is she going to be here today?'

I gulped slightly. 'Victoria actually left the company,' I said, crossing my legs and attempting to present my most professional self, but neither of those things was easy in a pencil skirt. Both men looked at me with alarm as I shuffled uncomfortably in my seat until one knee was successfully over the other. 'It's just me and Shona on the events side now.'

'Shona? Who's Shona?' Christopher perked up. 'Are we meeting Shona?'

'No, I'm going to be taking care of you,' I said, trying to sound reassuring and not wonder whether or not I would have to pay to replace the now cracked screen of my iPad. 'You don't need to worry about anything at all. Other than your baby. Not that you need to worry about your baby. Probably. I don't know.'

Sharaline burst through the door carrying four glasses and a bottle of Bollinger.

'Here we go,' she said, placing the bottle in the middle of the table while Andrew and Christopher pursed their lips like cats' arses. 'Shall I pour?'

'Please,' I nodded, clearing my throat and shuffling my papers. If this was going to go tits up, I was at least getting a drink out of it. 'I was just about to ask Mr and Mr Dickenson to tell me all about their baby.'

The couple shared a look and a shrug and accepted their champagne. Clearly they had the same attitude towards this situation as I did.

'We're having a little girl, Audrey Dickenson,' Christopher said as Andrew pulled up a picture of a sonogram on his phone. Sharaline and I ahhed in unison. When did it become socially acceptable to show any old person the inside of someone else's uterus? I didn't get it. 'Our surrogate is due in three weeks and so we were hoping to plan the party for some time at the end of July.'

'OK.' I nodded sagely as Sharaline took down notes. 'And you want to do it on a weekend?'

'Yes, on the 25th ideally,' Andrew confirmed.

One week before Lauren's wedding, I scribbled down in my own notepad. Not to worry. Perfectly fine. Entirely achievable.

'So I'm going to show you a presentation of some events we've organized,' I said, cueing up my presentation, 'but is there anything in particular you're thinking about? A certain theme or location to get things started?'

'There is,' Andrew said, whipping out his own, undamaged, iPad. 'We're both very detail-oriented people, so we've done quite a lot of research already.'

He wasn't joking. Before I could so much as pull up my PowerPoint, he was scrolling through a Pinterest board showing me photos of floral arrangements that would cost two thousand pounds apiece, cakes that I couldn't get made for less than a grand, and venues that didn't even exist in the UK.

'We know exactly what we're looking for,' he said, swiping through the pictures far too quickly for me to take them in, but the general feeling I was getting was that these men would consider one of Elton John's parties a bit cheap. 'Afternoon tea in an English garden with a storks and roses theme.'

'Storks and roses,' I repeated, making a note on my pad.

'The ceremony will take place amongst the roses and the colours will be peach and pink. All the roses need to be peach and pink. All the food should be peach and pink. All the decorations should be peach and pink. Then we want a wonderful, wonderful party for the grown-ups and the children but it should be classy, not tacky. And Christopher has coeliac disease, so everything will need to be gluten-free. Oh, and there can be no balloons. I have globophobia.'

I clucked my tongue and tried not to cry. 'Riiiiight.'

Sharaline picked up her champagne glass and knocked the whole thing back. Maybe she wasn't as dense as I thought.

'Obviously we're looking for something out of the ordinary,' Andrew said, pausing on a picture of the Mad Hatter's Tea Party from Alice in Wonderland. 'Something extravagant and surreal and spectacular. It has to be something that will blow people's minds.'

'OK.'

'But child-friendly.'

'OK.'

'But totally insane.'

'OK.'

'But beautiful.'

'Right.'

'But fantastical.'

'Brilliant.'

'And money is no object.'

'Great.'

'But we're talking within reason.'

'OK.'

'Does that sound like something you can manage?'

'You want a beautiful, fantastical, spectacular party in a pink and peach rose garden without any gluten or balloons that will blow everyone's minds but not scare the babies?' I said. 'Piece of piss. I mean cake.'

They turned to look at each other. Andrew grasped Christopher's knee and gave a curt nod.

'If this isn't something you think you'd be able to put together,' Gluten-Free Christopher said, looking almost relieved, 'we can always, you know, do it ourselves.'

'We talked about this,' Andrew hissed. 'You're too busy to plan a party. You can't do everything, Christopher.'

'Really, this is completely fine,' I said, trying to sound more confident than I felt. 'Nothing I haven't done before.'

'Really?' Christopher said, beginning to look hopeful. 'Truly? You've done something on this scale before?'

'A thousand times,' I exaggerated. 'At least.'

'Hello, everyone.'

The door opened and Shona strode in, blonde ambition ponytail swinging around on the top of her head, black-and-white checked trousers so tight even Christopher and Andrew would have been able to pick her vagina out of a line-up.

'How's it all going?' she asked, leaning over the empty chair at the head of the table. 'Has Maddie wowed you with her vision?'

'We're only just starting,' I said, all my bravado falling away. 'I'm showing the presentation.'

'I'm Shona.' She strode round the table to my clients, shaking their hands so hard I thought their arms were going to fall off. 'You must be Andrew and Christopher. Congratulations on the new baby – you must be so happy.'

'Thank you,' Andrew said, his eyes shining brighter

than his wedding ring. 'We're so glad you're going to be joining us.'

'Oh no.' Shona's smile was so wide her face nearly split in two. 'I just came in to grab Sharaline.'

Christopher nudged Andrew. 'I told you that was her name.'

'I'm taking notes for Maddie,' Sharaline said, waving her notepad at the boss.

'Sharaline is taking notes,' I repeated, trying to sit up as straight as the compression bandage I was wearing as a skirt would allow. 'We won't be that much longer.'

'We really won't,' Andrew confirmed.

'You don't need Sharaline,' Shona purred, glaring at our new assistant. 'You're very good at taking notes – you were taking mine last week, after all.'

Sharaline closed up her notebook and shuffled out of her chair, throwing me an apologetic grimace as she went. Patting the younger girl on the shoulder as she scuttled out of the meeting room, Shona gave Andrew and Christopher one last winning smile and then winked in my general direction.

'You're in good hands,' she said as she walked out. 'I taught her everything she knows.'

And then the door slammed shut.

'I think we might want to go away and think about this,' Andrew said, draining his champagne. 'Thank you for your time.'

'No,' I said, staring at my notepad. 'We're not finished.'

'It's fine,' he said, gesturing for Christopher to drink up as he stood. 'We'll be in touch.'

'Do sit,' I said loudly, standing up and staring them down. 'Please.'

I was not going to give up. I was not going to be

intimidated by an impossible party or a size six bottle-blonde and her stupidly monikered minion. The only things Shona did that I didn't was put on a show. I was the one who did all the work, I was the one who looked after the logistics. And if you can take care of the shitty end of the stick, the sexy end shouldn't be any trouble.

I could do this.

Probably.

Andrew sat down slowly, holding Christopher's hand underneath the table.

'Fantastic!' I said, accessorizing my slightly too loud voice with my finest jazz hands and the strongest smile I could muster. 'Shall we take a look at my presentation?'

'Yes please,' Christopher said. 'Could we have another drink?'

'Absolutely,' I said, turning on my laser pointer. I wasn't messing about. 'Have the bottle – go crazy.'

One hour later, thanks to a combination of utter bullshit, a show-tunes medley (that Andrew loved but Christopher hated) and two more glasses of champagne, I managed to convince them to let me send over a proposal for their baby-naming ceremony by the end of the week. For the first time since Matilda had suggested I apply for this job, I was more excited than I was scared. In fact, I was so busy researching peach and pink rose gardens where I could hold a spectacular, baby-friendly, mind-blowing party with storks but no gluten, it was past four before I realized I hadn't heard from Will. Hadn't he said he wanted to do something on Wednesday night? Wasn't it Wednesday? I pulled out my desk drawer to check my phone. Nothing.

Right, I thought, pulling an Independent Woman pout.

I'm not in the mood for being dicked around today – I'm just going to text him. And before the wimpy, wet, 'what will he think?' mind-fuck could take hold, I sent the message. And before I'd had a chance to regret it, my phone lit up with a response.

Result!

'Alright, gorgeous,' I read. *'Work's still crazy, let's hang out at yours. Be there at 8.'*

With the smug grin of a woman who had received an immediate reply from a new not-quite-boyfriend, I texted back with a *'K'* and shoved my drawer shut. I was a woman in control, a woman in charge. I was a woman who had to cost out whether or not it was affordable, never mind ethically acceptable, to dye two dozen white rabbits pink for the world's most ridiculous party.

At least it's not sea lions again, I told myself, shuddering at the memory. You might think they would be an adorable addition to a summer pool party, but no, they are not.

I was reading up on vegetable versus chemical dyes when an appointment appeared in my calendar: 5.00 p.m., new client consultation. It had to be a mistake.

'All right, Sasha,' I called out to our receptionist, who had scheduled the appointment. 'I've got a new client thing in my diary for five, but Shona's already left for the day.'

'It's not for her,' she replied happily.

Sasha had been our receptionist for three years, but Shona still insisted on calling her Michelle because that was the name of our old receptionist and she couldn't be bothered to learn a new one.

'It's for you,' she said. 'He asked for you specifically.'

'He?'

'He,' she replied. 'And he's fit, as well. Just sent him up to the meeting room. Brush your hair and get your arse in there.'

Curiouser and curiouser.

'My hair doesn't need brushing,' I said after she'd already hung up. I grabbed my notebooks and a pen, pausing after catching sight of myself in the window and throwing it all back down while I scrabbled around in my desk for a hairbrush.

'Hello again,' I said, as I walked into the meeting room to come face to chest with Tom the Usher.

'Hello,' he said, looking down at me.

I stood in the doorway hugging my notebook to myself and sucking my stomach in. I hadn't forgotten the panda comment.

'Are you going to sit down?' he asked.

'Yes?' I replied, not sitting down.

'Are you going to sit down in here?' he asked.

I pursed my lips and shuffled over to the opposite side of the conference table, dumping my notebooks and pens and sitting as carefully as possible in my pencil skirt. Tom sat down across from me, white shirt, grey trousers, messy hair, briefcase on the chair next to him. A briefcase! A proper one! I didn't even have a proper pen; they were mostly a collection of promotional biros I'd nicked from the bank.

'What are you doing here?' I asked. 'I mean, what can I do for you?'

'My mum's sixtieth birthday is in September,' he said, taking a hardback diary out of his briefcase and flicking through the pages. 'And I wanted to do something special for her. A party. You organize parties.'

'Yes, I do,' I said. I opened up my notebook and scribbled down 'mum', 'birthday', 'sixty' and 'briefcase'. All pertinent information. 'So you want us to plan a birthday party?'

'Yes,' he nodded. 'Surprise party. She's never had one.'

I pushed my hair behind my ears, glad I'd given it a quick brush but wishing I'd thought to bother with a bit of lip gloss. Not that it mattered, but I hated thinking it might get back to Will that I looked anything less than fantastic when we were still in the shaving-your-legs-every-day stages of our relationship.

'Is your dad in on it or is it a total surprise?' I asked.

'That would be a surprise,' Tom said. 'He's dead.'

'Right,' I replied. Event planning 101 – never ask directly about family members. Lots of them are dead. I am a lip-gloss-less imbecile. 'Sorry.'

'That's all right,' he said, giving me a smile. 'You didn't kill him.'

I gasped. 'Oh my God, did someone kill him?'

'No, I just meant . . . it's a figure of speech.' Tom cut himself off with a sigh. 'He had a heart attack years ago. It's fine. Don't worry about it.'

'I'm sorry,' I said again. 'I mean, I'm not sorry for killing him or anything, just sorry in general anyway how about this party.'

My second ever meeting was going brilliantly. Almost as well as the first.

'Tell me about your mum,' I said, clearing my throat and aggressively crossing out the note 'dead dad'. I smiled sweetly at my prospective client. 'What sort of stuff does she like?'

'Um, mostly mum stuff,' he offered unhelpfully. 'Cake,

flowers, John Nettles, Poirot. Oh, and snooker. She really likes snooker.'

Visions of Steve Davis jumping out of a green baize cake ran through my mind.

'You want a snooker party?' I asked. 'Because I think we can get Ronnie O'Sullivan for a fair price.'

'Interesting suggestion, but no – I was thinking just a nice, regular party,' Tom said. 'Fancy cake, all her friends, presents, gin, that sort of thing.'

'Gin I can definitely help with,' I replied, flipping my pen between my fingers. 'It sounds like you're after something relatively simple, though. At the risk of getting fired, do you really think you need an event organizer for this?'

He reached an arm behind his head and massaged the back of his neck, the fabric of his shirt straining round his bicep as he squeezed. And very nice biceps they were too. Biceps it was perfectly acceptable for me to objectively notice as a woman with eyes. His fiancée was a lucky woman.

'I know it's not as big a deal as a wedding,' he said, 'but I'm so busy with work right now I haven't the time to do it properly, and I want it to be genuinely special. She deserves something wonderful.'

'Then let's do something wonderful,' I said, softening.

I'd sat beside Shona for long enough to know this wasn't something we'd usually take on. Our events were expensive show-stoppers, not afternoon tea for Mum and her mates. But how could I say no to that face? He looked like a giant puppy. A really tall, good-looking puppy with big brown eyes you could get lost in. Again, objective observation only.

With one eye on the clock and the knowledge that I

needed to clean up, make the bed and shave my legs before Will could come over at eight, I took Tom through our basic presentation, skipping over the firework displays, water features, ice sculptures and chartered yachts as quickly as I could, pretending I couldn't see his face getting whiter and whiter as we went along.

'If there's anything you like the sound of, just stop me,' I said, pausing as he chugged a big glass of water. 'Or if you've got any questions?'

'Did you really get an animatronic dragon for that birthday party?' he asked.

'I got three,' I replied. 'They actually breathed fire. It was a *Game of Thrones* theme. Does your mum like dragons?'

He shook his head. 'We don't need dragons.'

'No fire-breathing dragons,' I noted. 'That's going to make finding a location much easier.'

'Is that the most mental thing you've done?' Tom asked, leaning forward across the desk. 'The dragons?'

'I wish.' I rolled my eyes. 'Where do you want to start? Recreating the goblin ball from *Labyrinth*? Dressing little people up as cherubs then hoisting them up over the aisle for an entire wedding ceremony? Mermaids?'

'Seriously?'

I clicked my mini remote control to the next page in our presentation.

'Behold the underwater kingdom of King Triton.'

'Christ almighty.' He stared at the screen. 'That's incredible. How long have you been doing this?'

'Ten years nearly,' I said, clicking through a decade of my life. The Secret Garden birthday, the Harry Potter bar mitzvah, the nudist wedding. 'Although I was an assistant until, well, today actually.'

'Am I your first client?' he asked with bright eyes.

'Second,' I said. 'If the first ones actually sign my proposal. Which they might not. So maybe.'

'Well, that's exciting,' he said, the exact opposite reaction to the Dickensons. 'What was the worst party you've done?'

'Worst?'

'Most disastrous,' he expanded. 'The one you would like erased from your memory for all eternity.'

'We did a *Breakfast at Tiffany's* birthday party once. Very glam, very sophisticated.' I pressed my hands against my eyes. It hurt to even think about it. 'But the sister of the birthday girl got very jealous and very drunk and decided she wanted to give a speech where she explained to everyone that it was a much more appropriate theme than they realized because Holly Golightly was a heartless whore and so was her sister.'

'Wow,' he breathed.

'Yeah,' I nodded. 'Turned out she really was a prostitute. Lovely party, though. She gave everyone a present from Tiffany's.'

Tom laughed. 'Maybe I'm in the wrong business.'

'Exactly what I said,' I agreed. 'I'd be making more money and getting a shag out of it.'

Tom stopped laughing with a squeak and his face flushed beet-red.

Hmm. Maybe I'd taken it one tiny baby step too far.

'But I digress.' I closed the presentation and held out my hands. 'Next steps would be for you to give me some dates and an idea of budget, then for me to send over a proposal and we'll go from there.'

'Sounds good,' he said, combing his hands through his hair. 'I just want to do something nice for her. She always does things for other people – she's worked so hard all her life.'

'Not as hard as the hooker,' I assured him. 'That party cost two hundred grand.'

'As far as I know my mother has never turned tricks,' he said, sliding his diary back into his briefcase. 'So we can lower that budget somewhat.'

'It's not the sort of thing a mum would mention, is it?' I replied. 'Not that I'm saying your mum was ever a prostitute.'

'Of course not.' Tom stood up. 'You'd never put your foot in your mouth like that.'

'Of course not,' I repeated. 'Can I get the presentation to you by Monday?'

'That's fine.' As he picked up his briefcase, he was so tall he looked like a giant holding a handbag. 'Any exciting plans tonight?'

I watched while he shrugged on his jacket and considered my answer. I was doing something nice: I was seeing Will, but it felt wrong to talk about him to Tom. Whatever their issues were with each other, I needed to keep things professional and not fuck up this job.

'Yes.' I waved my notebook at him and strode past purposefully to open the meeting-room door. He blinked twice and then shook his head. 'Well, I've got your email. I'll get back to you with the proposal and you can tell me what you think.'

I stood in the doorway and waited for him to leave. But he didn't. He just stood there, looking at me.

'Well, thank you,' I said. 'I'll email you tomorrow.'

'Great.'

He paused for a moment before sticking out his hand. I looked at it for a moment before I realized he expected me to shake it.

'You want me to shake your hand?' I asked.

'It's traditional,' he replied. 'But never mind.'

With that, he legged it out of the meeting room and straight down the stairs.

And that was Wednesday.

'I was thinking . . .'

Will had been at my flat for an hour, we'd already done it twice, and were now enjoying a post-coital Papa John's in bed. I was basically in heaven.

'Maybe we could go out for dinner on Friday.'

I wasn't sure if it was the double-sexing or the stuffed-crust pizza, but for some reason I was feeling very brave.

'I might have to work late, but yeah,' he replied, stuffing three potato wedges into his mouth at the same time. So hot. 'Sounds nice.'

'We could do Saturday?' I suggested, running through my weekend plans in my head. I'd scheduled a hair and make up trial for Lauren, but that was in the afternoon; dinner would be OK. 'If you have to work Friday?'

'Friday's better.'

What was he doing on Saturday? What was he doing on Saturday?

'Friday it is,' I said. 'There's one of those cool pop-up restaurants above the pub near my office. I could try to get a reservation there?'

'I like this restaurant a lot,' he said, popping a wedge into my mouth. I smiled and chewed, trying not to choke on the dry potato. 'You've hardly eaten anything.'

'Not that hungry,' I said, covering my mouth with my hand. It was such a lie – I was starving when I left the office, but as soon as we ordered that pizza I knew I wouldn't be able to eat it. He was the best diet: as soon as I was near him, I completely lost my appetite. Who needs to eat actual food when you're feasting on hormones and compliments?

'Did you have a good day?' I asked.

'Shit day.' Will picked up the pizza box and dropped it onto my bedroom floor. 'You don't want to hear about it.

'Yes I do,' I argued. I did. I wanted to know about all of it – who he liked, who he hated. I wanted to know who broke the photocopier and who always brought the same sandwich in for lunch every day. I wanted to know everything. I wasn't hungry for pizza, but I was ravenous for Will.

'No,' he said again, correcting me with a little kiss on the nose. 'You don't.'

So learning the names of his colleagues could wait.

'Mine was a bit stressful,' I said, pulling his arm underneath me and resting my head on his shoulder. Because I could do that, because he was my boyfriend. 'Actually, you know your friend Tom, who was an usher at the wedding?'

He rubbed his stubble against my forehead in that way that men think is adorable but actually just makes your face a bit sore. 'I wouldn't call him my friend, but yeah?'

'He came in today.'

I pulled the covers up over my bare legs and stroked the black fuzz on his flat belly. How could someone eat almost an entire pizza and still have abs?

'To your work?'

'Yep.'

'Why?'

I looked up at him. Was that a hint of jealousy I heard? Please God, let it be a hint of jealousy. I was not a mature person. I needed it.

'He wants me to organize a party for his mum,' I said. 'It's her sixtieth.'

'But you're a wedding planner?' Will said, stretching until his toes tapped the end of my Ikea bed frame.

'I'm an events organizer,' I clarified. 'I don't just do weddings.'

It's an easy mistake to make; even my parents didn't really understand what I did. And I was sure he was doing something very boring on Saturday, which is why he couldn't tell me exactly what he was doing.

Not that I was thinking about that at all.

'Isn't his mum dead?' he asked, his forehead creased with the effort of remembering. 'I thought he was the full Harry Potter?'

'No, that's his dad,' I said. 'He's not an orphaned wizard.'

Will shrugged and settled back down against my clean pillowcases. 'Whatever. He's such a geek,' he replied. 'You're not going to do it, are you?'

'It's only work,' I said as his hand wove its way into my hair and my skin started to prickle. 'It doesn't matter.'

'Yeah, I suppose,' he said, kissing my neck. Even though the room smelled like pizza, he smelled like heaven. Sweaty, post-sex, lingering hint of some expensive aftershave heaven.

'What aftershave are you wearing?' I asked. I was all about the important questions in life. 'You smell so good.'

'I've got a ridiculously early meeting in the morning,' Will said as his hands busied themselves underneath the covers instead of answering my question. 'So I can't stay over.'

'Really?' I closed my eyes and tried not to sound too disappointed. 'But I've got leftover pizza for breakfast.'

'No you haven't, I'm taking it with me,' he replied. 'But dinner on Friday, yeah?'

'Yeah,' I agreed, melting into the pillows as he went for third time lucky. 'Dinner on Friday.'

Two planned dates in one week. I was this close to adding him on Facebook.

This.

Close.

One of the most exciting stops on your bride's journey will be the day she finds The One – no, not her husband, her dress! Whether it's a precious family heirloom or an exquisite new gown, many will tell you the wedding dress is what transforms a woman into a bride.

If you are already married, paste a photo of your wedding dress below. If you have yet to take that magical step, clip out a picture of a gown you love or sketch your dream dress in the space below!

12

Saturday June 13th
Today I feel: Very, very tired.
Today I am thankful for: Red Bull and Sky Plus.

'I don't believe you don't like any of the dresses,' I said, clutching the powder-blue wedding ring binder to my chest. 'This is insane, Lauren.'

'I thought I'd know when I saw it,' Lauren said as she did a twirl on the raised dais in the middle of the room and frowned at her beautiful reflection for the fifteenth time that afternoon. 'But something's off with all of them.'

Me, Sarah and a very tired-looking sales assistant were standing in the middle of a divorcée's worst nightmare, surrounded by some of the most extravagant wedding dresses in the world while Lauren frowned at herself in a floor-length mirror.

'Let's work out what you do like about this one,' Carol, the incredibly patient assistant, suggested. 'You liked the sweetheart neckline of the first one and the ball-gown fit of the second one. What is it here that you like?'

'I like that it's simple,' Lauren said, staring at herself. 'I like that it makes me look really skinny.'

'And what don't you like about it?'

'It looks too much like a wedding dress.'

Carol the assistant turned to give me a look of death. I'd had to pull several strings and sell the soul of my first-born to get Lauren an appointment at this boutique on a Saturday afternoon in June. I was certain she'd walk in and buy the first dress she tried on – there were dozens of dresses in her wedding binder, she'd done her research, and yet here we were surrounded by hundreds of thousands of pounds' worth of designer gowns and she'd suddenly decided she didn't want her wedding dress to look like a wedding dress.

'If we killed her, we could just stuff her body in a bin bag and all our problems would be solved,' Sarah whispered. 'I don't mind sticking some crystals on it if that would help.'

'You know, it can be fun if you let your bridesmaids pick a couple of dresses out for you,' Carol said, helping Lauren off the platform in her borrowed four-inch heels. She hadn't even chosen shoes yet, and Lauren loved shoes. 'My bridesmaid actually chose my dress. It can be helpful to get someone else's perspective.'

'I guess.' Lauren mooned at the mirror. 'I had such a clear idea of what I wanted.'

'Sometimes your friends know your style even better than you do,' Carol said with a smile. It was a smile that said, 'Why don't you go and pull out ridiculously heavy frocks that she's never going to buy while I have a sit-down, you bastards.'

'Don't think too much,' she instructed us. 'Grab whatever you like the look of and bring it back to the dressing room while I get our bride out of this one.'

Sarah and I leapt to our feet, excited to be standing again after nearly two hours on a very hard-on-the-arse sofa. Wedding dress salons are such strange places. Blindingly white, eye-wateringly expensive and full of women screaming. I wondered if the government had considered bringing terrorists here for questioning.

'You know in *Return to Oz* when she's walking through that room full of decapitated heads?' Sarah said, running her hands over the dresses as we walked. 'I'd rather be doing that.'

'Let's just pick two and get this over with,' I said, pausing in front of an especially frothy confection of a frock before moving on. Too poufy, too sparkly, no sweetheart neckline. 'I've been here before – she's not going to choose one today.'

'How can you tell?' Sarah asked, pulling out a skintight mermaid dress with crystal detailing all over the boobs. I shook my head and she put it back.

'I've done this a million times,' I said with a sigh. 'When a woman really wants to find her dress, she finds it. It's the one thing she wants to get locked down, and yeah, all these dresses seem totally different, but in reality they aren't. You know what shape you want, you know what fabric you want. Lauren hasn't decided on a single thing and she's tried on, what, twelve dresses?'

Sarah stopped, pulled out a simple A-line lace dress with a silk sash at the waist and held it up for me.

'Too basic,' I replied. 'Actually, it looks a bit like your—' Cockitywankbollocks.

'Oh, bloody hell.' I grabbed Sarah's own wedding dress out of her hands and tossed it onto the chair behind me. 'I can't believe they still have that.'

'Banana,' Sarah said, frozen. 'Does the safe word still work? Banana me, Maddie.'

'Do you want to go outside?' I asked, poised to catch her in case she collapsed. 'Do you want to leave?'

'I do,' she said with wet eyes. 'But I can't seem to move at all.'

'How about a sit-down?' I suggested, pointing over to a pink, puffy sofa. 'That's better, isn't it?'

'I think I'll just do the floor if that's OK with you,' she said, her legs folding up underneath her. 'Banana.'

'I'm sorry,' I said, dropping down beside her and pulling her head onto my shoulder. 'We should never have asked you to come. I'm an idiot.'

'I wanted to come,' she said, sniffling, her eyes fixed on the wedding dress still tossed over the back of a chair. Her wedding dress. 'Honestly, I did. I was sitting at home last night thinking how much fun it was when I bought my wedding dress.'

Well, that just proved she had gone completely cocking mad. Shopping for Sarah's wedding dress was two straight days of her mother calling her fat and refusing to spend more than a grand on a dress unless she lost a stone, followed by tears and recriminations and secret bingeing on bags of Mini Eggs in the changing rooms.

In the end, she lost two stone and her mother had to pay a fortune to alter the dress, but yeah, Sarah, so much fun.

'I don't want to mess this up for Lauren,' she whispered. 'But I wasn't expecting that.'

'Don't worry about Lauren,' I told her, pulling a dubious-looking tissue out of my pocket and dabbing at her eyeliner. 'I'll do that. You worry about you.'

She gave me a half smile and nodded.

'Stephen's at the house now.' She wiped her face with the sleeve of her jumper and tried to smile. 'He's getting the rest of his stuff. Didn't want to do it while I was there.'

'Sounds wise to me,' I said, remembering Seb's and my last encounter in the flat. He was so polite and jovial, like someone I'd met once at a work do and then bumped into on the street. I hadn't even cried – I was just empty. Apart from the moment when he'd told me he was leaving – that was the worst part. That was when he stopped being my Seb and became my ex.

'Seriously, though, thank God for iTunes,' she said. 'If we'd had to sit and separate all the CDs I would have killed myself.'

'No, you would have killed him,' I corrected her, shaking off my own break-up memories. 'You're not slashing your own wrists over who bought the Coldplay CD.'

'That would be him,' she sniffed. 'Wanker.'

I nodded thoughtfully for a moment. Sarah's shoulders heaved with the effort of trying not to cry. As a friend, it was heartbreaking, and as a wedding planner who had called in fifteen favours to get this appointment, I was very anxious about having someone wearing that much black eyeliner so close to so many white dresses.

Do you know what I realized yesterday?' she asked, her eyes and nose all red and blotchy. 'He must have been planning it for ages. All that time I was thinking it was just a bit of a rocky patch, he was getting ready to go.'

'Don't make yourself feel worse,' I said, squatting down beside her and hoping my bum wasn't hanging out of the back of my jeans. It usually was. Damn you, Topshop. 'How could you have known if he didn't tell you?'

'Because he wasn't telling me anything?' she replied. 'We used to talk for hours, about everything. When we first got together, we would lie awake in bed at night and talk about everything. I knew everything about him, I told him everything about me, and then, out of nowhere, I couldn't even tell that my husband was planning to leave me. How sad is that?'

I flashed back to the last night in bed with Will before chasing the thoughts away. We'd get to the bit where you share stories of childhood trauma at three a.m., once we'd got past the rampant shagging and eating pizza in bed part.

'It's all the stupid little things that are killing me,' she said. 'You know what's really pathetic? I went out and bought new toothbrushes to put in the holder next to mine, just so I wouldn't have to see my sad one on its own first thing in a morning and last thing at night.'

'That isn't pathetic,' I said. 'It's totally understandable. I remember when Seb left he took the toothpaste. I think I cried about it for a week.'

'It's bloody pathetic,' Sarah corrected. 'I wish I could go back in time and work out what I did wrong.'

'You know you haven't done anything wrong,' I said, trying to remember all the things she'd said to me two years ago. 'You never cheated on him, you were never cruel to him, you always put him first. What's happening now is horrible, but . . . God, I don't want to say it because it sounds like such a cliché, but—'

'It's for the best?' Sarah finished for me. 'It is what it is? You can't change the past? All you need is time? I know, Mads – I've heard all of them. I just wish I could wake up and wipe it all out. Isn't there a pill for that yet?'

'Yes, but it only wipes out about twelve hours and it's

usually administered by very, very bad men,' I said. 'I'm not going to let you get roofied every night for the next six months. Drunk, yes, drugged, no.'

'I can't do any more hangovers,' she said, screwing up her face. 'And it's only been two weeks.'

'You say that now,' I said, stroking her hair. 'Let's not make any bold claims we might regret later.'

'What am I going to do?' She lay back on the carpet, closing her eyes as I waved a confused-looking sales assistant on before she could get involved. 'I'm thirty-one. I'm going to be thirty-one and divorced. I'm never going to meet anyone else, I'm never going to have kids. He's going to meet someone else next week or something, if he hasn't already.'

'That's not true,' I lied. As far as I could tell, she was entirely correct. In the last two years, Seb had got engaged, married and babied up and it had taken me that long just to find a nice man who would have sex with me on the regular. The evidence was not in our favour. 'You're going to be fine and you're a hot piece who looks about twenty-three.'

'But I'm not twenty-three,' she said. 'None of us are twenty-three. We're going to die alone.'

'Thanks for the reminder,' I said, lying down next to her. It was actually quite reassuring. 'We're not going to die alone.'

She sniffed a big, dirty, sloppy sniff. 'Oh yeah – you're in love now. You're sorted.'

I let out an attractive choking sound. 'I wouldn't say I was in love.'

Only I would. I would totally say it. I would stand on the roof of my house and shout it to the passersby if it wouldn't get me arrested and locked away in the loony bin. I was completely and utterly in love. But this wasn't the time to have that conversation.

'I should probably go back in and check on madam,' I said, bouncing my hand up and down on her topknot. 'Would you do me a massive favour and get me a Diet Coke from somewhere? I'm dying.'

'Course.' Sarah blinked the last of her tears away and smiled, seeing right through my ruse. Obviously I was giving her an out but at the same time, I really was parched. 'How's my make-up?'

Her make-up was a terrible, terrible mess.

'You look fine,' I said, taking the tissue to the worst of the eyeliner smudges. 'Just a bit smudged here . . . OK. Yep, now you're fine. Go and find me some pop. I'll tell Lauren I sent you to fuel my caffeine addiction.'

'I'll go and find you some pop,' she said with a grateful smile. 'Thanks, Mads.'

'Whatever,' I said, grabbing a random blush-coloured one-shouldered gown from the rack beside me. 'Go on, you daft mare.'

'I pulled this – oh my God, what's wrong?'

I wasn't sure if I'd walked back into Lauren's changing room or some terrifying time-loop worm hole. The bride-to-be was sitting hunched up in a little ball in the corner of the room, wearing nothing but her undies and a pair of four-inch glitter heels, mascara streaks that made Sarah's look like a subtle nod to goth. She looked like the saddest stripper ever, and if you've ever seen a stripper, you'll know that's quite an achievement.

'I hate all the dresses,' she replied in a tiny voice. 'I hate them.'

'Then you don't have to buy any of these dresses,'

I said, hanging the new gown on the hook in the wall and resuming my position beside a sobbing friend. Seriously, couldn't we keep it to one life in crisis at a time? 'No one is going to force you to wear something you don't like. We'll find another dress.'

'It's not the dress,' she said, wiping a hand across her face and smearing her mascara as she went. I stuck my hand in my pocket, but Sarah had made off with my nasty tissue. 'It's everything.'

'Everything?'

'It's all happening so quickly – I don't know what I'm doing,' she said, her bottom lip trembling while she talked. 'I know his grandmother is ill, but I'm freaking out, Maddie.'

'But you want to marry him, don't you?' I asked. 'That's all that matters.'

'I don't know,' she laughed. Lauren dropped her head to my knees and groaned. 'I'm being stupid, aren't I? Tell me I'm being stupid. Tell me to get my shit together and that it will all be fine.'

I shuffled closer to her, ignoring the stabbing pain in my knees, and took her hand in mine. 'You have to do whatever you want to do,' I told her. 'This is not the fifties – you do not have to marry someone if you don't want to, just because you said you would. If you're not one hundred per cent, it's going to be much easier to postpone things now than it will be afterwards. Or on the day.'

At work, we never said 'cancel', always 'postpone'. 'Cancel' made women panic. 'Cancel' made them feel like they were letting people down, costing people money and ultimately doing something bad. 'Postpone' was just putting it off for a little bit until they had thought of a better way of explaining there was no way in hell they were going through with the wedding.

'I love him,' Lauren repeated once more. 'I only wish I had a little more time to figure it all out. Why is this so hard?'

'It only gets harder as we get older,' I said, pulling a fresh tissue out of the box on the side table. 'Everyone thinks women over thirty are desperate to get married, but to me, anyway, it's harder now to compromise and settle. When I was younger, I put up with a lot more shit than I would put up with now.'

'Yeah,' she sighed. 'You're right, I guess.'

'And more importantly, you know how *you* feel.' I squeezed her hand, stood up – with some difficulty – and picked up the wedding dress that lay on the floor beside her. 'In this room, right now, it only matters what you want. If you ask me to take this away and never, ever speak the "w" word again, I'll do it. I'll deal with everything. You wouldn't even have to think about it.'

'What would I do without you?' Lauren asked, another smile breaking through a shit-storm of runny mascara. 'You're amazing.'

'I know,' I said modestly. 'Now you get dressed while I go and tell Carol we're done for the day.'

She nodded, fumbling with the buckle on her shoe as I slipped out of the changing room and collapsed on the chair outside.

'Everything OK, Maddie?' Carol asked, appearing out of nowhere.

'No, Carol,' I replied, exhausted. I pressed my hand against my forehead and shook my head. 'No, it most definitely is not.'

13

Sunday June 14th

Today I feel: Confused.
Today I am thankful for: My brother. Hence the confusion.

'Hello, madam, I wasn't expecting to see you here.'

As if spending half of Sunday ploughing through the Internet looking for a company that could make a hundred pairs of personalized flip-flops by the first Saturday in August wasn't enough of a treat, I looked up from my desk to see Shona standing in the middle of the empty office.

'What are you doing, working on a weekend?' she asked, as though it wasn't something I did all the bloody time.

'Just taking care of some bits and pieces,' I said, running a hand through my messy Sunday hair and wondering if she actually woke up looking like a Barbie doll. I knew her boobs always looked like that because I'd covered for her the week she'd had off to have them done. 'I'm leaving soon.'

'Don't go on my account,' she said, sipping from a Starbucks cup the size of her head. 'Great that you're showing some ambition. And look at you working on a Sunday without me begging you first!'

I smiled tightly, swallowing down a scream so loud anyone would have thought there was a One Direction concert happening in the office.

'How is your thing going?' Instead of going into her own office, Shona sat down at Sharaline's desk, directly opposite me. 'The baby-naming party?'

'OK,' I said, shuffling two Coke cans and three empty packets of Wotsits into my bin. I hadn't expected to be in the office quite so long, but that was what happened when you got distracted by make-up tutorials on YouTube and gifs of Daniel Craig taking his top off. 'It's fine.'

'You can talk to me about it, you know,' she said, sipping her coffee, eyes on me all the time. 'I'm not the enemy.'

HA.

'Do you remember just after you started here, we did that first-birthday party?' She put the coffee down to pull off her jumper, and then smoothed out her hair, smiling. 'God, that one was mental. The one with the carousels? Do you remember?'

'I do,' I said. It was a hard one to forget. 'The Fergusons?'

'Yes! The Fergusons! I don't know how you remember all the details.' Shona laughed and leaned back in Sharaline's chair. 'They were mental. One hundred per cent completely and utterly mental.'

'Just because grown men and women want to dress as babies doesn't mean they're mental,' I replied, wincing at the memory. 'A bit messed-up, maybe, but we mustn't judge.'

'Faking a first birthday party so you can have a sex party dressed in nappies and babygros is where I draw the line between messed-up and mental,' she said. 'How long was it until they let us use that venue again?'

We've never used it again, Shona,' I reminded her. 'Even if they would let us, I couldn't. The things I saw . . .'

'Fair.' A big, sticky-looking stain began to spread around the bottom of her coffee cup, seeping into Sharaline's notes. 'I'll never forget walking in on that woman changing her husband's nappy.'

'And nor should you,' I said, raising a can of Coke in a toast. 'I wonder if they're still together.'

'Oh, couples like that never break up,' Shona said. 'No, the weirder your fetish, the more likely you are to stay together forever. It's like lesbians.'

I winced – something Shona couldn't do due to her Botox treatments. 'I don't think lesbianism counts as a fetish.'

'Oh yeah, your sister's a lezzer, isn't she?' she replied. 'Sorry, didn't mean it like that. Just meant how lesbians couple up forever.'

'Eleanor says that's a stereotype,' I said, trying not to remember any of the other things Eleanor might have said recently. 'She says that's not actually true.'

'Didn't she get married when she was sixteen?'

'Twenty-two,' I replied.

'First girlfriend?'

'Yes,' I replied, without a leg to stand on. 'But Eleanor isn't all lesbians.'

'Must be weird, having your little sister married off already.' Shona rifled around in Sharaline's pencil pot and produced an emery board. 'Is your brother still with that make-up artist?'

'Yes,' I said, my shoulders stiffening. 'Rachel.'

The relationships you forge at work are always strange. It doesn't matter how you feel about someone: when you spend upwards of sixty hours a week with them, it's inevitable that you'll become involved in each other's lives somehow. But, given my feelings towards Shona, it made me very uncomfortable when she talked about my real life. She had a memory like a steel trap when it suited her, and it was unnerving to hear the names of my friends and family coming out of her mouth.

'Rachel, that's it,' she repeated slowly as though committing it to memory. 'Do you still see Seb? Are you still friends?'

'We're Facebook friends,' I said, tapping my fingers on the cold Coke can. 'Why?'

'Just wondered.' She clicked the emery board against the desk. 'It's hard being single when everyone else isn't.'

I sat back in my chair and nodded.

I wanted to tell her I wasn't single. I wanted to tell her I had met a wonderful man who made me feel amazing and always replied to my text messages and was very handsome and had a job and all his own hair and no apparent physical or mental defects, but I just didn't trust her.

'It's one thing to meet them, but it's another one to find one worth keeping, isn't it?' She ran the emery board back and forth over her nails, and I noticed they weren't painted for the first time in forever. 'And all this online stuff has only made it harder. Easier to get a shag, but impossible to meet a decent man.' I nodded again, afraid to contribute to the conversation.

'Organizing all these weddings and christenings and anniversary parties –' she kept her eyes trained on her nails as she spoke – 'and then it's either home to an empty house or going on another pointless date with another pointless wanker.'

'That is difficult,' I agreed. It wasn't like Shona didn't had boyfriends but they never lasted that long, and not just because she was one of the seven worst people alive today. She always ended things. Somehow, every single man she met ultimately managed to bore her or disappoint her or fail to meet some unspecified criteria she refused to share with anyone.

'All my friends are married now,' she said, finally meeting my eyes. 'Apart from you, I mean.'

'That's hard,' I said, wondering if she really did think of me as a friend or if she was just being polite. I hoped it was the latter because if I was a friend, God help her enemies. 'Lauren is getting married.'

'Your American friend Lauren?' she asked. 'Are you helping her plan it?'

'Eh.' I shrugged. No more personal details than necessary. 'When I can.'

'Friends can be so selfish,' she said, shaking her head. 'They forget it's your actual job. Like you want to go home and start working again for free. You should tell her no.'

'I can't, though, can I?' I said, dazzled by the very idea. 'She's my friend.'

'Doesn't mean she can treat you like a doormat,' she replied. 'What was the last thing she ever did for you?'

Hmm, let me think. She had woken me up at three a.m. to apologize for her matrimonial meltdown, and then again at four a.m. to ask if I could schedule another appointment with the same boutique. And then again at four-thirty to apologize again.

'She's not been that bad, considering,' I lied.

Shona raised an eyebrow to the best of her Botoxed abilities. 'You must have your work cut out with that baby party, anyway. Sounds like a nightmare.'

Having a civil conversation with Shona was like talking to a sympathetic shark. I wasn't sure if we were having a genuine conversation or if she was just looking for a weakness before she went in for the kill.

'It's fine,' I said. 'Why, what have you heard?'

'Oh, nothing,' she replied, blowing it off. 'Sharaline mentioned the dads were a bit of a handful, that's all. How's it all going? You on top of it?'

'It's not the easiest party ever,' I said. 'It's going to be a challenge.'

That was not a lie. Now that I was approaching things from Shona's perspective, there was more work involved than I had realized, and since she was monopolizing Sharaline's workload, I didn't even have an assistant to help me out. Where was that cloning machine when you needed it?

'Well,' she said, poking around in the top desk drawer. 'If you need any help, you just let me know.'

I looked out of the window. Nope, zero flying pigs.

'Thanks?' I said, nearly choking as I took a sip of my Diet Coke.

'But I am talking to a woman who organized a sex party for a load of adult babies.' She dropped the nail file onto the desk and stood up, leaving her coffee cup to stain Sharaline's work. 'How hard can this be?'

'Oh my God, it's happening again, isn't it?' I asked, the colour draining from my face. 'There's no baby, is there? It's another nappy-fetish orgy.'

'Part of me wants it to be,' she laughed. 'But even I'm

not that evil. It's going to be fine – you just need to believe in yourself.'

Believe in myself? Had she hit her head on the way into work?

'I know I was a bitch when you first said you wanted Victoria's job.' Shona hadn't taken her eyes off me and I was terrified to move. Any sudden movements and she could attack. 'But when I thought about it, it made sense. I don't want a complete stranger coming in and trying to take over. We're a good team, Maddie – there's no reason why that can't continue, is there?'

'No reason,' I said, worried my eyes might pop out of my head at any second, they felt so wide.

'And I like Sharaline – she's on top of things,' she said. 'You like working with her, don't you?'

'As soon as I get over her name,' I replied, 'I will love her.'

'Ha, I know.' She tapped the top of Sharaline's monitor. 'Her parents must hate her. Thank goodness she has us to look after her now. We're basically her work parents.'

'God help her.' I watched as she stood up, helping herself to the Kit-Kat on Sharaline's desk. 'I hope we don't have to pay her therapist bills when she leaves.'

'I'm trying to be gentle,' Shona said, slinging her handbag over her shoulder. 'Anyway, like I said, if you need any help with the party, just ask.'

'I will,' I replied. Did she mean it? Had Colton told her to be nice to me? Was this her long-lost good twin? 'Thank you.'

'I've just got a few bits and pieces to do,' she said, nodding towards her office. 'We could get a drink when you're done if you're going to be here for a while.'

'I was actually just leaving,' I said, almost regretting it. 'But we should definitely do that soon.'

'We should,' Shona agreed. 'We should take Sharaline for a welcome-to-the-team drinks or something.'

'Drinks,' I echoed. 'That would be nice. I think Jen from finance is having a drinks thing tomorrow night for her birthday, actually. Maybe we could go?'

'That old slag?' Shona gagged and looked at me with pity. 'Please, Maddie – when will you learn that hanging around with the sad and desperate is catching. You do not go to that or I will personally drag you out by your hair.'

Relieved, I nodded and felt myself relax. Well, thank goodness for that.

'How come the flat isn't as much as a shit-tip as normal?'

My brother Dan stood in the middle of the floor casting a suspicious eye over my semi-tidy living room.

'I don't know what you're talking about,' I lied, kicking an empty takeaway container under the sofa. 'It's always tidy.'

In reality, since Will had taken to 'stopping by' unannounced every so often, I'd had to start making a bit of an effort with the place. And with myself. I couldn't remember the last time my legs had been shaved on so many consecutive days.

'You're such a bad liar,' Dan said, flicking through the masses of paperwork on the dining table. 'What's all this?'

'For Lauren's wedding,' I replied, slapping his hand away. 'Don't touch anything – it's organized.'

'Looks it,' he said with a quirked eyebrow. 'Get the kettle on, Sis. I'm parched.'

Narrowing my eyes, I filled up the kettle with suspicion. Dan never just 'popped in' for a cup of tea. Dan always wanted something. And wasn't Dan supposed to be in Tokyo?

'So, what do you want?' I asked, cutting directly to the chase.

'Coffee?' He settled down on the sofa and put his massive size sixteen boots on my freshly dusted coffee table. 'No milk, two sugars.'

'No, really,' I said. 'Why are you here? What do you want?'

'A brother can't come to say hello to his little sister on a Sunday night without an ulterior motive?'

'No,' I replied. 'Out with it or I'll spit in your coffee.'

'Fine,' he said with a sigh. 'I've been thinking. Rachel's birthday is coming up and I've decided I'm going to propose.'

'Oh, Dan!' I clapped my hands together and threw myself at the sofa to give him a big hug. 'That's brilliant.'

'Yeah, yeah,' he said, pushing me off. 'Get off. I was thinking I want to make it special.'

'Have you got a ring?' I asked, bounding back over to the whistling kettle to make our coffees. 'When are you going to do it?'

'Well, little sister, I thought that might be where you could help me.'

I turned round to see Dan looking over the back of my settee with a big cheesy grin on his face.

'You're the expert, after all.'

'Oh, now I'm the expert?' I said, hands on hips. 'Because last weekend I was a vacuous, unpokable tart with a pointless life.'

'In my defence,' Dan replied with his hands held out in surrender, 'it wasn't me who said that.'

'You didn't exactly leap to my defence either, did you?' I asked. 'I know she's my sister, but she can sod right off.'

'You've got to cut her some slack, Mads,' Dan said. 'She's having a hard time with this baby – she's pretty miserable every time I speak to her. When was the last time you called her for a chat?'

I tapped a teaspoon in my palm and opened my mouth to defend myself. But I couldn't remember. Oh bugger.

'You're not telling me you've never put your foot in your mouth when you've not had a proper night's sleep?' he said. 'Let alone when you've got a miniature human being hanging off you twenty-four hours a day? Imagine that for a minute.'

Eleanor hadn't said anything to me about having a hard time. Eleanor hadn't really said anything to me at all. Before I could reply, my phone started to buzz on the coffee table.

'It's Lauren,' he said. 'Shall I answer it?'

'Give it here,' I commanded. 'You're not allowed to talk to my friends.'

With a sulky face he held it out in exchange for his coffee.

'Hello?' I answered, while Dan pulled a face at the mug of instant he'd just been handed. 'Yes. It's been ordered. Yes, it'll be here next week. No, there isn't time to change the colour. No, we don't have the budget to just get new ones. I'll call you tomorrow, Dan's here. All right, love you.'

Hanging up, I shoved the phone into the back pocket of my jeans and flopped down into an armchair.

'You're planning her wedding?' Dan asked.

I nodded. 'And it's a nightmare. One minute she's

freaking out about place settings, the next minute she isn't even sure she wants to go through with it, and two minutes after that she's obsessing over the colour of the flower girls' dresses. She hasn't even got a dress for herself yet, and the two flower girls have three each. It's ridiculous.'

'I'm not exactly shocked,' he said. 'She's got high maintenance written all over her, that one.'

'Rich English dad, posh American mum,' I shrugged. 'She was up against it from the beginning. Anyway, about this proposal?'

'Is it weird, talking to you about it?' Dan asked, shifting in his seat. 'It feels weird.'

'It's not weird,' I said as my phone buzzed into life again. This time Sarah's name flashed up on the screen with a text message. 'Hang on a minute, I've got to reply to this.'

'You know what your problem is,' he said, tasting his coffee once more and then pushing it away on the table with a sour look. 'You take on too much. No wonder you haven't got a boyfriend – you're too busy holding your friends' hands all the time.'

'She's going through a hard time.' I kept my eyes on my phone, tapping out a response to Sarah's miserable Monday-dread text as I talked. 'She needs me.'

'Someone's always going to need you,' Dan replied. 'But sometimes there's a difference between being needed and being taken advantage of.'

'Isn't it mental that I might not know the difference, coming from such a loving and non-judgemental family?' I said, putting my phone back down. 'And as I mentioned, I do have a boyfriend, actually, so eff you.'

'Really?' Dan looked genuinely surprised. 'I assumed you were making that up to keep Mum quiet.'

He was such a great big brother.

'No.' I shook my head. 'He's real. His name is Will, he's a lawyer, he plays rugby, he's got all his own hair, eyes and teeth, and as far as I can tell has no major mental defects. It's early days but I think it's going well.'

Buzz-buzz. Another text.

'Do you always answer your phone when he's here?' Dan asked.

I reached for my phone and saw Tom's number on the screen. A little fizz of nervous excitement ran through me as I swiped to read. 'Yes?'

'Then it's probably not going as well as you think.'

'Shut up – this one is work,' I said, reading, re-reading, and then putting the phone on silent. Just confirming our meeting, very polite and totally professional. 'I've got a meeting on Wednesday – the client was just confirming.'

Dan clucked his tongue. 'At eight on a Sunday evening?'

'It's not a nine-to-five job,' I replied. 'You're a photographer – you should understand that.'

'Fine.' He picked up his coffee and gave it another brave sip. Poor Dan, so spoiled with his fancy espresso machine Mum and Dad had bought him for Christmas. I'd got a 'proper coat' because clearly I couldn't be trusted to dress myself. The fact that said coat was something my Nan wouldn't be seen dead in was another matter entirely. 'You always seem so rushed off your feet. You need to learn how to say no. I'm only thinking of you.'

'I suppose you've got a point,' I admitted as Lauren's name came up on my phone. I discreetly sent it to voicemail and gave my brother a tired smile. 'I'm basically doing two jobs at the moment as well as organizing

Lauren's wedding. And Sarah's round here every other night. I am knackered.'

'Just say no,' Dan repeated. 'I used to be the same. I'd take every job I got offered, but you end up not doing your best work. You need some downtime, Mads.'

'Just say no.' I took a swig of my own coffee. God, it was pretty rank. 'Now. Engagement. Spill.'

'I want to do something amazing,' Dan said, his eyes lighting up. 'Something really extravagant and memorable and brilliant.'

'OK,' I said, excited to see him so excited. 'Like what?'

'Well, I was thinking you could help with that.' He gave me a cheery grin. 'What would you do?'

I stared at him, unblinking, unsmiling.

'What happened to "just say no"?' I asked.

'I'm your brother,' he scoffed. 'I didn't mean say no to me, obviously.'

'Obviously.'

'I've had some ideas,' he said, whipping out an iPad. 'Let me know what you think.'

I sighed as he opened Pinterest and wished I'd had something stronger than a Nescafé. This was going to be a long night.

Everyone knows that falling in love is the most amazing experience in the world, but the path to that magical moment is different for everyone. Use this part of the journal to record your happiest memories.

How does it feel to fall in love? Giddy and exciting and confusing and generally like I'm going mental.

What's your favourite thing about being in love? The warm, fuzzy, buzzy feeling when you're alone together.

How do you know when love is real? When you feel totally safe and secure and you trust him completely and you feel understood and heard and cared for and you know he isn't going to run off with that girl from his company and knock her up.

14

Wednesday June 17th
Today I feel: Umm . . .
Today I am thankful for: The tiny, tiny amount of natural grace I have been blessed with.

One day I'll sit down with this journal and write about what a lovely, non-eventful day I've had. Only I probably won't because I have quite a few non-eventful days, and at the end of them I don't have the energy to pick up a pen. Today was a test. Today I came home so exhausted and confused, I took the remote control with me to the toilet and then couldn't find it for half an hour.

In the future, historians are going to look at Twitter and Facebook and think we were an entire generation of people dealing with a mass bipolar disorder.

Nothing about today was simple. I was on the phone with flower farms all morning trying to source pink and peach roses for the Dickensons and red roses for Lauren, while simultaneously trying to text-talk Sarah out of the toilets at work after one of her co-workers left a

Lindsey Kelk

copy of *Divorce: Think Financially, Not Emotionally* on her desk.

It's a rare occasion when I'm relieved to be meeting a client, but when I saw Tom waving at me outside the Palm House this afternoon, I could have kissed him. I hadn't seen him since his impromptu appearance at the office but we'd spoken over email, and, in spite of Will's repeated warnings, he didn't seem to be too much of a knobhead. More importantly, he wanted to spend money on an event he wanted me to plan.

'We would put round tables in here,' I said, waving my arms around the big empty room, trying to give the impression of a lot of furniture without falling over. 'And do the afternoon tea, which we can have served or as a buffet, depending on the budget, and then we would use this space for dancing.'

I led Tom through the grand glass doors into the neighbouring room and gave a little flourish. 'You usually want the dancing and the bar close together. People drink more that way.'

'Do we want people to drink more?' he asked.

I could hear my fuck-up echoing around the empty room.

'The venue does,' I admitted. 'But you can either set a limit for the open bar or have people pay as they go. Sorry, that's not me trying to pump you for cash, honest.'

'Hmm.' Tom looked over at the bar. 'I reckon Mum's friends can put it away.'

'Then maybe set a limit for the open bar,' I suggested. 'Or just serve wine and beer.'

He frowned. 'I reckon mum's friends can put beer and wine away.'

'Moving on, we'd do five tables for eight in the main room, which means we can seat forty of your mum's fabulous friends.' I whisked him back over to the other side of the venue before he could get too anxious, a trick I'd learned from Shona. Don't let them think about anything budget-wise too long or they'll talk themselves out of it. Sell them on how it's going to feel, not what it's going to cost. 'It'll be so beautiful, Tom, she'll love it. Flowers everywhere, soft lighting, music. Our caterers are amazing – the food is to die for.'

'We might never get them out again.' He looked over to the huge windows that lit up the room. 'This place is fantastic. I must have walked past it a million times and I never would have known it was here.'

'Well, that's my job,' I said. It's hard to sound humble when you're feeling very smug. 'I've been waiting for the right party to come along and use this place – it's so romantic.'

Tom coughed and nodded, hands deep in his pockets.

'And perfect for your mum's birthday,' I added, flapping my cracked iPad around. It turned out I would have to pay for it if I wanted it fixed. I'd decided to go with the lived-in look until next pay day. 'Anyway, like I said, this room for food and toasts and then next door for dancing, making this the chill-out-and-chat area.'

He didn't say anything. He was the complete opposite of the Dickensons; I had absolutely zero idea of what he wanted.

'We'll choose a colour scheme that will be reflected in the linens and the flowers,' I went on regardless, ticking off items on my mental checklist. 'And I'll speak to some lighting designers about the best way to get this place looking pretty once the sun goes down. I'm thinking lots of fairy lights and low lamps, nothing overbearing and harsh. Just a very flattering soft glow.'

'Sounds good,' he said.

Don't be too enthusiastic, I thought.

'Thanks,' I said. 'And as for entertainment, do you have a preference about a band or a DJ?'

'What's the sound system like?' he asked, springing to life. 'Can I see the amp? Where are the speakers?'

'Um, I've got the technical specs here,' I said, rifling through my notes. 'Why don't we sit down and have a look.'

With newly bright eyes, Tom followed me to the small table set up by the window and pulled out one of the chairs. I stood in front of it for a moment, wondering what he was doing. He was just standing there, looking at me.

'Oh, thank you,' I said as I realized.

Awkwardly, I sat down in the chair and stared down at my iPad. His mum deserved a party; she'd raised him terribly well.

'So, we've got a projector, a DVD and BluRay player, iPod dock, 5.1 surround sound, three wireless microphones and audio set up for live music. Does that sound good?' I asked.

He pouted. 'I mean, yeah, I suppose so.'

'Audiophile, are we?' I smiled politely as a waitress appeared with a three-tier tray of goodness and a giant pot of tea. This was quite clearly the best part of the job. Tastings. 'You're into all that stuff?'

'Passing interest,' he said, leaning back from the table as the tea was poured. 'I was in a band at uni and I always got lumbered with the set-up.'

'Rock god, roadie and lawyer?' I shook out my napkin and placed it delicately in my lap. I had to remember I was at work and not shovel all the delicious food directly down my gullet. 'That's an impressive CV.'

'Jack of all trades,' he said, waiting for me to select a mini strawberry tart before taking one of his own. 'We weren't very good. Or any good, actually.'

'I would very much like to see you in a band,' I said, laughing. He was so neat and tidy and buttoned up, I couldn't imagine him letting it all out on stage.

'You've already met the other members,' he said, shaking his head but still smiling at the memory. 'Ian was on drums, Will on bass, I sang and played guitar.'

'Will was in your band?' I asked, slightly surprised. 'That's funny.'

Tom poured the tea and raised an eyebrow. 'Funny because Will wasn't the main man or funny because we don't get on quite so well now?'

'Both?' I said through a mouthful of shortcrust pastry. He gave me a shot of side-eye and then picked up his teacup.

'What's funny?' Tom asked, taking a sip from his cup while I covered my mouth with my hand.

'It's just that the teacup is so tiny and you're so big.' Never try to smother a laugh if there's a risk of it coming out of your nose. Cackling is more attractive than snorting. Only just, but still. 'It looks like a doll's tea set.'

Narrowing his eyes, he stuck out his little finger and carried on drinking.

'You tit,' I said, sipping my own tea and smiling.

'Sorry, I should remember to carry a massive great mug around with me everywhere I go,' he apologized. 'Or, you know, a bucket.'

'I could do a bucket of tea right now,' I said, refilling both our cups. 'I'm gasping.'

'Big night last night?' He took a finger sandwich from the cake stand and nibbled it delicately.

'You are an idiot,' I said, shaking my head at him. 'Not an especially big one, but I shouldn't drink on a school night.'

Or stay up until four a.m., binge-watching American TV shows. Baltimore was off the to-do list forever.

'I'm appalled at your lack of professionalism,' he said drily.

I shrugged, opening up my notebook. 'Now, what do you think of the sandwiches?'

'Have you seen much of Will?' he asked abruptly.

I gave a short, fake laugh and looked away. 'Isn't it a bit weird to talk about him to you? Anyway, the sandwiches?'

'Hmmm.' He put down his tiny teacup and pushed up his shirt sleeves. Such good arms. Really. Even when I was trying not to notice, I couldn't help it. They were huge. 'Look, I know it's not my place.'

'No, it's fine, I'm sorry,' I replied, studying the remainder of my tiny tart. 'I don't want to be horribly unprofessional but can I ask you something?'

'You've already called me a tit and let it slip that the venue is going to try and fleece me on the booze,' Tom pointed out. 'Ask away.'

'Right.' I bit into the cupcake and swallowed. Might as well get a taste before he walked out and cancelled the party. 'Um . . .'

I really wanted to know what had happened between the two of them. Every time I saw Will, I could feel myself falling a little bit deeper and it bothered me to know that there were people out there in the world who didn't like him and I wanted to know why. I wanted to know everything about him, from the name of his first pet to his shoe size, it was a sickness.

Tom looked at me expectantly across the table in a way that made me think I had something on my face. Oh, wait, I did – there was icing everywhere.

'Here you go,' Tom said, whipping a clean white cotton hanky out of his top pocket as I started pawing at my sugary cheeks. 'What did you want to ask?'

'Obviously we'll have lots of napkins on the day,' I said, taking it from him and dabbing at my red, icing-covered face. 'Thank you.'

Tom gave a curt nod.

'So—'

'Maddie.' Mr McDonnell, the manager of the venue, strolled across the room, resplendent in a plum velvet suit and blissfully unaware of the awkward interruption at our table. 'How is everything?'

'It's all great,' I assured him, shaking his hand as Tom stood. 'This is Tom, I mean, Mr Wheeler. We're planning a party for his mother's birthday.'

'How lovely.' Mr McDonnell reached upwards to shake Tom's hand; he was a good foot shorter than the stony-faced man in front of him. 'Any questions?'

'Tom, I mean Mr Wheeler –' I corrected myself again – 'had some questions about the audio set-up.'

'Of course.' He gave Tom the respectful nod of a man who knew things about electronics. 'Would you like to take a look?'

'Sounds good,' Tom said, resting his briefcase on his knees and pulling out a shiny silver iPod. 'Can we try it out?'

'Absolutely.' Mr McDonnell took the iPod with a gracious nod and held out an arm to guide us into the other room. 'Shall we?'

The second room had the same beautiful picture

windows as the first, and as the two chandeliers on the ceiling weren't lit up, the three of us cast grand, late-afternoon shadows across the dance floor.

'All the electronics are through here,' Mr McDonnell said, walking us over to what looked like a small cupboard at the back of the room beside the stage, and opening the door to reveal a techie's wet dream. I was perfectly capable of hooking up a satellite box and BluRay player to the telly at the same time, but this was beyond me. Not beyond Tom, however. He pressed a few buttons, flipped a few switches, stuck a cable into the top of the iPod and, just like that, the room was filled with music.

'Let me go and see if I can sort the lights out,' Mr McDonnell said, easing past Tom and giving me a quick wink. 'So you can get a proper idea of the room. It's always a little darker in here after teatime.'

'Who is this?' I asked, swaying slightly to the music crooning out of invisible speakers. 'It's gorgeous.'

'Etta James,' Tom said, carefully placing his briefcase on the floor. 'Mum's a big jazz buff. I grew up on this stuff.'

'Lucky you,' I replied, closing my eyes. 'We listened to a lot of Phil Collins in my house, and there is no cultural enrichment to be found in Su-Su-Sudio.'

Before I could open my eyes, I felt a hand take hold of mine and Tom pulled me out into the middle of the room.

'What are you doing?' I asked, panicking. He was so strong and so big and, as far as I could tell, really quite mad at me. But his stony expression had broken into a smile that started in his eyes and almost found its way down to his mouth.

'Do you dance?' he asked.

'What?' I looked up at him, feeling a strain in my neck from being so close. 'Do I what?'

'You know, you're quite rude,' he said, taking hold of my hand and placing it on his shoulder. 'You've got terrible manners.'

'I was a middle child,' I replied as he took my other hand in his. 'I apologize for nothing.'

'Can you waltz?' he asked, taking a step forward.

'I don't know,' I said, letting him shuffle me backwards towards the door. 'Am I doing it now?'

'You are,' he replied, sweeping me round in small circles. 'Don't think too much, just go with it.'

'OK,' I said quietly. 'I won't think.'

An easy thing to say and an impossible thing to do.

Don't think too much? What a bloody joker. Two minutes ago I thought he was going to walk out, cancel his mother's party and possibly knock Will on his arse into the bargain, and now he was whisking me around a dance floor like an old-fashioned gent in a black-and-white movie. Where was McDonnell with those lights? Why was it so dark in here? How was a girl supposed to think straight when a very tall man who smelled nice and had very good hair was dancing, actually properly dancing her around in a beautiful ballroom?

I mean, this was the kind of behaviour that made a Disney princess fall in love with an actual beast. What chance did I have?

'You're a natural,' he said as we picked up pace and he pushed me away into a spin. Tripping over my own feet, I was relieved when he caught me. Relieved and confused.

'Thanks,' I replied, folding myself back into his arms far too easily. 'You're not so bad yourself.'

When you see couples dancing together on TV, all you see are sweeping camera angles and lush dips, but when it's happening to you, it's completely different. I was painfully aware of every step, every stumble, every time I swore and then immediately apologized for swearing. Audrey Hepburn, I was not. The one thing that was just how you would imagine was when I leaned in and let myself rest against Tom's chest. I could hear his heart beating.

While he looked calm and composed and completely in control, his heart was beating so hard and so fast, I had to hold my breath until the song was over.

As the music faded away, he came to an elegant standstill. Reluctantly, I pried myself away from his chest, looking down at my feet and repeating the mantra 'bloody hell bloody hell bloody hell bloody hell' over and over in my mind. I forced myself to look up at him, only to see him staring down at me. Neither of us said a word. After a moment, I realized I still had my hand in his, and I couldn't tell who was the one with the clammy palms; but I had a feeling it was me. Behind us, the sun was low in the sky, framed by the huge windows and casting reddish shadows onto Tom's hair, and it was all far too much in the best possible way.

'That was lovely.' Mr McDonnell's voice broke the silence before Etta James could fire up another track. 'We get a little bit more proper dancing these days, but not as much as I would like. Just lovely.'

I cleared my throat as I stepped away from Tom and shook my hand free, but instead of a quiet cough, my voice came out as a melodramatic bleat. Classic. Before anyone could react, McDonnell flicked a switch and the room was filled with bright yellow electric light, flooding any romance out of the moment.

'I think that's everything,' I said, rubbing my palm against my jeans. 'Is that everything? It's everything, isn't it?'

'I think so,' he replied, looking as startled as I felt.

'So that's everything,' I confirmed to a confused-looking Mr McDonnell. 'I'll be in touch very soon. With both of you. About the party. For your mum. I'll be off, then.'

Dazed, I marched straight out of the door. One foot in front of the other. I could just about manage without a partner, but only just.

'Ms Fraser,' McDonnell called.

I held on to the chair and spun round, a big beaming smile on my incredibly professional face. 'Mm-hmm?'

'That's the door to the kitchen.'

'Yes,' I replied. 'Yes, it is.'

'And your bag is over there on the table.'

'So it is.'

Burning bright red from head to toe, I slunk back across the room with far less grace and purpose than I had previously exhibited.

'Maddie?' Tom called my name and I looked up to see him not quite smiling, one hand shoved in his pocket, the other raking his hair back from his face. 'This place is perfect. Let's do the party here.'

'OK then,' I replied, picking up my coat, my bag and my iPad. 'I'll be in touch. Thanks, bye, thank you.'

Waving blindly, I gathered myself together and marched out of the front door.

Maddie Fraser, consummate professional.

'We have the venue, we have the catering, the invitations are printing, Michael has his suit, we've done the wedding list.' Lauren paused to take a big mouthful of salad. She was the only one eating the salad, which she'd brought with her. 'We're pretty much there, right, Maddie?'

'More or less,' I replied, taking a big bite of pizza and leaning my back against the settee. The three of us were sitting on my new rug. She was only missing the wedding dress, bridesmaids' dresses, photographer, videographer, the music, the flowers, the linens, lights, table plan, the favours, registrar and the cars. No big deal. And at some point we should probably discuss the epic emotional meltdown she'd had at the bridal shop, but whatever, no rush. It wasn't like the wedding was in six weeks or anything. Oh wait, yes it was.

'And we're all booked for next weekend,' Sarah said, pulling the cheese off her slice and eating it. Disgusting habit. 'I'm picking you both up here after work on the Friday for the Bachelorette.'

'Can't wait,' I said as Lauren nodded. 'You're not going to make us wear matching T-shirts or anything, are you?'

'How tacky do you think I am?' Sarah asked, wrinkling her tiny nose. 'Hens on Tour? Lauren's Getting Married in the Morning? Please.'

'I got us matching tracksuits,' Lauren said. 'Mine says bride across the arse and yours both say bridesmaids. They're very classy.'

'She's joking,' Sarah said. 'She's definitely joking.'

'She'd better be,' I warned.

'You know, I still have to pick your bridesmaid dresses,' Lauren replied. 'Just keep that in mind. This could go badly for you two.'

'You're not leaving here tonight until they're picked,' I replied, pushing a pile of catalogues across my coffee table, butting against two pizza boxes on the way. 'We can get any of these in the next month. Did your sister give you her measurements?'

'She did,' Lauren replied, opening the first catalogue and pulling a face. 'But they don't sound right. I've got to ask my mom to measure her again.'

'I need to order them by next Friday,' I told her, focusing on forcing as much pizza into my mouth as I could manage, trying to smother my feelings with carbs. 'So tell her to get a move on.'

'She's being all pregnant and dumb,' Lauren said with a grimace. 'Not that she wasn't dumb before she was pregnant, but now she has an excuse she's really working it. Total baby brain. Your sister didn't suddenly lose twenty IQ points when she got knocked-up – what gives?'

I stretched out my legs and wiggled my toes. 'Well, no, but my sister did tell me she thinks my life is empty and pointless. I think I'd prefer baby brain.'

Both women turned to stare at me, mouths wide open.

'She said what?'

'That I – we, actually,' I corrected myself for extra emphasis, 'are wasting our lives worrying about pointless things because none of it will matter once we have a baby.'

'Woah,' Lauren breathed, putting down her salad and grabbing a garlic-butter-smothered dough ball. 'That's so shitty.'

'So shitty,' I agreed. 'And so unfair.'

'I don't know,' Sarah said slowly. 'Maybe she's right?'

The room fell silent as we both turned to look at the woman who had once referred to pregnancy as 'the easiest-to-cure STD you could catch'.

'It's like your phone,' she said. 'You know how you

only have so much storage for all your apps and photos and songs and stuff? I think it's like that, having a baby.'

'Oh really,' Lauren said, unconvinced. 'Please elaborate.'

'Well, I mean . . .' Sarah clearly was not entirely sure Sarah knew what Sarah meant. 'You've got loads of photos and songs and things that you love, but then you run out of space so you have to delete some stuff to make room for more important things. It doesn't mean you don't still love those other things or think they're important, it's just that maybe, for a while, the LinkedIn app is more important than the Instagram app. At that moment.'

'The LinkedIn app will never be more important than anything to anyone,' Lauren replied. 'The LinkedIn app is for weirdos.'

'You know what I'm saying,' Sarah said, looking to me for help. Help she was not getting.

Sarah let out a frustrated sigh. 'I'm not saying what Eleanor said was right – of course Maddie's life isn't stupid or pointless just because she doesn't have a baby, but you have to look at it from her perspective. I'm sure anything that isn't a four a.m. feed or worrying whether or not she should vaccinate her baby is stupid right now. It's hard to commiserate over whether or not a boy has called someone when you're trying to keep another person alive.'

'Firstly, vaccinate your goddamn baby,' Lauren said, moving in on a second dough ball. So much for her salad. 'And secondly, promise me you guys aren't going to disappear as soon as you get babied–up. I couldn't cope.'

'Can't see that being a problem any time soon,' Sarah said. 'Hello – divorcée over here.'

'I'm sorry,' Lauren apologized, taking a kick to the thigh for her troubles. 'You know what I mean.'

'It's not your fault,' Sarah said. She was considerably more together than she had been the last time I'd seen her, but I still felt as though she was on a knife's edge: she could go at any second. 'I'm doing all right. Just keep telling me how pretty and thin I look.'

'You're the best person I know at Scrabble,' I said as quickly as possible. She stared at me, stony-faced. 'And you look like you've lost weight.'

'One of the benefits of not cooking at night is not eating,' she replied. 'Hand me more pizza.'

'You're a shit cook anyway,' I reminded her. 'Just make sure you can still fit into your bridesmaid dress.'

'I never heard back about the job, you know,' Sarah said in between thoughtful chews. 'You did give my CV to HR?'

The CV that had sat on my desk for a week? The CV with all the brilliant and relative experience that would almost certainly get her my job? Did she mean that one?

'Of course,' I said, barely missing a beat. 'I heard there's been a recruitment freeze. Don't worry.'

Lauren looked at me, confused. I flashed her a look and tried to force down the feeling that I might be sick in my mouth.

'Ohhh,' Lauren said, her eyes widening with realization. 'You don't want to work there. We don't even want Maddie to work there, remember?'

'She can leave and I can stay,' Sarah shrugged. 'Perfect solution.'

'Not until she's finished organizing my wedding,' Lauren countered. 'Don't be so selfish, Sarah.'

'Do I get a say in any of this?' I asked.

'No,' they replied in unison.

I love my friends, I told myself. I love my friends, I love my friends.

'I had no idea how stressful it was planning all this shit,' Lauren said, considering the dough balls but reluctantly turning back to her salad. 'It's morning, noon and night.'

I eyed her carefully, looking for a sign that she was putting on a brave face, but no, there was nothing. Maybe it had just been a wedding-dress wobble. Maybe everything was OK.

'Thank God you don't have to actually work for a living,' Sarah said. It was a bit of a low blow but I wasn't about to defend Lauren, given that she'd done bugger all and I was spending every spare second working my arse off for nothing. And given that I had no spare seconds, that was quite the accomplishment.

'I so work,' she squealed. 'You know I work.'

'You post Twitter updates for your dad,' Sarah said. 'That's not working.'

'I am the social media director for one of the southeast's leading boutique estate agents,' she replied. 'It's Twitter, Facebook and Instagram.'

'No Pinterest?' I asked.

'I'm not superwoman, Maddie,' she replied. 'I can't do everything.'

I bit my tongue. Hard.

'Shall we talk about something else for five seconds?' I suggested before someone got the slap they were so clearly asking for. 'I mean, anything?'

'What's going on with Will?' Sarah asked immediately.

'Anything else?' I asked, looking at Lauren. For the first time I didn't want to talk about him.

Her mouth full of uncooked kale, she shook her head and pointed at Sarah. 'Spill,' she demanded. 'Is he coming to the wedding?'

'I haven't asked him,' I replied, bothering my phone until I could see the screen glowing in the darkness out of the corner of my eye. 'I think it's too soon.'

'You're seeing a lot of each other, though,' Sarah said. 'It's been, what, a month?'

'Something like that.'

A month and three days. If you were someone who kept track of that kind of thing.

'So is he officially your boyfriend now?'

'We've been through this,' I reminded them. 'We're too old for this nonsense. We are two grown-ups who like spending time together and doing it. Loads. It's a perfectly fine state of affairs without weighing everything down with labels.'

Sarah tightened her topknot and raised an eyebrow and I forced myself not to slap her hands as hard as I could. I didn't feel like adding that I hadn't seen him in a week. We'd rescheduled that Friday dinner three times now, and although he'd managed to drop by for some on-the-hoof shagging a few times on his way home from the office, his work plans always meant that he had to leave the same night to make an early start in the morning. And since he'd cancelled dinner again last Friday and had been too busy to see me over the weekend, we hadn't made new plans. He was still texting, but things were definitely slowing down and I didn't know what to make of it.

'What's his place like?' Sarah asked, placing a cushion from the settee under her head. But, once again, not getting onto the settee. 'Is it a super-fancy bachelor pad or a boy version of this shit-hole?'

'I imagine it's nice,' I said, preparing myself for what was definitely coming. 'I haven't been there yet.'

'You haven't been there?' Lauren didn't even try to keep the judgement out of her voice 'At all?'

Sarah wasn't nearly so careful. 'What's that all about? What's he hiding?'

'It's not a big conspiracy,' I said, staring up at the ceiling. 'He's renting out his spare room to one of his friends while he looks for his own place. I don't have a flatmate, so . . . so that's all there is to it. And my flat is closer to both our jobs.'

'Well, that's convenient,' Sarah said.

'Exactly,' I replied.

Sarah gave me the look. 'Not the kind of convenient I meant, and you know it.'

They looked at each other for a moment before coming to a silent agreement.

'Aren't we supposed to be choosing our bridesmaid dresses?' I asked before one of them could start on me again, pushing the catalogue at them and watching as it magically fell open on the lilac strapless number I'd already chosen. 'Can we get on with that, please?'

'I want to meet him,' Lauren said, pushing away the catalogue. 'I can't wait, Maddie.'

'You're going to love him,' I said.

Sarah sat bolt upright. 'Oh my God, do you love him?'

'That's not what I said,' I wailed, covering my face with a cushion. 'I don't know, I don't know anything. I've had the weirdest day.'

'What has Shona done now?' Lauren asked. 'Or was it the lovely Sharaline?'

'Neither of them,' I said from underneath my cushion. 'If I tell you, you're not allowed to make a big deal out of it.'

'We promise we will not make a big deal out of it,' they sang together.

'You remember Will's friend, the usher who I met at the wedding?'

'The one who fancies you?' Sarah asked.

'He doesn't fancy me,' I said without nearly as much certainty as I'd used before. 'I'm planning a party for his mum, and this afternoon, when we were checking out the venue I want to use, he made me dance.'

'The pervert,' Sarah gasped.

'Are you being, like, super euphemistic?' Lauren asked.

'No!' I pulled the cushion away from my face but kept it handy in case I needed to smack someone with it. 'We were testing the speakers, and while the music was playing, he made me dance. We danced.'

'Like, dance, monkey, dance?' Sarah just wasn't getting it. 'Should we call the police?'

'We waltzed,' I said, cringing as I spoke. 'I danced a waltz, like a lady.'

They stared at me, Sarah's mouth a tight, hard line, Lauren's hanging wide open.

'And then what?' Sarah asked.

'And then I left,' I said, leaving out the part where I walked into the kitchen and a cleaning cupboard before I found the exit. 'That's it.'

Apart from the email that had come in about fifteen minutes ago.

'That's the most romantic thing I've ever heard,' Lauren said with a sigh. 'I love a man who can dance. My dad dances.'

'I bet he's an amazing dancer,' Sarah sighed. 'What a man.'

'Don't *even!*' Lauren threw a cushion across the room and caught her square in the boob. 'Do not start talking about my dad.'

'Fine.' She wiped the dreamy look off her face and tuned back to me. 'Seriously, Mads, what's *wrong* with this weirdo? Do we need to call the police?'

'If we're being entirely honest . . .' I put my pizza down and cradled my can of Diet Coke, my shoulders creeping up around my ears . . . 'it was quite nice.'

'Wait, you're planning a party for his mom?' Lauren asked. 'Like, for work?'

'Yes,' I said, wondering if either of them ever listened to a word. 'I do that, you know. It's not that strange.'

'At the risk of sounding like Sarah, it's one hundred per cent strange,' Lauren corrected. 'You met him at the wedding, right? The same night you met Will?'

I nodded confirmation.

'And then he came to your office that time to pick stuff up for his fiancée, and now you're planning a birthday party for his mom and waltzing around some ballroom together? Is his mom the Queen? Are you living in *The Princess Diaries?*'

'It's her sixtieth,' I explained. Of course it was going to sound dodgy when you put it like that. 'He wants to do something special for her because his dad died when he was younger and they're really close.'

Sarah shuddered. 'Bates Motel close?'

'Shut up.' Lauren gave her a swipe, taking the tally of Sarah-slaps to two for the evening. 'I think it's sweet. But I don't understand why he needs to hire a professional events planner to do his mom's birthday.'

'He's a barrister,' I replied, batting my hands against the floor. 'He's busy.'

'Another goddamn lawyer,' Lauren muttered. 'I'm staging an intervention.'

'He's a barrister and he's trying to get into your knickers,' Sarah countered. 'Just out of interest, what were you wearing at this wedding where you pulled *everyone* in attendance?'

'He's engaged!' I was too tired to shout but I definitely had enough energy to raise my voice over the *EastEnders* theme tune. 'It's nothing! He's not trying to pull me! This is why I said you couldn't make a big deal out of it.'

'That means he's potentially a twat,' Sarah said. 'But it doesn't mean he isn't into you. Have you told Will? What does he say?'

I frowned. 'Nothing much. He just says he's an arsehole. They don't get on.'

'Do you think he's an arsehole?' Lauren asked.

I breathed in and breathed out loudly. The sweaty reality of our *Come Dancing* two minutes had already been through at least twenty-five internal Instagram filters in my brain until it was this epic, intimate moment I would remember forever. The more I replayed it, the more the rough edges wore away, leaving a perfectly polished diamond of a memory.

'No,' I said. 'He's nice. He cares about his mum, he's funny, he's very thoughtful. He always asks me a lot of questions.'

Lauren stroked my hair. 'But—'

'He's engaged.' I finished her sentence. 'I know.'

'I was going to say you're going out with Will,' she said, biting her lip, eyebrows raised.

'Oh, yeah,' I muttered, hitting myself in the face with the cushion.

We all reached for the pizza at the same time.

'Haven't you got a wedding dress to get into?' I said, fighting Lauren for the last piece of pepperoni.

'Actually, we don't have it yet, remember?' she replied, slapping my hand. 'And I'm good, I'm at my goal weight. I just need to tone up my arms a little. By lifting my arms to eat the pizza.'

'We order it by Friday the 26th or we don't order it at all,' I replied. 'Easy.'

'My goal weight is four pounds less than this, and then whatever Chris Hemsworth would weigh lying on top of me,' Sarah said, picking up the bridesmaid dress catalogue that had found its way underneath the pizza box. 'Oi, Lauren, what about this lilac dress?'

I picked up the last half-slice and smiled.

Well, thank God for that.

It was an evening well spent. After the pizza and the bridesmaid dress decision, we looked at pictures of otters that look like Benedict Cumberbatch and scoured the Internet for flattering swimming costumes to buy for a beach holiday we weren't going on. By the time *Newsnight* began, Lauren was leaving in an Uber and Sarah was passed out on my spare bed for the second time this week. Curling up under my duvet, I plugged my phone into the charger and took a last minute turn around the Internet.

There was an email from Tom.

Dear Maddie,

Formal, business-appropriate, weirdly hot.

Thanks so much for the tour of the venue today. It seems perfect for the party and I would love to go ahead and book for Saturday September 13th.

So far, so whatever.

With regards to music, I would be very happy to use a pre-selected playlist. The audio set-up in the venue was quite satisfactory.

Quite satisfactory? Oh, I am glad.

I look forward to hearing from you in due course.
Best,
Tom Wheeler

And that was it.

Seriously, that was it. No 'Oh, I'm sorry I went the full *Strictly* on you, wasn't that terribly inappropriate' or 'Well, that was an uncomfortable two minutes of your life you can never get back. LOLZ'. Just a straightforward, slightly too formal email. At least I now know he doesn't fancy me, I told myself. Just as well since he's engaged, I'm going out with his friend and we have to work together. But it really did feel a bit, you know. *You know*.

Because maybe I do fancy him a little bit.

Although I obviously don't. It's just because he made me dance with him, that's all. Even though he is funny and quite handsome and has lovely hair and big hands and he danced with me and he's very tall and clever and loves his mum and oh bollockingbollockingbastard.

15

Sunday June 21st
Today I feel: Murderous.
Today I am thankful for: Waterproof mascara.

'All right.' Will rushed me as soon as I opened the door, pushing me up against the wall and kissing me so hard I could taste blood when he pulled away. 'You look good.'

Usually I would be very welcoming of this kind of hello. It had been so long since I'd received this kind of welcome that I had been openly encouraging it by way of suggestive text message and one or two potentially regrettable-should-I-ever-choose-to-run-for-office photographs, but my evening with my friends and my Strictly Come Swooning dance-off with Tom had got me thinking. Never a good thing.

The last month had been fun but I was ready for more than a sexytimes fling and I wanted that 'more' with Will. It was time to move our relationship out of the bedroom and into the outside world. And then back into the bedroom again with occasional, but optional, adventures outside.

'Thanks,' I squeaked as his hand travelled up my thigh and under my skirt. Probably should have put jeans on. My plan would definitely have been easier to execute in jeans. 'How was work?'

'Boring,' he replied, rubbing his face in my hair. Jeans on and hair up. 'You don't want to know.'

'You always say that,' I said, contorting my body so that I was face to face with him. Those eyes . . . 'I do want to hear about it.'

'I'll tell you after.' He started kissing my neck, hands travelling. Dear God this was difficult. 'You bum is brilliant. Has anyone ever told you how brilliant your bum is?

Using all my strength and more willpower than I knew I had, I pushed him gently but firmly away. 'It hasn't come up, actually. Can we talk?'

'What's wrong?' Will asked, adjusting his crotch area. 'Are you pissed off at me or something?'

'Nothing's wrong,' I said, leading him into the living room. 'I just want to talk. It's like we never talk.'

'You're too distracting,' he said with a sexy smile. 'It's your fault.'

'That's only a little bit threatening,' I said, ducking under his arm and opening the fridge. 'Do you want to go and get something to eat? I haven't got anything in.'

Will cocked his head to one side, loosened his tie. 'Maddie, what's going on?'

Underneath my bright kitchen lights, I could see how knackered he really was. His stubble was three days deep and he looked exhausted. When I looked tired and had three days of stubble, I looked like Dustin Hoffman in *Tootsie*, only less convincing. He looked like a God. Thor, to be exact, without the blond hair. I wondered if

I could get him to take off his shirt and swing a hammer around . . . no. NO.

We were leaving this flat if it killed me.

'I thought we could nip out to the pub round the corner.' I picked up my handbag and slung it onto my shoulder with purpose. Immediately knocking a candle off the hall table and onto my foot.

'Bloody hell,' I mumbled, picking it up and clutching it in front of me, all the while trying to look determined. 'I'm hungry.'

'We'll order a takeaway,' he suggested, taking off his tie. 'I'm tired.'

'The thing is, you're always tired,' I said. Nothing like a little bit of boundary pushing on a Sunday evening when your new boyfriend had worked all weekend. 'I don't think we've ever actually left my flat together.'

I didn't think it. I knew it. And it was bothering me.

'If you want me to leave, just say.' Will rolled his tie up and stuck it in his pocket. 'I've had a shit week, followed by a shit weekend. I'm sorry for wanting to spend time with you, not half the city and their dog.'

'I'm sorry,' I said automatically, not sure that I was. Or why I was still holding the candle. 'But don't you think it's funny that we don't go out?'

Even saying 'we' made me feel physically ill. Maybe I didn't need a boyfriend, maybe I needed a therapist.

'No,' he said, sticking the tie in his pocket. 'I can't do half the things I want to do to you if we go out.'

'I don't know,' I said, wrapping my arms around myself. 'We should be going out?'

'Says who?' Will asked.

I shrugged. He had a point.

'Compromise.' He planted a softer kiss on my lips and

took the candle out of my hand. 'We'll stay in, light this candle, and I will do terrible, wonderful things to you, and then next weekend, I'll take you out for dinner. Wherever you want to go.'

Weren't relationships all about compromise? I wanted to stand my ground and insist he take me out right then and there, but at the same time I knew that when I'd been working on the weekend, the last thing I wanted to do was trek back out to the pub and listen to other people's arguments and kids and wait half an hour for dodgy scampi. He wasn't being unreasonable.

'I'm going away for the weekend on Friday,' I reminded him. 'Can you do Wednesday?'

'I can.' He kissed me again. 'We'll go somewhere nice.'

I closed my eyes and revelled in the kiss for a moment – still a novelty, still so different from Seb's kisses. 'So what do you want for dinner?'

He answered with a raised eyebrow and a maddeningly confident grin.

'I've got some menus in here.' I took hold of his hand and pulled him out of the hallway and into the other room. 'Indian, Chinese . . . I think the sushi place is open on Sundays. Let's have a look.'

'Fine.' He followed me, chucking his coiled-up tie on the settee as we went. 'Whatever you want, I don't mind.'

It's not like I'm stressed about the fact that a very attractive man wants to have sex with me all the time. It's fun, it's exciting and it's excellent cardio, but it had been more than a month and I wanted more. I felt like Oliver Twist or the Little Mermaid. Actually, not so much like the Little Mermaid. Let's not forget she was a sixteen-year-old princess living in a castle with her own personal singing coach and a doting father and a secret room full of shit and she *still* wanted more. All I wanted was for the man I'd been banging for five weeks to express an interest in my general wellbeing.

That was definitely more on a par with a starving orphan asking for a bit of porridge.

'What are you working on at the moment?' I asked, rooting around in a kitchen drawer and taking considerably longer to find the menus that were already in my hand than was strictly necessary. 'Is it a big case?'

'Yeah,' he replied, decidedly non-committal as he sat down on the settee. 'Have you got any beers?'

'I have.' I pulled a Becks out of the fridge and handed it to him along with the menus. He pulled a face but took it anyway and started to leaf through them. 'Tell me about the case?'

'I would, but it would take forever and you'd be bored shitless in two minutes.' He gave me the Chinese menu back and nodded. 'Anything off there is fine by me. I'm not trying to fob you off, it's just boring corporate stuff.'

'I had a busy weekend,' I told him as I pulled out my phone and tapped on the takeaway app. I hardly ever had to speak to people in the real world any more, it was wonderful. My great-great-great-grandchildren would be born mute with very nimble thumbs. 'I had to work yesterday and me and Lauren went to look at dresses again today.'

He sipped his beer and kicked off his shiny shoes. 'You went shopping?'

'For Lauren's wedding dress,' I clarified. 'I'm helping her plan her wedding, remember?'

The beginnings of relationships are strange. You go from not knowing anything about a person to them being such a big part of your life so quickly you forget they weren't always there beside you. It's jarring when they don't know something that's so everyday in your life.

'That's right. Lauren,' he said, rolling his head from side to side, stretching his neck. 'I don't know how you can spend all day planning people's weddings. It's my worst nightmare.'

'I don't just do weddings all the time, I've told you,' I replied. 'I'm helping Lauren because she's my best friend.'

One more three a.m. text from her about the new seating plan and that would no longer be true.

'When is the wedding?' he asked, his gaze resting on me, stress levels noticeably lowered. It's amazing what a beer and a snog can do.

'August,' I said. Was this the moment? Should I ask him? 'First weekend in August.'

'Rather you than me,' he replied. 'Thank God I haven't got to go to any more this year.'

No, it was not the moment.

I stared at the bridesmaid dress catalogues on the coffee table and screwed my wedding-date fantasies up into a tiny little ball, shoved as far down as they could go, until they were lodged between my dreams of meeting and marrying Johnny Depp and the idea that I might one day be a person who could wear over-the-knee socks without looking like a hooker.

'What's up with you tonight?' Will reached over and brushed my hair out of my face before squeezing my shoulder. 'You're being weird.'

'Just Monday dread,' I lied, promising myself I'd be extra assertive tomorrow to make up for it. 'Tomorrow's going to be a nightmare.'

'Tell me about it,' he said.

And just like that, he made it all about himself again. Maybe Lauren and Sarah were right. Maybe I should be on guard. Maybe he wasn't the one.

'No, I mean it. Tell me why it's going to be a nightmare.' He took my hand in his and inched round on the sofa until he was facing me. 'Why's it going to be so bad? Who can I kill?'

And there it was. That was all it took. The soft look in his eye, the smile on his face, the casual threat of murder. It was everything a woman dreamed of.

'I've got a meeting with these two blokes who want a party for their adopted baby,' I said, shuffling along the sofa towards him. 'And I'm not certain I'm going to be able to give them what they want.'

He wrapped his arm round my shoulders. 'What do they want?

'Everything?' I replied. 'I'm currently trying to locate a unicorn.'

Will looked at me. It was fair; I don't imagine he gets that many requests for unicorns in court.

'No, really.' I pulled up the last email from the Dickensons complete with photograph of unicorn. In case I needed a visual reference for the mythical beast they required at their daughter's do. 'I don't know what they're smoking, but I want some.'

'Can't you tell them no?' he asked. 'And then tell them that they're totally barking?'

'Normally, we would "push back" at this point.' I applied judicious air quotes. 'But this is sort of my interview to be a full-time event planner instead of an assistant, and I don't want to give them any reason to be pissed off at me.'

'I get that.' Will laced his fingers through mine and

kissed the back of my hand. It was working! Talking to him like a person instead of allowing him to treat me like a vagina with a lady attached was working! 'But I think you need to manage their expectations. Nothing fucks a client off more than promising them the world and then under-delivering.'

'I am worried I've taken on too much,' I admitted. 'I'm getting stress lines. Now I understand why Shona gets so much Botox.'

He laughed. It was a lovely sound. 'I don't believe that.'

'I'm really good at getting things done, making sure all the logistics are taken care of and everyone is doing what they're supposed to be doing. I'm a really, really good events assistant,' I said, shrugging and squeezing his tree trunk of a thigh. 'Maybe I'm not a very good manager.'

'You did look hot in that little waitress uniform,' he said. 'Actually, do you have it handy?'

I slapped his tree trunk of a thigh.

'I thought I looked nice today?' I asked, smoothing down my dress. 'Maybe I should wear the waitress outfit more often.'

'You always look good.' He pushed me back against the sofa, the weight of his body on top of me. 'But I'm not against the idea of dressing up.'

There is something brilliant about having a man lying on top of you. The weight of his body made me feel warm and safe and wonderful.

'And what are you going to wear?' I shifted so that I could press my forearms against his chest. However lovely this was, there was still Chinese on the way, and, in this rare instance, sweet and sour chicken was higher up on my list than doing it.

'A smile?' he suggested.

'Weren't we having a very important conversation about work?' I asked. 'Weren't you pretending to be vaguely interested in my job?'

And then there were hands, hands everywhere.

'I've got a job for you, right here,' he whispered into my ear.

'That's the least sexy thing I've ever heard.' I rolled out from underneath him, landing in a wildly attractive heap on the floor. 'And I cannot believe you said it.'

Will stretched out on the sofa and unfastened the top three buttons of his shirt, a big smile on his face. 'You know you love it.'

Sitting on the cold, slightly less than spotless floor, I looked up at him and wondered.

Did I?

'It's a lovely house you've got,' I told Mr and Mr Dickenson as I lowered myself carefully onto their pristine white settee the next day. What sort of idiot has a white settee? Weren't they having a child? 'Did you decorate yourselves?'

'Christ, no,' Andrew replied. 'If it had been left to us, the whole place would have been five cans of Dulux Magnolia Moments and wall-to-wall Ikea. Andrew's sister is an interior decorator.'

'We're not very good gays,' Christopher said, looking left and right to make sure no one was listening. 'I hate Kylie.'

'I'm just sad for her,' Andrew qualified. 'Put some trousers on and lay off the fillers, love.'

'Well, hopefully we won't take up too much of your time,' I said, so pleased that they'd saved up all their imagination to make my life more difficult. You couldn't choose your own side tables but you could insist on me finding an eight-foot fountain that spouted strawberry margaritas? Brilliant. 'I'm sure you've got lots to do with Audrey on her way.'

'I can't believe she'll be here in less than a week,' Christopher said, finding his husband's hand with his. 'I've always wanted to be a dad.'

'I'm just so nervous.' Andrew squeezed his shoulders up around his ears. 'Excited but nervous. We've been dreaming about this and planning for it forever, and now it's actually going to happen. It's freaking me out.'

'She's a very lucky little girl,' I replied, backing it up with a semi-genuine smile this time. Maybe they weren't massive wankers with a unicorn fetish after all. Maybe they were nice men who had got a bit overexcited and wanted a memorable party for their baby. If only I weren't the one organizing it.

'I'm going to make some tea,' Andrew announced, standing up abruptly and swiping at his eyes. 'Everyone wants tea, yes? Yes.'

Christopher rolled his eyes as his husband marched out of the living room. 'He's getting all emosh about the baby,' he said, crossing his legs and leaning back into his beautiful, baby-unfriendly white sofa. 'Don't worry, carry on.'

Nodding, I unpacked my iPad and notebook (anyone who can rely solely on an iPad clearly never had a Walkman run out of batteries during a long car ride, and I cannot deal with them) and swiped around until I found the right pages.

'So, I thought I'd take you through where I'm up to. We'll get as much as we can locked down,' I said, as Sharaline sat mute beside me, pen poised, pad at the ready. Shona had insisted I bring her along 'for moral support', but so far all she had done was tread on the back of my shoes twice and point out a spelling mistake in my proposal document that it was too late to change. But it was going to be OK, I could do it. I was so tense, there was a chance I might have a stroke but as long as I had it on the way home, it would all be fine. 'Venue-wise, I have the Matlow Club on hold for the 18th. Let me show you some pictures . . .'

As I leaned across the table towards Christopher, a shrill ringing sound sounded somewhere around my feet. Heart pounding, I jumped, and my iPad flew out of my hands and hit my client squarely in the nuts.

'You're not very handy with that, are you?' Christopher groaned, clutching his groin.

'It's your phone,' Sharaline hissed, rootling around in my handbag to find the offending article while I remained frozen over the mid-century coffee table, arm still outstretched, and showing my knickers to anyone who passed by the window behind me. It was a classical and beautiful tableau. 'It's Lauren.'

'Send it to voicemail,' I nodded, standing back up slowly. 'It's not urgent.'

'I'm so sorry – another client,' I said, hands out in front of me, not sure what my next move should be. I'd never assaulted a client before, but Mr Colton often told us we needed to break new ground to achieve new heights. 'Are you OK?'

'No,' he choked, and held my iPad out to me. 'Why don't you just show me the pictures?'

'Why don't I do that?' I agreed. Oh God, oh God, oh God. I just hit a client in the bollocks with an iPad. However little and light they are these days, it still had to sting. This was definitely the kind of thing that came up on a feedback form. 'As you can see, the venue is just what we were looking for. Lots of light, airy inside spaces and then beautiful grounds outside that we can transform however we like.'

Christopher grimaced and gave a grave nod.

'The venue has a preferred caterer, but I've met with them and they're very happy to meet all of our menu requests. If you'd like, we can arrange a tasting prior to the event, but since you're going to be so busy with baby Audrey and I've worked with them before, I don't think we need to do that unless you desperately want to. And, really, are you all right?'

'Let's just be happy I've already got a baby on the way,' he replied, straightening up inch by inch. 'I can't imagine there's any permanent damage.'

'I'm not usually a clumsy person,' I said. 'I thought my phone was on silent. It just made me jump.'

'Then as long as no one else calls a phone anywhere near you ever again when you're not expecting it, the world will be safe,' he said, a tight expression on his already surgically tightened face. 'I don't think we'll have time to do a tasting. Next.'

'I've got the storks and the rabbits organized,' I said, keen to impress my first client and not to maim him any further. 'And we're having special cupcakes handmade and iced in all your colours.'

'In what way are they special exactly?' he asked.

'In the way that all cupcakes are special?' I suggested.

Once more, my phone trilled into life and Christopher instinctively covered his crotch.

'Lauren's calling again,' Sharaline said, waving my phone in my face. 'Should I answer it?'

'Fine, yes,' I said. 'Get a message and tell her I'll call her back in a bit.' She nodded and dashed out into the hallway.

'Tea's ready,' Andrew sang from down the hallway, trotting back into their living room carrying a terribly elegant silver tea tray. 'Maddie, milk and sugar?'

'Just milk,' I replied. 'Thank you.'

And-a-Valium-if-you've-got-it-thanks.

'We're just looking at the venue,' I explained as they exchanged looks and Christopher attempted to communicate that I had just used the latest tablet technology to turn him into a eunuch with nothing more than one raised eyebrow and a single shake of the head. 'It's perfect for your celebration, very Alice in Wonderland.'

'We don't want anything cheesy,' Andrew said quickly. 'We definitely don't want anything garish or ridiculous.'

I covered my frustration with my most professional smile. 'Of course not,' I reassured them. Just candy-pink rabbits and the odd unicorn running around. And let's not forget the storks that I would personally have to keep out of the strawberry margarita fountain or risk being sued by the RSPB. 'It's going to be magical.'

'I'm so sorry about that.' Sharaline skittered back into the house on her high heels, blue hair flying behind her. She threw the phone down on the sofa and madly tapped me on the shoulder 'Maddie, can I have a word?'

'Can't it wait?' I asked, wishing I had a Shona stare for moments like this. That was definitely something I was going to have to work on. 'We're just about to go over the entertainment.'

'Is something wrong?' Andrew asked. 'Can I get you a cup of tea . . . Sharaline?'

'Nothing's wrong,' I replied in a high-pitched screech,

the most attractive and alluring of all the weapons in a woman's arsenal. 'She'd love a cup of tea.'

'Lauren is freaking out,' Sharaline hissed in my ear as I smiled a smile brighter than the sun. 'You need to call her.'

'I can't call her right now,' I said. 'What could be so dramatic that it can't wait five minutes?'

'Something about her mother? She's arrived early and wants to go over the wedding plans?'

Oh dear God.

'I need to make a very quick phone call.' I snatched my phone out of Sharaline's hands and stood up carefully. 'I will be right back. Sharaline, could you show the gents the pictures of the venue? And, well, everything else? I might be a couple of minutes.'

Stalking down the hallway, I pressed call back and Lauren picked up before it could even ring.

'Maddie, code red, my mom is here,'

'She isn't supposed to be here for another month,' I said, gnawing at the already bitten-down nail on my little finger. 'Why is she here now?'

'My sister has been having some trouble with the pregnancy and so they wanted to come over early and get settled,' she said, clearly hyperventilating. 'Maddie, I'm freaking out. I. Am. Freaking. Out.'

'Right, calm down,' I commanded. 'Is your sister OK?'

'*My sister is fine,*' she shouted. 'She's *got morning sickness, it's nothing. She's being a melodramatic douche.*'

'Then we don't need to worry about that,' I said, mostly to myself. Lauren's mother was bad enough, but a potentially poorly pregnant bridesmaid would not have been ideal. 'It'll be fine. It might even be nice.'

'It will not be nice,' she choked. 'Mom wants to get together with you tomorrow and go over everything we've planned so far.'

I caught a glimpse of my reflection in an oversized mirror and blanched.

'I'm very busy tomorrow,' I whispered. 'And the day after that and the day after that.'

'Every day until my wedding?'

'Pretty much.'

Mrs Hobbs-Miller had never been my favourite person. There was a reason Lauren chose to live in the UK with her dad when they got divorced, and the last thing we needed while trying to pull together a last-minute wedding, was her mum looming over us and picking everything apart. She made my mother look like a saint.

'She came over for dinner last night to meet Michael,' she said, her breath still raspy and uneven. 'She was not keen.'

Hmm. Maybe he had told her about the Swiffer.

'I showed her some dresses I liked and she hated them, I showed her the flowers I want and she said no. I'm freaking out, Mads.'

'I don't care what your mum wants,' I replied, trying to keep the quaking terror out of my voice. 'It's your wedding not hers.'

Lauren whimpered down the phone.

'Will you speak to her?' she asked. 'Will you call her and tell her?'

Fuck no, I thought.

'I will sort it out,' I promised. 'I will.'

'You'll call her?'

'I will sort it out.'

Clearly I was not going to call her. I would be sending

a well-crafted and very polite email and hiding from this particular sixty-year-old American woman from now until the end of eternity.

'It's going to be fine,' I said. 'Just out of interest, what did she say about Michael?'

'It wasn't so much what she said as what she did,' she explained. 'He tried to hug her and, well, let's say it didn't go well.'

Lauren's mother was not a hugger.

'I've got to go, Laur,' I said, trying to sound soothing. 'I'm in the middle of a meeting, but I'll call you back later.'

'Yeah,' she said weakly. 'I'm going online to look at some more wedding dresses.'

'If I don't have one chosen by the end of the week, you're going down the aisle in Primark,' I threatened. 'I'll call you tonight.'

'Um, one more thing,' Lauren said quickly. 'I gave her your number. And she might call. Talk later! Bye!'

She hung up before I could scream down the phone and deafen her forever. Why? Why would she do that? I felt a shiver run down my back. Lauren's mother was in town. I should have known – the temperature had dropped nearly ten degrees last night. The ice queen cometh.

'So.' I walked back into the living room beaming and sat back down on the sofa. 'How's it going?'

The beautiful living room was silent, every carefully placed throw cushion, ornamental bowl and gay husband judging me. Sharaline sat beside me in silence.

'We don't love the flowers,' Christopher announced. 'Or the performers. Or the venue.'

There had to be a way to get this back. If anyone was

going to cock this job up, it was going to be me. I could fuck it up all on my own; I didn't need anyone else's help, thank you very much.

'All of that can be sorted out,' I said. 'Shall we have a look at some unicorns?'

'Lets,' Andrew said crisply. 'Did you manage to sort everything out on your call?'

'I think so,' I nodded. 'Lots going on at the moment – wedding season is in full swing, you know?'

'Oh, it must be a nightmare. I understand,' his tone of his voice inferring quite the opposite. 'It must be such a stressful job.'

And that's when my ear-piercingly shrill phone rang one more time. And that's when I threw my cup of tea up into the air. And that's when I threw myself underneath it, as though it were a Tetley's tea bomb, to protect the troops.

'That's really fucking hot,' I screeched, collapsing onto the hardwood floor with boiling liquid seeping through my blue silk blouse and burning my chest. 'Is the settee OK? Did I get tea on the settee?'

'No, but . . .' Andrew reached into the depths of the decorative cushions to retrieve my phone. And my pen. My pen that had leaked blue ink all over the pristine white sofa cushions. Andrew handed me both, bottom lip quivering. 'This is probably worse than tea.'

He stepped away. I looked at the screen – unknown number with an American dialling code.

The ice queen ringeth.

'I probably don't need to answer it,' I answered in a mouse voice, still in a heap on the floor, shirt stained, skin slowly melting away from my body. 'But thanks.'

I rejected the call, brushed my hair out of my face and looked over at the fathers to be.

'Of course, there's always the option to hire me as a clown,' I suggested. 'That would cut back some of the budget.'

Things were going better than I could have ever imagined.

Are you excited? It's time for the bachelorette party! Did you know that, before we adopted the term 'bachelorette', this pre-wedding ritual was called a hen party? In 1897, the Deseret News said there was 'a time-honoured idea that tea and chit-chats, gossip and smart hats constitute the necessary adjuncts to these particular gatherings'.

Today's bachelorette parties are a little different, right? Use this space to remember your bride's big night, before her big day!

The bachelorette party took place: In Bath.
The invitees were: Me, Sarah and Lauren's mum.
Our party favours were: Sleeping pills from Lauren's mum.
The games we played: Seething family resentment and Cluedo.
Most memorable moment: getting hammered in the dodgy nightclub, Sarah getting off with a nineteen-year-old and Lauren telling me she didn't want to get married.
We can't tell the groom about: getting hammered in the dodgy nightclub, Sarah getting off with a nineteen-year-old and Lauren telling me she didn't want to get married.

16

Friday June 26th
Today I feel:
Today I am thankful for:

Lindsey Kelk

Saturday June 27th
Today I feel:
Today I am thankful for:

Sunday June 28th
Today I feel:
Today I am thankful for:

Monday June 29th
Today I feel:
Today I am thankful for: Oh, just fuck off.

I am home from the hen weekend from hell.

And let us never speak of it again.

Actually, no, let us speak of it because if we don't speak of it, no one will ever, ever in a million years believe that it happened.

'This place is so nice,' Lauren marvelled after we had been shown to our hotel suite. 'Look at the bathroom.'

'And the view,' Sarah yelled, throwing open the curtains.

'And the beds,' I said, dropping my suitcase in the bedroom. 'Of which there are only two. When we are in fact three.'

'I have to spend the entire rest of my life sharing a bed with the same dude, so I think I should get my own,' Lauren said, throwing her handbag across the room like a thousand-dollar missile and still missing the other bed completely. 'There's a big couch?'

'It's hardly the first time we've bunked down together,' Sarah said, clambering up onto the giant bed and stretching out. 'And look, it's so big you'll hardly know I'm in it.'

I didn't want to cause an argument and I didn't want to sleep on the settee, so instead, I opened up my suitcase and began hanging my clothes in the wardrobe. After much deliberation, Lauren had decided she didn't want a traditional hen do. All she wanted was 'a quiet weekend away with her two best girlfriends', and so, after work on Friday night, we all squeezed into Sarah's mini and headed west. After four hours, three very wrong turns, two bathroom stops and a dirty McDonald's en route, we finally arrived at the hotel, deep in the heart of the Somerset countryside.

'I'm knackered,' Sarah announced. 'And we've got a busy day tomorrow. Bagsy first go in the shower and then I'm going to bed.'

Lauren, busy hanging up outfits that might have been better suited to a weekend in Vegas, waved her into the bathroom, ignoring the overexcited swears that followed Sarah's discovery of the roll-top tub.

'So.' I sat on the edge of my bed and tried to tread carefully. 'How are you doing?'

'Awesome,' Lauren replied without looking at me. 'Everything's perfect.'

Hmm. I wasn't sure that was entirely true.

'Everything's going all right with your mum?'

'She wanted to know if I had invited the Obamas.' Lauren pressed her hand to her forehead. 'Not because she thought they would come, but because she thought it was disrespectful not to.'

'And that's why I'm not involving your mum in the wedding plans,' I replied. 'This week has been ridiculous enough without those kinds of suggestions.'

'Oh, Maddie,' Lauren smiled and laughed. 'You're so wound up all the time. Anyone would think you were the one getting married. You need to learn how to relax – it's only a job.'

'You're such a good friend,' I said, trying to convince myself of this as much as her. 'Thanks for the advice.'

'Sure thing,' she replied, missing the irony completely. 'Any time, honey.'

So, yes, things got off to a brilliant start.

'That meal was amazing,' Sarah announced, pushing her plate away. 'I'm so full I think I might die.'

'So great,' Lauren agreed. 'You two are the best.'

Sarah and I exchanged a look. It was true, we were. It had been a successful day, full of food and drinks and naps. Well, I had a nap. Sarah and Lauren went for mani-pedis but sleep was far more important to me than the state of my trotters.

Lauren clapped her hands and grinned. 'And where are we going now?'

Sarah and I exchanged a look. Huh?

'What do you mean where are we going now?' Sarah asked. 'Bed?'

'We're going out, right?' Lauren picked up her wine glass and emptied it in one gulp. 'Like, to a club or a bar or something?'

Neither of us said anything. Which said everything.

'We're not going anywhere?' she asked. 'It's just dinner?'

'You said you didn't want to go out,' I reminded her gently. 'You said you wanted a relaxing weekend away.'

'But it's my hen party,' Lauren whined. 'This is it?'

'Because an amazing day at one of the fanciest and most exclusive spas in the country and dinner at their equally fancy and even more exclusive restaurant isn't exactly what you asked for?' Sarah asked. 'Are you serious?'

Her little face fell and I could hardly stand it. 'So we're not going *out* out?' She looked at me like she might cry.

'Of course we are,' I said, whacking my hands on the table and making Sarah jump. 'We're teasing. Go upstairs and get changed. We'll meet you back down here in fifteen minutes.'

'I might need twenty,' she said, jumping to her feet.

'Even better!' I replied. 'Go on!'

'Now who's gone mad,' Sarah hissed across the table.

'We haven't planned anything. She said she wanted a quiet night in. What are we going to do?'

'You're going to go and tell the concierge that it's our friend's hen night and that something tragic has happened to the person who was supposed to be bringing all the hen-night accessories,' I ordered. Sarah looked sceptical. 'I don't care what you tell them – traffic accident, dead dog, traffic accident caused by dead dog. Just see what they can do.'

'I don't think they're going to have any penis straws or bride-to-be sashes,' she said, balling up her napkin and throwing it onto the table. 'You're not really going to make me do this, are you?'

'Or you can sit here and call every cab company, cocktail bar and nightclub in a fifty-mile radius and try to pull a fabulous hen party out of your arse.' I suggested. 'Totally up to you.'

Scowling, she stood up. 'I'll be back,' she said, heading out of the restaurant.

An hour later, we were sprawled out across the benches of a shady-looking pink limo with half a dozen mini bottles of Bollinger, a selection of promotional sex toys and enough gummy sweets in a plastic bag to bring on diabetes.

'I can't believe they had a screening of that bloody film last week,' Sarah whispered, pawing through the handcuffs, whips and riding crops. 'They couldn't get rid of these fast enough.'

'Fifty Shades of Yay,' I said. 'The party gods are on our side.'

'I don't really have to wear the tiara, do I?' Lauren asked. 'It's going to mess up my hair.'

'Yes,' I replied, another fifty quid short after buying it from an eight-year-old girl celebrating her birthday with her too-rich parents in our hotel. 'You do have to wear it. Possibly forever.'

'I know it's dumb,' Lauren said as Sarah popped the first bottle of bubbly, 'but I kind of wish we'd done the matching T-shirts now. This is super fun. I knew you guys wouldn't let me down.'

'Banana,' Sarah whispered. 'Maddie, banana.'

'You're banned from saying that for the rest of the night,' I said. 'Normal service resumes tomorrow.'

'I intend to get so drunk, I don't see tomorrow,' she replied, handing me a bottle and a straw. 'Cheers.'

'We're here.' Todd the driver lowered the screen he had put up the instant we asked him to put on the Dirty Dancing soundtrack. 'What time do you want me back?'

'Midnight?' Sarah suggested.

'Four!' Lauren shouted, looking at her phone. 'They're open until four!'

'In half an hour?' Sarah said, revising her offer.

'Can we say two, and if it's any later, we'll pay you double-time?' I asked as Lauren hurled herself onto the street.

'We can,' Todd the driver said. 'Good luck.'

I nodded grimly and followed my friends out into the night.

It had to be at least three and a half years since I had set foot inside an actual nightclub. Not a nice bar with a bit of a dance floor or an East London hipster thing where a DJ with a giant box full of vinyl played songs from his phone, but an honest-to-God nightclub. That streak had ended at Tramps in Bristol city centre on this

Saturday night in June, and I was afraid.

'Hello,' I shouted over the music to the woman manning the coat-check booth. 'I called about an hour ago – we're here for my friend's hen night and the person on the phone said he could reserve us a booth? I think I spoke to a Gareth?'

She clacked her gum and stared.

'Is Gareth here?' I asked.

She shrugged.

'I'll go and find Gareth, shall I?'

I wasn't nearly drunk enough for this. Unlike Sarah and Lauren, who had already taken to the light-up dance floor and were spanking each other with black plastic riding crops in the middle of a bus load of Welsh teenagers.

'Hi!' I hurled myself at the bar, smiling politely at the first bartender I could find. 'Do you happen to know if there's a Gareth working tonight?'

'That would be me,' he replied, straightening his clip-on tie. 'What can I do you for?'

'My name's Maddie.' I stuck out my hand, only for Gareth to take it in his and kiss it. Eurgh. 'We spoke on the phone, about my friend's hen do.'

I wiped my hand on the arse of my jeans and tried to keep smiling.

'Oh yes!' He ducked under the bar and gave a flourish. 'Welcome!'

I glanced over my shoulder. Fifty or so sweaty teenagers in next to nothing were vibrating madly to a song I'd never heard under three disco balls and a selection of epilepsy-inducing flashing lights. It was everything I'd ever dreamed of.

'Let me show you to the VIP suite.'

Gareth took four steps and stopped in front of a red vinyl booth at the side of the bar.

'This is the VIP suite.'

I crossed my arms in front of me and gave him a look he'd probably last got from his mother when he failed his GCSEs.

'Let me send over a round of shots, my treat,' he said as I threw my jacket and handbag down, squeaking against the sticky plastic as I utched myself round the table. 'How many of you are there?'

'Thr— seven,' I replied. 'There are seven of us.'

'Seven shots on the way,' Gareth promised. 'You're going to have such a fun night.'

Maybe, I thought, after I've downed half those shots.

'And I said to him, Steve, I said, you're not being fair. This is hard enough without you trying to take the telly as well as the settee.' Sarah's head lolled back against the vinyl booth. 'And he didn't reply. I mean, he can afford a new TV – he makes more than I do. It's not fair, is it? Maddie, are you listening, Maddie?'

'I am,' I said, patting Sarah absently on the knee while I watched Lauren force her way into a dance circle with half a dozen eighteen-year-old girls and out-twerk every one of them. 'It isn't fair.'

'Take a selfie with me.' Sarah fumbled for her phone and held it at arm's length. 'Look sexy.'

'How's this?' I asked, pressing my face against her and pouting.

'You're not doing it properly,' she said, squinting into the camera and fussing with her hair. 'Do it properly.'

Gareth's shots were about as strong as a premature kitten, and an hour later I was still stone-cold sober. Probably because I'd eaten three courses for dinner and was so full of steak I could barely move, so the idea of drinking on top of all that food made me feel quite sick enough, thank you very much. Sarah and Lauren were fighting their food-forced sobriety the sensible way. By mixing their drinks and consuming every alcoholic beverage known to man.

'I hate him, Maddie,' Sarah said, abandoning our photo and dropping her phone on the floor. 'I hate him so much. I can't believe he's gone. I still wake up every day and expect him to be in bed, and he isn't, and he's a shit, and I feel sick.'

'Do you want some water?' I asked, retrieving her phone from the very sticky floor. Sarah nodded.

'He's a bastard,' she mouthed.

'Such a bastard,' I agreed. 'I'll be back with your water – don't go anywhere.'

By the time I had battled my way to the bar and returned to our booth with two bottles of overpriced Evian, Sarah was nowhere to be seen.

'If she's throwing up, I'll kill her,' I muttered, leaving the water in the 'VIP' booth and venturing off to find the toilets. 'It's another hundred quid if we're sick in the limo.'

Walking into the ladies was like being transported into another world. It was amazing how quickly you forgot what these things were like. One £12-a-pop cocktail bar and your brain erased any memory of queuing for the loo in a lurid red lav with mirrors screwed into the wall and covered in teenage graffiti. *Je ne regrette rien.* It smelled of hairspray and cheap bodyspray and one too many alcopops. One whiff and I was seventeen again.

'Excuse me,' I called, almost drowned out by aggressive spritzing of dry shampoo. 'I'm looking for someone. She's about this tall and has blonde hair in a topknot and—'

Lindsey Kelk

'Maddie?'

Someone called my name in a low, choked American accent from inside one of the toilet cubicles.

'Maddie, I need you.'

'Lauren?' I shouted. 'Where are you?'

'In here,' she replied. 'I need you.'

I excused myself as I cut through the queue and gently pushed on all the toilet doors until one gave way and I found her. Slumped in the corner of the loo, sequinned skirt up round her waist and lipstick smeared across her left cheek.

'Oh Lauren.' I couldn't work out how much I'd need to have drunk to think sitting on the floor and propping myself up on the lav could possibly be a good idea. 'Are you OK?'

'I was sick,' she said, pointing into the toilet. 'But now I feel awesome. Do I look OK?'

'You look brilliant,' I told her. 'Fantastic, actually.'

'You're so pretty.' She reached out for my hair but I pulled away before she could make contact. 'Your hair is all long and nice and your eyes are like crazy green. You know that? They're so green. Like, the greenest.'

'Thank you.' I let out a loud sigh and tried to remember how to do this. 'Shall we get you out of the toilets?'

Lauren shook her head. 'I think maybe I might be sick again,' she whispered loudly, punctuating each word with a flap of her hand. 'We should stay here.'

With the greatest reluctance, I lowered myself onto the toilet floor, accepting that I would have to throw these jeans away in the morning.

'Are you having a nice time?' I asked. 'Are you enjoying your bachelorette?'

'Yes,' Lauren replied before promptly bursting into tears.

Oh, bloody hell.

234

'What's the matter?' I scooted closer, stroking her hair back from her sticky face. 'Do you want to go back to the hotel?'

'It's not the bachelorette.' She wiped a hand across her face, smearing her mascara as she went. I quickly grabbed a piece of loo paper to clean up her mucky paws. 'It's everything.'

And here we go.

'It's too quick,' she said with a hiccup. Lauren always hiccupped when she cried. If it weren't so frustrating waiting for her to finish a sentence, it would be adorable. 'Way too quick. And all that stuff with Michael's grandmother being ill, it's, like, so much.'

'But you want to marry him, don't you?' I asked.

Lauren didn't answer nearly as quickly as I might have liked. 'I love him,' she replied. 'But I'm really, really scared.'

I took her hand and smiled. 'That's natural,' I said. 'Everyone gets nervous before they get married.'

'But what if I mess it up like my mom and dad?' she whimpered. 'What if I have to get divorced like Sarah?'

'Not everyone gets divorced,' I reminded her. Just most people, I said to myself. 'You and Michael love each other – that's all that matters. You can't ask for more than that.'

'We've only been together for a year,' she said, tracing a lipstick-smeared love heart on the tiles. I wondered whether Gav and Caz were still together. 'What if that's not long enough? It's not long, Mads.'

'That's true,' I said, my mind running over everything that had already been arranged and paid for while trying to wipe away my best friend's tears. 'But you know, you've been around the block a couple of times. It's not like you don't know the difference between something real and something, well, not.'

'But I'm not sure,' she said, fresh tears spilling over her cheeks. 'I should be sure and I'm not.'

'Do you want to marry Michael?' I asked. 'And you're allowed to say no.'

'I love him,' she replied. 'But it doesn't feel the way I thought it would feel.'

There wasn't a lot to say about that. I have no idea how it's supposed to feel; I've always assumed I'll know. Fuck, what do you do if someone asks you to marry them and you don't know? I can't even turn down a cup of tea if someone offers but I'm not in the mood.

'How do you feel?' I asked softly.

'I love him,' Lauren slurred again. 'He's handsome and clever and he always remembers what kind of cereal I like when he goes shopping and he gets on well with children and he has a huge—'

'They're all good reasons,' I interrupted before she could go any further. I really didn't want to know. 'Does he make you laugh?'

'Oh yeah,' she replied, dilated eyes wide. 'He's so funny. He's the funniest person I know.'

I cocked my head to one side. 'Really?' I asked. 'Because I have not seen that side of him.'

'You haven't seen what's in his pants, either,' she pointed out, hitting me in the nose with her index finger. 'He's a keeper.'

'I think you've got your answer,' I said, slapping her hand away from my face. 'You love him, you think he's funny, and apparently he's packing. It's just cold feet, Lauren. It's going to be fine.'

'Maybe you're right,' she said, her head lolling back and hitting the cistern. 'That hurt.'

'I'm going to find Sarah,' I said, rubbing the back of

her head. 'Can you meet me outside in a few minutes?'

She gave me a blissful smile and blew me a kiss with an outstretched hand. 'I love you,' she shouted as I opened the door to let myself out.

'I love you too,' I called back, blocking an angry-looking girl with dyed black hair from going into the cubicle. 'There's someone still in there,' I explained. 'And even if there wasn't, you wouldn't want to go in.'

Outside the toilet, the club had filled up quickly and I couldn't see Sarah anywhere. Pausing on the balcony, I took out my phone to text Todd the driver, asking if he could come and pick us up early. How was it possible that it was only one a.m.? After a fruitless five-minute double lap of the club, I gave up and headed back to the table. Where Sarah was snogging someone's face off.

'Um, hello?' I said, poking her in the shoulder. She pulled away and looked up at me, confused. The man she was sitting on top of gave me a filthy look. And when I say man, he couldn't possibly have been more than nineteen.

'What?' he asked. 'Is something the matter, like?'

'Yes,' I said, wrenching my jacket out from underneath him. 'That's my friend.'

'And?' he replied.

And I didn't have anything else.

'Sarah, Lauren's ill, so we're leaving.' I decided to ignore the rude child my best friend was straddling. 'Can you please meet us outside in a minute?'

'Who shoved a stick up your arse?' he asked. 'We're having a conversation.'

'No you're not, actually,' I replied. 'You might be getting off with my thirty-one-year-old friend, but you're definitely not having a conversation.'

'You're thirty-one?' he said to Sarah. 'Wicked. Cougar life, man.'

The smile fell from Sarah's face. 'Let's go,' she said, gracelessly clambering off his lap, kneeling on his nads as she disembarked. 'Where's Lauren?'

'She'll be outside,' I said as my phone started ringing. 'That'll be the driver.'

But when I looked down at my phone, it wasn't my driver.

'What's wrong?' Lauren asked, ignoring the noisy writhing of her manchild as she tried and failed to get her arms into her leather jacket. I held out my phone and showed her the name flashing on the screen.

Tom Wheeler.

'Wait, that's the usher?' she said, grabbing one of the unopened bottles of water from the table. 'He's calling you? At one a.m. on a Saturday? What's wrong with him?'

'What do I do?' I panicked.

'Answer the fucking phone?' the boy in the booth suggested.

'Clearly you can't do that,' Sarah said, rolling her eyes. 'Let it go to voicemail. It might be a butt dial.'

'It must be a butt dial!' I agreed, full of hope. 'Thank God. Can you go to the lav and get madam? I'll go out and find the car.'

'And listen to three minutes of the hot usher heavy-breathing and groping his hot fiancée in the back of a cab?' she asked. 'Whatever. I need to puke before we leave anyway.'

Sarah had always been a pro drinker. Hammered one minute, fingers down her throat and back on the shots the next. It was disgusting. And probably why she worked in PR.

The limo hadn't arrived yet when I exited the club, ecstatic to be told that there was no re-entry. Fizzing with curiosity, I pressed the voicemail button, preparing myself for the drunken worst.

'Maddie, it's Tom.' It was not a butt dial. He didn't sound drunk, he sounded panicked. 'I got your text. Where are you? Are you OK? Let me know where you are and I'll come and get you.'

He'd come and get me? With a horrible, horrible, career-destroying realization, I pulled my phone away from my ear and swiped through my texts. I had not asked Todd the driver to collect us from Lauren's hen do, I had sent Tom the Usher a text message saying '*so sorry, pls could you come and get us right now?*'

Oh, Maddie Fraser, what a cockmonkey you are.

My finger hovered over the screen, ready to reply, but I didn't know what to say. Just as I was about to send my very best apologetic emoji, his name lit up the screen again. Gritting my teeth, I answered.

'Hello?'

'Maddie, it's Tom, are you OK? Where are you?' He sounded so genuinely concerned, I couldn't help but be a little bit touched.

'Tom, I'm fine,' I said quickly, trying to get the mortification out of the way as quickly and as painlessly as possible. 'I'm so sorry, I texted the wrong number. I'm on a hen night and our driver is called Todd and I messaged the wrong person and, you know . . . eek. So, so sorry.'

There was silence on the other end of the line for a moment. I grimaced, waiting for a response while I watched a man throw up round the back of a kebab van.

'I see,' he said. Awfully calm for someone who was ready to get in the car and collect a girl he barely knew from an undisclosed location at one in the morning. 'I was a bit worried.'

'Well, I can see why you would be,' I replied, awkward laughter in my voice. 'But I'm fine. Honest. We're all fine. But thank you.'

'Not at all,' he said, his voice crisp and stiff again. 'Have a lovely evening.'

'You doing anything nice?' I asked, immediately slapping my palm against my forehead.

'Sleeping,' he said. 'Or at least I was.'

'I'll let you get back to that then,' I said, shaking my head at myself. 'Sorry about the text. And the call. And waking you up. Just, generally, sorry.'

'Noted,' Tom replied. 'Goodnight, Maddie.'

Brilliant, I thought to myself as Lauren and Sarah staggered out of the club in each other's arms. Maybe I should call Matilda while I was at it and have her add embarrassing late-night text messages to clients to my CV.

That would definitely help my case with Mr Colton.

17

The next morning, according to Sarah's itinerary, we were supposed to be up at nine for breakfast and then take a brisk walk around the grounds. When neither of my friends had pulled their heads out from underneath their pillows at ten, I took myself down for breakfast and then embarked on a very steady, hungover wander to the nearest bench, right outside the breakfast room.

The hotel grounds were lovely, all rolling hills and green fields. I just wished I could get the throbbing pain in my right eye to go away. Alcopops were made for those with high metabolisms and the devil; I hadn't had a hangover like this in years.

Because nothing went with a hangover quite so well as personal shame, I took out my phone and swiped through last night's messages. I couldn't believe I had texted Tom. I couldn't believe I had spoken to Tom. I desperately wanted to text him again and beg him not to tell my bosses about it, but he wouldn't, would he? Will might have him pegged as some sort of uber wanker, but he'd only been polite to me. Bloody hell, he was prepared to get in his car at one in the morning when he thought I was in trouble; that went well beyond the duty of a Nice Man.

Distracting myself with some Instagram shots of the beautiful Somerset scenery worked for about three minutes, but soon enough I was panicking again. And with both my best friends unconscious, I did the only sensible thing I could think to do.

I called Will.

'Hello?'

'It's me,' I said, awkwardly realizing this was the first time I'd ever called him on the phone. 'Maddie.'

'That's what it said on my phone,' he replied. 'What's wrong?'

'Nothing's wrong,' I lied. 'Just thought I'd call, say hello.'

'Aren't you on your girls' weekend?' Will asked. I could hear a lot of manly shouting in the background. 'Isn't it no blokes allowed?'

'I'm on Lauren's hen weekend,' I said. 'The others are still in bed. Last night was a rough one.'

'Ouch,' Will laughed. 'It's nearly eleven. You must have been caning it.'

'Yeah,' I agreed. 'What did you do last night?'

'I can't chat right now, Mads,' he said, the shouting getting louder. 'I'm at rugby, we're going on in a minute. Can I call you back later?'

'I'll be home tonight if you want to come round?' I suggested. 'About seven or something?'

'I'm busy tonight,' he said. 'But tomorrow could work?'

'Sounds good,' I replied, not at all wondering what he was doing. 'Tomorrow.'

'All right, see you then—'

'Will.' I had to say it, I needed reassurance that this wasn't a firing offence or I'd be feeling like shite all day. 'Last night, I accidentally sent a text to Tom.'

'Tom Wheeler?' he asked, the rush gone out of his voice. 'Why have you got his number in your phone?'

'I'm doing that party for him, remember?' I know it's childish to enjoy your boyfriend being jealous, but fuck it, I hadn't had the pleasure for such a long time

'I thought you weren't doing that,' Will said. 'I thought you said no.'

'I never said that,' I replied. 'You don't need to worry about it. I was trying to text Todd, our driver, but I texted him by mistake and I think he's a bit mad about it. You don't think he'll call my boss or anything, do you?'

Will sniffed. 'I wouldn't think so. Do you want me to call him? I'll call him.'

My knight in tiny rugby shorts.

'No, not if you don't think he'll do anything,' I said, relief taking the edge off my headache. 'It was my fault anyway. I did text him at one in the morning.'

'Nothing salacious, I hope,' he replied. 'Those texts are only meant to be coming to me.'

'Hardly.' I smiled to myself. 'He thought I was asking him to come and pick us up from somewhere. And he was going to come! Isn't that mental?' As soon as the words were out of my mouth I felt weird about them and about what it might have meant that Tom was prepared to get out of bed and come find me, wherever I was, without even asking why.

Will did not seem to think it was mental. 'Just be careful around him, Mads,' he said, an edge to his voice. 'I don't like him hanging around you. He's a snake.'

'I know you're busy,' I said. 'But sooner or later you're going to have to tell me what went on with you two.'

'Just be careful,' he warned gently. 'I'm only thinking about you. He's had it in for me since college – he needs to grow up and get over himself. We're not eighteen any more, but he's still got a chip on his shoulder. I wouldn't trust a word he says.'

'Right.' I thought back to the dance, the party for his mum, the awkward charm. It was all so lovely. Was it just an act all calculated to look like charm when really it was nothing but sneakiness? 'I'll be careful.'

'You should tell him where to stick his party,' Will advised. 'I've got to go, Mads. I'll call you tonight, yeah?'

'Tonight,' I confirmed. 'Talk to you later.'

Sticking my phone into my jacket pocket, I stared off into the blue sky. Thank God I'd found Will, I thought, allowing myself a five-second fantasy of our wedding on these beautiful lawns, the rolling hills behind us.

Thank God I had someone looking out for me for a change.

'Hey, Maddie, smile.' Lauren clicked a picture of me staring blindly into her camera. 'Hmm, not your best.'

'So, this is nice,' I said, sitting back as a waiter in a starched white shirt poured me a cup of freshly brewed Earl Grey from a silver teapot so shiny I could see every single one of my burgeoning wrinkles in its reflection. I wondered how many had been caused by Lauren's wedding.

'It's so nice,' Lauren agreed. For whatever reason, her expression didn't seem to agree with her words. She looked as though she had been dug up and dragged to the table, her usually glowing skin was grey and sallow and her hair was a rat's nest of tangles, accessorized by her cheap Claire's Accessories tiara, that I had insisted she wear. Sarah didn't even reply. She sat opposite me, completely silent with her lips glued together, her face green.

There is no such thing as a dignified hangover when you're in your thirties. I had never been so thankful that I'd laid off the alcopops when I took a look at my BFFs, both about ready to chuck at any second.

'Are you having a nice time?' I asked Lauren, diving straight into the scones. 'Yay, hen weekend?'

She nodded with grim determination. The tiara really set off the black circles underneath her eyes.

'The hotel is lovely,' I continued blithely. Was there ever such a thing as too much clotted cream? No. The answer is no. 'I wish we didn't have to leave tonight.'

'How are you eating?' Lauren whispered. 'How are you putting food inside you?'

I shrugged. 'It's delicious? And I'm a greedy fucker?'

'Madeline, language!'

With a mouth stuffed to bursting with warm scone, half a pot of cream and lashings of freshly made jam, I turned slowly, hoping I was having a delayed aural hallucination. It couldn't be. It just couldn't be.

'Looks like I'm just in time for the party.' A tiny, blonde woman with a huge smile on her face stood behind me eye-balling Lauren. 'Don't just sit there catching flies, baby, come and give your mama a hug.'

Lauren stood up slowly. 'Mom? What are you doing here?'

I looked at Lauren. Lauren looked at me. Sarah closed her eyes and rested her forehead on the table.

This was not good.

'And so, when Sarah invited me to join you guys, I just knew I had to come along,' Mrs Hobbs-Miller twittered, settling herself in the seat between myself and her daughter before any of us could find a thing to say. 'But I have to tell you girls, it wasn't easy to find this place and goodness me, the price of the taxi was extortionate.'

'You took a taxi all the way from Bristol?' I asked as she beamed in my general direction.

'No, dear.' She shook her head, brushing her long pale blonde hair over her shoulders. Unconsciously, Lauren did the same thing across the table. 'From London.'

'You took a cab all the way here from London?' Lauren asked. 'Mom, that's crazy. It's like, a hundred miles.'

'It's not *like* a hundred miles,' she corrected carefully. 'It is one hundred and fifteen. Lauren, darling, whatever do you have on your head?'

Lauren grabbed blindly at her tiara and tore it out of her hair, taking several tangled blonde wisps with it. Her mother smiled, pleased.

'Thank you,' she said. 'You look like a twelve-year-old at a tea party, silly thing.'

Which was funny because that's exactly how I felt.

'So, Sarah invited you?' I asked. Sarah still hadn't spoken but her eyebrows drew together in confusion. 'What a nice surprise.'

'Yes, I was a little disappointed not to have heard from you, Madeline, it's been such a long time,' Mrs Hobbs-Miller gave me a reproachful look. She wasn't angry, just disappointed. 'But I was so pleased to be included, it's been such heartache watching my little girl go through with this shotgun wedding when I've been so far away.'

'It's not a shotgun wedding—' Lauren began, only to be shushed by her mother.

'I brought something for you, Sarah,' she said, passing a little gift bag across the table. 'Just to say thank you for thinking of me.'

Sarah moistened her lips and took a deep breath. 'Thank you,' she whispered before swallowing hard. She reached inside the bag and pulled out a packet of Hershey's Kisses and a Maybelline mascara.

'Your favourites,' Lauren's mum said. 'I remember how excited you girls used to get when you came to visit. Of course, it's been so long since you've been over to me, I don't even know if they're still your thing.'

'They are, Mrs Hobbs-Miller,' Sarah reassured her. 'Thank you, Mrs Hobbs-Miller.'

'How many times am I going to have to remind you guys to call me Vivienne?' she said with a sparkling laugh. 'Oh, it's so nice to be with my girls again.'

We girls glanced around the table at each other. Nice? Hmm.

'Perhaps don't eat all those candies at once,' she said to Sarah as she stashed the bag underneath the table. 'Lauren tells me your husband left you. The last thing you need right now is to be gaining weight, trust me. Are you a little bigger than the last time I saw you?'

Sarah's bottom lip began to tremble.

'You know what?' Mrs Hobbs-Miller took Lauren's hand in hers and squeezed it before turning it over to check out her engagement ring and raising an eyebrow. 'I'm going to run to the ladies' room and wash up. Be a doll and order for me?'

'What would you like?' Lauren mumbled, twisting her diamond around her finger.

Her mum smoothed down her cashmere sweater as she stood. 'Oh, whatever you're having, honey. Only no milk. Or gluten. And of course I'm watching my weight so I don't show you up on your big day. So anything is fine. I'm just so happy to be spending time with you gals.'

'Oh my *god*,' Lauren spat in Sarah's general direction. 'What the hell, Sarah?'

'I didn't invite her,' Sarah protested, poking herself in her flat stomach. 'She sent me a nice card when you asked me to be a bridesmaid and so I emailed her to say thank you and she asked what we were doing for the bachelorette and I told her and honestly, Lauren, I didn't invite her. I don't even remember if I mentioned the name of the hotel.'

'She didn't send me a card,' I said, pulling a face.

'Not about you, right now, Maddie,' Lauren snapped. 'I can't do this right now, I can't. I've been avoiding her since she got into town and I'm way too hungover to deal with it now.'

'It won't be that bad, will it?' Sarah asked pleadingly. I was still sulking. Why hadn't I got a card? I was a bridesmaid *and* an unpaid wedding planner. Surely that warranted the price of a stamp? 'I mean, *my* mum is hardly mother of the year but it would have been weird if she hadn't been involved in my wedding, wouldn't it? This is just the same.'

'Sarah, my mom only just got here and she already called you fat,' Lauren replied. 'She called me a twelve-year-old and has Maddie sulking like a teenager because she didn't send her a card.'

'I just don't see what I did to *not* deserve a card,' I muttered.

'Shut up about the card, Maddie,' Lauren warned. 'Right now, we just have to get through this alive.'

'She looks so sweet,' Sarah said, staring at the doorway as though she was waiting for an axe murderer to return from the lavs. 'I just want her to give me a hug and tell me I'm pretty.'

'Yeah but afterwards you'd find a business card from her plastic surgeon in your pocket and a knife in between your shoulder blades.' Lauren pasted a smile on her face as her mother reappeared. 'You can't win, it's easier not to try.'

'Did you order for me?' Mrs Hobbs-Miller asked, settling back into her seat.

'Not yet,' Lauren replied. 'Sorry.'

'Hmm,' she sniffed, still smiling. 'I hope this husband of yours is an organized soul. You'd forget your head if it wasn't screwed on, sweetheart. Thank goodness it's so pretty.'

'Lauren told us you've met Michael,' I reached for the sugar bowl before snatching my fingers back. I didn't need telling I was a porker when I already had jam all over my face. 'Isn't he lovely?'

'He's a delight,' she confirmed without hesitation. That wasn't Lauren's recollection of the evening but whatever. 'And such a good man to take on a project like this one.'

Lauren looked down at the tablecloth while her mother signalled the waiter.

'Maddie.' Mrs Hobbs-Miller turned her attention to me. I sucked in my stomach, combed my fingers through my hair and smiled. 'Lauren tells me you're planning the wedding.'

'I'm helping Lauren,' I said, nodding. 'She's had some amazing ideas. It's going to be beautiful.'

'That's so wonderful and goodness knows she needs the help,' she said. 'It's so nice to see you girls still so close. And planning a wedding can be so hard, have you done it before?'

'Well, yeah,' I said, looking over at Lauren. 'It's sort of my job.'

'I thought Lauren said you were an assistant?'

'An events assistant,' I replied. 'I plan weddings. At work. For a living.'

'That's so lovely,' she said, a genuine look of pride on her face. 'When did you start there?'

'Uh,' I reached out and grabbed two sugar lumps before she could say anything. 'I've been there a while.'

'And you get to do a lot of the actual planning, do you?' she asked. 'As an assistant?'

'Lots,' I confirmed. Lauren was still refusing to make eye contact. 'Honest.'

It was like being trapped in the headmaster's office with a hangover and no bell was going to ring, ever.

'I'm sorry,' she said, patting my hand. 'I don't mean to keep asking, I just want to make sure my baby's big day is perfect. I'm sure Sarah will agree with me, planning a wedding can be so stressful.'

'Yeah,' Sarah said, chewing her bottom lip.

'Oh, I'm being so silly,' she said. 'I'm sure you don't want to talk about your wedding right now, do you?'

'No,' Sarah said, chewing her bottom lip.

'Because you're getting divorced.'

'Yeah,' Sarah said, chewing her bottom lip.

We sat in silence for a moment while the waiter poured her tea.

'So how are you getting along at work, Sarah?' she asked.

'I think I might have to pop to the loo,' Sarah said, wiping a dot of blood from her lips then abruptly pushing her chair away from the table and walking out of the room.

'Oh no,' Mrs Hobbs-Miller pressed her hands to her chest. 'I should go after her, I shouldn't have said that.'

'It's OK, Mom,' Lauren said. 'She'll be fine.'

'It's best to leave her when she's upset,' I added. 'Sarah doesn't like a fuss.'

'Remind me never to come to you two if I need help,' she said, laughing. 'Poor Sarah. You can't even begin to imagine what she's going through, you know.'

Lauren took a deep breath. 'Here we go,' she whispered.

'When your father left me,' she began, 'I didn't know what to do with myself. All alone with two tiny, wilful children.'

'Mom, I was eighteen,' Lauren replied. 'And Jessica had already left home.'

'Please don't speak with your mouth full, Lauren,' she replied. 'I would lay awake at night, trying to work out what I could possibly have done wrong. How I could have made things better. I felt like we had let him down.'

'We?' I asked. Lauren shook her head vehemently.

'But it's not your fault when things go wrong,' Mrs Hobbs-Miller took our hands in hers. 'Sometimes it just doesn't work out. Of course, the two of you don't need to worry about that. Yet. Are you still with that dashing lawyer, Maddie?'

'No, she's with a different dashing lawyer,' Lauren answered for me. Her help was not appreciated.

'Oh.' Her mum gave me a bittersweet smile. 'Well, I guess that's something. What happened?'

'He met someone else,' I said. My face felt hot. 'It's fine, it was a long time ago.'

'Then it's for the best,' she said, rapping my hand briskly. 'Just make sure you don't make the same mistakes again.'

She was a wonderful woman.

'None of you are getting any younger,' she added in a sing-song voice. 'Now, tell me everything about the wedding, I can't wait to hear all of your ideas. Half of the things Lauren has shown me seem quite ridiculous. She tells me she wants an ice cream truck at the reception, don't you think that seems terribly tacky? Before you know it, all the children will be running around with sticky hands, Lauren's dress will be ruined, there'll be bees everywhere . . .'

Under the table, Lauren grabbed my knee.

'Yeah, um, I already booked that,' I said. 'It's usually very popular.'

'They do that sort of thing a lot at the weddings you plan, do they?' she asked, a curious look on her unlined face. 'Fascinating.'

'Lauren thought it sounded fun, didn't you, Lauren?' I said, nudging my friend.

'Michael wanted it,' she mumbled. 'I don't know. I guess I don't know if it's a great idea.'

'Michael wanted it,' Mrs Hobbs-Miller squeezed a lemon slice into her tea. 'Well, that explains everything. Clearly I've arrived at just the right time.'

Sipping my sweet, sweet tea, I wondered whether it would be considered impolite to suggest that two weeks after the wedding might be a better time for her to arrive. Or even never.

'Don't worry, Maddie,' she said, leaning her head to one side and smiling. 'I'm here to help. We'll get everything ship-shape in no time now.'

*　　*　　*

'Has she gone?' I asked as Lauren appeared in the doorway of the spa, clad in a fluffy white robe.

She nodded, holding her arms around herself tightly. 'She's gone,' she confirmed. 'I told her that we were taking a pole dancing lesson and she couldn't get out of here fast enough.'

'I'm so sorry,' Sarah said, holding her arms out for a hug which Lauren threw herself into. 'I'd totally forgotten how scary she can be.'

'And she likes you,' she replied with a sniff. 'Let's just pretend it didn't happen. She was never here.'

'I still don't know why I didn't get a card,' I said, pouring myself a glass of spa water.

'I can't believe I'm still hungover,' Sarah said, changing the subject swiftly. Cow. 'I feel like a skunk crawled down my throat and died.'

'I can't believe you got off with a child,' I replied. 'How old was he? Eighteen?'

'Twenty-two,' she threw me a filthy look. 'And we don't ever need to talk about that again, thanks.'

'You made out with a twenty-two-year-old?' Lauren clucked. 'Oh my God, Sarah, that's nasty.'

'I may or may not have called Steve,' she said, holding out her hands to cut us off. 'And don't ask because it did not go well and I don't want to talk about it. So yes, I snogged a twenty-two-year-old. Clearly it's both of your faults because you weren't there to stop me.'

'Then it's Lauren's fault,' I said. 'I wasn't the one puking my guts up and telling everyone who would listen about the size of my boyfriend's wang.'

My phone beeped quietly in the pocket of my dressing gown, but not quietly enough for Eagle Ears Hempel to miss it.

'Ooh, speaking of wangs,' she grinned. 'Who is it? Is it Will? Is it another photo of his knob? I want to see it.'

'It is not another photo of his knob.' I should never have shown her the first one. 'Don't say it like he's sent me hundreds.'

He had sent me six. It might seem like a lot written down, but they all made sense at the time and he was awfully proud of it. Eleanor has sent me about a thousand photos of her baby and she's only been in my life two weeks longer than Will's penis, so I think that number is fine.

'Is it from Will?' Lauren asked.

'Yes.'

'Is it a photo of his penis?' Sarah asked.

I sighed.

'Yes.'

'Can we see it?' Lauren asked.

There just didn't seem any point in arguing with them, so I handed over my phone.

'You can never tell him I showed you,' I said. If he had shown pictures of me to any of his friends I would have killed him, but this seemed to be one situation where double standards really did exist. As I said, he was very proud of his penis. 'Now give it back.'

'What angle is he taking it from?' Lauren asked, turning the phone round in her hand trying to work it out before the picture resized itself on the screen. 'Are you sure it's not his thumb?'

'Bloody big thumb,' Sarah said, pulling a face. 'Look, that's his leg and that's his—'

'OK, we've seen enough.' I held my hand out for my phone. 'Give it back.'

'Can I send him a photo of my tits?' Sarah asked. 'Let's all send him a photo of our tits!'

'Oh my God, yes!' Lauren clapped her hands, spilling her orange juice all over her white robe. 'Guys love tits!'

'No one is sending him a photo of anyone's tits,' I said. I hated having to be the matron of the group, but there was No Way. 'Will doesn't want a photo of anyone's tits – he's just being silly.'

He did want a photo of someone's tits. He wasn't being silly.

'What's going on with the other one?' Sarah asked through a mouthful of cheese. 'Tom?'

'Nothing,' I said, twisting my hair into a ponytail on top of my head, still utterly confused after my conversation with Will earlier. 'I'm organizing a party for him and that's all.'

'And texting him at one a.m.,' she reminded me. 'Classic Maddie.'

'I still can't believe he danced with you,' Lauren said, falling into a mock swoon. 'It's so romantic.'

'It wasn't romantic,' I said, lying to her and myself. 'It was uncomfortable. What kind of bloke does that?'

'A romantic,' Lauren argued. 'I'd rather someone took me dancing than sent me a photo of his semi-erect penis.'

'Yeah, like, at least get a full hard-on,' Lauren sniffed, turning to Sarah with a confident nod. 'That's why I thought it was a thumb.'

'Oh, definitely,' Sarah replied. 'A semi is such an insult.'

'It's so offensive,' Lauren said with a sour face. 'Don't you think it's strange to send someone a photo of your penis? Who is it working for? What girl is getting a photo of a penis from a guy and saying "he's the man for me!"?'

'I think some men just like showing off their penis,' I said with a shrug. 'I don't think there's any more to it than that.'

'Women have the concept of "the one" shoved down their throats from birth, all that princess fairytale shit,' Sarah theorized confidently. 'And all men are looking for is "the one who will".'

For a bitter cynic with divorce paperwork in her handbag, she made a good point.

'Men aren't only looking to get laid, though,' Lauren said. 'Men do want to get married. Michael wants to marry me.'

'And Seb wanted to marry not me,' I added. 'They're not all evil shag machines.'

'Yeah, they are,' Sarah said, wrinkling her nose and biting her bottom lip. 'They get bored of having to make so much effort after a bit and that's when they decide to give marriage a whirl, but they'd all be out shagging everything that moves until they were drawing their pensions if they could get away with it.'

In the interests of not giving up and killing ourselves there and then, Lauren and I maintained our doubtful expressions.

'Two words,' Sarah said, taking a deep breath and regaining her composure. 'Hugh Hefner.'

'Mmm. Have you been on any dates yet?' Lauren asked. 'Or are you just making out with teenagers in nightclubs.'

'No,' she admitted, pulling her robe around her. 'I registered with a bunch of online dating sites, but I can't do it – it's still too weird.'

'There's no rush,' I told her, trying to sound as though I meant it. 'There's no point starting something if you're not ready.'

'Yeah, I don't know,' she said. 'Honestly, I thought it would be easier. No one I fancy has even messaged me anyway.'

And then Lauren said the one thing that you're absolutely, positively not supposed to say to a single woman over thirty.

'It's because you're a single woman over thirty.'

Sarah turned on our best friend so quickly I thought she was going to knock her out. And might I just add, she would have been completely within her rights to do so.

'Excuse me?'

'It's not your fault,' Lauren qualified, as though that would make it better. 'But they're filtering you out. No guy in his thirties using online dating looks for women over thirty. They assume you're desperate.'

'Do you really believe that?' Sarah asked. 'You think all women over thirty are desperate?'

'Doesn't matter whether or not it's true,' Lauren said with a shrug. 'Men believe it. As soon as they hear that you're over thirty, they assume you're dying to get married and push out babies with the first man who says yes, so they don't even get involved.'

'That's so depressing,' I said, thanking my lucky stars for my boyfriend once again.

'It's true, though,' Lauren pushed on. She threw out her painful truths with all the confidence of a woman wearing a Tiffany engagement ring and a half-cocked Claire's Accessories tiara. 'It was easier before online dating because they couldn't write you off without meeting you. Now they don't even need to see your picture. You turn thirty, you fall out of the algorithm, and you literally don't exist. You, Sarah Hempel, do not exist.'

'Oh, right,' Sarah replied, stung. 'You do believe it. Is that why you're trying to convince yourself you want to marry Mr Swiffer when you're crying in the toilets and throwing up on yourself?'

In the immortal words of Cher, if I could turn back time . . .

'No wonder Steve left you,' Lauren said, her eyes burning. 'You are such a bitch, Sarah.'

Because saying something like that was definitely going to help.

'Now then.' Apparently I thought the best thing to do at this moment was an accidental impression of my dad. 'Come on, ladies.'

'Better a bitch than a fantasist,' Sarah snapped. 'Oh my God, someone asked me to marry him! I'd better say yes before he realizes what a pathetic excuse for a waste-of-space daddy's girl I am and changes his mind!'

Lauren sat up straight. 'Better a waste-of-space daddy's girl who's getting married at thirty-one than a fat, lonely bitch who's getting a divorce.'

'*I am not fat!*' Sarah yelled.

It was fair, she wasn't, but I couldn't help but feel as though that wasn't the most offensive part of that statement.

'Can we calm down?' I asked in a quiet voice. 'Please?'

'Fuck this.' Sarah stood up and stared at me. 'I'm not pissing my day away on her. This is all pathetic. You're both pathetic.'

Apparently we could not.

'Why am I pathetic?' I yelped. 'What did I do?'

In her temper, Sarah threw her juice glass into the plush carpeting, where it landed with a soft plop, and stormed out of the lounge and back into the dressing room.

'Bloody hell.' I buried my face in my hands. 'You do realize she's our lift, don't you? And, you know, our best friend?'

'I can't believe you didn't stand up for me,' Lauren said, snapping. 'I can't believe you let her say those things about me.'

'To be fair, you both said some fairly unpleasant things,' I reminded her. 'You know she's sensitive right now.'

'She's never sensitive,' she shouted. 'She's a robot. That's why Steve left her in the first place. He told Michael. He's sick of it.'

And then, you know, I had to ask. Against every ounce of my better judgement, I had to. 'What else did he say?'

'That's pretty much it.' Lauren looked almost as disappointed as I felt. 'He said he was bored and that she's more invested in her job and her friends than him. He felt like he didn't exist and he wants someone who's going to put him first, stay home with the kids, be a real wife.'

Oh, damn you, conflicting emotions. On the one hand, of course everyone wanted to feel valued by their partner, but on the other, it sounded ever so slightly awful. Like Stephen believed that Sarah shouldn't be invested in her career and her friends. I hoped that Lauren was telling the story wrong and that Sarah hadn't inadvertently married a sexist pig who belonged back in the fifties with a desperate housewife pumped full of Valium.

'He told Michael they had this huge argument a while back, where he wanted her to quit work to have a baby and he said he would take care of them both,' she went on. 'But she refused to give up, and he said he thought mothers ought to make their kids a priority and not their jobs, and she went crazy, and that's when he decided he'd had enough.'

Oh, fuckityfucknuts.

I remembered that argument. Sarah and I had drowned it in G&Ts the next night and I'd reassured her that he couldn't possibly mean it and that it wasn't the past and that he was just giving an extreme example. It was six months ago.

Stephen had been planning to leave her for six months and she hadn't known.

'He's totally right to be pissed with her,' Lauren said confidently. 'He wanted to take care of the family and she was just a big old bitch about it.'

'*No way,*' I screeched so loudly even I was shocked. 'You can't seriously think that Sarah should have to give up her job to have kids because that's what her husband wants?'

'She doesn't like that job anyway,' she rationalized. 'And he makes enough money to pay for everything. Marriage is about compromise.'

'I can't believe you're saying this.' I watched as she calmly crossed her legs and sipped her juice; it was as though the last five minutes had never happened, never mind the last fifty years. 'Especially after yesterday.'

'Like you said, it was just cold feet,' she replied. In that moment I realized she might be a daddy's girl, but she could just as easily be her mother's daughter. 'Maybe if you had spent more time on your relationship instead of at work, Seb wouldn't have left either.'

'Excuse me, ladies.' The locker-room attendant stuck her head through the door.

'I would love another drink, thank you,' Lauren said, the picture of suffering.

'Actually, that's not what I was going to say,' the attendant said, the picture of awkwardness. 'I'm going to have to ask you to keep your voices a little lower. You're upsetting our other clients.'

'Oh my God, I'm so sorry,' Lauren replied immediately. 'I apologize.'

The woman smiled sweetly and disappeared back into the locker room.

I stared hard at my friend.

'What?' she asked. 'Why are you looking at me like that?'

'I don't think I'm in the mood for a massage now,' I said. 'I'll see you back in the room.'

'You can't leave,' Lauren called after me. 'It's my hen party.'

'Bloody funny party if you ask me,' I muttered under my breath.

The wedding is getting closer! By now, all the major details are arranged and your bride needs your support to make sure she hasn't missed anything. The checklist below will make sure you're not missing anything – however big or small!

Bridal gown [✔]
(Ordered with an additional 'premium' fee to make sure it's ready on time that is so extortionate, it would more or less pay for your average wedding.)
Bridesmaid dresses [✔]
(Ordered against Lauren's wishes.)
Transport for the bride and groom [✔]
(The last vintage Rolls Royce available in all of the British Isles.)
Venue [✔]
(Private home bribed into letting us host there with the promise of a spread in a top bridal magazine.)
Catering [✔]
(All done except for Lauren's mother and sister who have decided they are gluten-free, lactose-free, sugar-free pescatarians, i.e. wankers.)
Flowers [✔]
(As long as someone can find a thousand pink peonies in season in August, we're laughing.)
Photographer [✔]
(At last, having a photographer brother pays off.)
Officiant [✔]
(At last, having a mental friend who had himself ordained on the Internet pays off.)
Table and chair hire [✔]
(The only thing that was easy.)

Entertainment [✓]
(Couldn't get Beyoncé, daren't tell Lauren.)
Table plan [✓]
Subject to final approval. Again.
Place cards [✓]
Favours [✓]
(Disgusting Hershey's kisses as long as Lauren's cousin remembers to bring them. Which she won't.)
Anything else you need to add?
Flip-flops for dancing [✓]
Fireworks [✓]
Bubbles instead of confetti [✓]
Convince bride and bridesmaid to start speaking to each other again [ ]

18

Wednesday July 22nd

Today I feel: Ask me again tomorrow.
Today I am thankful for: British reserve.

'So tell me, how are things going with the Dickenson party?'

'It was a bit of a rough start,' I said, quickly combing stray strands of hair behind my ears. 'But it's all under control now. It's this Saturday.'

It was almost two months since Matilda had pulled me into the bogs and insisted I apply for the promotion. I'd been so consumed with planning the Dickenson party, planning Lauren's wedding, counselling Sarah and trying to remember how to be a girlfriend to Will, I'd forgotten I was technically still interviewing for the job.

Being dragged into the meeting room for an impromptu catch-up with her and Mr Colton was not how I wanted to be reminded.

'Are you sure?' Matilda asked. 'I've noticed you putting in a lot of late nights and early mornings.'

'The Dickenson party is fine,' I insisted. Since when was it a bad thing to work late? 'It's going to be great. They had some very elaborate ideas that I had to manage, but we're all on the same page now.'

Meaning they decided they didn't need Michael Bublé to perform when I told them how much he charged per hour and Christopher said he'd want a blow-job for that money and Andrew started to cry and dear God that was a long afternoon.

'Do you feel as though you could take on all the responsibilities of an event planner full time?' Mr Colton asked. Matilda, sitting beside him, was giving me tiny little nods.

'I do,' I said, trying to look very confident and excited about the opportunity. 'I'm very confident and excited about the opportunity.'

'Very glad to hear it,' Mr Colton said, a stern smile on his face as he stood up and headed for the door. 'We'll speak again after the event on Saturday. I look forward to hearing all about it. I'll leave you with Matilda to go over the next steps.'

'Next steps?' I asked as he closed the glass door carefully behind him and went straight over to Shona's office. Eurgh. 'I don't just get the job?'

'We have to interview,' Matilda said. 'Because we advertised. And Mr Colton always likes to talk to outside candidates, even if we're planning an internal hire. It's good to get perspective.'

'When are the interviews?' I asked. I wanted to be on top of my game on the day my competitors were coming in and not caught out unawares like I had been today. I also wanted to be wearing a considerably more professional outfit than a crazy cat lady T-shirt your boyfriend has bought you as a joke and a tartan mini kilt.

'They're today,' Matilda replied.

So much for that.

'Don't worry,' she said, gathering her notebook and coffee mug and standing up. 'It really is just procedure. The candidates are interesting, but, without wanting to get myself into trouble, all you need is a glowing reference from this party on Saturday and you're fine.'

'As long as I don't need a glowing reference from Shona.' I looked over at her office and seized up when I saw Colton knocking on the door and letting himself in. 'She's been extra twatty lately.'

'That's because she's a twat,' Matilda replied. 'I didn't say that.'

'What am I going to do?' I asked. 'Go to HR?'

With a reassuring pat on the shoulder, Matilda left me in the meeting room with a plate full of biscuits. So I did what any woman would do who had two days to pull off a party that would make or break her career. I settled in to eat those biscuits.

In the three weeks since the hen from hell, things had gone from bad to worse with Lauren and Sarah. Lovely, funny, generous Lauren had become a fully-fledged Bridezilla, incapable of discussing anything unrelated to her wedding, and reserved, witty, dry Sarah had become incapable of discussing anything at all. It didn't matter how many times I reminded her I had been on her side at the hen, that I was Team Sarah, she was still avoiding me, answering my texts with one-word responses and claiming to be too busy to see me when I suggested we hung out. And I'd spent the last three weeks doing some call-dodging of my own, as Lauren's mother rang every day, sometimes several times a day (like mother, like daughter) and so I was constantly on red alert for unknown numbers. Imagine if I accidently answered it . . . The horror.

I hadn't realized how much time I spent talking to the two of them until all that talking went away. No texts, no tweets, no Facebook posts, Instagram tags, IMs, emails, phone calls, nothing. On one hand, it gave me enough time to stay on top of my job and catch up with the last season of *Downton Abbey*, but it also left a gaping friendship-shaped hole in my life that could not be filled by my sister's occasional passive-aggressive texts and Sharaline's attempts at daily conversation. Although, to be fair, I now knew a lot more about Snapchat and could use the phrase 'on fleek' in conversation

Breaking my second chocolate Hobnob in half, I opened my inbox on my phone and scanned. Supplier, supplier, Lauren, Lauren, Lauren, Topshop, supplier, Tom Wheeler.

Tom.

I'd almost forgotten about him. Him and the most awful one a.m. conversation I had ever had with a client. Worryingly I'd had a few of those, but usually because they were freaking out and not because I was drunk and not paying proper attention to who I was texting.

Without Sarah or Lauren to bring him up constantly, he really hadn't crossed my mind. His event was two months away and I had a globophobic baby-naming ceremony and the wedding of a woman who – whisper it – I wasn't convinced was entirely sure she wanted to get married to get out of way before then. Two months felt like a lifetime.

Dear Maddie,

Might as well eat the rest of that Hobnob, I reasoned as I read on.

Just checking in on the sixtieth birthday party. I've had some ideas and I'd love to discuss them with you. Would a meeting tomorrow after work be possible?
Best wishes, Tom Wheeler

The last message Will had sent me was a photo of a pack of condoms and a smiley-face.

I was still debating my response, my third Hobnob hanging out of my mouth, when I walked out of the meeting room and right into Matilda and the first interviewee.

Sarah.

'Hi,' she said. 'You've got chocolate on your, well, everywhere.'

It's hard to talk with a chocolate biscuit wedged in your mouth. I shoved my notebook between my knees to free up a hand and took it out.

'Hello,' I replied, wiping my face with the back of my hand. 'You're here?'

'For the interview.' She glanced over at a confused-looking Matilda. 'For the event planner job.'

'Right,' I said, totally blindsided. 'You didn't tell me?'

'Friends don't tell each other everything,' she said, turning her back on me. 'I'll let you get on. I'm sure you're busy.'

'Maddie, you've got a little something,' Colton said, pointing at his face as he left Shona's office and followed my best friend and the head of HR into his.

Instead of going back to my desk, I did what all women do when they're losing their minds at work. I went to the disabled toilet, threw my stuff on the floor, sat on the lav and cried.

Sure, Matilda had said they were just talking to people because they had to, but after ten minutes in a room with Sarah, that would all be out the window. She was completely qualified for the job, and she was wearing a suit instead of an outfit Miley Cyrus wouldn't be seen dead in. And without Shona trying to sabotage her every fifteen minutes, she'd probably be a lot better at it than I was. She was definitely going to get it. I was definitely going to get fired. And then I'd be unemployed and then I'd be homeless and then I'd be living on the streets and then I'd get eaten by Alsatians and no one at Lauren's wedding would even notice.

Or even worse, Mum and Dad would make me go back to uni to get my PGCE and I'd have to be a teacher. All those kids, every single day?

I couldn't do it. I'd rather be eaten by Alsatians.

A sharp rap on the toilet door, followed by the voice of the last person I wanted to speak to. 'Maddie, are you in there? Can I see you in my office?'

'Yes, Shona,' I replied. 'One minute, Shona.'

Well, at least the day was about to hit its lowest point. Things couldn't get any worse after this.

'Come in, shut the door.'

Shona was all smiles when I sloped in five minutes later. She always made a huge show of making everyone shut the door when they came to her office, even though the walls were glass and everyone could see and, thanks to her seagull-like squawk of a voice, hear everything that went on inside. 'Sit down. It's ages since we had a proper catch-up.'

'I haven't got my notes with me,' I said, holding up my empty hands. 'What do you want to catch up about?'

'Just things in general.' She motioned for me to sit down. 'You're still getting on fine with Sharaline? Things are working out?'

'I haven't worked with her since you pulled her out of the Dickenson meeting,' I said. 'Which I'm sure you already know.'

'Well, I find she's very good,' Shona replied. 'You would never believe she's so young. She's picking things up so quickly, she'll be taking my job before you know it.'

'Right.'

I hoped it was true; she'd more or less already got mine. Maybe I could be Sharaline's assistant.

'Mr Colton came to ask how I thought you were getting on with your new responsibilities.' She pushed a box of mints towards me and I shook my head. 'No, really, have one,' she insisted, wrinkling her nose. 'No one wants coffee breath.'

I took a mint and sighed. I hadn't had any coffee.

'I'm probably not supposed to talk you about this, am I?' she asked, dropping her voice to a theatrical whisper. 'It's probably supposed to stay confidential.'

'I don't think it matters.' I folded my arms in front of me. 'You don't have to tell me if you don't want to. I'm sure I'll survive.'

'No, I'm sure it's fine,' she said. She flapped away her concerns and closed the box of mints without taking one herself. 'I told him I hadn't had any complaints.'

That was big of her.

'But I did have to tell him that Sharaline's been shouldering the bulk of your responsibilities so you have had an awful lot of time to dedicate to your one project,' she added.

'What haven't I been doing?' I asked, fully aware that I was spoiling for a fight. 'I'm still doing all the invoicing, all the scheduling, I'm at every event two hours before you and at least one after you leave. What exactly is she doing that I'm not?'

For once, I was too tired and too annoyed to mince my words. I was fucked off and I didn't care who knew it.

'I've been giving Sharaline some elevated responsibilities.' Shona flinched slightly then carried on, her outstretched fingers curling up into claws. 'They're not things I would have given you to do. They're more creative than the usual admin stuff.'

'I'm sure she's doing a fabulous job,' I said, standing up to leave. When neither of us wanted to back down, our meetings were usually brief. She only really enjoyed making me feel like shit when I lay down like a doormat and let her. 'Is that it? I've got quite a lot to do.'

'Best to get things all wrapped up,' she agreed. 'Before the party, I mean.'

'Yeah, OK.' I shook my head, breathing out wearily. And it was only half-past ten. 'Whatever, Shona.'

'Oh, Maddie.'

'Yes?'

'Was that your friend Sarah I saw going into HR just now?'

I turned back to look at her.

'Yes.'

'Interviewing for the event planner job?'

Shona was smiling.

'Yes.'

'That must be uncomfortable, competing with your best friend for the same job,' she said. I turned back, but she was too busy checking something in a notebook on her desk to look at me. 'Her CV was amazing. She's got to be a contender.'

'It was amazing,' I agreed. 'She's very good.'

'I'd definitely hire her, anyway.' She scribbled in her notebook and then looked up at me, mini skirt, crazy cat T-shirt, chocolate-covered face and all. 'That's all. Didn't you say you had a lot to do?'

'How did you get her CV?' I asked softly.

'It was on your desk,' she said, not even attempting to lie. 'You've been so busy, I didn't know whether or not you'd remember to pass it on yourself.'

I didn't say a word.

'What?' Shona looked so pleased with herself. 'I was doing you a favour.'

'It wasn't on my desk,' I said. 'It was in a drawer, in my desk.'

'And in your emails,' Shona added. 'She sent it through, what, seven times? She really wants that job, doesn't she? And she's definitely qualified.'

I stood in front of her in the same spot I'd stood in for the last decade and looked down at her in her over-sized leather executive chair. And I'd had enough.

'What is wrong with you?' I asked. 'Seriously? What is actually wrong with you?'

'Excuse me?' Shona blinked, her giant tarantula lashes flapping up and down.

'I don't get it,' I said, as much to myself as to her. 'Are you fundamentally damaged in some way, or do you just get off on being a massive bitch?'

Now it was Shona's turn to be struck dumb.

'No, really, just tell me.' My voice was getting louder and I caught Sharaline looking over out of the corner of my eye. 'What is it? What exactly did I do to make you behave like such an utter shit?'

'I don't know what you're talking about,' she replied. 'But I would appreciate it if you would lower your voice.'

'I'd love to, but I don't seem to be able to right now,' I said. 'I don't know what to do any more – I'm at my wits' end with this. Whatever did I do to you to make you treat me like this?'

'I don't treat you any differently to anyone else,' she said, leaning back in her chair as though I'd actually hit her. 'If anyone has a problem, it's you.'

'No, I'm fairly certain it isn't,' I replied. 'I work my arse off, I do everything you ask me to do, I never complain, I never mess up, and yet you still talk to me like I'm some reality TV reject. Nothing I do is good enough, nothing I say is clever enough. I don't get it.'

'I'm sorry you're sad that I don't want to be your best friend,' Shona said, standing up and placing her hands on either side of her computer keyboard. 'But I haven't got time for BFFs in the office. You think I'm a bitch? I'm not a bitch. This is what it takes for people to take you seriously. I don't care if you don't like me.'

I shook my head. 'No,' I said. 'I don't believe that. I don't believe that women have to treat each other like shit to get ahead. You are basically the anti-Beyoncé. You can't treat people the way you do and expect no one to say anything.'

'But no one ever has,' she replied triumphantly. 'And I'm still your boss.'

'I'm saying it now.' I pushed my chair into her desk, letting it clatter to a standstill. 'This stops. The way you talk to me, the way you talk to Sharaline. It stops. We're not idiots, we're not your whipping boys, we're not your slaves – we work for you. Why, I'm not quite sure.'

'Because no one else would have you?' she suggested. Her voice was steady as ever, but two high-spots of colour lit up her heavily powdered cheeks.

'I know that's what you want me to believe,' I said, smiling and pointing at her as I made for the door. 'But it's not true. I'm good at my job, Shona, and that is because I learned what to do from you. And what not to do. But I don't want to be you. Sorry if any of this came as a shock – I should have said it years ago.'

Before she could say anything else, I walked out of the door and shut it carefully and quietly behind me. Every single face in the office was staring at me, jaws gaping, and there was barely a sound, save the odd phone ringing in the background.

Without a word, I sat down at my desk, my heart pounding, waiting for retribution. I risked a glance up at Shona's office just in time to meet her eye as she dropped her blinds with one swift, sharp movement.

'Maddie . . .' Sharaline coughed across the desk, her voice breaking as she spoke my name. I'm not sure why she would struggle with it – it was a perfectly normal name. Oh. That was probably why. 'I just wanted to say something.'

'Can you make it quick?' I asked, a bright, brisk smile on my face as I grabbed a pile of paperwork and unopened mail and shoved it in my handbag.

'I know you think I'm an arse-kisser.' Her eyes were gleaming with admiration. 'But I'm not. I'm sorry if I've made things difficult while I've been here.'

'Don't worry about it,' I replied. 'The only person who has made "things" difficult is Glenn Close in there.'

'I don't know who that is,' she said.

Of course she didn't.

'I'm not trying to take your job,' Sharaline said, finally finding her voice. 'It's just that, Shona . . . man. She scares me shitless.'

Handbag on shoulder, heels switched for flats, I was ready to go. I had to get out of the office before Sarah came out of her interview. 'That just proves you're not mentally deranged and that you're far too good for this place. You'll be fine,' I told her.

'She said she thought I was going to be a scouse stripper before she met me,' she whispered. 'It was so mean. It's not like my name is that weird, is it?'

'It is quite weird,' I said, shrugging. No point in lying to the poor girl. 'But it doesn't matter. You're going to be fine.'

It seemed like the right thing to say at the time, even if it was a flat-out lie. I shrugged at her look of disbelief and ran for the back stairs.

Working from home was my favourite because working from home really meant putting on my pyjamas, turning on the telly and not giving a single fuck about anything for the rest of the day. I'd managed a whole three hours of truly appalling television before I even bothered to get my phone out of my handbag. Alongside the assorted receipts, half-full packets of chewing gum and tampon after tampon after tampon, there was a small square package in the middle of the mail I'd taken from my desk. Interest piqued, I tore open the brown paper to find a CD case.

The Best of Etta James.

A small square of white card fluttered to the floor, and, rather than touch it, I leaned over the edge of the sofa to read it from a safe distance.

'*Dear Maddie,*' I read aloud. '*A small thank you for all the work you've done so far. I hope you enjoy Etta's music as much as I do. Best wishes, Tom Wheeler.*'

Oh.

Bloody hell.

Still hanging half off the settee, CD in my sweaty paws, I heard a knock at the door.

'Not today, thank you,' I muttered, unable to tear my eyes away from Tom's note. The little buzz I always felt when he sent me a text spread across my shoulders and shivered all the way down my back.

'Just a nice gesture,' I told myself, shaking off any other possibility and wondering where on earth my CD player might be. 'What a gent.'

Whoever was at the door had no time for my duvet day. The knocking turned into banging, the banging turned into hammering, and then, just as I was considering calling the police, it stopped. And then my phone beeped with a new text.

Answer the bloody door, you slag.

It was Sarah.

Sitting up, I tossed the CD onto the coffee table, rubbed any stray mascara away from under my eyes and tried to straighten my hair. Sarah had seen me in every single state possible, but I felt weird seeing her now, looking such a mess.

'Maddie, I know you're there,' she shouted through the letterbox. 'Bloody let me in.'

'How do you know?' I shouted back.

'Because I saw you screaming at your boss and storming out of the office and where else would you be? Your parents' house? Open the bloody door. I can't let myself in – I forgot my key.'

'And it's usually considered a bit rude to let yourself into someone's house when you've been ignoring them for two weeks,' I said, opening the door. 'Hello.'

'Hello yourself,' she replied, massive Tesco bag in her hand. 'Nice PJs.'

'Nice suit.' I watched from a safe distance as she emptied the bag on the kitchen surface. Biscuits, teabags, milk (I never had milk), tonic water (I always had gin). No visible weapon. I closed the door and followed her into the kitchen. 'I can't believe you didn't tell me you were coming in.'

'I did!' She filled the kettle and gave me a funny look. 'What are you talking about?'

Hmm. I checked my phone and reread my last message from her. *Can't talk, Mat just called. Prepping for tomoz. Thank you!!!*

Ohhhh.

'You meant Matilda,' I said, opening the biscuits. Priorities.

'Who did you think I meant?'

'A random man called Matt?'

'And why did you think I was thanking you?'

'I assumed it was a general thank you to the universe.' I couldn't really add that I had been engaged in some sexting with Will and hadn't read her message properly.

'You thought I would be so happy to get a text message

from a man called Matt that I was shouting "thank you" out to the universe?'

I shrugged.

'Oh, piss off and drink your tea.'

Snatching up the biscuits, I hurled myself onto the settee. No biscuits for Sarah.

'Sounded like you and Shona were having a very healthy conversation,' she said, settling herself in her favourite chair. 'Are you all right?'

I paused mid-dunk. 'You could hear it?'

'Maddie, there are wallabies in Australia tweeting about it,' Sarah replied. 'Everyone could hear.'

'Do you think Mr Colton heard?'

She blew on her tea before speaking. 'Maddie. Wallabies. Tweeting.'

'Fuck.'

It probably wouldn't work for me when it came to my promotion.

'The interview went well, though,' Sarah said, smiling and looking generally happier than I'd seen her in months. 'I think they liked me. I know I keep going on about it, but how cool would it be for us to work together?'

'You've stopped sulking now then, have you?' I asked, dodging her question. Because it would not be cool. Because it would be horrible. Because it would take about seven seconds for Shona to tell her I had never handed in her CV and had tried to keep the event planner job for myself.

'I'm sorry,' she said. 'I needed to spend some time on my own, work some stuff out.'

'What did you work out?' I asked.

She grabbed one of the biscuits from out of my lap. 'That I'm going to die alone.'

'That's not true,' I said. 'We'll get you some nice pets. What lives for ages? A nice tortoise or something.'

'Brilliant.'

'Eat that biscuit,' I ordered. 'You look horribly thin.'

Her face brightened immediately. 'Thanks!'

'It wasn't a compliment,' I replied. 'If your bridesmaid dress doesn't fit, I'm going to kill you.'

'We both know it's a compliment,' Sarah said, sucking in her cheekbones and prodding them happily. 'And this feels very weird to say, but I haven't actually spoken to Lauren since the hen night. I don't know if she still wants me to be her bridesmaid.'

'Let's find out, shall we?' I asked, waving my phone at her as Lauren's name lit up the screen. I'd say it was awfully convenient, but she had taken to calling me at least ten times a day to ask wedding questions, and I was overdue.

'Hi,' I started, putting her on speakerphone. 'What's—'

'My mom just called and she needs to know what colour butterflies you've ordered.'

'Why?' I asked.

'Because she wants them to match her hat?' she replied as though it was obvious.

If I was being entirely honest with myself, if anyone should be applying for the wedding-planner job right now, it was her. She had questions I'd never even dreamed of. No, I didn't have the ingredients list for the liquid we were putting in the bubble machine. No, I didn't know whether the floors of the venue were being cleaned with oil or wax. No, I didn't know if the fireworks we were using at the end of the night had been ethically sourced. I didn't know if fireworks could be unethically sourced. When I asked if it genuinely mattered, she gasped and hung up on me. I know being morally sound is important, but there was a time and place. I'd never been convinced that the doner kebabs at the end of my street were one hundred per cent lamb, but I choose not to ask questions. I wish she would adopt the same bloody attitude.

'I don't know off the top of my head.' I rolled my eyes at Sarah who replied with a 'what do you expect' eyebrow raise. 'Let me get my emails up and check.'

'Are you home yet? I'm just round the corner from you,' Lauren replied. 'I'll come over. I've got some more stuff I want to go through.'

Sarah began vehemently shaking her head and very, very nearly spilt her tea on my new rug. Not cool, Sarah.

'OK, I'm home,' I said, slapping Sarah away. 'But—'

'I'll be there in five minutes,' she said, cutting me off. 'I can't stay long, I have plans, so if you could have my planner ready, that would be great.' And she hung up.

What was that I was feeling? Oh, that's it, over-whelming rage. There's nothing like being treated as though you're an employee by one of your alleged best friends. Especially when she's not paying you a penny.

There was a long pause.

'She talks to you like that? When you're doing her a favour?' Sarah raised an eyebrow at me and for one small second I felt slightly less alone.

Rather than answer Sarah, I slowly lowered my head until it was resting on the coffee table and banged it gently a few times. Then I turned my head and looked at Sarah. Time to take advantage of this détente.

'You guys are going to have a talk. Now.'

'Right, so I'll see you later.' Sarah chugged her tea and stood up. 'Hopefully at work.'

'You can sit right back down,' I demanded. 'If you can talk to me, you can talk to her.'

'You didn't tell me my husband left me because I'm a bitch,' she replied. 'Until she apologizes, I'm not talking to her.'

I shook my head. 'Well, that's going to make the wedding very difficult, isn't it? Sit your arse down. We're sorting this out.'

Sarah narrowed her eyes until they were just bright blue slits and grabbed the biscuits from the settee. By the time Lauren knocked on my door, she had eaten five caramel digestives and not spoken a word.

'Hey, so Mom emailed me a long list of questions and I need to get back to her before my great-aunt Evelyn books her flight,' she said, pushing past me up the stairs. 'She's gluten-intolerant, lactose-intolerant and she has a peanut allergy so—'

She stopped dead in the doorway at the sight of Sarah stuffing her face in the living room.

'Hi,' she said, tossing her hair like a slightly put-out pony. 'I didn't know you were here.'

'Ta-da.' Sarah waved her hands around in the air, biscuit crumbs going everywhere.

'I'll go and get the organizer,' I said, shoving Lauren into the living room while she continued to flip her hair around like a tit. 'You two play nicely.'

I closed my bedroom door, pressing my ear to the wood. I don't know what I was hoping to hear exactly; just not blood-curdling screams.

'You're looking well,' Lauren said, her painfully polite upbringing getting the better of her and breaking the silence.

'Thanks,' Sarah replied. 'Turns out you eat a lot less when you're not cooking for someone else.'

'Yeah.'

'Yeah.'

Come on, kids, I thought, crossing my fingers. You can do it.

'I've been busy too. I kept meaning to call you but all this wedding stuff kept getting in the way.'

'Like you being a knob?'

Nice one, Sarah. I banged my forehead gently against the wall.

'More like you being a knob,' Lauren replied. 'You, like, totally ruined my bachelorette.'

'I, like, totally ruined it?'

Silence. I hoped neither of them was stabbing the other. I really did like my rug.

'I guess the whole thing was kind of a disaster,' Lauren relented. 'I said some pretty horrible things.'

'Yeah, you did,' Sarah agreed. There was a slightly too long pause and I nibbled at my thumbnail. 'And so did I. I'm sorry.'

Phew.

'I maybe kind of overreacted about things,' Lauren said slowly. 'I'm sorry too.'

'Are we all done now?' I left the sanctuary of my bedroom, armed with Lauren's wedding planner, and found the pair of them sitting side by side on the settee, happily eating the last two biscuits in the packet. 'Are we playing nicely?'

'I finished the biscuits,' Sarah said, holding her hand over her mouth. 'Sorry.'

She wasn't really.

A wedding is a beautiful occasion, not just the union of two people beginning a life together. It is a time to celebrate happiness and love, not only for the bride and groom, but for everyone – our friends, our family, those we have lost, those we will find.
Use this section to celebrate the love in your life!

I am grateful for the people who have brought love into my life:
Sarah
Lauren
Mum & Dad
Dan & Eleanor
Jon Hamm
The blonde lady in Starbucks who always get my name right and remembers I want soy milk.

Will?

Three things that make me happy are:
Sleeping in
Using the spirit level app on my iPhone
Watching *Bake Off* with my friends and saying we're going to bake cakes for each other but then not doing it and ordering pizza instead

What does love look like to you?
Michael Fassbender

Describe your dream partner (of if you're already with them, stick in a photograph!):
Tall, all his own hair, piercing eyes, strong arms, excellent

at hugs, clever enough to read a newspaper every day but still watches telly. Makes me laugh, can cook, drives (and has nice car), knows when to take me to bed and make sweet, sweet love and when to bend me over settee and give me a good seeing-to. Loves animals and children. But not in a creepy way.

19

Thursday July 23rd
Today I feel: Bleururuueuugh.
Today I am thankful for: Bleururuueuugh.

I really wish Lauren had never given me this journal, I really do. If you looked at my Facebook page from the last couple of months (which I like to think Seb still does from time to time), you would think I've been having the time of my life. Girls' nights out with Sarah, wedding planning with Lauren, quick jaunt to the country, carefully alluded-to burgeoning romance, artfully shot cocktail after artfully shot cocktail, and yet, open these pages and HAHAHAHAHAHAHA, giant pile of wankery upon giant pile of wankery.

And yet the best is still to come.

Behold! The greatest pile of wankery ever to be committed to paper!

'Sorry I'm late. Tube nightmare,' I said, peeling off my jacket as I walked into the Plumtree to find Tom sitting in the same seat Sarah and I had occupied two months before.

'Not a problem,' he replied, handing me the drinks menu. 'Glad you could do this late. Sorry it's out of hours.'

'All part of the job,' I said. 'Not many people can meet in person from nine to five.'

That part was true. The tube being a nightmare was not. After our 'chat' Shona had decided to 'take meetings out of the office' for the rest of the week, leaving me and Sharaline up shit creek with no paddle. Which is a funny sentence until you realize it means you're going to be up to your elbows in shit, trying to row to shore.

By the end of the day today, Sharaline had cried twice and I'd had to go on an emergency doughnut run just to stop her from quitting. We were thirty-six hours away from the Dickenson baby-naming ceremony and everything that had come together was falling apart. The last thing I had time for was a drink with Tom, but, bugger me, here I was. Because I still didn't know how to say no. It was a sad day when I had to accept that my big brother had given me good advice, even if I wasn't following it.

'At least we can have a drink.' Tom stood up, leaving me at hip height. Awkward. 'What can I get you?'

'Oh, um, gin and tonic, please?' I supposed I should have been buying the drinks – it was a meeting, after all, and I shouldn't have been drinking at all – but after the day I'd had, a day that wasn't even nearly over, I didn't think one drink could hurt. Because I would never learn. 'Thank you.'

'You're welcome.' He strode off to the bar, and yes, I looked at his bum, but no, it didn't mean anything.

'I'm so sorry about the text message the other week,' I said when he returned from the bar with two stiff drinks and two bags of crisps. 'Totally unprofessional of me.

And thank you for the CD. And sorry for not thanking you for it sooner. Also unprofessional.'

'Not at all,' Tom said, attacking the cheese and onion and shaking his head. 'All fine. Glad you got the CD.'

I didn't dare tell him I still hadn't managed to find the disk drive so I could load it onto my computer, but still, he seemed fine with everything.

'How are the plans going for your friend's wedding?' he asked. 'It's soon, isn't it?'

'Next week,' I confirmed, ripping into the salt and vinegar. 'We've got the bridal shower on Sunday, the rehearsal dinner the Friday after, and then it's just the wedding and . . . done.'

'I don't know what either of those things are,' he said. His fiancée clearly wasn't American. Or she was sane American without a crazed WASP mother entirely up in the air.

'A rehearsal dinner is just that – everyone who's taking part in your wedding shows up for a walk-through at the venue, and then you all have dinner the night before the ceremony. And the bridal shower – well, we've already had the hen night, but . . .' I shuddered involuntarily at the flashbacks. 'Shall we just say it didn't go that great? So we're having a bridal shower too. As far as I can tell, it's afternoon tea with friends, with booze and with presents. I'm just happy it's almost all over.'

'I can imagine weddings aren't easy,' he said, shaking his head. 'So much to organize.'

'Well, yeah – you must know,' I replied, surreptitiously wiping my hands on my skirt underneath the table. This didn't feel like a lick-them-clean kind of situation. 'My mum always kicks off whenever I complain about it. She likes to give me the whole "in my day" speech. Apparently weddings have become horribly overcommercialized.'

'She's in the church service and a buffet in the village hall brigade?' he asked. 'Yeah, mine wasn't that amused when there was talk of hiring an entire hotel for the weekend.'

'Really not that rare these days. I tried to explain that those overcommercialized weddings keep me in a job, but she doesn't get it,' I said, tucking into another crisp. 'Maybe your mum will be more positive about fancy parties after her lovely birthday.'

'Only fancy parties that are for her,' he said with an uncomfortable laugh. 'But at least you won't be a waitress at your friend's wedding.'

'No penguin or panda this time.' I shook my head. 'Posh frock and everything.'

At least, I hoped so. Right now I wouldn't put anything past Lauren.

'You're never going to let me forget that, are you?' he asked, smiling.

It was just a throwaway comment, but it struck me that 'never' didn't mean what it should have, because we weren't an 'us', he was my client. We weren't even friends. He wasn't even my boyfriend's friend. Realistically, after his mother's party, there was literally no reason for us ever to see each other again.

Hmm.

'Shall we catch up on where we are with everything?' I asked, washing down my crisps with a far too large swig of gin and trying not to splutter all over my notebook. 'I'm sure you don't want to be here all night.'

'It's fine.' Was it my imagination or did he look a tiny

bit deflated? 'No exciting plans other than to pick up something for dinner that I can't ruin in a microwave.'

I laughed politely. His fiancée didn't look like much of a cook in those Facebook photos from the wedding. You couldn't possibly have such well-toned arms and be a good cook. Unless you were doing a lot of risotto. All that stirring.

'Are you doing anything this evening?' he asked, sipping his pint.

I shook my head. 'Quiet night in,' I told him. He probably didn't want to hear about my plans to send his not-a-friend a photo of my tits. And I probably didn't want to tell him. 'I've still got some work to do, so it's going to be laptop, bubble bath and then bed.'

'Sounds lovely,' Tom replied. 'I mean, not for me, obviously. Can you imagine me in a bubble bath?'

I didn't say anything because if I put my mind to it, I could. This was all Will's fault – why hadn't he been over all week? You can't start giving a girl a regular seeing-to and then disappear on her for six whole days; it wasn't fair. I was running around town with a dangerous level of hormones and it wasn't safe.

'I'm so sorry, I haven't even asked,' I said, turning the conversation back to a nice safe topic that made me want to do a sick. 'When is your wedding?'

Tom choked, spitting a mouthful of bitter back into his pint. 'Excuse me?'

'Your wedding?'

'Are you trying to be funny?' he asked.

'Hardly ever,' I replied.

'There is no wedding,' he said, his face falling. 'We broke up two months ago. At Ian's wedding. When I met you.'

Thank God I had a big glass of gin and a full bag of crisps in front of me.

'You broke up with your fiancée when you met me?'

'No, no, I didn't mean it like that,' he corrected himself. I was still thankful for the gin. 'I meant we broke up during the wedding at which we met.'

'That's shit timing by anyone's standards,' I said, relieved, and, as the daughter of two English graduates, appreciative of his proper use of grammar. 'I'm sorry.'

'It's for the best.' Tom looked down at the table and then back up at me with renewed certainty. 'Especially since she'd been shagging someone else.'

'I won't ask whether or not you're going to get back together, then.' I bit my lip and curled in my shoulders. What do you say to a man when he's been cheated on, dumped at his mate's wedding and has cancelled his own? I couldn't hug him and give him ice cream and tell him his ex was a bastard. Oh, wait, I could do that last bit.

'She must be a right bastard.'

'I'm sorry, I thought you knew,' he said, pushing a salt and vinegar crisp around the table. 'What with Will . . . well, you know.'

Oh. There was that awful sense of vomitty terror I hadn't been missing ever.

'He didn't! Not with your fiancée?'

'Oh God no,' Tom's eyes widened. 'Well, not with her, anyway. He did shag my girlfriend at law school after I dropped out when my dad died, but those things happen.'

I choked on my gin. Was that what Will was talking about? The chip on Tom's shoulder? It was a perfectly understandable bigger than average chip, but he seemed fairly OK with it at this moment.

'No, he didn't do the deed with this one,' he went on,

Always the Bridesmaid

'but he was the one who decided to tell me all about it,' he said. 'He thought I knew, apparently.'

'But he didn't really?' I asked, recognizing the tone in his voice.

'No,' Tom replied. 'No, he did not.'

Eurgh. That was such a Shona thing to do. I didn't like hearing that about my boyfriend, but Tom had no reason to lie. It wasn't as though Will had shagged his missus, just chosen to be the bearer of bad news. He wasn't a scumbag, just a bit of a shit. Although, from the sounds of it, he was a scumbag at uni.

'She shagged Ian. The groom.'

'What?' I asked. I couldn't have heard him right.

'The groom,' he repeated. 'By all accounts, they'd had a drunken thing just before he got engaged when we were on a break, she thought it meant more than it did, she asked him to leave Emma and he said no, so she decided to stick with me. Until I found out.'

This was not the kind of thing I wanted to hear a week before my uncertain friend's wedding. Where were all the fairy-tale love stories? I thought back to Will's best man speech, how he'd said Ian hadn't even looked at another woman from the moment he'd met Emma and how I'd swooned. What a liar. And what a lie.

'Hang on a minute.' I folded my arms across my chest. 'Your fiancée had been sleeping with the groom?'

'Yes.'

'And you were his usher?'

'Yes.'

'And Will, the best man, knew all about it?'

'That's right.'

'Jesus Christ.'

'It was an age ago,' he said, breathing in and then out,

very hard. 'I'm sure it all would have stayed buried if Will hadn't decided to share it with me on the way out of the church.'

'Christ almighty,' I muttered. 'And you would have been happy with that?'

'I was happy before I knew,' he shrugged. 'No point wondering now, is there? I suppose in some twisted way, Will did me a favour.'

'He's all heart,' I said weakly. 'I'm sorry.'

'Don't be,' he said. 'It's not your fault and it's all sorted now. Me and Ian had it out, no harm done.'

'I've got to say,' I said, sitting back in my chair and resting my glass on my chest, 'you seem to be dealing with this incredibly well.'

'It's been two months – I've had some time,' he replied, rubbing his left eyebrow. 'And I knew things were on a rocky road. I suppose I just didn't want to admit it to myself. I think I always knew we wouldn't actually get married. I'm not sure why we ever got engaged.'

I pushed my hair out of my face and sighed. Everyone's story is different. Everyone's story is the same. But something didn't add up. Either Tom was an amazing actor, or he didn't have nearly so much of a problem with Will's past behaviour as Will seemed to think he did.

'How come everyone else always knows something's wrong?' I asked. 'I didn't know anything was wrong. Am I just incredibly stupid?'

He winced and pushed the cheese and onion crisps towards me. 'So you know about it, then? Christ, I'm sorry, Maddie.'

'How it feels to have someone cheat on you?' I clucked. 'Yeah. Got that covered.'

'I really am sorry.' Tom rested his hand on the table

for a moment before placing it over mine. I looked up at him, Kettle Chips' finest halfway into my mouth. 'I know I should have said something earlier, but it was so awkward, and I didn't know if it was my place, and I didn't want you to be angry at me because, well . . . oh, sod it. Because I like you.'

Before his words could settle, I watched the door open to reveal a beautiful blonde.

'Don't look now,' I said, gripping his hand tightly, 'but your ex just walked in.'

I sat up straight, eyes on the stupidly pretty woman as she parted the waves of lawyers just like Christian Bale did the Red Sea in the Bible. Red Sea? Dead Sea? Someone definitely parted a sea, anyway. I fell asleep halfway through the film. Tom ignored my instructions and looked.

'That's not my ex,' he said. 'That's Vanessa.'

'She was a bridesmaid at the wedding?' I said.

'Yes, Vanessa,' he said again. 'My ex is Maria.'

'But Vanessa was the one who was supposed to pick up the stuff from my office when you came instead,' I told him in case he didn't know.

'I came because she couldn't be bothered and because Will told her he couldn't,' he said. 'Presumably because he knew he would have to go to your office to collect those things from you.'

'I'm not following,' I said, confused, but not too confused to eat another crisp. 'Why wouldn't Will want to see me at work?'

'Because Vanessa is Will's girlfriend,' Tom explained. 'You . . . said you knew?'

Ha, what a joker that Tom was.

'No,' I smiled, glancing across at the blonde woman. 'I'm Will's girlfriend.'

Lindsey Kelk

Tom pressed his mouth into a very, very thin line until it completely disappeared.

'Maddie, we should leave,' he said after a moment's consideration. 'Come on.'

'Why?' I asked, still very confused. 'Why should we leave?'

He was right, we should have left right then.

Tom was still looking at me, clinging to the wooden arms of his chair, when Will walked in through the front door.

'Will!' I jumped up out of my seat and threw myself into his path. 'Hi!'

Will stood stock still, his jacket halfway off his shoulders. 'Hi.'

'Fancy seeing you here. We're going over a few things for Tom's mum's party,' I said, pointing at the angry-looking giant in the tiny chair across from me. 'And then I'm done. With work. And with Tom.'

'Maddie,' Tom said quietly. 'Sit down.'

'What are you doing here?' Will shrugged himself back into his jacket and glanced over at the bar before turning on Tom. 'And what the fuck are you doing here?'

'What she said – we're going through some things for my mum's party and having a drink.' Tom picked up his pint to make his point. 'Don't make a scene.'

'It's a meeting,' I said hastily. 'We're in a meeting.'

'Hi, Tom.' The blonde appeared at Will's side.

'Hi, Vanessa,' Tom replied.

Vanessa smiled at my boyfriend. And then Vanessa kissed my boyfriend. And then I thought I was going to be sick.

'Will?'

'Uh . . .' He looked at his very shiny shoes and didn't

294

say a thing. 'I need a minute, Van, can you go and get us a drink?'

'Yeah, right,' she laughed. 'You go and get the drinks.'

Her legs were so long. I wondered if she had to pay more for her jeans. They clearly had to use so much more material than they did on mine; surely I should be getting a discount? And then she slid her hand into Will's and I forgot about getting shafted by the great designer denim conspiracy and remembered how much I wanted to vomit on her lovely shoes. Why was she touching him? Why was he letting her? When did it get so hot in here? I shouldn't have started that second bag of crisps.

'Are you OK?' Tom reached out to touch my hand but I snatched it away before he could make contact. Hands. Touching. Bad.

'Why are you holding her hand?' I asked. 'Will?'

His name sounded weird in my mouth, as though it didn't mean the same thing any more.

'Why shouldn't he be holding my hand?' Vanessa asked. 'Who are you?'

I mean, it was one thing not to wait to be introduced properly, but that was just downright rude.

'Van, I just need a minute,' Will said again. Maybe it *was* hot in the bar – he looked awfully sweaty. And uncomfortable. And trapped. 'Please.'

She replied with a look that suggested 'Van' didn't appreciate being told what to do and really wasn't used to it.

'Well played, Tom.' Will wiped a hand across his forehead and glared at him. 'I suppose you think this is clever?'

'No, I don't,' Tom replied. 'I'm not you.'

Three years ago, I met Seb's now wife at his firm's

summer party. Even then, I knew she was into him. All touchy-feely and little in-jokes intended to make me feel bad about myself, but I didn't say anything because I genuinely didn't believe he would cheat on me. Whenever I think about that moment, when I was nothing but polite to a woman who was clearly flirting with my boyfriend, I still get angry at myself.

I wasn't going to make the same mistake twice.

'I'm Maddie.' I held out my hand, pushing past Will and Tom to get to the tall, attractive lady. She shook it like a wet fish for a split second then pushed it away. Unpleasant.

'Will, what's going on?' she demanded, throwing her hair around as though we were all trapped in a very bad shampoo ad. 'I'm thirsty.'

'I'm Maddie, I met Will at Ian and Emma's wedding,' I said, answering on his behalf. 'Will? Do you want to say something?'

He guppied his mouth open and closed a couple of times and then shook his head.

It genuinely seemed so impossible. How could this grey-skinned, angry-looking man be the same person who had been naked in my bed just a week ago, wearing my knickers as a hat and reading an article about the importance of exfoliation out loud from the latest issue of *Marie Claire*? All the nights we'd spent together, all the text messages, all the emails and the conversations, and all of it had been a great big load of bollocks.

'Are you his girlfriend?' I asked.

'Yes,' she replied. I'd never heard the word sound more like a threat.

'Then this is horrible,' I said, taking a deep breath and visualizing the scene five minutes from now when we would be knocking back shots at the bar, glad to have the truth out in the open and this wanking, shitting, tosspot of a cheat out of our lives, 'but he and I have been seeing each other. I didn't know he had a girlfriend.'

Other than me, I added silently.

'Are you seriously shagging her?' She turned to Will, pointing at me with a very nice little handbag. 'Her?'

I've got to say, I didn't care for the insinuation in her voice.

'Vanessa, it's nothing, let's not—' He pushed her arm back down by her side. 'She's not—'

'Oh my God.' She screwed up her very pretty face until it wasn't very pretty any more and took a big step back. 'You are. You're shagging that slag.'

This was not the united front of sisterhood I had envisioned. Vanessa turned so she could look at both of us, spreading the full weight of her sneer that turned into a snarl that turned into pure, unadulterated disgust.

'I'm not a slag,' I retorted, jumping to my own defence since there was no one else here to do it for me. 'I didn't know about you.'

Will stared at the floor, very interested in his own shoes.

'How fucking dare you?' she spat.

At me.

It's fair to say I was a bit taken aback. 'Sorry?'

'How dare you shag my boyfriend?' she said, pushing Will out of the way and poking me in the shoulder. 'You absolute slag.'

'Hey!' I held my hands out in front of me, warding off further angry prods. 'Can we drop the "slag" stuff? It isn't helping.'

'You're the one sleeping with my boyfriend,' she

replied, squaring up to me. 'Sounds like a slag to me. A fat, desperate slag.'

'I thought he was my boyfriend,' I snapped back, beginning to lose my temper. Why do women always call each other fat when they really want to cause upset? Such a low blow. 'I didn't know about you.'

'Yeah, whatever,' she said, pushing me backwards. 'You should be ashamed of yourself. I would never do this to another woman.'

'Vanessa.' Tom elbowed his way in between us, but not before she was close enough for me to see what a lovely job she'd done on her eyeliner. Even Sarah would be impressed by that. 'She didn't know. Seriously. It's Will you should be angry with.'

'Don't worry, I am,' she said. 'But this slag needs to know who she's dealing with.'

'We're officially taking slag off the table,' I said, standing on tiptoes to talk to her over Tom's shoulder. 'I'm not a slag, you're not a slag. I didn't know, you didn't know. When you think about it, he cheated on me too.'

'Oh, that is it.' She turned quickly, ducking under Tom's arm – one of the perils of being so tall: he was easy to sneak around – and lunged at me, fists flying.

In all my thirty-one years, brotherly and sisterly slaps aside, I've never actually been hit. Turns out, it really, really hurts.'

'Bloody hell!' I lurched across the table, bashing my hip on a chair for good measure as I went down, and landed heavily on my arse. I pressed my hand to my eye, trying to stem the insane throbbing sensation that started immediately.

Even though I knew the bar was noisy and Vanessa was shouting and Will was shouting and lots of people were looking, everything had gone very quiet in my head. I sat on the floor, holding my face and looking up at two men I thought I knew, trying to hold back a woman I'd never met in order to stop her from kicking the shit out of me. It wasn't the Friday night I'd imagined by a long shot.

I blinked, or rather winked, since my left eye wasn't working, and suddenly someone turned the volume back on and the world resumed normal speed.

'Get off me!' Vanessa was wild with rage, her long hair flying around like a sexy lion. 'I'm going to kill her.'

If it weren't directed at me, I might have been impressed. I've always been the kind of girl who gets bad news, goes home, feels hard done by and then bottles up all the feelings of rage and resentment until they presumably turn into a tumour, but she was incredible, all arms and legs and thrashing Def Leppard hair. I wanted to say something or do something, but I didn't quite know what.

So I just sat there on the floor, nursing my bleeding eyebrow and staring at her.

My boyfriend's girlfriend.

'What are you looking at?' she screamed. 'How dare you? Don't look at me! You don't get to look at me!'

'I'm going to go,' I said, attempting to stand up and then immediately falling back down. Who knew a punch in the face would impact your legs? This is what happens when you wait until your thirties to get decked. I've always been a late bloomer.

Not knowing how long the boys would be able to hold on to her for, I grabbed my bag and, for the want of a pair of working legs, crawled underneath the table and out towards the door.

'Excuse me,' I squeaked as I pushed past the ankles

of a group of very confused drinkers. I hoped they didn't think this was some sort of weird S&M thing as they cleared a path. 'Thank you.'

Happily, it was quite a nice evening to be sitting on a street in London, nursing a newly blackened eye and even newer scuffed-up knees. I rolled over, leaning against the window of the pub, and even though I was outside and on a main road, I could still hear that woman screaming inside.

It was quite a lot to take in. Of course she was angry. I'd been shagging her boyfriend. But I didn't know I'd been shagging her boyfriend and I was angry as well. I felt angry and guilty and upset and disappointed and hurt and oddly proud that a man with a girlfriend that hot would still want to have sex with me, and that feeling sent me right back to the part where I felt guilty again.

'You all right?'

Tom crouched down beside me as a big red bus went past.

'Not really.' I poked my cheekbone gingerly. 'My face hurts.'

'You're going to have a cracking black eye in the morning,' he said, peeling my hand away from my eye and wincing. I wasn't quite sure what he was looking so green about – it was my face that was buggered. 'Should look nice for that bridal shower.'

'Even better for work tomorrow.' I poked it again. It still hurt. Who knew?

'Shall we get you off the floor?' Tom suggested. I glanced around at all the cigarette butts and broken glass and God knows whatever else and nodded. 'Come on.'

He reached down and grabbed me under the arms, pulling me gently to my feet. It was a bit problematic, since he was a good foot taller than me and my legs weren't working properly, but after a couple of near falls, I was more or less vertical and clinging to his arm. Tom stuck his other arm into the road and whistled for a taxi while I made the epic mistake of turning round to look back at the bar.

There they were, Will and Will's girlfriend, sitting in the seats Tom and I had occupied only five minutes earlier. And they were holding hands. He had his big manly hands wrapped around hers, and whatever he was saying, he looked terribly earnest and passionate and every sentence was punctuated with intense nose-to-nose face smushing and heartfelt kisses. The kind that looked amazing in the movies but tasted of salty tears in reality and made you self-conscious that your nose was running.

Or was that just me?

Tom looked back to say something to me and got an eyeful of the live show in the window before I could start to whimper.

'Maddie,' he said, pulling me away from the scene that would haunt my nightmares for months to come. 'Get in this taxi.'

'Why are they kissing?' I asked, struggling to put one foot in front of the other. 'Why isn't she shouting at him?'

'Just get in the taxi.' Tom scooped my legs out from underneath me and rag-dolled me into the back of the black cab, dropping me in my seat and fastening the seatbelt around my lap.

I heard him give the driver directions to an address I didn't recognize and kept my eyes trained on the window. Any second now she was going to reach out and punch him. Any second now he was going to stand up and race out after me, realizing I'm the one he loves. He was probably explaining to her that it was over. He was explaining to her that I was the one. Just before the taxi pulled away, he looked out of the window and caught my eye. And immediately looked away.

As we moved into traffic, all the nonsense churning in my stomach began to settle until all that was left was a great big knot, wrapped up with a great big bow of feeling like an imbecile. And there aren't many things worse than being made to feel like a fool.

'I'm sorry,' Tom said, reaching out for my hand. 'That was terrible and all my fault.'

'Yeah,' I croaked. 'It was.'

'It shouldn't have happened like that,' he said. 'I can't apologize enough.'

I shook my head. Silence was fine, but if I talked, I was going to cry. My eyes burned and tears trembled on the edges of my eyelids as I tilted my head upwards, praying that the tears I had already sprung could be sucked back into my tear ducts. It would all be OK as long as I stayed quiet.

'He's such a wanker.' Tom shook his head. 'I'm so sorry.'

'Don't be,' I said, sucking in the air as I spoke. I would not cry, I would not cry, I would not cry. I would go home and call Sarah and Lauren and scream hysterically while they said all the right things, but I would *not* cry. 'It's not your fault.'

'Yeah, well, it's not yours either,' he replied. 'I wanted to say something way back, but . . .'

Sod it. Too late.

'Why would he do it?' I wailed, tears coming thick and fast. It turns out that getting punched in the face is painful, but sobbing uncontrollably after you've been punched in the face is excruciating, and that just made me cry more. It was the most painful lose-lose situation I'd ever experienced. 'And my face really hurts.'

'Don't cry . . .' Tom tapped my back with ineffectual staccato pats as I hurled myself at his pale blue shirt. 'He's not worth it.'

And I knew he was right, but it didn't help. I wasn't just crying about Will. I was crying about Seb and Shona and my job and my sister's aggression and my parents' refusal to be proud of me and Lauren's wedding and every last shit little thing that had happened to me from birth, from the big disasters like puberty, to the things that didn't even seem to matter at the time, like when I put milk in my tea last Thursday and then found out it had gone off.

Eventually we pulled up outside somewhere and Tom paid the taxi driver while I carried on crying. I'm not much of a crier, honestly – the John Lewis Christmas ads do nothing to me – but now I'd started, I couldn't stop. When Tom prised my arms from around his neck, his shirt was completely covered in mascara and lipstick and whatever else had come from my face that didn't ever need to be spoken of again.

'Do you want a drink?' he asked, keys rattling in the nice-looking door of the nice-looking building.

I wiped my arm across my face and nodded, dragging one foot in front of the other. Normally when devastated and/or mortifyingly embarrassed, I would go home, run a bath and sit in it, trawling through every element of the experience until it was fully committed to memory for future emotional flagellation, but since Tom had already seen me get punched in the face and knew I was shagging a man who already had a girlfriend, going home felt a bit like locking the stable door after the horse had bolted.

'Bloody hell.' I dropped my tote bag on the very shiny hardwood floor and clung to my handbag while I gaped at Tom's house with the one eye that wasn't already swollen shut. Because it was a house, not a flat – a great, big, lovely house with doors and furniture and an actual landline phone and everything. 'Are we still in London?'

'What do you mean?' he asked, hanging his coat on an actual coat rack.

'Where are we?' I scrubbed some of the smudged make-up from my face, swapping grey stains for red splotches, and combed my hair with my hands. 'It didn't feel like we were in the taxi for that long.'

'We weren't, we're in Queen's Park,' he replied. 'Sorry, did you want to go home?'

'No,' I said, my arms pressed closed to my sides. I was afraid to breathe too hard in case I broke something. He had a bowl on a side table and there wasn't even anything in it. This was a grown-up's house, and my scuffed knees and swollen face did not match the décor in the slightest. 'Is this your house?'

'Bit worrying that I've got the keys if it isn't,' he said. 'Let's get some ice on that eye – it looks bloody painful.'

'That's funny,' I said, following him closely. 'It feels bloody painful.'

Even though I could only see out of one eye, it was impossible not to notice how beautiful Tom's house was. Clean, simple, classic and very, very expensive. I knew lawyers made a lot of money, but it hadn't occurred to me that he could be rich.

'Here, you take this.' Tom handed me a clean tea towel full of ice cubes freshly dispensed from the ice machine

in the front of his megafridge and directed me to a chair
next to a great big reclaimed wooden table in the middle
of his kitchen. 'Hold it against your cheek, but don't
push it in or you'll make it hurt more.'

'Get punched in the face often, do you?' I asked while
he rattled around in a cupboard.

'More often than I'd like,' he replied. 'But thankfully
it's been a while.'

'Fight club?'

'First rule of fight club –' he went back to the cupboard
for glasses and then back to the fridge for more ice – 'we
don't talk about fight club. Now, I've got a couple of
beers, some whisky, gin—'

'Gin, please,' I said quickly.

He poured a generous measure of mother's ruin into
a tumbler and set it on the table in front of me, turning
back to the fridge. 'I'm sure I've got some tonic in here
somewhere.'

I put the empty glass back down on the table, dabbing
at my mouth sheepishly.

'Do people actually drink neat gin?' he asked, looking
somewhat alarmed.

'No,' I replied. His alarm was justified.

'Would you like a more socially acceptable drink this
time?'

I pondered it for a moment and then shrugged. Why not.

'Should my face still hurt?' I asked once I was sipping
my second drink, so as not to look quite so much like
someone with a problem. 'Because it's really throbbing.'

He swirled some whisky around in his glass and
nodded. 'I'd like to say keep drinking until it stops, but
since we're adults, I suppose I just have to say yes, it's
going to hurt for a while.'

'Most of your face-punching happened in your younger days, then?' My eyes flickered down to his mottled black and blue shirt. If you ask me, the Dalmatian spots of mascara added a little something.

'Something like that,' he said. 'I had a temper when I was younger. I was in a boxing club for a while.'

'So you really were in fight club,' I said. 'Not that we can talk about it.'

'I packed it in when I went to law school the first time,' he explained. 'It's quite difficult, training to become a lawyer when you're coming to school with a thick lip every other week. Doesn't go down very well.'

'So you dropped out of law school to be a vigilante?' I threw back the rest of my drink and hoped he would get the hint to pour me another. 'That's impressive.'

'I was the Batman of Richmond,' Tom replied, pouring me another gin.

As soon as he went to get more ice, I pulled my phone out of my handbag and fumbled it into life, but there was nothing from anyone. A new wave of disappointment flooded over me as Tom carefully placed two ice cubes into my drink, the tiniest drop splashing onto the screen of my phone as they settled.

'There's nothing I can say that won't sound like a terrible cliché,' he said, sitting back down beside me. 'But in this instance, they would all be true.'

'He's an arsehole, he's not worth it, I deserve so much better?' I suggested, wrapping my fingers round the glass but not raising it to my lips. The first two I'd shotgunned were starting to hit home, and it was bad enough that I was sitting in this beautiful home looking like something Tom had dragged in off the streets; the last thing I wanted to do was to throw up in his *House Beautiful* show home.

'He is an arsehole, he's not worth it.' Tom emptied his glass and poured himself another. Someone wasn't quite so worried about his alcohol tolerance. 'And you do deserve better.'

'I'm not likely to get it, though, am I?' I replied. 'I never do.'

Tom's lips pressed together in a tight line again, an expression I'd seen on him before. It meant he was forcing himself not to say something, and I didn't like it. If he'd said something about Will earlier, I wouldn't be in this mess.

Well, I most likely would, but I might not have got decked.

'Whatever you're not saying, please just say it,' I said. 'You can't possibly make feel any shittier than I do now.'

'Whereabouts do you live?' he asked. 'I can give you a lift home if you want. The car's outside.'

To be fair, that wasn't what I'd been expecting him to say. He was kicking me out? 'Just down the road,' I replied. 'Back down the road where people get robbed and don't live in mansions.'

'This was my mum and dad's house,' he said. 'Mum moved out to the country to live near her sister after my dad died, so it's just me now.'

'Sorry, I didn't mean that to sound rude.' I shook my head at myself. 'It's a beautiful home. And there must be lots of room for your bat cave.'

'Loads,' he replied. 'And the fight club.'

'We don't talk about fight club.' I slapped his hand on the table and he grinned. 'Remember?'

He had a lovely smile. You know who else had a lovely smile? Will, the lying, cheating shit who didn't want me, and that was even worse than knowing that he was a lying, cheating shit, and, oh my God, what was wrong with me?

'I'm sorry about your shirt,' I said, glancing down at my own messed-up sleeves. Nothing got that mascara out, as my pillowcases would attest. 'I'll get it cleaned for you.'

'Collateral damage,' he shrugged. 'Better make-up than blood.'

'I think there might be a bit of that in there too,' I said. 'I'll just buy you a new shirt. I feel like such an idiot.'

'I don't think you're an idiot,' Tom said, setting down his drink and coming over to where I was sitting, shaking. 'I think you're pretty great, actually.'

'Funny,' I replied. 'Because I feel like an idiot.'

'These things happen,' he rationalized, wiping out three months of me being played for a fool with three words. 'It's not your fault.'

'OK then,' I said, all the fight fading out of me when I felt the weight of his hands on my shoulders. 'I'm not an idiot, these things happen.'

'That's right,' he nodded. 'You're not an idiot, but you are funny and interesting and clever, and I could listen to you talk about anything, all day long.'

'Right.'

'And I think you're beautiful,' he said, taking a stray strand of hair between his fingers and brushing it back, away from my bruised face.

No one in all my years, not even Seb, has ever called me beautiful.

'I've got a black eye,' I pointed out. 'My face is a mess.'

'I know.' Tom started to smile. 'And it might be the most beautiful you've ever looked.'

I put my hand to my hair, touching the strands he had just touched. 'You're just saying that to be nice.'

He shook his head. 'I'm not that nice.'

'You are quite nice,' I argued. 'You were going to come and pick me up from Bristol at one in the morning.'

The big, bright, airy kitchen became very small as I spoke, and somehow, Tom grew even taller as I seemed to shrink. Oh no, I wasn't shrinking, I was just falling over.

'Shit, Maddie.'

He caught me before I hit the floor, nursing me on his knees.

'Do you want to lie down?' he asked. I let go of my handbag and heard it make a soft thud on the kitchen floor as I gave something like a nod.

My brain was telling my legs to move, but the message got lost on the way, possibly somewhere around my liver, and before I could protest, Tom scooped me up off the floor and carried me out of the kitchen and straight up the stairs. I wanted to make some sort of protest about how I was a grown woman who didn't need to be carried, but since I couldn't actually use my legs, I kept my mouth shut.

'This is my room – the spare bed isn't made,' he said, kicking open one of several doors on the second floor and tipping me out of his arms onto a bed. I landed with all the grace I imagined he had come to expect from me, legs akimbo and trying not to throw up. 'Do you want some water? I'll get you some water.'

'Thank you,' I said, all politeness as I pulled my skirt back down over my knickers. 'That would be lovely.'

Thinking about it, I had hoped to end my night on a lawyer's bed with my skirt up round my waist, but not like this.

Oh, fuckknuckles.

20

Friday July 24th
Today I feel: Like everything happens for a reason if that reason is I AM CURSED.
Today I am thankful for: I don't even know. Kittens?

The idea was, I'd close my eyes for five minutes until Tom came back with the water, chug it down and then ask him to call me a cab. Of course, the plan didn't quite come off. The next time I opened my eyes, or one of them at least, the clock on the bedside table blinked 8.30 at me: 8.30 Friday morning.

'Shit.'

Making words was an ambitious move, even single swear words. My tongue was a magic carpet away from passing for the Sahara desert, and my left eye was still completely swollen shut. For a brief, blissful second all I could feel was the physical pain of my messed-up face, but then, just like magic, the events of last night all came flooding back.

The only thing worse than waking up with a black

eye and a badger's-arse mouth and the knowledge that you got smacked in the face in a bar by your boyfriend's real girlfriend is having all those things happen in someone else's house. I didn't know where the bathroom was, I didn't know where my handbag was, and, most disconcerting of all, I didn't know where Tom was.

After a few false starts, two walk-in wardrobes and a bathroom, I eventually found my way downstairs to the kitchen and, hallelujah, my handbag.

'Good morning.'

Through my one good eye I saw Tom, still wearing his stained shirt but without his trousers. His arms were folded and he looked incredibly sheepish. I threw half a packet of TicTacs in my mouth and waved.

'How did you sleep?'

'Like I'd been punched in the face,' I replied, desperate to leave. 'Can you please do me a huge favour? My phone's dead, can you call me a taxi?'

'I'll drive you home,' he said, rubbing sleep from his eyes and padding across the kitchen, keeping a wide berth, to switch on the kettle. 'Tea?'

'I don't have time for tea,' I snapped, panic rising. 'I need to get to work. I've got twenty-five pink rabbits being delivered to my office before midday and God knows what will happen if I'm not there to sign for them.'

'I don't actually know what to say to that,' he replied as the kettle began to whistle. 'Let me have a cup of tea and then we'll get you home.'

If I hadn't been utterly manic, I might have said something about the fact that he had one of those fast-boil kettles, but instead I rooted round in my make-up bag looking for something to help with my eye. Like concealer or a balaclava or the number of a plastic surgeon.

'This is the worst day this could have happened,' I replied, opening up my powder compact and immediately wishing I hadn't. 'I haven't got time to go home, I haven't got time to get changed. I cannot believe this is happening.'

'There are still some of Marie's old clothes in the spare room,' he said, taking two mugs out of the cupboard. 'I reckon they'll fit.'

'Marie's clothes? Because that wouldn't be incredibly weird,' I poked at my purple cheekbone and subconsciously filed away the name of his former fiancé for future Internet stalking. 'Please just call me a taxi.'

'You can't go to work looking like that,' Tom said, waving in the general direction of my creased, blood-spattered, make-up-stained ensemble. Clearly he didn't know I worked in East London; I could absolutely get away with this. 'At least let me get you one of my T-shirts or something.'

'I don't want one of your T-shirts,' I said, beginning to lose my temper. Why couldn't he see the urgency of my situation? 'I want to leave. I need to leave.'

He dropped a teabag in each of the mugs. 'Look, I know you're angry about last night—'

'Of course I'm angry,' I replied. 'I just found out my boyfriend has another girlfriend. That I'm the other woman, Tom, and if that wasn't enough, because of you, I got punched in the face twenty-four hours before the most important day of my entire career.'

'I'm very, very sorry,' Tom said as I pressed my palm against my face. Jesus *Christ* getting angry was painful.

'We apologize to each other a lot, don't we?' I said, blinking through the pain in my face. 'It's starting to feel like a very bad sixties sitcom.'

'We do.' He rubbed his hand over his face and frowned. 'I shouldn't have asked you to meet me at that bar. It was a terrible idea, I knew it as soon as he walked in.'

'It wasn't your responsibility to tell me Will had a girlfriend. It's not like we're actually friends, is it? I work for you.' I looked to the heavens to try to work out whose responsibility it was but was distracted for a moment by a lovely skylight. 'I mean, it's not as though you knew he was going to be at that bar with his actual girlfriend.'

Saying the g-word made me want to be sick in my mouth. Then I looked up, saw the expression on Tom's face, and was almost sick in my mouth.

'You did know he was going to be there,' I said slowly. 'You knew they were both going to be there.'

He didn't reply. He just looked down at his enormous feet and stayed silent.

'That's why you wanted me to meet you there.'

'The more I thought about it, the more I thought you ought to know,' he said simply.

'And you thought the best way to tell me was to drag me out to a pub where I could be publically humiliated?' I asked. 'After what Will did to you at the wedding?'

'I didn't know she was going to hit you,' he replied, rubbing his nose and looking wounded.

'I'm not talking about being hit,' I said. My heart was pounding. 'I meant being made to feel stupid and small and cheap and horrible. Didn't that even cross your mind?'

'No?' he replied.

'It had nothing to do with you.' Oh yes, it was time to raise my voice, face ache or no. 'And if you really felt it was your civic duty, a quiet word or an email might have been better.'

'But you wouldn't have believed me!' Tom banged an

empty mug down on the kitchen counter. 'And I would have sounded like a jealous dickhead.'

'You don't know that,' I shouted back. 'Anything would have been better than this, Tom – anything. I'm so sick of people treating me like an idiot.'

'I don't think you're an idiot,' he said. 'I would never treat you that way.'

'That's funny,' I said, 'because you did.'

He didn't look at me, just kept his eyes on his hands.

'I'm not a joke.' My hands were shaking, I was so angry. 'It's not OK for people to keep shitting on me. Why does no one take me seriously?'

'I wasn't trying to shit on you,' Tom said, but I was not in the mood to be placated. 'Truly.'

'Why can't anyone just wake up and think, oh, Maddie, she's all right?' I kicked backwards out of my chair, preparing for a dramatic exit. 'Why am I not good enough for anyone as I am?'

'I think you're good enough,' he said slowly, as though I was a horse that might bolt. 'I think you're brilliant.'

'I'm not a pair of trousers!' I yelled triumphantly, pleased with my own analogy.

'You've lost me.' Tom scratched his head, looking right at me for a second.

'I'm not a pair of trousers,' I said, reaching for my handbag and missing. Only having the use of one eye meant my perspective was off. 'I'm not something you buy, thinking you can take them up a bit and take them in a bit and alter them until they're perfect. I can't be altered, I can't be taken up. I am what I am.'

'OK.'

'No,' I replied, completely ignoring him. 'My parents think I'm not ambitious enough, my sister thinks I'm pointless, my boss hates me, my big boss is making me jump through two months of hoops instead of just giving me the job I deserve when I've been there ten bloody years, Seb cheated on me, Will cheated on me, even my best friends take the piss. I don't understand why people think it's OK to treat me like this?'

'It isn't,' he said. 'And I really am sorry.'

'Well you should be,' I yelled, my fingers wedged between my eye socket and my cheekbone. 'Because this is all your fault.'

He stepped back, stung, as the kettle boiled into life.

'Right.' He poured boiling water into one of the mugs, then took the teabag out of the second mug and popped it back in the caddy. 'I see. It's my fault.'

He carried on making a single cup of tea, pushing the other mug, my mug, across the kitchen counter. My victory wore off quickly. Suddenly we were locked in an uncomfortable silence, me breathing heavily and Tom piling sugar into a mug of tea that was not for me.

'I'd better get you a taxi then,' he said, pulling out the teabag and dropping it in the sink. 'They usually beep when they're here, they're very quick. I'm sure you can let yourself out.'

Without looking at me even once, he picked up his mug, walked straight out of the kitchen and back into the living room, and closed the door loudly behind him. It wasn't quite a slam, but there was purpose behind it.

Grabbing my bag, I hobbled out of the kitchen and down the hallway to fanny around with the eighteen different locks he had on the front door. I didn't have time for damaged male egos – I had to get to the office and save my rabbits before Shona had them turned into a pink fur coat.

*   *   *

'Oh, Maddie, what happened?' Sharaline stared over the top of her computer monitor as I limped into the office half an hour later. 'What's wrong with your face?'

'There was a thing,' I muttered, dropping my bag on my desk and ignoring the stares from around the office. 'I might possibly have completely destroyed any chance I ever had at happiness. But, you know, it's nothing, I've got a lot to do.'

'There have been some calls,' she said, sloping round to my desk and handing over a handful of paper slips. 'I can help, though. Shall I get you a coffee?'

'Yeah, please,' I said, setting the slips down, popping two Nurofen Plus and swallowing them with yesterday's water. 'And any make-up you can find. I need to get changed and then see where we're at with everything, and—'

'The venue cancelled,' she blurted out. 'For tomorrow.'

I turned on her with one wild eye. The other was too swollen to be wild.

'What?'

'They called this morning,' Sharaline said. 'Something about permits not coming through in time.'

'We've got all the permits. I got all the permits.' I turned on my computer, barely breathing until I heard the annoying Mac chime and started searching my emails. 'They're all here. I did them myself. Exactly what did they say?'

'Just that the permits weren't received in time,' she said. 'And something about the insurance. Let me get you a coffee and we'll sort it out.'

It wasn't possible. I'd double-checked everything we could possibly need and we were insured up the arse. I had alcohol permits, fireworks permits, large gathering permits, animal permits, and I'd cleared the DJ with the noise pollution people. We were insured for fire, flood, thunder, lightning, terrorist attack and any act of God the insurance company could think of. A ninja assassin could storm the party and chop off Andrew Dickenson's head and I would still be covered. What could they possibly be complaining about?

'I'm going to call them,' I shouted across the office. 'By the time you're back with the coffee, it'll all be fine. They can't cancel.'

Four minutes later, Sharaline placed a venti mocha latte on my desk.

'They cancelled,' I said. 'The whole thing is buggered. I'm going to get sacked.'

'No you're not,' she said with the kind of confidence that could only come from a twenty-two-year-old with blue hair. 'We're going to fix this. We'll get a new venue, a new caterer and God, I can DJ.'

I looked up, tears in my eyes. 'We lost the caterer and the DJ?'

Sharaline winced. 'You didn't read the other notes?'

I shook my head.

'Also, we need to find new rabbits.'

'What happened to my rabbits?' I whispered.

'You don't want to know,' she replied, a distasteful look on her face. 'But they're gone.'

My poor, poor rabbits.

'The venue called the vendors and told them they'd cancelled and then they cancelled. I managed to convince the furniture hire people we were moving to another space and that we'd let them know this morning, but the caterers said they couldn't switch venues last minute.'

'I'll call them,' I muttered, trying to make sense of

something that made no sense at all. 'They can do as they're bloody told.'

'Drink your coffee, read your emails, and then we'll get started. It's not impossible, Maddie. You can pull it off.'

'Really?' I asked. 'I don't know what's given you that impression.'

'Of course you can,' she said as though I was an idiot for asking. 'Look at all the stuff you've done before. How many times have you saved Shona's arse?'

'One time I caught her before she tripped and fell into a barbecue pit,' I replied. 'I literally saved her arse.'

'You should have pushed her in,' Sharaline said, sipping her own giant frappuccino. 'You know, I bet she wouldn't believe you could do this. Shona would love to see you mess this up.'

Oh, clever girl.

'Normally, reverse psychology will get you everywhere with me,' I said. 'But this is bad.'

'We've got an entire day.' She slammed down her huge, frothy drink and gave me a determined look. 'And I really want to stick this up Shona's arse. Tell me what you need me to do.'

Looking across the desk at her eager young face, I felt like I was looking at myself ten years ago. If I'd been unbelievably pretty and had cool hair and a backbone.

'You're right,' I said, almost believing it. 'We can fix it.'

'Yeah, we can,' she whooped, pumping her fist in the air, before catching the look on my face and lowering it slowly. 'Sorry.'

'We *can* fix it,' I said, pulling out my phone and opening a new email at the same time. 'But not on our own.'

* * *

If there was one thing guaranteed to take your mind off having your heart ripped out of your chest and shredded into taco meat in front of you, it was a career emergency. Even when I was at my busiest I could still find five minutes to linger over Facebook, but today was a master class in time management. Even when I went for a wee, I was sending emails instead of checking Twitter.

'This place looks great,' I told Lauren as the furniture hire team pulled up outside the house. 'You're a life saver.'

'It's been on the market forever,' she said, handing me the keys to the empty house. 'I think Daddy is pricing it a bit too high. Who knows, maybe someone from the party will like it so much they'll decide to buy it?'

'Miracles apparently can happen,' I said, looking round at the space. It was perfect. Maybe even better than the original venue. The downstairs was one huge open-plan space with huge French windows that opened out onto a beautifully landscaped English garden.

'Sharaline is transferring all the insurance and stuff over to this address, so you're totally covered,' I said. 'Not that anything else is going to go wrong.'

'I believe you,' Lauren said with a shrug. 'Of course it's going to be great. Now, other than find you a change of clothes, what else can I do?'

'How are you at filling *vol-au-vents*?' Sarah asked, staggering into the house underneath five huge bakery boxes. 'The cavalry has arrived.'

If my left eye hadn't been completely swollen shut, I could have cried.

'You're amazing,' I said, taking two of the boxes to reveal my other best friend's sweaty face. 'How did you get out of work?'

'I cried and told them I had to see my lawyer,' she said, dumping the other three boxes on a spare chair. 'For the first time in ever, this divorce is working for us. Good God, Maddie, what happened to your face?'

'It's a long story which I will happily share as soon as I've spoken to the florist, the lighting design team and the man who is bringing the storks and I've finished dip-dyeing two dozen giant rabbits, because that's all on me now.'

'Stalks?' Lauren asked, concern crossing her face. 'Or storks?'

'Let's get this food into the kitchen, shall we?' Sarah suggested, pushing her out of the room. 'Maddie has a lot to do.'

'Thank you,' I mouthed at her as Sharaline bounded through the door.

'This place is fantastic!' she said, clapping her hands happily. 'I said you could do it.'

'Save the "I told you so"s for tomorrow,' I warned. 'Where are we?'

'I've called all the guests and couriered out new invitations, all the paperwork has been changed to this address, and the margarita fountain is being delivered at four,' she said. 'The florist has been reconfirmed and they're bringing all the floral arrangements tomorrow morning. Oh, and I've got fifty loo rolls in the car. Do you think that's enough?'

'Unless we give everyone food poisoning, it should be,' I said, waving the AV guy in.

'Don't say that,' Sharaline blanched. 'Did you tell the baby daddies that the caterer cancelled?'

'I did not,' I replied, flashing back to our very tense phone conversation an hour earlier. 'Out of everything going on, that's the last thing they need to worry about, and between you and me, once the crusts are cut off, every single sandwich is the same. Sarah is buying up every M&S in the county. The food will be fine.'

'And the waitresses?'

'I'm pulling in some favours,' I said. 'Worst comes to the worst, we'll put on our pinnies and do it ourselves. It's only tray passing.'

Sharaline nodded, standing back as two large men came through the door with a settee on their shoulders.

'It's going to be the most beautiful, fantastical, spectacular baby-naming party in a pink and peach rose garden without any gluten or balloons ever,' I said. 'Even if it kills me.'

'Don't say that,' Sharaline said. 'If you die, I'll be on my own with Shona.'

'I'll give it my best shot,' I said. 'I will try not to die.'

But I was making no promises.

'How long do you think it will take for this pink dye to wash off?' I asked, staring at my stained cuticles. 'It's supposed to be temporary.'

'Are you asking for you or the rabbits?' Sarah said. 'That is a vision that will stay with me for a long time.'

'Well, if you will walk into a bathroom without knocking, you should expect to see a woman sitting in the bath in her knickers dyeing white rabbits,' I replied curtly. 'Welcome to my life.'

'Have we got any more edible glitter?' Lauren asked, blowing her hair out of her eyes. 'I'm almost out.'

'I think that was the last of it,' Sarah said, combing through the boxes and packets and mixing bowls that covered the kitchen counter. 'These last few will have to be glitterless. They'll survive.'

'I honestly don't think there are enough words to thank you two,' I said, yawning into my shoulder as I squeezed a perfect rosette of peach icing onto a pink cupcake and passed it down the production line to Lauren. 'You've literally saved my life.'

'We've literally saved your job,' Sarah corrected. 'And you don't have to thank us. Just buy us presents instead.'

'I will buy you both a pony,' I promised. It was almost two a.m. and we'd been sitting cross-legged on the kitchen floor, icing five hundred gluten-free cupcakes, for the last three hours. Who knew making delicious treats could be so soul-destroying?

'I never want to see a cupcake again,' Lauren said, flicking a brand new blusher-brush-turned-cupcake-glittering-tool over my icing. 'Are we having them at the wedding?'

'We were,' I replied. 'But I'm swapping them for cookie platters.'

'Thank God.'

'Don't punch me for asking –' Sarah circled her arm back and forth for a moment, cupcake-decorating RSI setting in, before reaching for the final un-iced bun – 'but have you heard from Will at all?'

I shook my head, automatically reaching for my bruised face. 'Nope,' I replied. 'Nothing. Not even a text.'

'What a weasel,' Lauren breathed. 'I'm so glad we didn't include him in the seating plan.'

I offered a tight smile and carried on frosting.

'You should go to the police,' Sarah said. 'Report his bitch girlfriend. It's not as though you don't have any evidence.'

'I can't see how that would help,' I lied. It would help

tremendously. 'All I want is to forget it ever happened, the whole thing. I wish I'd never met him. His name is officially stricken from the record books.'

'Thank God you didn't add him on Facebook,' Lauren said.

We all nodded at once. Trust lovely Lauren to find a bright side.

'And have you heard from Tom?' she asked.

Bloody Lauren, never knew when to keep her mouth shut.

'I haven't.' I poked my bruise a little bit harder until it hurt. 'He can do one as well.'

'Yeah,' Sarah said. 'How dare the good-looking, tall, lovely man take you back to his palatial mansion and take care of you?'

'If it weren't for him, I wouldn't have got punched in the face in the first place,' I pointed out. 'And I wouldn't have needed taking care of, would I?'

'While I will admit his methods were questionable,' she said, 'I don't think his motives were. I don't think he's a bad dude.'

'You don't think he was using Maddie to get his own back on Will?' Lauren asked. 'Because the dude clearly has a grudge against Will the Weasel.'

'No,' Sarah argued. 'I think he didn't want her to blame him. Everyone knows you shoot the messenger. And, you know, bro code. Blokes are weird. Even if they don't like each other, they won't throw each other under the bus.'

'Not like women, you mean?' Lauren commented.

'I just mean he probably wasn't being malicious or manipulative,' Sarah said. 'Imagine that you knew something that would hurt someone you cared about. It's difficult trying to find the right way to tell them.'

I shrank into myself, watching Sarah finish icing a cupcake at two in the morning and inadvertently run herself out of a job I hadn't told her I'd applied for.

'I guess sometimes it's better not to tell them,' Lauren admitted, her own guilt all over her face. We'd agreed it was better she keep her Steve stories to herself. Sarah didn't need to know the tales he'd been telling the boys; it couldn't help anyone now. 'I think he was right to stay quiet.'

'While I am enjoying this debate,' I said, dusting off my hands and staggering to my feet, 'I think we could probably go home now.'

'If I'd known suggesting you'd overreacted on the Tom front would have got me out of cupcake duties, I would have done it hours ago,' Sarah said, rolling onto her back and yawning. 'Because, you know, you did.'

I kicked her lightly in the boob. 'You're not getting a pony.'

I didn't need reminding that I'd fucked up. Whatever Tom had done wrong, I shouldn't have attacked him the way I did. And now it was done, there was no way to take it back. I'd let Will screw me over twice. Quite impressive.

On the other hand, as I looked over the kitchen, I couldn't help but be proud of myself, of us. All the food was laid out on trays, ready to be cooked or handed out at the party, the main room was decorated, and every toilet in the entire house was stocked with loo roll. Other than a boyfriend who wasn't shagging an almost supermodel behind my back and a client whose crush had led me to getting punched in the face, what more could a girl ask for?

21

Seven hours after I'd left, I arrived back at the house showered, changed and wearing more make-up than all five Kardashian sisters combined. There was no way to completely cover the black eye, but at least the swelling had gone down and I could actually see.

Sharaline had beat me to the venue and was already showing the floral designers into the back garden with their buckets of rose bushes. She gave me a wave, tapped at her headset to let me know she was online, and carried on. That girl was a star. I took back every bad thing I had ever said about her. Apart from the stuff about her name.

As soon as the party was over today, and as long as I got through Lauren's bridal shower alive tomorrow, I would call Tom, and then I would settle down to work out how I could ruin Will's life.

Like I said, priorities.

'Hey.' Sharaline materialized in front of me, iPad in hand. 'Great job on the face.'

'Thanks,' I said. 'Is it fleek?'

'Uh, yeah.' She looked away awkwardly for a second

before pointing over at the kitchen. 'Did you get everything sorted with the rabbits?'

'They're in a very spacious and luxurious holding pen in the shed with all the carrots they could ask for,' I nodded, holding up my still tinted hands. 'And they're all pink.'

She pulled a face. 'Is it OK, you know, dyeing rabbits for a children's party?'

'I called PETA and they said that it sounded morally questionable, but as long as the animals weren't being harmed there wasn't anything they could do,' I shrugged. 'So, yes.'

'Fair enough.'

'Right.' I clapped my hot pink hands together, fuelled by the energy of four hours' sleep and three shots of espresso. 'I'll go and check on the storks and the rabbits. Can you look after the margarita fountain?'

She saluted and headed off into the garden. Watching her go, I really did feel as though I was watching myself, only ten years younger. And wearing clothes that would have made me look like a deranged bag lady. And with blue hair. So, not that much like me at all but still, it was nice to be the one giving directions and having someone follow instead of the other way around.

By midday, everything looked amazing. The main room was all decked out in fairy lights and there were flowers everywhere, but nothing cheesy or garish or ridiculous. Outside, the gardens were an absolute wonderland, although not the Disney kind because nothing was cheesy or garish or tacky. The food all looked delicious, our cupcakes passable, the band I'd hired had, for an extra hundred quid, agreed to wear peach lounge suits with pink ties, which was slightly tacky and garish, but they looked amazing so I didn't care. Comfy sofas and over-stuffed armchairs were dotted between the pink and peach rose bushes and a pretty flower-entwined fence kept two dozen powder-puff-pink bunnies away from the five real-life storks that were patrolling the pond.

It was the first time I had ever executed my own event from beginning to end, and I had to say, it looked bloody brilliant. And that was before you took into consideration that, on top of two-thirds of the event having been pulled out of my arse inside twenty-four hours, I still had a black eye, my left knee had seized up and my heart had been taken out, torn up, freeze dried and then shoved in my pocket for safe-keeping.

I was on my hands and knees winding an audio cable round a whimsical hat stand in the middle of the garden when I heard Sharaline yelling my name across the lawn. I blinked up into the sun, still on all fours, when a large, three-headed silhouette appeared in front of me.

'Andrew! Christopher!'

Brilliant. The baby daddies, two hours early.

'And this must be Audrey! Look at her, she's beautiful.'

'Isn't she?' Andrew cooed as Christopher thrust a tiny baby in my face. 'Isn't she the most beautiful little girl you've ever seen?'

'She is,' I agreed. 'Well, apart from my niece.'

Their faces fell.

'Actually she might be cuter than my niece. All she does all day is shit herself and throw up.'

Their expressions turned black.

'Did I tell you my sister is gay?'

'Why don't I show you inside?' Sharaline raced down the garden and rested her hands on the baby daddies'

backs, leading them away before things could turn nasty.
'You have to see what a beautiful job Maddie did with
the ceremony room.'

'Has she got a black eye?' Andrew whispered to
Christopher in his not terribly quiet at all voice. 'I could
swear she has.'

'She's very pretty,' I shouted after them. 'Best baby ever.'

I definitely had a bright future as an event planner, as
long as I never had to actually talk to the people who
were paying for them. Perfect.

The ceremony itself went without a hitch.

Andrew and Christopher looked spectacularly dapper
and baby Audrey barely made a sound, officially
promoting her to the top of my favourite baby list. The
guests all made the appropriate effort, and my roving
photographers clicked away, capturing every moment of
Audrey's official welcome to life as a Dickenson. And as
the party moved outside, guests were handed paper para-
sols to protect them from the sun and ate themselves
into a sugar coma at the candy bar, while the babies were
ditched with the team of childminders or dragged off to
pose in a field full of rabbits.

'The band are going on break.' Sharaline's voice crackled
through my headset from the other side of the party while
I liaised with the caterers in the kitchen, preparing to bring
the cake outside. 'I've got the DJ ready to go.'

'Great, I'm bringing the cake out in five,' I told her,
standing back to admire the incredible creation. Our
cupcakes were pretty, but this was remarkable. The cake
was three feet of deliciousness: amazing red velvet cake
covered with a swarm of peach sugar roses tumbling all
the way from the top to the bottom and accented with

glittery pink ribbon woven all around the blooms. Part of me wanted to take it home and put it in my living room forever, and part of me wanted to stick my face in it and eat the entire thing. 'Can you clear a path?'

'Done,' she replied. 'I'll get Big Daddy and Little Daddy to the table.'

Given that it had been quite the twenty-four hours for surprises, Sharaline proved to be one of the biggest of all. She was quick, she was intuitive and she was incredibly helpful. Most importantly of all, she hadn't asked me about my face all day and she was constantly making me laugh. Actually, that wasn't brilliant because my cheek was still pretty painful, but it turned out we both much preferred laughing through our days than crying in the toilets.

I heard the band wrapping up their set and gave the waiters their cue – no penguin or panda waitresses today, only very attractive out-of-work male models in need of a few quid – and it took four of them to pick up the cake and carry it out to the garden. I watched them like a hawk. Every second it was in the air was a second I thought I was going to faint.

'Today our family is complete.' Christopher was halfway through his speech when I tiptoed into the back of the crowd.

'We'd like to thank Colton-Bryers for bringing our vision to life today.' Andrew waved his arm with a flourish, not at me, of course, but at his party. 'And to all the staff who have made things go so smoothly.'

Whatever, Andrew, whatever.

'But just because we've got a baby doesn't mean we don't still know how to have a good time,' Christopher announced.

'Fountain is go,' I whispered into my headset. 'I repeat, fountain is go.'

'Let's get the party started,' Andrew crowed as the enormous stone fountain in the middle of the lawn sprang into life, spurting out frothy pink liquid. 'Who wants a drink?'

'That's disgusting,' Sharaline crackled into my ear. 'Are they really going to drink from it?'

'I think they are,' I said, watching the guests line up with their plastic margarita glasses. 'I had them run it through with disinfectant and then distilled water for a couple of hours, but still. Gross.'

'Totally,' she agreed. 'Also, I just got a weather warning that there are showers on the way. Should we start moving people inside?'

I looked up at the clear blue sky and frowned. Everything looked fine, but this was the middle of summer and we were in England, so you never could tell.

'Let's get the canopies up over the petting zoo and the fountain,' I directed. 'And I'll let Andrew and Christopher know we might need to move things back in.'

'Done and done,' she replied. 'It's all going so well.'

'Famous last words,' I warned. 'We're going for the biggest drink after this.'

'As long as it's not from that fountain,' she replied.

I slipped through the crowds to find the baby daddies enjoying their first margaritas now that their nanny had taken baby Audrey off their hands. Something I imagined she'd need to get used to.

'Hey, guys,' I said, leaning in to give each a brief hug. 'Great speech.'

'Thanks,' Andrew beamed. 'It's all going so well. We're so pleased. And these drinks are very strong.'

'The whole thing was such a great idea,' Christopher

said to his husband, ignoring me completely. 'Maybe you should go into event planning.'

'You totally should!' I agreed, a great big fake smile plastered across my face. It was a typical reaction whenever anything went well – the client always gave themselves credit, and every time something went wrong, it was our fault. But there would be time to make voodoo dolls of them later.

'Now, I don't want to spoil the fun but we've had a weather warning, so we need to get some tents up to cover the food and drink and the animals, and if we get anything more than a shower, we'll need to move everyone inside.'

'Oh, boo,' Andrew complained. 'I think partying in the rain sounds like a great idea.'

'It does,' I said, nodding enthusiastically. 'Unfortunately, if it rains and someone slips and breaks their neck, I'm going to get sued, so we we're going to pop up some canopies just in case.'

'I'm sure it isn't going to rain,' Christopher said, draping his arm over his husband's shoulders. 'Don't worry about it.'

'It's my job to worry,' I reminded them brightly, resisting the urge to slap the backs of their heads, 'so you don't have to. Just wanted to give you a heads-up. Now, get back to enjoying your party.'

For the first time in a long time, Siri had the weather forecast dead on. Not fifteen minutes later the sky was turning a threatening shade of purple-grey, not unlike my left eye, and I helped shepherd the very drunk people back towards the house while Sharaline supervised the canopies.

'I'm going to have a fag, love,' a short, unpleasant-looking man informed me, sparking up as the first rain began to fall. 'And then I'm going home. Are there goody bags? Do you want to pop off and get me one?'

'You can't actually smoke out here,' I said. 'You'd need to go outside onto the street. Sorry, it's a non-smoking venue.'

I wasn't sorry. I was quite clearly not sorry.

'You're not serious?' he said, ignoring me and flicking his lighter again,

I was serious. Definitely serious, definitely not sorry. Wanker.

'If you wouldn't mind putting out your cigarette and moving inside, that would be great,' I said. 'Thanks so much.'

The man levelled his bloodshot blue eyes at me, took a deep drag on his Marlboro Red and then chucked it behind him, shoving me shoulder to shoulder as he pushed past to get inside.

'I didn't ask him to murder his mother,' I muttered under my breath, looking for the dog-end to put it out. 'I asked him to put out a cigarette.'

And that was when I learned something new, something everyone at that party will take with them to their deathbed.

Strawberry margaritas are incredibly flammable.

Now, this is a great life hack if you're ever trying to light a barbecue and you haven't got any lighter fluid to hand, but it's not that brilliant when you have a six-foot stone fountain suddenly spurting fire instead of sticky strawberry liquor in the middle of a children's party.

The screaming started even before the canopy caught on fire, and they should have waited until that happened because that was when things really started to get out of hand. The storks, unnerved by all the running and screaming and occasional yell of 'we're going to die' all turned at once and caught sight of the flames. In spite of their handler's assurances that nothing could startle them and that they were quite tame and hated flying, they immediately began flapping their enormous wings and took off into the sky. Storks are quite scary when they're flying, you know.

And then people started to really panic.

And panicked people and panicked storks meant panicked rabbits. And panicked rabbits can easily jump over a two-foot fence. Like, incredibly easily.

Less than one minute after asking a man – very politely, mind – to put out his cigarette, I was standing alone in front of a flaming fountain of death, surrounded by circling storks and madly hopping pink rabbits. It was like being in a Lady Gaga video. Did you know rabbits make a high-pitched squealing noise when they're distressed? No, me neither. They do. It's loud and it's scary and I don't like it.

I'm still on the fence as to how thankful I am that Sharaline came tearing across the lawn with a fire extinguisher, covering me in anti-flammable foam as she attempted to put out the fountain fire, but I suppose foam is preferable to flames. And of course seconds later, in one of those fun 'the universe hates me' moments, the instant she unleashed the extinguisher on the fountain, the heavens opened and the rain put out the fire in a heartbeat, leaving the two of us standing in the middle of the garden in front of two hundred terrified guests, wet, miserable and surrounded by patchy pink and white damp rabbits.

Now there's something I never thought I would say.

The bridal shower is a time-honoured tradition among brides, where the bride's best friends and family come together to celebrate this special woman and the journey on which she is about to embark.

As the bride's mother and future mother-in-law are often in attendance at a bridal shower, these tend to be a less risqué event than the bachelorette party, although it is not uncommon for the bride to be showered in gifts that include lingerie for her wedding trousseau!

22

Sunday July 26th
Today I feel:
Today I am thankful for:

As you can imagine, once you've set the garden alight halfway through a party, it sort of kills. Once I'd talked to the fire brigade and the police and everyone else who 'wanted a quick word', the breakdown was actually pretty swift. No one was really in the mood for a chat and a drink while they took the tables apart, not like they usually are. I was mostly relieved that no one, rabbits and storks included, had been hurt in the production of this party, although I imagined the RSPCA might want to reappraise the situation if they caught wind of it. That was the last time I ever had animals at one of my parties.

If I ever had another party.

After Lauren's bridal shower, of course.

'There.' Sarah took a step back to survey her handiwork. 'You can hardly see it now.'

I peered in the mirror and she was right – her impressive

make-up prowess had covered up my black eye magnificently, but I still looked like death warmed over. Even though it was almost twenty-four hours since the Dickenson debacle, I couldn't move on. Every time I closed my eyes, I heard those rabbits screaming. One of the guests had referred to it as a live-action remake of *Watership Down* only more distressing, and he wasn't far off.

For some reason I couldn't quite put my finger on, I hadn't slept very well.

'I'm sure it's not as bad as you think,' she said, chucking her make-up back in her handbag and smacking her lips together to redistribute her gloss. 'It was hardly your fault.'

'Maybe.' The flames from the fountain were burned into my retinas, regardless. I was happy it was just my retinas and not my actual face, but it was still a concern. 'The clients were quite upset. That's not a good thing.'

Upset didn't really cover it. Christopher had done a lot of shouting while Andrew ran around his guests, hugging them and smothering sobs as though we'd all just lived through the actual war as opposed to enduring a freak accident that was over faster than it had begun. As far as I was aware, no war had ended in its participants being given goodie bags and a cupcake to take home with them.

'It wasn't your fault,' Sarah said again. 'No one got hurt and nothing got damaged. Now if we can say the same at the end of today, we'll both deserve a prize.'

'Did you buy prizes?' I asked.

'I bought gin,' she replied. 'Secret gin I'm not going to offer to anyone else. That's a prize.'

'Do me a favour and don't mention any of it to Lauren?'

I asked, receiving a quirked eyebrow in response. 'I haven't talked to her yet, and since she stuck her neck out to let us use her dad's house . . . you know how she is. She'll overreact. There's nothing wrong, anyway – by the time the cleaners left, you couldn't even tell we'd been there.'

'The plan is you're just not going to tell her?' she asked. 'Ever?'

'Not right now,' I said. 'Maybe after the wedding, when it'll all seem hilarious.'

'I've got to be honest, it seems pretty hilarious to me now,' Sarah said. 'I wish there were pictures.'

'Oh, there are,' I said, closing my eyes. 'We were quite the social media sensation for five minutes yesterday afternoon. Thank God whats-her-face went out without her knickers on this morning.'

Sarah smiled, positioning a peony.

'Everything looks great,' I said, looking round the living room. 'Honestly, it looks like a pro set this up.'

'Well, if I get the job at your place, I will be.' She arched her eyebrow and smiled. 'It was fun putting it together.'

Sarah's flat had always been very East London hipster chic, but for today she had transformed it into a bridal-shower fantasy. The furniture had all been moved to the edges of the room and covered in baby-blue blankets, one of Lauren's wedding colours, and there were different stations set up for the guest book, the gift table, food, drinks, sweets, all accented with bundles of pink peonies and oodles of tealights. Naturally, after yesterday, I was very nervous about the tealights.

'She doesn't deserve us,' Sarah said, beaming with pride at her production. 'I cannot believe she set up a gift registry for her own surprise bridal shower.'

'Yes you can,' I replied. 'And better that than someone get her the wrong thing and then have to endure her "this is brilliant but I hate it" face.'

'Why can't she just be over-polite like an English person?' she asked, fiddling with a vase of peonies. 'And take it back to the shop afterwards?'

'Hey, you guys!' On cue, Lauren burst through the front door, laden down with bags and a great big smile on her face. 'Oh my God, look at this place, Sarah – it's, like, the cutest.'

'No, you're the cutest,' Sarah replied, leaning in for a half hug and cheek kiss. I approached for mine and got battered in the boobs by half a dozen bakery boxes for my efforts. 'What's in the bags?'

'I brought some snacks.' She unloaded five boxes carefully onto a table I knew Sarah had set up especially for the lovingly designed homemade cookies that she had waiting. And when Lauren opened said boxes, they were full of cookies, iced with L ♥ M. 'Aren't they adorable?'

'Yeah,' Sarah said, raising her eyebrows. 'But so are the ones I've got in the kitchen, because I'm supposed to be organizing this, not you.'

'There can never be too many snacks,' Lauren said with a wave of her hand. 'I'm just helping out. I thought, after we sat up icing cupcakes until stupid o'clock in the morning on Friday, you'd appreciate the help.' I couldn't help hearing a note of steel in her usually sunny voice.

'Perhaps if you'd told me before I sat up until stupid o'clock again on Saturday?' Sarah replied in her super-polite voice. 'Everything is already organized.'

Lauren shrugged. 'I know cooking isn't your thing. I wanted there to be something, you know, else.' With my eagle eye, I noticed she looked tired.

'You think my cooking is shit so you brought your own cookies?' Sarah looked over Lauren's shoulder where I was opening one of the boxes and sneaking a cookie. 'Thanks.'

'Are you OK?' I whispered. Lauren ran a hand through her very slightly less than perfect hair and nodded.

'I'm sorry,' said the bride-to-be, closing up the box and slapping my fingers. 'I'm sure your food is awesome and we won't even need to put these out.' Even tired and irritated she had better diplomacy skills than anyone else I knew. 'Oh, and by the way, my mom and my sister are coming.'

'What?'

Surely not. Surely, surely not.

'But you said your mum wasn't coming,' I pointed out, trying to stay calm. 'Because, you know, she's completely cocking mental.'

'Don't exaggerate,' my friend replied, still concentrating on getting the peonies into the exact formation she was looking for and refusing to look me in the eye. 'And I would have thought after yesterday's stress, you'd be appreciative of the help. And hey, Sarah, Mom had an idea. Sounds kind of crazy, but how would you feel about going back to your natural colour for the wedding?'

Oh, Mom and her ideas.

'Excuse me?' Sarah reached up to her blonde topknot.

'Yeah, because Mom was looking at some photographs, and since Maddie and my sister are both brunette and you're a bottle blonde, she thought my photos would have more visual impact if I was the only one with light hair. What do you think?'

Without saying a word, it was quite obvious what Sarah thought.

'You want me to dye my hair for your wedding?' she asked.

Lauren shrugged and gave a big smile. 'Maybe it would be a fun change for you.'

'Maybe it would be a fun change for me?'

'New start and everything,' she said. 'Fresh.'

'Doesn't Sarah's flat look lovely?' I said loudly. 'Where did you get the throws from? They're so soft.'

'I'm not dyeing my fucking hair,' Sarah replied.

'Haven't heard of that place,' I said. 'Is it in Dalston?'

'OK, Sarah, don't be such a drama queen.' Lauren shrugged off her coat and threw it on the settee without so much as a glance at the lovely throws. 'I think you'd look great as a brunette. Mom just likes to throw some blue-sky ideas in.'

'I am going into the kitchen to check on my shit food,' Sarah announced. 'The other guests will be arriving very soon, I'm sure. I might just stay out of the way until they get here.'

Lauren looked at me and rolled her big blue eyes. 'What got into her today?'

'Oh, she's probably feeling sensitive,' I said, trying to be tactful as I picked up her coat and folded it tidily. 'It's a big deal for her to have a bridal shower in her flat this soon after Steve moved out. And telling her that her hair looks shit probably didn't win you any points. Blue-sky ideas? You knob.'

'So it's not about the cookies?' she asked, chewing her lip.

'I don't think they helped.' I frowned. 'Could you go into the kitchen and say something nice to her?'

Thoroughly chastened, she sucked in her cheeks and sloped off out of the room.

'Your hair doesn't make you look washed-out,' I heard her say before turning my attention to my phone. 'And your cookies are probably fine.'

Nothing from anyone at the office.

This meant one of two things – either I had completely got away with the Dickenson Debacle, or they were saving my punishment for Monday morning. I was definitely going to have to hit the Night Nurse if I wanted to get any sleep tonight.

'OhmygodMaddieyouburntdownthehouse?'

Lauren flew through the living-room door, her face flushed, her eyes wide.

'What?' I held my phone tightly in both hands.

'Did you burn down my dad's house?' she screeched at half the speed but twice the volume. 'Sarah said—'

'Sorry,' Sarah shouted from the kitchen. 'It just slipped out.'

'Thanks,' I shouted back. 'Massive help.'

'Maddie, the house.' Lauren clicked her fingers in my face, definitely not a move that made me want to kick her in the vag. 'Is it OK?'

'The house is fine,' I replied. 'There was a slight inci-dent with the margarita fountain and an absolute wanker who wouldn't put his fag out, but it was never not under control.'

'Tell her the bit about the rabbits going mental,' Sarah said, hanging off the doorframe with a tea towel over her shoulder. 'You may as well, now she knows.'

'I can't believe you weren't going to tell me.' Lauren looked as though she had just found out I was actually her mother. 'I trusted you, Maddie. My dad's gonna kill me.'

'Your dad isn't going to know,' I said. 'The house is fine, better than fine. It's spotless and shiny and every

Lindsey Kelk

bathroom is again full of toilet paper. If that isn't a selling point, I don't know what is. I'm sorry – I thought you'd have enough on your mind with the wedding.'

'Yeah, as if that isn't what's freaking me out now,' she said, pressing her hands to her face. She actually looked tearful. 'Your first party and you basically blow up the house? Should I be concerned about my wedding?'

'What's that supposed to mean?'

'I mean, I didn't want to say anything when we had to save your butt on Friday,' she said, hands on hips. 'But do I need to, like, check things? Make sure everything is what I asked for? Am I going to be icing my own cupcakes at two in the morning next weekend?'

'I reckon everything's fine, Lauren,' Sarah said, holding the tea towel in front of herself. 'Maddie's on top of it.'

'Like she was on top of the baby party?' Lauren asked. There was no stopping her.

'And we're not having cupcakes,' I reminded her. 'Cookie platters, remember?'

'I've tried not to be on your arse about this, Maddie, because you're supposed to be a professional . . .'

'I. Am. A. Professional,' I replied. It was happening again. Whatever had come over me in Shona's office was creeping up on me again. I was two seconds away from Hulking out on my best friends. 'And you haven't just been on my arse, Lauren, you've been so far up it, I can hardly sit down. Pain in the arse doesn't even cover it, and you haven't said thank you once.'

There was a chance I was shouting.

'There is nothing wrong with the house, and there is nothing wrong with your wedding,' I told her in a voice that was a bit louder than necessary. All right, I definitely was shouting. 'Everything has been booked, checked and

342

double-checked and it was all out of the goodness of my heart. We would usually charge thousands for the work I've done, let alone the midnight texts and crazy requests. Do you know how hard it is to get actual 3D printed renderings of you and Michael for the cake toppers? Do you? No. Now I've had a properly shit few days and I would like to sit down, eat some cake and drink some drinks. Just for today, if that's all right?'

I stopped. My heart was beating uncomfortably fast and my face felt hot, sweaty and red. There was a long pause. And then . . .

'Sure, sit down, take a load off, enjoy your Sunday,' she erupted, equally furious. 'It sounds to me like you don't have what it takes to get that event planner job. It sounds to me like it would be best if Sarah got it.'

My eyes opened so wide I thought they might fall out.

'Eh?' Came a voice from the side of the room.

'Nothing,' I said quickly. 'Ignore her.'

'Why would you get the job?' Sarah asked, clearly not ignoring her.

'Because Maddie –' Lauren yelled, stabbing her finger towards me – 'applied for it too, and she didn't want to tell you.'

'What?' Sarah blinked at me. 'Mads?'

'Only because you've had so much going on,' I protested. 'I wasn't not telling you just to not tell you. They asked me to apply at work. Matilda in HR told me I had to.'

'So why did they interview me?' Sarah looked confused. 'And why would you give them my CV if you were applying for the same job?'

I looked at the floor and offered her a non-committal shrug, struggling to come up with a good excuse.

'You did give them my CV, didn't you?' she asked.

'And why would you lie to me?' While Lauren still looked furious, Sarah just looked hurt, and that was the worst part by far. 'If you wanted the job that badly, why wouldn't you just tell me? Why would you lie?'

'Why wouldn't she tell me she tried to burn down my dad's house when I was just trying to do her a favour?' Lauren asked.

'Oh, shut up, Lauren,' Sarah snapped. 'You're not helping. This is not about you – can you get that into your head for once?'

Lauren's face went red. And then white. And then red again.

'I'm sorry I asked my best friend to help me organize the most important day of my life,' she exploded. 'And I'm sorry that I don't trust her lying ass. It's my wedding and I want it to be perfect.'

'It's not going to be perfect, is it?' I pointed out. 'It's hardly going to be a dream wedding when half the time you don't even want to get married in the first place.'

Apart from Sarah's perfectly timed gasp, the room was silent.

'Maddie.' Sarah spoke first but I didn't say a word. 'Lauren, she didn't mean that.'

'Yes she did,' Lauren said, staring me down. 'Thanks, Mads.'

'Whatever,' I muttered. I felt sick. I felt tired. I felt weirdly hungry.

'I think we all need to calm down,' Sarah said, folding her arms around herself. 'We're all just stressed.'

'What do you have to be stressed about?' Lauren asked. 'Go back to your shitty cooking and stay out of this.'

I did a double-take. Did she really say that?

'I've got plenty to be stressed about, actually.'

And Sarah was off.

'You've probably forgotten because your head is wedged so firmly up your own arse, but I'm in the middle of a divorce, and I did just find out my supposed best friend has been trying to shaft me for a job I really want, and my fucking cookies are *not* shit.'

'Will both of you just pack it in!' I screamed. 'Honestly, I don't want to hear it any more. I'm sick of it.'

They both turned to look at me, their mouths wide open, both revving up to start again.

'No, don't say a word,' I said, grabbing my handbag off the settee. 'I've done nothing but bend over backwards for the two of you for as long as I can remember and I'm done with it. I ask you to help me with one thing, and then you both just throw it back in my face. Yeah, I did apply for the events planner job, but only after they asked me to, and no, I didn't tell you because I thought you were going through enough shit, to be honest. And I wanted it. I knew if I told you, you'd talk me out of applying, so I didn't. And I thought probably you'd get it and I wouldn't. That was selfish – I'm sorry. But it is my work and my only chance at a promotion, and I didn't see, for once, why I should just hand it over to someone else just to be nice. I've been there for you every second, Sarah – I've made your tea and given you gin and my spare room is basically your bedroom now. I've answered every single middle-of-the-night phone call, I've sat up watching Challenge TV until four in the morning. This is the only time I've ever put myself first.'

Sarah busied herself folding her tea towel into a very small square.

'And I'm sorry I said that about your wedding,' I said to Lauren. 'But I have worked my tits off organizing it and replying to texts also at four in the morning and pulling miracles out of my arse to get it all done on time when you were having a meltdown, so yeah, a thank you might have been more appreciated than you throwing me under the bus as soon as you heard about the baby-naming, panicking about your dad's house, insulting me and implying I can't organize shit. I've worked nights and begged any number of favours to get your three-month countdown wedding how you wanted it, when any other planner would have laughed in your face.'

I took a breath.

'So from now on, you can sort it out, because I don't give a shit any more. And thanks for all the support on the Will stuff. And Tom stuff. Silly old Maddie, what a fool she is.'

I pulled two beautifully wrapped blue boxes out of my handbag and threw them in their general direction, then burst into tears. 'Matching necklaces,' I said, heading for the door. 'I thought they might be a bit silly, but hey, what do I know? Have a very lovely wedding and a very lovely life.'

I yanked the front door open to find Lauren's mum, sister and the rest of the bridal shower guests standing wide-eyed on the doorstep. 'Hello, Mrs Hobbs-Miller,' I said, pushing past her and down the front path. 'Bye, Mrs Hobbs-Miller.'

'Well, what was that about?' she asked loudly.

'Your daughter is a selfish, spoiled cow,' I shouted back from the street. 'Congratulations, you must be very proud.'

23

Monday July 27th
Today I feel: Oh, piss off.
Today I am thankful for: Seriously, go away.

'I imagine you know why you're in here?' Matilda sat across from me in the HR meeting room first thing on Monday morning.

'Are you giving me some kind of prize?' I asked, my hands clasped in front of me on the table in order to stop me crying.

Matilda did not crack a smile. Matilda looked as though she might not ever crack a smile again. And yet there was a plate of biscuits on the meeting-room table.

'The incident at the Dickenson party,' she said. 'Do you want to tell me about it?'

I pushed my shoe around the floor. 'Which one?'

I didn't mean to be rude to Matilda, but after my showdown with Sarah and Lauren the day before, I was done. Done with everyone and everything.

'Why don't you just talk me through it?' Matilda suggested. 'From the beginning, so I have all the details.'

'Well, I'm guessing you've seen the pictures, so I can keep it brief,' I replied.

She had. I was fairly certain everyone in the office had. The photographer had emailed me a link to the look book late Sunday night. After I'd finished sobbing all the way home from Sarah's house, I'd spent a good couple of hours wailing at photos of Seb and his baby on Facebook, then stalking Will and his girlfriend on Instagram, and finally, when I was catatonic on the settee, I necked half a bottle of gin and watched last year's *Downton Abbey* Christmas special. And during all of that, somehow, a work email had managed to pass me by. Thankfully, Shona had been awake, had been in a far more productive mood, seen the email, down-loaded all the photos and forwarded them to half the company.

'The original venue cancelled on me the day before the event, meaning I had to find a new venue and several new suppliers at the last minute. Everything was in place on the day and the event was going well right up until some dickhead threw a lit cigarette into a fountain full of tequila – I'm assuming that's the incident you're refer-ring to?' I was angry and hoping it didn't show.

Matilda nodded.

'Well, that's it, in a nutshell. Tequila is, curiously enough, very flammable. Turns out no one mentioned that when we hired the fountain or researched the idea. There was a brief fire risk, but between Sharaline, the fire extinguisher and a lovely British summer shower, it was out before anyone or anything could get damaged. We even got the full deposit back on the fountain. No one was injured, the fire was contained, it was just very unfortunate that the skies opened and rained on everyone as well.'

'The Dickensons sent over a slightly more detailed email this morning,' Matilda said, pulling a piece of paper out of her notebook. 'They mentioned something about "demented storks terrorizing the party guests" and "rabbits that looked like they were covered in blood giving the children nightmares".'

'They asked for pink rabbits!' There didn't seem to be a lot of point in defending myself, but if you'd spent three hours dip-dyeing two dozen rabbits by hand, it would have annoyed you too. 'The storks got upset by the rain, the storks upset the rabbits. As I said, it was unfortunate.'

'So it wasn't the fire that upset the storks?'

I considered it for a moment. 'Could have been.'

'Maddie, you must agree this looks terrible for us as a firm. Your role is not only to deliver the clients' dream event, but to make sure nothing gets in the way of a great experience for them. With all due respect, it couldn't really have been worse.' She paused, and held up a hand when she saw me open my mouth again, ready to protest.

'The Dickensons have suggested they don't feel comfortable paying the second half of their bill,' she said. 'Which as you know is a considerable sum.'

'Oh, Christ, you're not going to make me pay it, are you?' I asked, visions of my overdraft spinning through my head. Lauren's wedding had cost me a bloody fortune – I was almost stony broke.

'No, but I'm afraid we're going to have to terminate your contract with the company,' she replied gently.

'Oh,' I whispered. 'Bugger.'

'We're eliminating your position,' she said. 'There's

going to be a restructure, with Shona taking over as director of events and a new events manager reporting in to her and a team assistant. Mr Colton confirmed the plans this morning.'

'Oh.' I glanced across at the plate of cookies. 'Then I think I will have a biscuit.'

'Maddie, I get the feeling you're not taking this terrible seriously,' Matilda said, snapping out of HR mode for just a moment. 'I pushed you for this. I honestly thought you were capable of it.'

'I was,' I said, taking a cookie anyway. 'I am. I dealt with the cancellation of the first venue and I pulled off an amazing party. And now you're telling me none of that matters because of something I had absolutely no control over. To be honest, Matilda, I feel like punching someone in the face, but I don't think that would help right now, would it?'

'Not really.' Matilda looked doubtful. 'What reason did they give you? For cancelling?'

'They said the permits and insurance weren't filed correctly,' I admitted. 'But they were. I checked them and double-checked them myself. I've done that same paperwork a thousand times over.'

'It doesn't matter now,' she said, pushing a manila envelope across the table. 'We're letting you go because of the restructure.'

I looked at the envelope but refused to touch it.

'I'm serious, Matilda. Look at the pictures before the bloody margarita fountain burst into flames, which, by the way, was not my fault and could not possibly have been predicted. All the guests were told the party was no smoking and we put the fire out before anyone got hurt. What else could I have done? We should be suing the arse off that guest who was smoking.'

I broke my cookie in half and scoffed it while I waited for her response.

'It doesn't matter now,' she said with a resigned sigh. 'You should have done a proper health and safety assessment on the margarita fountain, I expect. But Colton won't be talked round on this. It's way past formal warning stage. I think it goes without saying that the company can't give you a reference, but if something comes up, you can use me as a personal one. Just don't tell anyone, for God's sake.'

I nodded, taking a deep breath and slowly reaching out for the envelope. I couldn't think of another time when I'd felt quite so much like shit. This was it. No friends, no boyfriend, and now no job. What was I going to tell people? And who were the people I was going to tell?

'I really did do a good job,' I said, sniffing. 'I know I did.'

'I am sorry,' Matilda said.

'Can you do me a favour?' I asked, standing up slowly. 'Can you make sure the Wheeler party goes to the new events person and not Shona?'

'I'll try,' she said. She looked at me a bit more sympathetically. 'Do you want to go out the back way?'

'No,' I said, in a terribly unconvinced tone. There was a silence. 'I need to get some stuff from my desk anyway.'

'Do you want me to come with you?'

'If I were to punch Shona right in the fake tits, what would happen? Hypothetically speaking.'

'Hypothetically speaking,' she replied. 'I imagine I'd carry you out on my shoulders.'

'Just checking,' I said, flexing my hands. 'Hypothetically speaking.'

It wasn't as though the office was usually abuzz with excitement on a Monday morning, but when Matilda and I walked across to my desk, me with cardboard box in hand, everyone was especially quiet. All I could hear was the clicking of a hundred keyboards, all locked in IM conversations, and all of them about me.

'In case you were wondering, the black eye isn't from the party,' I said loudly, resting the box on my desk. 'But thanks for your concern.'

'Maddie.' Sharaline stood up at her desk. 'This isn't fair.'

'Life's not fair,' I replied, trying to stay calm. 'If I hadn't applied for the promotion, I wouldn't be leaving. If I hadn't punched above my weight with Will, I wouldn't have been punched in the face. Learn my lessons, Sharaline – do not overreach.'

'But it wasn't your fault,' she protested, turning towards Matilda. 'Maddie did everything right. I checked again when I refiled the paperwork for the new venue. Someone must have called them or sabotaged us.'

'Someone?' I asked.

'If you checked someone's emails –' Sharaline stared at Matilda and cocked her head back towards the corner office – 'you might find out.'

'You read her emails?' I was impressed. 'That's awesome. Why did I never think of that?' Then I stopped. Shona would really go that far?

'She saves her passwords in a keychain,' she replied. 'She's an idiot. Anyway, it's not Maddie's fault.'

Matilda was looking increasingly awkward. I wasn't sure what the protocol was these days for wild allegations made by interns in an emotional situation, and I had a feeling that when it involved someone who was already sacked (and who had set fire to a fountain) there wouldn't be an inquiry.

'Sharaline, can you get in here, please?' Shona shouted from her office. 'Let HR deal with the situation. Don't get involved.'

Ten years working together and I was just a 'situation'. Brilliant.

'Are you just going to leave?' she asked me, clutching her notepad to her chest as though it were armour. 'Aren't you going to say anything?'

I looked over at Shona's office. She and her ridiculous pineapple of a ponytail were staring hard at her computer screen, trying not to look over. It wasn't like her not to be out here gloating all over someone else's misfortune. What Sharaline was saying all made sense. I chose to think that maybe Shona was suffering the side effects of remorse. It was unlikely, but stranger things had happened. Like dyed pink rabbits running amok at a baby-naming ceremony in Greater London.

There were a million things I wanted to say, a million things she needed to hear, but if I'd learned nothing else over the last few weeks, it was when to leave well alone. Shona wouldn't learn her lesson; some people never did. If I went in there, all guns blazing, it would just set her off. Look what had happened the last time I gave her a rollocking. I knew I was in the right, and I knew karma would bite her on the arse eventually. This was the universe doing me a favour.

On cue, Shona looked up, glancing over at my desk. With a perfectly straight face, I stretched out my hand and held up my middle finger, while mouthing the most unpleasant word I could possibly think of. Shona's eyebrows shot up and she reached out for her blinds, dropping them as fast as humanly possible.

'I think that covers it,' I said to Sharaline, emptying my top drawer into the waiting cardboard box. 'It would only make her feel better about herself, and the greatest thing to come out of this is that I won't have to work for her any more.'

'What are you going to do?' Her shoulders sank as she realized I was actually going.

'I don't know,' I said, resting my box on my hip, starting to find Shona's refusal to meet my eye almost funny. 'I've got quite a lot of telly to catch up on. I've been busy lately.'

'I'm going to miss you,' she said, her bottom lip quivering. Whether it was the thought of my departure or the thought of being left alone with Shona I wasn't quite sure, but I was touched nonetheless.

'Aww,' I said, giving her a sideways hug before striding over to the lift with Matilda by my side. 'I'm going to miss you too, Sharaline.'

Another thing I never thought I'd say.

Congratulations!

Today is the big day.

Everything that has happened since your bride asked you to join her on this journey has led to today.

You are her bridesmaid. You are her friend, her sister, her support, her shoulder to cry on, the person she trusts with her most precious secrets and the protector of her heart.

Enjoy your special day, bridesmaid, and treasure it forever.

24

Saturday August 1st
Today I feel: All of the feels.
Today I am thankful for: I don't know – what have you got?

By the time Saturday rolled around, I hadn't left the house in a week.

You'd think being unemployed, housebound and excommunicated by both your best friends would leave me some time to clean up, but no, I hadn't done that either. Since the second I had walked in on Monday morning, the only person I had spoken to was the Domino's delivery man, and our exchanges, though frequent, were not especially involved.

When my phone lit up with Lauren's name on Thursday afternoon I'd got a little bit overexcited, but it wasn't my best friend ready to make amends, it was her mother, ready to disinvite me to the rehearsal dinner.

I showered on Saturday morning, but only because I'd woken up when I rolled over in the night and smelled myself, and when I went to make a cup of tea I was completely out of milk. Finally I was going to be forced out of doors. Peering out of the window, I wondered if civilization still stood. The world could have been overwhelmed by zombies and I wouldn't have noticed. I could probably have passed for one myself; they wouldn't have bothered me. Especially if they could smell me.

My bridesmaid dress hung on the front of my wardrobe in its fancy grey garment bag, the lilac fabric giving me the finger through the little clear window on the front.

'Piss off,' I told it, rubbing my hair too roughly with my towel.

We hadn't spoken since the bridal shower, any of us. Well, for all I knew, Sarah, Lauren, Lauren's mental mother and horrible sister spent the afternoon eating crappy cupcakes and dressing each other up in toilet-paper wedding dresses, all the while debating which of them I had wronged the most, but neither of them had been in touch with me.

'I don't care,' I said to the dress. We'd become very friendly in the last week, but it didn't give much back on the conversation front. 'No job, no boyfriend, no friends. Fresh start.'

Only there was no start in sight. I was stuck with nothing other than a painful, protracted ending.

I sat on the bed, damp hair hanging down my back, wet towel in my hands.

'If this were a romcom, Will would be banging my door down about now,' I told the dress. 'He'd have realized the error of his ways or found out she was shagging someone else, at least, and be battering the front door in last night's suit with a dozen red roses in his hand.'

The dress just hung there.

'I don't want him anyway. It would just be so I could tell him to fuck off.'

Still nothing.

'No?' I asked, face falling. 'You're probably right. Maybe it wasn't my romcom. Maybe it was hers. Maybe I was the obstacle.'

I didn't bother with the bit I sometimes thought about, where Tom turned up on my doorstep with a bottle of Hendrick's and a packet of biscuits. And I didn't tell him to fuck off, since I'd already done that.

I stood up, letting the towel fall on the floor. Along with my pyjamas, my outfit from the baby shower, and the clothes I'd been wearing at work on Monday.

'Feels more like a horror story anyway.'

I mooched around my bedroom for a while, slathering on lotions and potions I never had time for, drying my hair carefully with the hairdryer instead of letting it poof up of its own accord, and finally, when there were no more things left in the bathroom to fanny about with, I went back, unzipped the garment carrier and pulled it off the most perfect bridesmaid dress that ever existed. It was one-shouldered, baby-soft lilac silk, fitted at the waist and then falling all the way to the floor with a slit from here to there. I had to hand it to Lauren – it took a brave bride to let her bridesmaids wear something as beautiful as this.

'Do you want to go and get some milk with me?' I asked.

The dress was playing things cool, but it seemed like it was into it.

Fifteen minutes later, I was sitting on the settee nursing a cup of tea, my computer on my lap, handbag by my side, wearing a £400 bridesmaid dress while I checked Facebook for the thousandth time that day. Neither Sarah nor Lauren had posted a single thing since Sunday, but there were a lot of well-wishers posting to Lauren's page. Because she was getting married. Because it was her wedding day. And I was sitting on the settee wearing a bridesmaid dress, contemplating going out for milk.

I clicked on my photos, scrolling back, back, back to the photos of Sarah's wedding. Thankfully it was before the days of Facebook, so we weren't captured and held up for judgement in real time, but Sarah had uploaded the photos afterwards. She had untagged herself in all of them, I noticed, but she hadn't taken them down, not yet. I remembered untagging myself in my photos with Seb. I had breezed through my pics, knowing they were still there, that if I really needed them they were only a search away, but the photos he had posted were another matter altogether. The whole purpose of that evening was to move on, but I'd spent hours crying over happier times and staring at photos to commit them to memory, knowing I would never see them again as soon as I clicked my mouse.

It took me a very long time to actually delete my photos. I wondered how long it would take Sarah to take down the wedding album.

'Oh God,' I moaned, pressing my hands against my face. 'I can't do this.'

It was ridiculous. Here I was, in a bridesmaid dress without a bride to maid, staring at the Internet and going slowly insane.

Picking up my handbag, I headed for the door. I couldn't sit here on my own all day, refreshing feeds and waiting for someone to upload pictures of the wedding. Yes, we'd had an argument, yes, it was a big one, and yes, we all needed a slap round the chops, but letting it fester on Lauren's wedding day felt all wrong.

It was my romcom. I would make the grand romantic gesture, only the gesture would be to the real loves of my life.

With a renewed sense of purpose and an elevated heartbeat for the first time in five days, I stuck my feet into my trainers and threw myself down the stairs, only to slam straight into someone outside the front door.

'It's you.' I rubbed my bashed-in nose. 'What are you doing here?'

'I kept calling your office and they kept saying you weren't available,' Tom said, rubbing his stomach as though my poor nose had hurt it in some way. It hadn't. He was rock solid, I noted at the back of my brain. 'So I found out your address.'

'You stalked me?' I said. 'You found out my address and then hung about outside, not ringing the doorbell? How long have you been here?'

'I saw you go out earlier,' he said, shoving his hands deep into his pockets. 'I thought I'd missed you. But then you came back so, I thought I'd give it another go.'

I pointed back up the stairs. 'I went out for milk.'

Tom Wheeler was standing on my doorstep.

He had actually stalked me, like in films and books.

I felt so special, even if he hadn't brought gin or biscuits.

'Bit dressed up for milk,' he said, nodding towards my frock, then frowning at my trainers. 'Going anywhere nice?'

The cardigan I'd thrown over my shoulders on the way out didn't especially go with the dress, but what can you do?

'Actually, I'm in a bit of a rush,' I said, hoisting my handbag onto my shoulder. 'Can we make this quick, I need to get a taxi.'

'Let me give you a lift,' he offered, pulling car keys out of his pocket and dangling them off his index finger. 'Where are you going?'

'East,' I said, snatching the keys from his hand. 'Is it OK if I drive?'

'No,' he said, snatching them back. 'It's the Range Rover across the road and you're not insured.'

'All right, Dad,' I muttered, following him across the street. 'Of course you drive a wanker mobile.'

'I'm so glad I decided to do this,' he said to himself as the car beeped to declare itself unlocked. 'Good move, Tom, great decision.'

'Not that I want to risk my lift,' I said, punching the address into Tom's GPS, 'but what are you doing here?'

'Do we have to have this conversation while I'm driving?' he asked, turning on the engine. 'Why couldn't I get hold of you at work all week? Why have they given my mother's party to someone called Sharaline?'

'Thank God it isn't Shona,' I sighed, relieved. 'I got fired. On Monday.'

'Oh fuck, really?' He pulled a face. 'Not because of the eye?'

'No, because I was kind of responsible for setting fire to a fountain and, well, there were some rabbits and some storks involved, but it's a very long story.'

He stared at me for a moment and then pulled out into traffic.

'*Stop the car!*' I shouted, slamming my hands on the glove compartment. 'Tom, Stop the car!'

'What's wrong?' Tom slammed on the brakes, a chain

of traffic honking and swearing behind us. 'Maddie, what is it?'

'Over there,' I said, unbuckling my seat belt and scrambling to climb out of the car. It was ridiculous – who needed such a huge car to pootle around London? 'In the dress.'

Outside my flat, a short, skinny blonde girl was pressing the buzzer and rummaging around in a lilac clutch bag that perfectly matched my frock.

'Sarah,' I screamed, hanging on to the car door.

'Get out the road, you silly cow,' a man in a white van yelled.

Offering him a middle-finger salute, I hurled myself across the street, barrelling down my front path and rugby-tackling my best friend.

'I was on my way to your house,' I said as we squeezed each other tightly and jumped up and down. 'I was coming to see you.'

'I was sitting on the settee, and it was so miserable, and I hated myself,' she said, breaking the hug to catch her tears before they could ruin her eyeliner. Which was, of course, perfect. 'I'm so sorry. I shouldn't have told Lauren about the fire – I just couldn't have her in the kitchen looking at me for another second. I thought I was going to—'

Sarah broke off, her hands gripping an invisible neck in midair.

'I'm sorry I said all that horrible stuff,' I said, struggling to get the words out fast enough. 'And I'm sorry I didn't tell you I was up for the job. They really did ask me to apply. I hadn't even considered it until they suggested it.'

'We were both a pair of fuckwits,' she said. 'Agreed?'

I nodded readily. 'Agreed.'

'They offered me the job,' Sarah said. 'At Colton-Bryers.'

They offered her the job. My job.

'Of course they did,' I said, trying a genuine smile on for size. 'Congratulations.'

'I didn't take it, did I?' Sarah said. She punched me hard in the arm. 'How weird would that be?'

'But you hate your job.' I was secretly pleased but outwardly confused. 'That was stupid.'

'Well, no, I was thinking—' she said as Tom's car beeped twice across the road. 'What if we went into business together?'

I looked at my best friend. It was a startling thing when someone you thought you knew inside out could still shock you. And not just because I realized her hair was in a messy chignon instead of a topknot.

'Are you serious?' I asked. 'Really? You would want to do that?'

'I liked the idea of doing proper event planning full time,' she explained. 'But I don't have your experience or your contacts. But I will have the money from my flat soon. We're selling it.'

'You can live with me!' I shrieked, grabbing her forearms and jumping up and down again. 'You can move into the spare room!'

'Well, no, let's not be silly,' she said. I stopped jumping.

'Are you serious?' I asked. 'You want us to work together?'

'After the way you saved Lauren's hen do?' she replied. 'And the baby party? And, I don't know, planned an entire wedding in three months *in your spare time*? Are you kidding? I'd be an idiot not to.'

'Well, yeah,' I said. This was no time for false modesty.

'As long as no one throws a fag into a tequila fountain, I am quite good.'

'But we've made a lot of money on that place, and I'm not going to buy anywhere right away. Fuck it, Mads, why not give it a go?'

'You're not in any way put off by the fact that my last party ended in a near rabbit-slash-stork-slash-flaming tequila massacre?' I asked.

'If anything, I'm intrigued,' she replied. I threw my arms around lovely, dry, funny Sarah and gave her a huge hug.

'I don't want to ask a silly question,' Tom said, fidgeting with his keys at the bottom of the path, 'but surely there's a reason why you're wearing matching dresses.'

'And you are?' Sarah broke the hug to give Tom the filthiest look known to man. 'Oh, wait, aren't you the usher?'

'I'm Tom,' he said, looking slightly perplexed. 'We haven't been introduced.'

'He is very tall, isn't he,' she said to me, ignoring him. 'Didn't seem *that* tall in photos. It's quite intimidating in person.'

'When have you seen me in photos?' Tom asked. 'Who are you?'

'I'm Sarah,' she said, pushing me out of the way to shake his hand. 'I'm Maddie's best friend.' She turned to me again. 'Why is he here?'

'I'm not entirely sure,' I said. 'But he was going to drive me over to yours.'

Sarah turned back to Tom. 'Why are you here?'

'Um, well, all right then,' he said, squeezing the back of his neck. 'I came to tell Maddie that I was very sorry about what happened last week, that I couldn't stop thinking about her, and that I very well might actually probably love her. A bit. Sort of.'

'That's the best you've got?' Sarah asked, arms folded. 'Seriously?'

'You love me a bit?' I asked, shoving her sideways to stand in front of him, leaning back to get a proper look at his face. 'That's ridiculous.'

'At the very least, intense and irrational like,' he said. 'Which I think translates into love. Or somewhere thereabouts.'

'But why?' I asked, trying to think of anything I could have done to him that was the slightest bit lovable.

'You actually want a list?' he asked.

I pinched my shoulders together in a small shrug. 'Actually, yes.'

'I don't want to be rude, but are you autistic?' Sarah asked. 'No, really? Because I worked with this guy—'

'Shut up, Sarah,' I said, still staring at Tom. 'Do you mean it?'

'I'd be a bit of a dick if I didn't,' he replied, his face red and flustered.

'Right then,' I said.

'Right then,' he repeated.

'I don't want to get in the way of a moment,' Sarah said, literally getting in the way of the moment, 'but we're not dressed like this because we're auditioning for *Britain's Got Talent*. Shouldn't we get over to Lauren's house?'

'Lauren?' Tom asked. 'There's a Lauren?'

'Is that offer of a lift still open?' I said, squeezing his wrist.

Not quite his hand, but still, I was getting there.

* * *

'She's not here,' I said, opening the passenger door to Tom's stupid car. 'I've knocked on all the doors, I've looked in all the windows, I explained to the neighbour that I wasn't trying to break in and they said she hasn't been home for a couple of days. She's probably staying with her mum or her sister or something.'

'She's not answering her phone either.' Sarah held up her own phone in defeat. 'I've left a message. Should we go to the venue?'

'There's nowhere for her to be at the venue.' I shook my head. 'The church hasn't got anywhere to wait, and the reception is miles away, that's why we were supposed to get ready here.'

'You can't ambush her at the church,' Tom reasoned. 'You'll have to wait until after the wedding.'

'Guerrilla bridesmaids!' Sarah exclaimed. 'Why not?'

'What, we just follow her up the aisle and force her to forgive us?' I asked. 'Actually, that's not a bad idea.'

'There are still a few hours,' Sarah reasoned. 'Let's go back to yours, have a drink and see if she calls us back.'

'I like how you slipped "have a drink" in there,' I said, resignedly clambering back into the car. 'Really, why do you need this?' I asked. 'It's ridiculous.'

'Because I'm six foot six and I'd look stupid in a Mini?' he replied. 'Now, where can I drive you to next, your majesty?'

'Oh, Maddie,' Sarah said, her seatbelt clunking closed. 'I like him.'

It took a while to find for a parking space big enough for Tom's Wank Rover on my street but forty-five minutes after we left Lauren's house and two hours before Lauren's wedding, we traipsed up my front path to find the front door wide open.

'Did you leave it open?' I asked Sarah as we hovered outside.

'I didn't even unlock it,' she replied, holding her clutch bag up in an attack position.

'You left in a rush,' Tom said. 'Maybe you forgot to lock it,' he said, running back towards the car. 'Hang on a second. Don't go in.'

'I never forget to lock it,' I said, pushing the door open cautiously. 'I'm thirty-one, I live alone, and I watch loads of police procedurals. I never, ever forget to lock it.'

Tom reappeared and edged in front of me, the steering lock he'd grabbed from his car in his hands, and stepped lightly onto the stairs.

'And they say chivalry is dead,' Sarah swooned.

'Chivalry might not be, but he will be if there's a murderer up there,' I replied. 'Idiot.'

'Better him than you,' she whispered. 'No offence, but, you know, for me.'

'No, totally fair,' I agreed.

But unless murderers had started screaming like terrified women and wearing ten grand's worth of embellished Jenny Packham, there was no murderer in my flat, just Lauren.

'Oh my God!' she screamed. 'Oh my God!'

'Calm down,' Tom said, still brandishing the steering lock. 'It's all right, calm down.'

'Lauren!' I rushed across the room to where she was sitting on my sofa, drowning in a puddle of tulle and gin. 'What are you doing here?'

'I can't do this,' she said, shaking her head and crying

fresh tears. Which followed the tracks of several rounds of sobbing that had come before. 'I can't.'

'It's OK,' I said, grabbing both of her hands. 'Tell me what's wrong.'

Sarah grabbed two mugs and a measuring jug from the cupboard and ran to Lauren's side. The clever girl already had the gin and tonic ready on the coffee table.

'I can't get married,' she said through a torrent of hiccups. 'I can't even organize a wedding without losing my best friends. How am I supposed to get married?'

'Don't be silly,' Sarah said, pouring the gin while she spoke. Sarah was all about priorities. 'We're here, aren't we? We're all here together now?'

'Where were you?' she asked, blinking at our outfits. 'You're wearing your dresses.'

'We were at your house.' I smiled gently and held the gin to her mouth as though she was a toddler. An alcoholic toddler wearing a dress that cost more than six months' rent. 'We were looking for you. We came to say sorry, about everything.'

'But it's all my fault,' she sighed before hiccupping again. 'I was so hung up on making the wedding perfect, I treated the two of you like shit.'

'You did,' Sarah said. 'But we forgive you.'

I gave her a stern look, but she sipped her gin out of the measuring jug and ignored me.

'I thought, if I could make the wedding perfect, make it my dream wedding, I would stop freaking out about it,' she said, nodding slowly and accepting another mouthful of gin. 'But it just made me more crazy. I'm so sorry, you guys. I was sitting at the rehearsal dinner last night and there were these two huge empty spaces that were driving me crazy, and I knew I couldn't do it. I want to marry Michael, but I don't want to do it if you guys aren't there with me. I'd rather run off to Vegas and elope.'

'Not after all the bloody work I've done,' I said. 'You're having that sodding wedding.'

'I'm trying to say none of that matters to me,' she corrected herself. 'Not that I don't appreciate it. I super appreciate it. But the wedding doesn't matter, does it? It's the people that matter.'

'Let's not use that as a slogan for the new business,' Sarah said.

'What did I tell you when we were in the loos?' I asked Lauren. 'This is all about you. If you don't want to go through with it, we don't go through with it. No one else has a say in it – not your mum, not your sister, not even Michael. If you want to run off to Vegas, I'll book the flights. But I'm going to need your credit card and your dad is still going to have to pay for today.'

Lauren looked at me and then at Sarah.

'Better to call it off today than ten years down the line,' Sarah said. 'Trust me.'

'You really went to my house?' Lauren asked.

'I can vouch for them,' Tom said, holding his steering lock aloft. 'They went to your house.'

'Who is that guy?' she whispered. 'He's so tall.'

'I wanted to say sorry,' I said, giving her a squeeze. 'About all of it.'

'So did I,' Sarah added, jumping onto the sofa and resting her head on Lauren's bare shoulder. 'To both of you. We've all been going through so much. Shall we promise to try one major life change at a time from now on?'

'We can try,' I said. 'But you're just tempting fate.'

'Guys, I'm sorry,' Lauren said, pulling me onto the settee and sliding her hand around my waist. 'I am. I missed you so much. I love your dumb faces.'

'Do you lot fall out often?' Tom asked. 'Is this normal?'

'Yes,' we all replied at once, with varying degrees of acceptance.

'Duly noted,' he said. 'Maddie, your flat is a disgrace.'

The best thing to do with that comment was ignore it.

With Tom off at the supermarket to pick up emergency supplies, we settled in on the sofa to calm Lauren's nerves.

'I can't believe you got fired,' she said, giving me a sympathetic sniff. 'That's so shitty. Can you sue? It's clearly unfair dismissal.'

'I bet my lawyers have someone who could look into it,' Sarah offered. 'We could get a group deal?'

'Are you doing OK?' Lauren asked her. 'I still can't believe I said all those awful things to you at the bridal shower. It's kept me awake all week.'

Sarah squeezed her face into an expression that didn't seem certain about anything. 'I will be,' she said with uncertainty. 'It's hard to stop loving someone because they've stopped loving you. But I'll be OK. I have you two wankers.'

'I'm back!' The front door slammed just in time and Tom thundered up the stairs. 'I didn't know exactly what to bring so I brought everything.'

He emptied three great big carrier bags onto the kitchen top. He was not lying. This man was a wonder.

'So, about the wedding.' I smiled at him and then turned back to Lauren. 'What are we doing? Are we off to the church or is it four tickets to Vegas?'

'I want to marry Michael,' she said confidently. 'But I'm so scared of my wedding.'

'There's nothing to be scared of,' Sarah promised, taking her hand. 'Maddie has everything under control, and we're going to be there every second of it.'

'I might have done some phoning around yesterday,' I confessed. 'Everything is going to be perfect. It's going to be the most amazing wedding ever. Even brides with years to plan get nervous about something this incredible, and Lauren, it's going to be incredible.'

'It is?' she asked, sniffing delicately and hiccupping one last time.

'The most incredible wedding ever,' I confirmed. 'Which I think you kind of deserve because you have the most incredible bridesmaids ever.'

'And I don't know about Maddie, but I'm in,' Sarah said, looking down at her frock. 'I got dressed up and everything. We might as well do it.'

'Me too,' I said. 'Although I need to do my hair.'

'And your make-up,' Lauren said. 'Or not! Whatever you want.'

The two of them heaved themselves out of my sunken sofa and began straightening each other's dresses.

'I don't suppose you fancy going to a wedding?' I said, leaning over the back of the settee to look at Tom.

'Bit of an intense first date.' He looked down at his black trousers and white shirt. 'And people might think I'm a waiter.'

'God forbid,' I replied, giving him a small smile. 'Can we at least get a lift?'

'So that's it, is it?' he asked, as I clambered upright and stared up at him. 'You just want me for a chauffeur.'

'Well, that and I sort of irrationally, intensely like you,'

I said, punching him in the arm. 'Now that I've come to think about it.'

The wedding, of course, was a complete success. Michael and Lauren both showed up, the butterflies were released on time, and no one died of a peanut allergy. It was genuinely everything we could ever have asked for.

The newly married couple were halfway through their first dance when the master of ceremonies invited the rest of the couples at the wedding to join them. Lauren's mum took the arm of Michael's dad, Michael's brother took the arm of Lauren's step-mum, and Sarah snapped up Lauren's dad so fast, I was worried she was about to start World War Three. But Lauren was so busy staring into the eyes of her husband, she didn't even notice. If I'd ever had my doubts about the two of them, they were gone in that moment.

'What's up with you, girl?'

Michael's ancient grandmother buzzed over to me on her electric wheelchair, a plaid blanket over her fuchsia skirt suit and a half-empty bottle of whisky that wasn't from my bar in her hand.

'No one to dance with?'

'Nice to meet you, Mrs . . .' I trailed off awkwardly, trying to avoid her bloodshot blue eyes. 'Are you having a nice time?'

'You don't want to sit there mooning after them,' she said, pointing to all the dancing couples. 'You want to get yourself a fella. None of you are getting any younger.'

'Thanks for the advice,' I replied.

'You'll end up like me,' she warned. 'More than a hundred lovers but never a husband to my name.'

'Oh, really.' I looked at her with a newfound interest. 'Doesn't sound that bad to me.'

'You want someone who's going to take care of you,' she warned, shaking the bottle of whisky in my general direction. 'Not someone who's going to knock your socks off in the bedroom.'

'Luckily, she's got both.' A hand reached out towards me and Tom stood there smiling. 'Sorry,' he said. 'I was having a whizz. Would you like to dance?'

I looked doubtfully at his outstretched hand.

'I washed them,' he said.

'All right then,' I said. 'And yes, I will dance, but only because I know you're good.'

Michael's grandmother nodded approvingly as Tom led me out to the dance floor.

'No fancy waltzing tonight?' I asked as he pulled me in close and we swayed lightly to the rhythm.

'The waltz isn't that fancy,' he said. 'You've been seriously deprived of dancing all these years.'

'I do a mean "Birdy Song",' I replied, affronted. 'You wait until that comes on – I'm going to blow your mind.'

He smiled gently and I was quiet for a moment, not sure of what to say next. He had been amazing all day, from driving us to the wedding to helping out when little things went awry. And now here he was, dancing with me at my best friend's wedding.

'Did you mean what you said just then?' I couldn't look at him, it was all too much. 'To Michael's grandmother?'

'About taking care of you or knocking your socks off?' he asked.

'Both?' I whispered.

'Both,' he replied.

Smiling, I pulled away from his chest and looked up. Standing in front of Tom, I brushed my own hair out of my own eyes and took his hand in mine. The girls weren't wrong – he really was ridiculously tall. It took him so long to lean down and put his lips to mine, I thought I was going to pass out from holding my breath for so long, but it was worth it. He pulled me into him, his huge hand on the small of my back, my whole body close to his, and it felt like something I'd been missing for the longest time.

'Question,' I said, my voice breaking as we parted. 'Did I ever get you to sign a contract for your mum's birthday party? Because Sarah and I are going into business together, and I think we'd do a very good job of it.'

'Will you please shut up, Maddie,' he said, pulling me into another kiss.

'My brother says I need to learn how to say no,' I replied, pulling away.

'He's right,' Tom said, pressing his lips firmly against mine. 'Start tomorrow.'

It wasn't bad advice. I decided to take it.

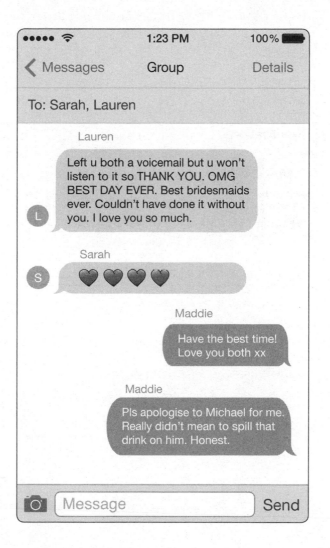

Notifications

Lauren Hobbs-Miller married **Michael Morgan**

Maddie Fraser and **Sarah Hempel** like this

See all notifications

David Hobbs <dhobbs@DavidHobbs.com>
To: Lauren Hobbs <lhobbs@DavidHobbs.com>

Hello Pumpkin!

Hope you're having fun in the sun.

Quick question – just back from a showing at the Teddington house and wondering if you could explain why there appears to be a family of pink rabbits living in the shed?

Lots of love,
Dad xxx

Atkinson & Associates

Dear Mr Colton,

As per our conversation on August 16th regarding the termination of Madeline Fraser's contract of employment, we will be representing Ms Fraser in this matter henceforth.

Following a thorough review of Ms Fraser's case, we will be pursuing compensation from your company for unfair dismissal.

We look forward to discussing the matter further.

Yours sincerely,
Andrea Atkinson

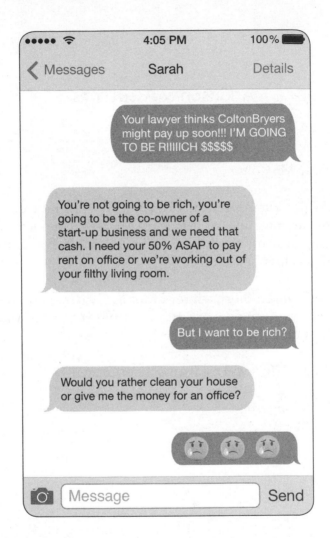

To our dearest darling Maddie,

We're so proud of you! Can't wait to 'like' FraserHempel on Facebook.

Lots of love,

Mum and Dad
XXX

Sharaline Michaels <sharaline@coltonbryers.com>
To: MatildaJacobs <matilda@coltonbryers.com>

Dear Ms Jacobs,

Please accept this email as notice of my resignation.

Thank you so much for the opportunities offered to me at Colton-Bryers but I have decided to pursue other opportunities outside of the company. Mostly because my manager is an unconscionable monster and I'm scared that she's going to shaft me like she shafted Maddie. That or kill me in my sleep.

As per my contract, my last day will be next Friday. If I live that long.

Yours sincerely,

Sharaline Michaels

PRESS RELEASE

FraserHempel Events

Dear Friends,

We are delighted to announce that FraserHempel Events will be open for business as of the end of the month. We can't wait to plan your next event and bring your dreams to reality.

For more information and to see examples of our previous events, please visit www.fraserhempel.com or contact our assistant: sharaline@fraserhempel.com

Matilda Jacobs <matilda@coltonbryers.com>
To: Shona Matthews <shona@coltonbryers.com>

Dear Shona,

I have just sent you an Outlook invitation for a meeting with myself and Mr Colton, in my office tomorrow at nine a.m.

In the absence of both of your assistants, I wanted to make sure you saw the message as this is a very important matter.

KR

Matilda

Director of HR
Colton-Bryers

Shona Matthews <shona@coltonbryers.com>
To: Matilda Jacobs <matilda@coltonbryers.com>

M

Would love to attend but, in the absence of both my assistants, am v v busy. Apologies.

Director of Events
Colton-Bryers

Matilda Jacobs <matilda@coltonbryers.com>
To: Shona Matthews <shona@coltonbryers.com>

Dear Shona,

You're in enough shit as it is.
Just be there.

KR

Matilda

Director of HR
Colton-Bryers

Dear Seb,
Here's your post from the last two years.
Hope there's nothing urgent!
Congrats on the baby!
                    Maddie x

●●●●● 🛜   12:03 PM   100% ▬

‹ Messages   **Dan**   **Details**

MADS! Check out this sparkler - your big brother is engaged! Thanks for your help, Rach loved the doves. They did shit on her new coat though, I'll send you the dry cleaning bill.

Congrats! But there's nothing attached. Aren't you supposed to be a photographer?

And I'm not paying the dry cleaning bill. JUST SAY NO, remember?

📷   Message   Send

Acknowledgements

If I had to list everyone who dragged me kicking and screaming through this book, we'd be here all day and you've just read an entire book, so the last thing you want to do now is listen to me harp on. But without these people, there would never have been a book – I know I say that every time but in this instance, it's very, very true.

Rowan Lawton, you're not just an amazing agent, you're an amazing human being. Literally couldn't have coped without you. Lynne Drew and Martha Ashby – sorry and thank you and sorry and thank you and sorry and thank you, repeat ad nauseam. I promise to probably never do this to you again.

To everyone at HarperCollins, thank you so much, I owe you cupcakes and booze and I couldn't be more grateful. Blaise, Georgie, Will, everyone at James Grant and Liane-Louise Smith (champion) at Furniss Lawton, thank you for being so impossibly tolerant. I don't care how much stick I take at home for #TeamKelk, you're f**king awesome.

388

There are a million people on Twitter, Facebook and Instagram who make my life easier but special shout outs go to my dead modern penpals, Lucy Robinson, Mhairi McFarlane and Rowan Coleman for reminding me we're not just women writers, we're women and we're writers and we're amazing. Well, you are, I'm mostly just tired. And falsely modest.

The last six months were the most difficult of my entire life and writing this book would have been impossible without the support, love and alcoholic beverages provided by these people: Della Bolat, Ryan Child, Kevin Dickson, Ilana Fox, Zainab Musa, Rosie Walsh, Terri White, Rachael Wright and Beth Ziemacki. This is a shit thank you, given what you gave me, I owe you all so much but can we start with a massive hug and go from there?

And thank you Jeff Israel for taking care of me, plying me with food and booze and generally being wonderful. It's a hard job, but someone has to do it.

Look out for Lindsey's

girl

series

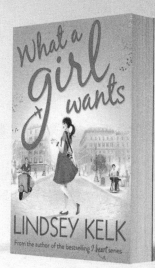

OUT NOW

OUT NOW

COMING
AUTUMN
2015

DISCOVER LINDSEY'S

I heart SERIES

LINDSEY KELK

Will Angela find herself
in the chapel of love?

I heart
Vegas

LINDSEY KELK

Angela's back on home turf –
and in her biggest romantic
scrape yet...

I heart
London

I heart
Christmas

Twelve days of Christmas –
and Angela's going to need
every one of them....

LINDSEY KELK

There are lots of ways to keep up-to-date with Lindsey's news and views:

Check out Lindsey's new website at lindseykelk.com

 Like her on facebook.com/LindseyKelk

Follow her @LindseyKelk